A BRIDE FOR THE WINTER KING

A DARK FANTASY ROMANCE

CURSE OF THE FAE
BOOK TWO

ANYA J COSGROVE

A Bride for the Winter King

Copyright © 2024 by Anya J Cosgrove.

Cover designer: Bewitching book covers by Rebecca Frank

A Bride for the Winter King/Anya J Cosgrove

ISBN: 978-1-7381056-6-3

✿ Created with Vellum

FOREWORD

Lovely readers,

Some stories are not everyone's cup of tea. The hero and heroine in this novel wrestle with more than one type of monster.

Here's the trigger list for this dark fantasy romance, so you can decide for yourself. Be advised that, when in doubt, I chose to include a trigger rather than skip it.

- Blood and violence
- Profanity
- Detailed sexual content (where consent is freely given)
- Light dubious consent situations (love potion style)
- Reality TV madness
- Love hate sex
- Morally gray situations
- Cheating (not by the MMC or FMC)
- Age gap (the heroine is nineteen and the hero is an immortal Fae)
- Threats
- Slut shaming (not by the hero)

- Misogyny (not by the hero)
- Mental illness
- Mention of physical abuse by a parental figure (no detailed descriptions)
- Mention of sexual assault (not by the hero, and no detailed descriptions)
- Voyeurism
- Masturbation
- Death of previous spouses
- Spiders
- Scars

This book ends with a HFN for our couple, BUT there will be big spoilers for book 1, so I highly recommend reading that first unless you're okay with that. Also, a particular plot point won't be resolved until later in the series and ends with a cliffhanger. You've been warned.

PLAYLIST

Another Love – Tom Odell (Almost single-handedly inspired the character of Elio)

Immigrant Song – Led Zeppelin

Don't Fear the Reaper – Blue Öyster Cult

Don't Blame Me – Taylor Swift

Iris – Goo Goo Dolls

If you're not into love/hate, scorching sex, turn back. Turn back now.

Unless it's you, Em. As my proofreader and best friend, you must go on. Love you.

MAPS

Map of the Fae Continent

Current Rulers of the Fae Continent:
Secret Springs - Freya Heart
Summerlands - Thera Summers
Red Forest - Eliza Bloodfyre
Wintermere - Elio Lightbringer
Solar Cliffs - Ethan Lightbringer
Shadowlands - Damian Sombra
Storm's End - Thorald Storm

COLD VOWS

"Elio Hades Lightbringer, you'll regret this. Your heart shall remain emptier than your promises, and your next bride will wither at your indifference. Mark my words, Winter King, for you shall never love again."

CHAPTER 1
BAD OMENS
LORI

S quelch. *Squelch. Squelch.* The soles of my feet dig in the mud, and the familiar rhythm soothes my soul. But whenever I close my eyes, I can still see them. The spiders.

Their crooked limbs and globulous eyes have burned my retinas. I see them crawl through the cedar hedges that flank my favorite running trail. Scurrying over the gardens to weave their webs. Dozens of them, with big fangs and disgusting darts.

I see them killing my friends.

My chest heaves at the vivid memories of poisonous silk clumping in my hair and clogging my mouth. Choking me. The wretched taste of venom and death sticks to my tongue, and I pick up the pace, trying—and failing—to outrun my own brain.

Trauma's an old friend I have no use for anymore. It makes me sappy and weak, and I swore never to let it rule my life again. So, I run. My shrink would say it's not healthy, but if worse comes to worse, I can always run *faster*.

Garlands of red fruits sag from the branches of the Shadow Court's Hawthorn. The sacred tree is almost barren by now, and flocks of raucous blackbirds burden the branches to steal a taste of its berries. A thin blanket of snow sticks to the bushels in powdery patches, and snowflakes fill the sky above my head.

Winter's coming...

A tingle of warning tickles up my spine. I'm a Shadow huntress, and like every skilled hunter, I can always tell when I'm running *from* something.

My heels slide in the mud as I come to an abrupt halt, and my breath frosts in front of my face. The air is ten degrees colder than it was a minute ago, and the loud thunder of boots trampling mud echoes behind me.

Not the nauseating click of spider legs, yet terrifying... An army nips at my heels.

A trickle of anxiety engulfs me. I slip into the shade of a cedar hedge, my magic coalescing into a dark, protective bubble around me. I have to assume that whatever's following my trail wants me dead. That's my lot in life.

Between rogue nightmares and psychotic ex-fiancées, unannounced visitors in these parts are rarely friendly. We're not expecting any guests for my best friend's wedding. It's a very secret ceremony.

What if Morrigan—the evil witch who made the soul-sucking spiders in the first place—discovered that the wedding was tonight and sent another wave of monsters upon us?

My shadow daggers flicker to life in my hands, light and lethal, and I draw in a deep breath. The spider bite that almost killed me tickles my ribcage, a splash of venom still embedded in the bone, but I dig the balls of my feet into the ground, ready to strike.

Nell deserves all the happiness in the world, and I won't let anyone ruin her big day. It's my duty as her bridesmaid to kill whatever's coming.

Wounded or not, I can still fight.

Goosebumps riddle my arms as I risk a glance around the corner of the cedar hedge.

A line of about twenty soldiers marches upon the Shadowlands in perfect unison, not one movement wasted. A well-oiled vision of doom. The men and women showcase the same hairstyle—half-buzzed heads that reveal the shape of their skulls. Silver zippers run down their form-fitting, sleeveless bodysuits, and white ski pants polish off the look.

Ice-blue tattoos have been carved rather than inked around their pointy ears, arms, and hands in intricate, swirly patterns peppered with snowflakes, and the subtle blue tint of their pale skins flips my stomach.

Grim reapers.

The only thing for certain in this life is that death comes to us all. When all is said and done, even immortals aren't impervious to its grip. Fae age in a slower fashion than us mortals, but when they don't have enough magic left to sustain themselves, they die. Or they get murdered by their enemies. Whichever comes first.

Are the reapers all here for me? Logic dictates one would have been enough, given my current state. I raise my arm to check on the spider bite in my side and hike up my jacket. An elongated M-shaped scar runs from the underside of my sports bra to my hip bone. My brown skin turned black and red and oozy over my bitten rib, but it's exactly the same as last night. It doesn't look like it festered, so why is a throng of reapers on my trail?

As if to answer my question, the reapers breeze past me, oblivious to my presence. Behind them, two men close the military march, and the bite of power rolling off the tallest one freezes the blood right in my veins.

By the spindle!

No matter how many gruesome nightmares I've hunted, or how many vicious Fae I've crossed paths with, nothing prepares you for the beauty of pure, unadulterated death.

The Winter King is tall and lean, but not one inch of him could be called skinny. Every single muscle looming under his white army uniform has been meticulously sharpened and toned into a weapon.

A long cape flows behind him, his blonde hair slicked back over his head, and a pure platinum mask—with no jewels or textures or irregularities at all—covers his eyes. The smooth surface reflects the gardens back to me as he angles his face to my hiding spot. A strange shimmer glides along the edges of the mask like it's made of liquid instead of metal, but the pressure of his gaze never finds me.

The squishy mud ices instantly beneath the soles of his boots, and the gardens glisten under the afternoon sun, most of the water in a fifty-foot radius now frozen solid.

My skin tingles all over, numb from the cold, as I take in the shape of his lips and the sharp angle of his jaw. I press my own mask in place to shield me from his hypnotic thrall and yank my full-face scarf over my long black hair.

According to the High Fae, death's never been so nicely wrapped up in a chiseled, angelic bow than under the command of Elio Lightbringer. I didn't give enough weight to this gossip, the High Fae known to exaggerate, but I truly don't understand how his rotten core could be overlooked in favor of his godlike aesthetics.

The cruel face of the reaper he sent after my dad's soul is branded in my memory, deeper than any spider could hope to burrow. The impatient curl of the monster's lips as he barked for me to step aside and the sting of his cold hands when he peeled me off his body haunt me.

The details live in my memory as heartbreaking and vivid as the day my father died. I remember how my tears iced over my cheeks, and the numbing grip of grief that didn't leave me for *months*.

All because of this power-hungry, soulless king...

If the Winter King knows I'm there, cradled in shadows, he doesn't let it show and turns his mask to the trio of blackbirds fluttering above our heads. After a few, long seconds, he starts walking again.

The man accompanying the king is wearing a reaper uniform, but with golden accents instead of silver. He holds one arm high in the air as the platoon reaches the shade of the Hawthorn. "Halt."

The soldiers stop near the Shadow King's balcony and widen

their stances, their arms now tucked behind their backs. I gape at the Winter King, unable to move from my hiding place.

Anger simmers at the back of my throat, and I tighten my grip on the hilts of my trusty daggers. *What are those creatures doing here, on our lands? Why couldn't they stay within the limits of their ice city where they belong?*

I'm almost mad enough to march over to them and air out my grievances, but a flash of brown hair stops me as Cece sticks her head out of the gym.

The fifteen-year-old girl stares at the reapers, and her hazelnut eyes widen. With her rosy lips parted in wonder, she appears eager to step onto the ice and introduce herself to our deadly visitors.

I dash across the trail to stop her. "Cece. Cece, go back inside," I order quietly.

A white puff of air rises between us, her entire body shaking from the cold. "What are they?"

The distinct pressure of a powerful Fae gaze prickles the hairs on the back of my neck. I wrap an arm around Cece's shoulders and pull her back inside the safety of the large training gym, closing the door behind us as quietly as possible. "Reapers," I whisper.

"As in grim reapers?" She twists in my grip and cranes her neck around to glance at them again.

"Yes."

Nell runs in from the opposite side of the room. A hood covers her white-blond braid, and a long dark cape reveals a glimpse of her wedding dress. Three pieces of black silk are woven and braided through the dress's sparkly bodice, and the off-the-shoulder ivory neckline makes her look like a fairytale princess—a true Shadow Queen.

"You're already dressed?" I check the clock on the wall and realize my melancholic run made me lose track of time.

"I couldn't just sit there, waiting. I keep thinking something horrible is about to happen."

"You and me both."

Nell peers through the diamond-meshed walls, the reapers barely visible between the thick branches of the barren bushes that crowd the sides of the gym. "Crops! They were supposed to come tomorrow."

Cece tiptoes closer to the wall with a dangerous smile. "They're so beautiful. Especially the tall one..."

"Beautiful?" I shake off the urge to scream and focus on her older sister. "You knew about this? And you didn't tell me?" I breathe.

Nell's eyebrows pull together. "I thought you knew. Damian said that they come every year after Morheim."

A hiccup quakes my throat, and I shake my head from side to side. "Believe me, Old World. If I'd seen an army of grim reapers before, I'd remember."

Nell squints like she's seeing me for the first time today. "Hey... Are you alright?" Her gaze falls to my side. "Is it the bite again? Has it ruptured?"

I shake my head. "It's fine."

But she reaches for the hem of my jacket anyway, and I hold up my arm to allow her to double-check. The tips of her cold fingers trace the angry patch of flesh, a crust of dried blood and fibrin still obscuring the center of the bite.

"The scab is stuck in this state, but it's not worse than it was," she says, her voice heavy with relief.

Nell's magic and Baka's salves brought me back from the brink of a horrible death, but their combined skills haven't been enough to extract the remaining spider venom from my rib. The rotten keepsake keeps the scar tissue in a constant loop of renewal and decay, and I haven't had a good night's sleep since.

I tug my jacket and shirt back down to cover the wound. "Told you so." I force a deep breath down my lungs. "Why is the Winter King here with an army?"

"His new reapers finished their training and came to get their masks," Nell explains.

She's still very new to this world, and I sometimes forget that she doesn't have all the baggage that comes with a life-long knowledge of Faerie. Or the truckload of prejudice associated with an upbringing similar to mine. Death hides from non-magic mortals, so she had probably never heard of reapers back home—except maybe in legends. She wasn't taught to dread the sight of them.

Her fresh point of view is part of why I love her, really, but I swallow hard at her naiveté.

After today, another flock of reapers will leave the Shadowlands with the power to walk the worlds freely. They will travel through glass—or even through reflections on ice or water—and wreak havoc on countless mortal lives. Their job is to collect souls as a gardener snaps flowers off their stems, plucking out the ones that catch their fancy.

The door to the courtyard blows open, and an icy wind gusts into the room. I slam it shut and jam a piece of wood through the lock to keep it secure.

Nell rubs the chill off her arms. "Brr— We'll just have to move the party inside."

Party is the word we use to talk about the wedding, and I throw my best friend a pointed glare. "What if they decide to stick around?"

She shakes her head and steals another glance at death. "They should be gone before sundown. It'd be too dangerous to postpone our plans, anyway. We'll make it work."

An army of grim reapers dropping in early, an hour before her wedding... talk about bad omens.

"Do you know why their skin is like that?" Cece asks.

I'd rather talk about anything else, but once Cece asks a question, she won't give up until she gets an answer.

"When reapers take their oath, the Winter King carves a special set of runes in their skulls. The glamor alters their appearance and grants them the power to act in his name," I sum up.

Cece slips her fingers through the diamond mesh wall. "Can we go and talk to them?"

"No!" Nell and I answer in unison.

I rub a path along my brow to the earrings decorating the round shell of my ear. "That girl is going to drive me crazy. I mean—I love her, of course, but fifteen-year-olds are the *worst*."

Cece braces her hands on her hips and lifts her chin. "Hey! I'm right here."

I offer Lil' Bit a wry grin. "It wouldn't accomplish anything to complain about you behind your back. Then you wouldn't know how to adjust your behavior."

She sticks her tongue out. "It's not fair. Baka and Damian never hold their age over me, and they're *way* older."

Nell and I share a giggle, which aggravates Cece even more. We shouldn't hold our narrow age difference over her, but it's just too tempting.

When she turns eighteen, she'll access the deep well of magic inside her. Until then, her powers are bound to remain as wild and untamed as her character.

Ignoring the painful sting between my ribs, I wrap an arm around Nell. "Come on. You have to help me get ready for the party."

The cold air vibrates with an entirely new pulse of magic, and all the hairs on my arms stand up at attention. A smoky cloud thickens into a man-shaped silhouette near the door.

"Crops!" Nell snatches a crossbow from the wall, and I summon my shadow blades back to life.

Seth Devine condenses into solid form, and the Fae prince rubs his hands together. "Did someone say, *party?*"

It's not the first time Seth has weaseled his way inside the castle, but with his ill-fated timing, it might be the last. The fiend is absolutely gorgeous—half his magic born out of lust itself. My mask protects me from his lure, but Nell's gaze loses focus, and Cece almost drools at the sight of him.

I raise my weapons in warning. "By the spindle! You've got a death wish, dude."

The corners of his mouth quirk. "It's *my prince* to you, Lori."

"I could probably kill you, you know."

His purple eyes dance. "Not if I kill you first."

Nell paws at the lace of her wedding dress with her free hand, her voice hoarse and croaky. "What do you want?"

The wedding dress... Seth has seen it. Fuck-fuck-fuck.

Seth holds both palms up in front of him in a carefree, halting motion. "Hey, I'm not the one leading with threats. I just want to chat."

Cece abandons her post by the window, the reapers all but forgotten in favor of the immortal piece of eye candy. "What's your name?" She raises her hand in greeting.

"Seth. What's yours, darling?" He presses his lips to her knuckles with a wink, and a deep red flush brands her cheeks.

"We're done here." Nell grabs her sister's arm and hauls her away with a grimace.. "I'll get Damian. Come on, Cece."

The young teenager stumbles behind her, her eyes never leaving the Fae prince.

Seth offers them a wave goodbye. "It was a pleasure to meet you, Cecelia."

"Likewise," Cece squeaks before disappearing from view.

After they're gone, Seth licks his lips, and his brutal, erotic gaze travels up and down my body. The curve of his lips reeks of sex, but the bite of power rolling off him—the taste of his magic—is desperate. "Alone, at last."

My eyes narrow, my daggers ready to draw blood. "I thought you wanted to talk to the Shadow King."

The prince's chuckle floods the empty room like heavy summer rain—warm and baring. "Oh no, Lori. You misunderstood. I want to chat with *you.*"

CHAPTER 2
GOT A SECRET
LORI

Wolves that march in with their teeth bared are dangerous. Snakes that lure you in are worse. Seth Devine is definitely a serpent. He's a particular beast, even for a Fae. He possesses both the charisma and mystique of a dark Fae coupled with the raw, blinding beauty of spring.

His mother is Freya Heart, the ruthless Spring Queen. The woman responsible for archers and love arrows... And my brother's doom.

I raise a blade to the fucker's nose despite the pain in my side. "I warn you. You're not my type."

"Oh, Lori. I'm everyone's type. That's the beauty of being me." He bats his eyelashes a few times, and the dangerous grin from before vanishes into a warm, boy-next-door type of smile. "You don't have to pretend otherwise. Where are you from, anyway?"

I blink and keep a straight-face, unmoved by his gigantic ego. "You of all people should understand what a trick question that is."

"Who are your parents, then? Maybe I know one of them."

Names and magic go hand-in-hand. I certainly won't help this

Fae get more information on me by revealing my heritage. "I doubt it. My parents are dead."

"Ooh, mysterious."

"You're the prince of nowhere at all." I show my teeth. "Well... I'm Lori of everywhere at once."

The mention of his illegitimacy doesn't ruffle him one bit, and he slithers closer. "Since we met, I've done my homework, and I've got a proposition for you, Lorisha Pari Singh."

My smile falters. *How in the seven hells?*

"I heard your brother was wasting away in my mother's court..." he trails off like we're talking about something as mundane as the next storm he plans to brew.

My pulse drums at my temples, and I flee toward the mirror. "You bastard! I don't know what kind of game you're playing, but I'm not listening to another word—"

"Too bad. Ayaan told me you'd hear me out."

I freeze, my heart about to explode. "You talked to him?"

"I might be called the prince of nowhere at all, but I'm still a prince. Crown or no crown, I could help you clear his name. Or at least save him from the noose."

I slip inside a shadow and dash over to Seth, the edge of my dagger soon grazing the soft skin under his jaw. "Noose? What are you talking about?"

He glances down at the weapon and extends his neck to taunt me, almost daring me to slice his throat. The motion causes the tip of the blade to pierce his dark brown skin, and I let the dagger fall to my side.

Seth rubs the blood from his neck and licks it off his thumb. "Your little brother has been marked for execution as part of the winter solstice celebrations."

My stomach lurches, my palms clammy and numb. "That's not— Why?" I squeak. "Selling arrows on the black market hardly justifies a public execution."

A contemptuous scoff quakes him. "Selling arrows on the black market? Is that what they told you? Lori, your brother associated with rebel dissidents and carved a *forbidden* arrow. I could get his sentence remediated...if you help me."

There's no way...

The urge to kick and scream and curse Seth and his family to the seven hells is almost impossible to quell. But even if the crown fabricated false charges, it doesn't change the facts. And the word *rebel* picks at painful, old memories.

"And how would I repay the favor?" I ask, stunned.

"Do you know that you're a ringer for a woman called Iris Lovatt?"

Iris Lovatt... The name sort of rings a bell, but I can't remember why. I squint at Seth, trying to see past his princely exterior and into the wicked inner workings of his brain. "You think I look like her?"

His smile doesn't quite reach his eyes. "You don't just *look like her.* You're the spitting image of her."

Fae can't outright lie, but most of them are very good at twisting the truth and omitting important information, so I can't quite believe his claim. "Who is she?"

"My cousin by blood—my aunt Irene's only daughter."

My grandmother was a Spring Fae, but she didn't have anything to do with the royal family. "And you want me to pretend that I'm her? You need me to kill someone or steal something—"

He cuts in. "Oh no. Iris died *decades* before you were born." The light in his eyes dims, and he looks me over like he's seeing his cousin in my place. "I was truly fond of her."

The obvious grief in the tremble of his voice makes me pause. Perhaps I've got this all wrong.

"She was a Spring princess?" I ask softly, stowing all my quick assumptions away.

"Yes. Irene's only child. Her father was the headmaster of Summers' Royal Academy. Have you heard of it? Almost all the royals in history have studied there."

"I've heard of it, but I still don't see what you hope to achieve. If she's dead, why does it matter?"

"Iris wasn't just any princess." He takes a dramatic pause, clearly stretching the suspense to rile me up. "She was the Winter King's first wife."

Holy fuck! I start shaking my head before Seth is even done talking. The gossip making its rounds through the Shadow Court about the Winter King's romance with his first wife makes Romeo and Juliet's fate sound like a fluffy fairytale ending.

"Why— Why would I look like her? My Fae heritage doesn't run as high as the lowest barony. My grandmother was a maid in a provincial town, for Morpheus' sake."

The platinum mask of the Winter King comes to mind, and I tremble at the thought of what might have happened if I hadn't crawled into the deepest shadow to avoid him.

"Who knows?" Seth shrugs like the reason for this resemblance isn't worth discussing. "But I suspect the Winter King is harboring a mutual *friend* of ours. If the woman responsible for that scar"—he grazes my bitten rib—"is hiding out in Wintermere, we catch her before she even realizes what's coming."

Jeez. Am I walking around with an "I almost died" neon sign written on my forehead? I look down at my side, but my jacket and shirt are still there, covering the mark. A dark hole at the pit of my stomach stirs to life. Revenge fills my blood, as slick and enticing as Feyfire wine.

"How would that work, exactly?" I ask, the sharpness in his voice too obvious for my taste.

His lips stretch in victory. "Every year, my mother sends in candidates for the Yule pageant. Your resemblance to Iris presents a rare opportunity for me to infiltrate Elio's court. I would present you along with the others, as nothing more than a Spring seed longing for a taste of immortality."

"You want *me* to enter the Yule pageant?" I paw at the front of my jacket, ready to melt into the floor.

"You wouldn't have to marry him in the end. And you'd get a generous dowry just for entering—"

"Keep your money. I don't need it. Why do you care so much about the Winter King, or Morrigan, anyway? What's in it for you?"

Seth grits his teeth. "Never mind that. If you get past the first few rounds of elimination, I'll make sure your brother survives. And I'll do everything in my power to set him free if we manage to track Morrigan."

The word *we* puts me on guard. A man like Seth doesn't go around making empty promises, but there's something he's not telling me. If anything, my resemblance to the Winter King's dead wife might put him off altogether.

"What's the catch? Why capture Morrigan? Why not kill her?"

Seth isn't supposed to know about Morrigan's blood link to Cece —a spell that prevents us from killing her without condemning Lil' Bit to the same fate.

The prince runs his thumb across his lips. "That's my business, but I need her alive. As for the obvious drawbacks, Elio's been suspected of killing off a few candidates over the years. But you...you can defend yourself. A spider like you, disguised as a rose, will be able to sneak around his castle without being seen."

Other courts call all Shadow hunters *spiders* because of our skills, but I shiver all over. This is a bad, *bad* idea. "You're mad! I could never pass for a Spring seed."

Seth tilts his head to the side, his tone all soft and quiet. "Don't sell yourself short, Lori of everywhere at once." His lips quirk. "With a little help, a woman like you could bring kingdoms to ruin."

My throat bobs, the certainty in his voice loosening something inside me. All my life, I've worked so hard not to stand out. To blend in with the mortals back home and shine only by my hard work here in the Shadow Court. Sparing male egos left and right.

Never shining too bright to attract the wrong kind of attention.

"It's a win-win-win situation. You're hungry for new adventures, Lori."

I am. I truly am. The business with the spider only reminded me how close to death we are here in the Shadowlands. It's my new home, but I don't want to die for the greater good. I want to fight and laugh and love...

Damian and Nell step out of the door-shaped mirror at the other end of the gym, interrupting my inner musings. And the Shadow King looks about to wrench Seth's heart out of his chest and serve it with a side of wedding cake.

CHAPTER 3
THE SERPENT'S PLUS-ONE
LORI

All mirrors connect us to the sceaware—the space between worlds that allows us to travel to and from Faerie. Equipped with an expansive knowledge of Fae runes and a mask, a magical being can easily walk in and out of different realms —or simply step from one room to another.

The Shadow King's arrival wraps the entire gym in darkness. Damian zooms toward Seth with incredible speed, but right as he's about to grab him, the prince dissipates into an airy mist. The king's arm shoots out toward the space Seth just occupied, and he wrenches the cocky prince out from the depths of his storm magic without hesitation.

"Seth." With a low hiss, Damian flattens his fellow Fae to the wall. "What did I tell you about coming here unannounced?"

I peer through the mesh walls to check on our deadly visitors, scared that the altercation might attract their attention. "Are the reapers still in the gardens?" I whisper to Nell.

"No. They're in the vault now," she answers, her emerald and gold mask tucked safely over her eyes.

My shoulders slack in relief. "This one hasn't stopped talking since you left."

"And what kind of fairy tales did he share with you?" Damian bands an arm under Seth's chin. "You came for the Yule pageant again? I warned you. My hunters are off limits."

I suck an audible gulp of air. Damian looks like he knows exactly what Seth wanted to talk to me about, and a hint of betrayal shows on my face. "You knew about this?"

"I did, and I told him that it's too dangerous."

"It's too dangerous for me to save my brother?" I say, my mouth opened in outrage.

"Your brother?" Damian frowns.

We stare at each other for a breath, and I realize he's still unaware of my brother's troubles. "Let's start again. Seth here offered to help my brother in exchange for my participation in the Yule pageant."

"How is your brother involved with this rascal?" Damian asks, but I shrug off his inquisitive stare.

"You're not the only one who's been keeping secrets."

He gives Seth an inch to spare. "How did you pierce the barrier without tripping the alarm?"

"I snuck in behind Elio, followed Lori, and overheard the single most juicy piece of gossip since my own birth," Seth chucks out. "I'd call that karma." His eyes roam over Damian with a mix of fear and respect. "What happened to you? You look...different."

"Never been better."

"I believe it." Seth licks his lips. "I'm not after your throne, D. I just need to find your phantom queen."

Nell's top lip curls in disgust at the mention of Morrigan's nickname. "She's not his queen."

The Fae rubs the curve of his jaw and corrects himself quickly. "*Erm. Not your* queen, obviously. Nell here is the only woman in your life worth mentioning. Congratulations on the wedding. I only wish you two the best— Truly."

Damian pinches the bridge of his nose with his free hand like he's about to lose his mind. "What am I going to do with you now? It's not like I can just enchant you to forget—"

Nell places a soothing hand over her lover's arm, and Damian finally releases his unforgiving hold on our visitor. "What can you do for Ayaan?" she asks Seth.

"Keep me around a little longer, and you'll find out." The Fae prince dusts off his jacket and shakes out the assault like he deals with threats and punches every day.

Given his behavior, I believe it.

The tension that had built up and up after Seth had revealed himself dissipates, and the potent scent of cinders—all the shadow magic clogging the air—goes along with it. Damian and Nell have a quiet conversation, the Shadow King and his future queen silently coming to an arrangement that'll no doubt affect Seth's survival chances.

"Alright. You're going to stay here—within Lori's sight—until the wedding. I'll deal with the reapers, and we can chat about the Yule pageant after the ceremony," Damian says. His shadowy aura thickens and drains the light from the room until the darkness becomes suffocating once more. "But if you pressure her in any way, or you say anything out of line, you're dead. I don't care what slippery shape you take, I'll find you. Clear?"

"Oh, I'm taking meticulous notes, and I'm with you. One hundred percent," Seth declares a little too formally. Damian spins around to leave, but the rogue Fae prince calls after him. "To sum up... You're inviting me to your wedding?"

The Shadow King slips his hand into Nell's without looking back. "Behave yourself, Seth, and I won't have to kill you before I leave for my honeymoon."

The bride and groom whistle out through the mirror, and Seth nudges my side. "We'll go together, then?"

Arms crossed over my chest, I raise a brow. "Where? I still haven't accepted your offer."

"To the wedding. Like a date."

My jaw drops, and I can't help but look him over. The damn prince is like a cardboard cut-out of a romance cover model. I can see his fucking abs through his shirt, and his dark skin looks perfectly smooth to the touch. "You *just* said that I'm a ringer for your *cousin*."

He shrugs, his hands tucked in his pockets. "So what?"

The mouth-watering shape of him fogs my brain, but I tear my gaze away. *A Fae prince. No, thank you.* Sleeping with him would without a doubt ruin me for all mortal men. My last sexual relationship was a long-lasting friends-with-benefits arrangement with a fellow Shadow hunter, so I'm familiar with Seth's *no strings attached* behavior, but I'm done with all that.

I have enough on my plate.

But the alarm bells ringing inside my head aren't enough to deter me completely. Seth is a welcomed distraction from the ache in my ribs and the unquenched thirst for revenge burning at the back of my throat, and a smile pierces my scowl. "You're a cocky jackass, aren't you?"

He wraps an arm around my shoulders and squeezes me to his side with confidence and ease, like we're already the best of friends. "That I am, Lori. That I am."

CHAPTER 4
MISS CONGENIALITY
LORI

The half-moon shaped balcony offers an unobstructed view of the pristine white gardens below. The Hawthorn towers in the center of the interior courtyard, the inch of ice and snow left by our afternoon visitors covering up all the imperfections of the shoulder season. A few snowflakes swing in the waning breeze, their slow drift unpredictable and mesmerizing.

Cece, Seth, and I stand by Nell on one side of the crescent-shaped space while the other Shadow hunters stand next to Damian.

The Shadow King's black tuxedo shimmers in the night. Nell's white-blond hair and ivory dress slice the darkness, the bride absolutely luminous under the glow of the last Morheim moon. The obsidian crown atop her head matches Damian's, the intricate piece of jewelry glimmering with iridescent teal, purple, and golden hues.

A thousand candles flicker over the floorboards of the balcony in all shapes and sizes, hot wax dripping down their sides. Three golden lanterns are set between the candles in memory of the people we lost in the last few weeks. I was almost one of them, and I swallow hard at the memory, discreetly wiping a tear from the corner of my eye.

"Mortal love wanes. Fae love cuts to the bone," Baka rasps in her thick accent. A beautiful wooden tiara sits atop the sprite's head, right between her thin, floppy ears. "Will ye cut yourself to honor yer commitment to each other, from this moment forth to eternity?"

I press my lips together not to squirm at the familiar phrase, and the wretched taste of spiderwebs fills my mouth. Even though this is a radically different wedding ceremony than the one during which I almost died, too much of it is similar—starting with the groom.

Damian takes the jeweled dagger from Baka's wrinkled hands, hikes up his sleeve, and rests the sharp tip of the blade on his lower arm until it draws blood. "Nell... When I met you I was broken. A mere shadow of the man I pretended to be. I was clutching to my bad habits with both hands, blinded by self-hatred." He smudges his thumb in his blood and traces her lips with it, his voice growing quieter and quieter. "You saved me in spite of myself, and I will spend the rest of my days fighting for you and our happiness the way I should have done from day one."

She takes the dagger from him and cuts a matching line in her arm. "You saved me too, Damian. You offered me a life I could have never dreamed of. A chance to love and laugh without shame. I vow to remind you of that, everyday, so that you never forget who you are. The most dauntless and stubborn—but also patient, kind and clever—absolutely enchanting king of Faerie."

They draw blood runes over each other's cheeks before Nell links their tainted fingers and tugs him closer. Their blood mixes, and the runes seep inside their skin with a flare of magic.

Fingers entwined, they stare at each other, eyes full of tears and adoration.

"They look quite taken with each other," Seth whispers in my ear.

He's standing way too close to me for his damn Fae-prince-ness not to quicken my pulse, and I roll my shoulders back. "That's because they're in love."

"So...you believe in love?"

My brows pull together. "You're the Spring Queen's son. Are you telling me that you don't?"

With his hands linked at his front, he switches his weight from one foot to the other. "Jury's still out. I've yet to witness a love that wasn't bred out of a thirst for power or fabricated by some flimsy magical arrows."

"You're totally ruining this for me."

He smiles like he's privy to an age-old secret. "No I'm not. I'm distracting you from the sting in your ribs and the dark memories eating away at you."

"How do you know about the bite, anyway?"

A cloud passes over his face. "I might be a Spring weed, but I'm more comfortable in a storm."

Weed is a derogatory term for illegitimate children born outside of the Spring Court, and the crude word makes my teeth grind.

Baka narrows her eyes in our direction. I offer her a sheepish grimace, and she clears her throat, ready to close the ceremony.

"Under the watchful eyes of the Seven...ye may now make sweet luv to yer bride," she says on a chuckle. Faerie folks do not shy away from telling it like it is, and her pink eyes gleam with warmth. "But maybe a dance or two, first?"

Damian curls a hand around Nell's neck and gives her a kiss so perfect, so intimate, that my gaze darts to the ground. I'd never dream to be loved so completely. Their romance is a tale for the ages.

Applause and cat-calls resonate on the balcony before we slip inside the mirror at the back of the room to wait for the newlyweds in the banquet hall. The secretive quality of the ceremony won't help get the party started, but we'll do them proud.

Jo, the leader of the hunter squad, inches toward us and gives Seth the stink eye. "Is he bothering you, little ninja?"

"We're fine, aren't we, Lori?" Seth chimes.

I pat my friend's shoulder to soothe him. "Right as rain. Thank you, Jo."

Beautiful champagne flutes are passed around by flying trays until we're all holding one, and the bride and groom walk to the center of the ballroom.

Damian raises his bubbly drink in the air. "Let's toast to new beginnings, love, and to my queen."

"In her name!" we all shout back in cheer—even Seth.

"Long live the king and queen!" Cece adds with a big smile plastered on her face.

We drink to their health, and Nell blushes a deep shade of red. "Thank you for being here. It means a lot."

"We love you, Nell," I declare loudly enough to start another round of pep-filled shouts and applause.

The staple of every Fae wedding starts to play, a heart-wrenching love song written by the most famous singer of all time, Elizabeth Snow. I take another long swig of champagne at the familiar melody, grateful to erase the lingering taste of spider silk on my tongue.

"What a lovely song." Cece dumps her empty glass on a magic tray and hooks her small arm around Jo's, pulling him forward. "Let's dance!"

Misha and Cary exchange a quick kiss before joining the other couples on the dance floor, and Seth holds out his hand. "It'd be rude not to."

I hold up my index finger. "One dance."

"I don't think this reception is supposed to last longer than a few songs, anyway." Seth pulls me close to him, the classic waltz suddenly very dirty-dancing. "In Spring, the bride and groom go straight to the honeymoon suite—a big, lavish tent set near the buffet. The guests drink to their health all night—along with the obligatory peeks through the tarps, naturally."

I chuckle at the absurdity of Fae traditions. "There won't be any *peeking* here, I assure you. But public sex sounds downright benign compared to the Yule pageant."

"Winter peeps need big, flashy drama to sweeten their cold hearts," he twirls me around. "It's a tradition that dates back a thousand years, at least—though they didn't use to last that long, nor come along every year."

I chew on that for a moment, wondering exactly how this egregious spectacle started in the first place. "Are you saying that the Winter King chose his first queen through a contest, too?"

Seth nods. "Back then, there were only four prospective brides—a princess from each of the first kingdoms. Winter, Spring, Summer, and Autumn. Elio was crowned king days before the solstice and scrambled to get married quickly. He and Iris had met before, at the Academy. Elio was already enamored with her, so his first Yule pageant barely took two hours."

"Wow."

Two hours to decide who to spend the rest of your life with. No pressure.

The music stops. Seth looks down at his wrist and taps an imaginary watch. "I'd love to chat with you until dawn, but if you're in, we've got to go. The Yule pageant starts in ten hours. If we are to pass you off as a Spring rose, you need your beauty sleep."

I gape at his confidence. He doesn't know half the story, and only glimpsed at my true hatred for Morrigan.

"Going once..." he trails off.

"Stop it!"

"Going twice."

My shoulders sag. "Alright. Let me talk to Damian and Nell alone."

There's no good option here, but I see no way around Seth's offer. Damian can't afford the necessary manpower to chase Morrigan throughout Faerie, and if I refuse, Ayaan will hang. The Shadow Court doesn't have much sway in Spring.

The happy couple stops swaying to the music at my approach, and Nell's face falls like she knows exactly what I'm going to say. "Are you sure you want to do this?"

"If I can help Ayaan..." I throw a quick glance behind me to make sure Seth is out of earshot. "Our mother was born on the fringes of

Spring. She never used the word *rebel*, but her tumultuous childhood landed her in jail. After her so-called friends left her to die in that place, she served her sentence and left Faerie to blend into the new world and change her life. She always made us promise never to disclose her name, so that *bad people* from her past could never track us down. If Ayaan was naive enough to be roped in by some rebel scheme... I have to do everything in my power to help."

"Then you have my blessing, of course," Damian says.

I'm proud to serve him, really. More than ever. With enough luck, I can help Seth capture Morrigan as a bonus. It'll feel good to take the fight to her instead of merely waiting for her to strike again.

I offer him a gentle bow. "Thank you, my king. I will strive to be worthy of your teachings." I punctuate the stuffy speech with a wink.

"I'm only a summons away. If shit hits the fan, pray for me," he says.

"Will do, boss."

Nell follows me to the outskirts of the dance floor and squeezes my hands. "If he tries anything you're not okay with, come home, and we'll find another way to save Ayaan."

I offer her a sad smile, her optimism endearing but not contagious. Seth is my only chance to save my brother's life. "Go and be with your man, Old World. You have until midnight to consummate this union."

Another silly Fae tradition, but oh-so-important if she wants to seal the deal, so to speak.

A deep shade of red brands her cheeks. "Be careful, okay?"

"I promise."

I grab Seth's elbow and drag him out of the banquet hall and into the tunnels underneath the castle. I'm going to sleep one last night in my own bed and offer Seth the floor. *I might lend him a pillow if he's nice.*

I risk a glance at him. "Tell me the truth. What kind of sick fuck marries and kills his bride every year?"

With his slick blond hair and his white, ghostly cape, the Winter

King possessed a striking villainous quality. I chew on my bottom lip, haunted by the memory of the strange shimmer gliding over his mask when he looked straight through me.

Seth's jaw ticks. "The worst kind, but he has to marry. The laws of Winter are all too clear on that. A queen has to participate in the solstice's sacred rites, or all of Faerie's magic would be in jeopardy. The Winter King's marriage is a matter of national security, so to speak."

"But he does kill his wives, right?"

"No one really knows, but yes. *Accidents* keep happening every year during the pageant...*and* after. You can't expect the reaper king not to be in on it."

My eyes narrow. "Let me guess: no one gives a damn when a mortal dies, as long as it's for the greater good of the realm? They used to enlist Fae princesses in the pageant, but after the murders began, they switched to mortals and called it a day?"

"That's about the gist of it," Seth admits.

My fists curl at my sides.

"You realize most of this process won't be about violence, right? It's a pageant, first. There'll be other girls there. Girls you'll have to fool as well as the king."

"I can fit in with them, no problem."

He nudges my side. "Are you sure? You wore a hoodie at your best friend's wedding."

I skim the hem of the vintage Chicago Bulls hoodie at my mid-thigh. "I was cold," I lie.

This hoodie is the last earthly piece of my father I still possess, and I really needed it tonight.

"If we want to pass you off as a Spring seed, your sense of style has to change." Seth scratches a line from his chin to his bottom lip with his index finger, appraising me like he's some fashion expert that finds me lacking. "The Shadow Court feels medieval compared to the first kingdoms. Winter and Spring follow the new mortal trends, and Spring fashion is all about bright colors, lace, and flowers."

Ugh. Lace and flowers? Kill me now.

We reach my bedroom door, and I hold it open for Seth.

The fire casts a soft orange glow over the queen-sized bed and dresser, and I immediately regret my decision to take him along. My little corner of the world looks so small and mundane... A pile of unread books clutters my bedside table. The drawers and panes of my jewelry box hang open, revealing an array of colorful earrings and necklaces.

I feel my resolve grow. A Fae prince doesn't belong in my bed— not even for one night.

Seth raises one perfectly plucked eyebrow, taking in his surroundings. "I didn't expect you to invite me in."

"Simmer down, Casanova. I want to keep an eye on you." I march over to the bed and hold out one pillow and a spare blanket. "You get the floor tonight, and I'll know if you leave this room, so you better not try to snoop around the castle."

He licks his lips, his jaw slightly askew. "You're serious?"

"Try me." I climb into bed fully clothed and cover myself with the duvet, turning away from my visitor. My nails sink deep into the pillow. *Am I being unreasonable?* I could die on this mission... Maybe I should treat myself with one more night of great sex?

Seth remains rooted in place for a good minute before he walks over to the side of the bed and crouches to meet my gaze. "Alright. Let's be friends."

"Let's keep things...professional," I offer, unsure I could ever become friends with someone who loves himself as much as Seth does.

"How about...professional friends?"

I crack a smile. "That sounds disingenuous *and* sexual."

An adorably sheepish smile curls his mouth. "Friends that share a large bed?"

I twist away from him, screwing my eyes shut, and enunciate a loud, "Nope."

"Why not?" Seth asks.

Maybe the prospect of joining the Yule pageant tomorrow irks my nerves, or I'm creeped out by the dead cousin, but I'm simply not in the mood—a phrase Seth has probably never heard in his adult life. "Because I need a straight head for tomorrow, and somehow I don't think you're the quickie type."

I leave out the part about me feeling hideous and sore because of the spider bite, because it's none of his business.

A light chuckle fills the room. "Is that a back-handed compliment?"

I adjust my head on the pillow once more. "Goodnight, Seth."

"Goodnight, Lori."

CHAPTER 5

TEACHER'S PET

LORI

At the break of dawn, Baka enters my room through the mirror. The sprite doesn't need a mask to travel through the sceawere, her bark-like skin and grainy wings rendering her impervious to the nightmares that roam the in-between. Her big ears move in time with the wings at her back, and her gaze darts to the sleeping prince. "I see ye've kept yer guest at arm's length."

Seth's light snores echo in the small room, his head buried in a pillow at the foot of the bed.

I sit up, my legs dangling off the edge of the mattress as I stretch. "What can I say? I wasn't in the mood for great sex."

Baka cracks a smile. She lands next to me, her weight barely making a dent in the duvet, and proceeds to hike up my shirt over my wound to check its current state.

Textured lids drape over her pink irises as she sighs, "It's not better."

"It's not worse."

The sprite covers the back of my hand with her wrinkled fingers, her skin soft to the touch despite its appearance. "Nell might not know what this means, but I do. If it ain't better by now, it's never going to be."

A soft tremble quakes my throat. "I was afraid of that."

Baka is kind, clever, and patient, but she says it straight like it is, and I can't bury my head in the medicinal roots anymore.

She grazes my chin with her bony claw. "Don't go chasin' ghosts and heartbreak. This poison is contained for now, but who knows what will happen if ye overexert yerself."

Her comment sparks an itch between my brows. "You think it might spread?"

She presses her lips together, and the worried curve of her mouth serves as an answer. My chest tightens, the ache in my ribs intensifying tenfold, but I jump to my feet and switch my hoodie for a long black t-shirt, the sports bra I'm wearing underneath perfectly modest.

I pat the fabric down over the scar, making sure it's covered. Out of sight, out of mind. "Don't tell Nell, please. I don't want her to worry about me any more than she already will."

Baka gives a small incline of the head, her bushy brows raised in understanding. "As ye wish. Be careful, my precious nightshade. And if ye find Morrigan, remember that revenge only hardens the heart."

I clasp her small hand in mine, grateful for her unwavering support. Baka is supposed to be our handmaid, but she's really the closest possible replacement to the mothers we've all lost. She takes care of us, and I'm going to miss her dearly.

"I'll come back in one piece, Tree Mama. I swear."

Her long black nail scratches my cheek as she cups it, her pink eyes wet with unshed tears. "There's always hope, even in the coldest of places. Remember that."

The sprite flies out of my room through the mirror, and I graze Seth's leg with the tip of my bare feet to shake him awake. "Wake up, sleeping beauty."

He yawns and stretches gingerly, his shirt riding over his belly button. "Morning, *friend*." The prince bounces to his feet with the verve of a toddler excited to play with his favorite toys, looking fresh as a morning glory. "Are you ready to go?"

I leave my father's hoodie on the bed, not willing to risk its safety by bringing it with me, but my fingers linger over the bull pattern for a moment. "As ready as I'll ever be," I mumble, moving away from the bed to lace up my boots.

Seth rolls up his left sleeve to access the runes tattooed on his arm and escorts me to the Winter Court through the mirror. Our short journey spits us out inside a modern bedroom with no windows.

An electric chandelier floods the space with warm light and casts inviting shadows upon the walls. The impressive piece is made of a series of gold and silver threads twisted together, reminiscent of the roots of a tree. The carpet, dressers, and king-sized bed are white as snow. Pink, lavender, and yellow pillows clutter the bed in an array of textures and sizes.

The first kingdoms' sense of style is closer to modern mortal trends, indeed.

Seth sighs in relief and removes his amethyst-crusted mask. "Welcome to the Spring quarters. We're not allowed to step foot outside these halls until the Yule pageant starts, and as long as we're here, we should be careful. The castle is crawling with courtiers in preparation for the wedding. Spying on the king should get easier on the road, when we tour the provinces." He holds out a hand. "Mask, please."

I peel it off and hide it behind my back. "I'd prefer to keep it close."

My mask is a part of who I am—a crystallized part of my soul. Without it, I can't travel through the sceawere. Without it, I can't escape.

Seth rubs the arch of his brow. "Spring seeds don't have masks, as you well know. Everyone has to believe I brought you here from the new world myself." He slips a small silver key from his jacket and twists open the lock to a small metal chest on top of his bedside table. "I'll take it with us on tour. And you don't have to worry about it being stolen, because the chest can't be moved by anyone but me."

I lay down the mask on the silk lining the bottom of the empty chest, and my fingers tingle from the loss.

"Here, you can keep the key." He tosses me the key, and I tuck it inside my bra. "The other girls are waiting in the dressing room at the end of the corridor. We have to make you presentable."

The large closet door slides open, full of pastel gowns, but a black tulle dress with embroidered flowers stands out among the colorful mass.

Seth holds a pink and orange number to my chest, but I wrench a different hanger from the pole. "This one."

"It's black."

"With *flowers*. Listen, if you expect me to seduce a Fae king, I have to feel confident." I slip inside the adjoining bathroom to change.

"We have fifteen minutes, tops," Seth announces from the other side of the door.

I strip from my uniform and boots and adjust the slim black straps over my shoulders. The sweetheart neckline dips between my breasts, and the skirt finishes at my mid-thigh. Not my style given that I'd never choose to wear a dress, but I look good.

Seth cracks open the door. "Can I?"

I give a sharp nod.

"Here. Let me." He reaches for the clip holding my hair.

"I didn't peg you for a hairdresser," I say.

Goosebumps raise along the back of my neck as he frees my long, dark mane and starts running his fingers through it. "Spring magic and all..."

"Right."

Under his influence, the knots and dry ends vanish, my hair perfectly straight and glossy in an instant. The result is twice as impressive as when Baka does my hair in the Shadow Court.

"Perfect." Seth meets my gaze in the bathroom mirror. "Now, look at me and close your eyes, partner."

I spin around and point my index finger at his face. "I warn you. No funny business."

He raises his hands in surrender. "I swear. Professional friends only." His fingers swipe across my closed lids, ghost along my cheeks, and trace my heart-shaped lips. "You know... Iris was considered to be the second most beautiful woman in Faerie."

The odd compliment sounds next to impossible, but I smile. "Only second, hey?"

This boy is mad... There's no way a woman who looks like me could be considered a standard of beauty. I check the result in the mirror and reel at his talent. The dark eye-shadow makes my clear gray eyes appear almost silver, and I've never looked so glamorous.

I smack my lips together a few times and blot the excess lipstick with a tissue, but to my surprise, the magic make-up doesn't smudge. *Nice trick!*

Feeling a little hot all of a sudden, I tuck my hair behind my ears. "Tell me about the Winter King."

"Elio's like all of his reapers. Cold. Unfeeling." Lips twisted in a grimace, Seth clears his throat and walks away. "Your voice is a problem. What about a high, friendly tone? Give it a try."

My voice? What the fuck. I roll my eyes. "Hi, I'm Lori Lovegood. I studied in the new world instead of Faerie because my mother was a bad-ass archer, and I'm *so* grateful to my prince, Seth Devine, for this opportunity."

The admiration sounds fake as hell, and Seth grunts. "You're not even trying. Most of the Spring seeds in the other room have been prepping for this their whole lives. They attended boarding school in Faerie to prepare for their future roles in my mother's court and fought for the chance to be here, so they know each other pretty well. They're going to scratch your eyes out if you're not careful."

"Why do they volunteer for this? Are they so broke that they'd prefer to be crowned queen and die rather than serve the Spring Court?" I ask.

Unlike Shadow seeds, Spring seeds come by the dozen, and not many of them wash out. My brother probably crossed paths with some of these girls during his studies. Like him, they're meant to become carvers, archers, or groomers after they graduate. All perfectly acceptable positions.

Seth averts his gaze. "I thought you knew—the top three women in the Yule pageant get a frost apple...and only one of them has to marry the king."

My breath catches in my throat. "Are you serious?"

"Considering Elio's reputation, they have to make it worthwhile for the brides to show up. Immortality is about the only thing mortals would willingly die for. Wouldn't you want it, given the chance?" He starts unbuttoning his shirt and returns to the bedroom. "I need to change, too."

Alone in the small, pristine bathroom, the nerves hit me all at once. A frost apple... I mean—I've been busting my ass to become the best Shadow huntress I can be, but I won't rise in the ranks quickly enough to claim immortality. There are four stages of training, and while the journey from seed to sprout took me ten months, twenty more years will most likely be needed for me to pass the next trials.

Becoming immortal would take a hundred more, and I haven't got that kind of time. The irony of being a magic-born mortal isn't lost on me. Endless possibilities, but time ticks by too quickly for us to reach our full potential. I touch the scar below the flimsy lace of my dress. *With that suppurating venom, I've probably peaked as a rough-edged, half-competent huntress.*

Before my confidence leaks out completely, I open the door and cover my eyes with my hand, rushing for the exit. "I'm ready to meet the girls."

"Wait!" Seth grips my elbow, and I catch a glimpse of his naked thigh. "I'll introduce you."

"Fuck, no! Don't single me out. It's only going to alienate me from them." Eyes still covered, I motion in the general direction of his crotch. "Get dressed, and be cool."

Without giving him another second to process, I escape to the hallway and slam the door behind me. *Oof.*

I force myself to slow down before opening the door leading to the women's dressing room. Twelve faces turn in my direction. A human bouquet of bombshells, with flawless make-up and colorful dresses that hug their beautiful bodies.

I force a smile on my face and inject a shitload of pep into my voice. "Hi, guys!" I give my fellow contestants a girly wave with both hands.

Major cringe!

A tall blonde wearing a long-sleeved dress made of colorful lace flowers sewn together pushes to her feet, her lips pursed in a pout. "Who are you?"

"I'm Lori." I plant my feet in the ground, and shadow magic tickles my palms.

Dude, you need to chill. They're Spring seeds, not nightmares. The worst thing that girl could do is scratch you with her fake nails.

Walking all the way into my bubble, the queen bee hones in on me like a shark and crosses her arms over her chest. "What's your story? Where did you go to school?"

"Chicago." Normally, I'd put the girl in her place. Scare her shitless. I know how to take care of bullies, but I'm not supposed to draw attention to myself. I've got a role to play, and Spring seeds usually don't threaten to maim the competition.

They scheme and stab you in the back instead.

"Someone dropped out at the last minute," I add with an affable smile. "They asked me to take her place."

The girl glares from her four-inch high heels, the shoes making her at least a foot taller than me. "Yes. She became mysteriously ill... so that *you* could replace her."

The others stare at us. Most of them look ready to reach for their popcorn, but none of them breathes a word.

A gorgeous brunette marches forward with her hands on her hips. The skirt of her red dress skims the ground behind her but finishes right below her knees in the front, the asymmetrical cut memorable and quirky. "Be nice, Daisy. It's not the girl's fault if your sister had a mental breakdown." She bee-lines for the floor-to-ceiling row of mirrors and powders up her nose with a flash of magic before meeting my gaze in the reflection. "Welcome, Lori. I love your earrings."

Another blonde wearing a pink dress joins Daisy's side. A golden pendant dangles in the valley between her breasts. "Always such a suck-up, Poppy."

"Bite me, Aster."

I switch my weight from one foot to the other. Twelve new faces... I'm going to need a pen and paper.

Seth enters the room with a pair of pumps hanging from his grip. "Um. Lori, you forgot your heels."

I glance down at my bare feet. *Fuck!*

Many of the women adjust their appearance at his arrival, straightening their bustiers or fluffing their hair.

The prince clears his throat and looks over his tributes. "We're all here and ready to go, wonderful! I expect you all"—he shoots Daisy a wink—"to make Lori feel welcome. Spring roses need to bunch together this year. There will be time to use your thorns later if you make it past the first few rounds."

"A teacher's pet, that's what you are," Daisy snickers under her breath. "You must be a reeeeal good friend of his."

I look her straight in the eyes. "I didn't sleep my way into this competition, Daisy. Did you?"

My confidence shakes her, and I slip into my heels with a smirk.

I spent two whole summers in a girls' camp, but that was with mortals. I had a big advantage there. The women here aren't sly, pimpled preteens. And they're magic. That multiplies the possibility for vicious pranks in an entirely new way.

The double doors in front of us open, and a winged Faeling—a human-shaped creature the size of Tinkerbell—hustles in. The navy tuxedo he's wearing must have been hard to tailor, given the size, and the round glasses resting on his nose are cute as hell. He holds a tiny clipboard close to his chest, his dark hair slicked back over his head. "Form a line, please."

"Hello, Byron," Seth says. "I missed you, too."

The little creature turns up his nose at the prince. "Hmpf."

The Faeling slaps a number over each of our chests in haste, not bothering to spare us a real glance. The numbers aren't one to twelve, as expected, but range in random leaps from one to fifty. A small *16* is now sewn into the front of my dress, and feels heavier than it should.

The night went by so fast—I almost forgot my hatred for this *tradition*. A beauty pageant where the winner has to marry a cruel king... It's barbaric. *How can anyone watch this nonsense, knowing their new queen is bound to die?*

"Spring brides. Follow me into your dormitory." Byron leads us to the adjoining room where the numbers we were just attributed are written across alcoved individual spaces.

Small cots radiate toward the center of the room, and long but narrow windows open to the gardens below, the dorms situated on the second floor of the castle's battlement.

"Please put on the provided accessories," Byron says flatly, not looking up from his clipboard.

My spine stiffens, and I force my jaw loose, slowly walking toward the number sixteen. A big hooded white and gray fur cloak is hanging by the head of the bed. All the other girls have an identical one in their alcoved lockers, with winter boots to match. I pick the heavy cloak off the hook and frown at the full-face mask hanging underneath.

The Spring brides exchange looks ranging from surprise to disgust, but we all put on the cloak, mask, and boots. I'm used to wearing a mask—just not one that could have been bought at the dollar store. The cheap plastic digs in the sensitive skin of my temples as I adjust the flimsy string at the back of my head to make the fit more comfortable.

My heart booms in my chest when a tall, slender Fae enters the room. The woman is pale as snow, her skin freckled with ice, and for a moment, I'm back in the Shadow Court's frozen gardens...watching death march in.

But the Fae's silver hair isn't buzzed on one side, and she's got no patterns carved in her skull. The bob haircut leaves her shoulders bare with the sides longer than the back. Her navy sequin pantsuit glitters under the electric lights.

Seth pecks her cheeks. "Sara, you're a vision, as always."

"And you my dear are still a shameless flirt." She embraces him with a smile and turns over to us. "Let me see your girls."

With the masks, the loose coats that conceal our silhouettes, and the big hoods over our hair, she's not going to see much.

"Spring seeds, hello. I'm Sarafina, the royal chief of staff. I'm responsible for the Yule pageant, so if everyone could form a line, we're about ready for the castle tour."

Daisy marches to the center with her hands braced on her hips. "Why do we have to wear masks?"

I bet she'd hoped to wow the king with her looks, poor thing.

Sarafina waves her concerns away. "The brides' reveal isn't until later, and we want to keep up the suspense. Now, follow me."

The Faeling lands on her shoulders and whispers something in her ear that makes her chuckle, and we all fall into step behind her.

"What a cute little fairy," Aster says. "I wonder where he comes from?"

"A Fae*ling*," I correct her. "Faelings are born out of a royal Faen's first laugh, and bound to him or her forever. They're incredibly rare and powerful allies, and if Sarafina's got one, it means she's royalty."

"Or used to be. The Fae courts' political landscape shifts quickly," Poppy adds. She lowers her voice and huddles up next to me. "Poor Aster, she was the only magic-born child in her family, and she's not the brightest flower..." she trails off with a chuckle.

According to Seth, a small fraction of the Spring brides are random seeds of magic that appeared in otherwise non-magic families, but most of them inherited their powers from a diluted Fae bloodline, like me.

Poppy's eyes shimmer with unabashed curiosity as she licks her lips. "But I thought you came directly from the new world, Lori. Have you seen a Faeling before?"

My heart falls in my chest at my mistake. "No, but I've studied... My mother would blush if I ever made the mistake of calling anyone a *fairy*."

During my short tenure as the Shadow Court librarian, I'd handled some of the rarest, most treasured volumes in the realm. But I was still only a sprout—a second-tier trainee. I wasn't allowed to read most of the precious collection, yet. Though, I did *occasionally* peek at a few of the books' secrets before sliding them back into the stacks.

Because of the restrictions placed on mortals and the rampant secrecy between courts, my general knowledge of Faerie is vast, but the specifics are still mysteries.

Poppy tucks her long brown braid inside the flap of her cloak and nods as though I'm making enough sense for her to pardon my cleverness. "Your mother was an archer, yes? That's why you went to school in the new world?"

"Absolutely," I lie. *Gods...* I tuck my bottom lip between my teeth. *Good job, Lori. At this rate, you'll be found out in less than a day.*

CHAPTER 6
IVORY TOWER
ELIO

Music blares down the stairwell of the tower as I hammer the white and black keys in a soothing, familiar tempo. The smooth ivories glide under my fingertips, cold and familiar, my soul never quite at peace but here, lost in the melody.

From the highest window of a castle frozen in time, I see them spread around the gardens below, crawling all over my lands like ants... Another year. Another wedding.

A fresh round of the curse that started in this very room.

I haven't slept in the baldaquin bed by the window in decades, and yet everything is still here. Wilted daffodils bow to my misery, Iris's hoop earrings still laying on the bedside table. I know what the other courts—even my own subjects—whisper about me.

They say I'm desperate to forget my first love.

They say I've gone insane.

They're not wrong.

I slam the key cover down and retreat to the depths of the icy tunnels and secret passageways running under my castle. In here, I don't have to hide who I am and take solace in these last few moments of clarity.

For the next seven days, I'll have to speak like a man. Dress like a man. Eat like a man and smile to the cameras. Fuck a pretty girl to appease my people—and the powers that be.

A girl I'll only end up killing. My kingdom needs a queen, and so I marry. Every year I marry, and suffer.

Every year, I lose her all over again.

This endless curse is meant to punish me for what I've done—with no hope of release. As Winter King, death shall never come for me. For me, death never ends.

CHAPTER 7
SNOW WHITE
LORI

Fresh, powdery snow peppers the roofs and turrets of the Winter castle. The stone fortress is perched at the foot of a snow-peaked mountain range, cradled between steep cliffs and the bustling city beyond the gates. The busy streets of Tundra, the Winter capital, are mere footsteps away from the castle. It's wild to witness that kind of proximity between the High Fae and the ordinary people considering most of the Shadowlands' citizens were barred from the grounds of the Shadow Court for decades.

The Spring brides drag their feet, taking in the splendid view. A gigantic frozen lake made of turquoise ice shines in the distance, smooth as a mirror. Awed whispers and delighted gasps buzz through the ranks as we walk along the parapet to the stairs leading down to an interior courtyard. Inside the castle grounds, the dramatic scenery is quickly replaced by secluded gardens that shield us from the icy wind.

A maze of cedar hedges crawls deeper and deeper inside the Winter stronghold, and Sarafina guides us through its corners and curves without hesitation. "Never enter the labyrinth without an escort. It protects the king's private gardens from uninvited visitors and stretches all the way to the mountains. Many powerful Winter Fae have lost their toes and fingers after getting lost in this maze. You'd never make it through on your own."

On the other side, steep rooftops create walls of packed snow around the inner gardens that extend past my head.

A dark frown obscures Seth's face, and I follow his gaze to the three uneven towers reaching out to the cloudless sky. The tallest of them is a little crooked, its blue stone shingles laden with ice instead of snow. I halt and blink a few times, my gut in knots. For whatever reason, the lonely window at the top gives me the major creeps.

Up ahead, Sarafina spins around to face us. "This is Winter's sacred tree, the only Hawthorn in existence to produce the infamous frost apples. If you're lucky enough to make it to the top three, you will receive one of these apples, and the healthy, long-lasting life that comes with it."

I'm at the back of the pack because of my quick stop and tilt my head to take a good look at the tree. Compared to the Shadow Court's Hawthorn, Winter's sacred tree is small and brittle. Ice coats the white trunk and branches, making them twinkle in the sun.

Beautiful, but barren. Almost sickly.

Sharp, deadly icicles hang from the network of gnarly branches right above our heads, and I gawk at their terrible beauty.

A handful of blood-red leaves hang on despite the frost, and tiny white apples dangle from a dozen branches. Some of them are bigger and slowly ripening into a deep, midnight blue.

Frost apples. The reason why mortal women flock to this mind-boggling contest in droves. The real treasure they covet. A six percent chance to taste the proverbial fountain of youth and see their lives expanded by centuries. No wrinkles. No sickness.

The one in fifty chance of actually marrying the king and dying at his hands is seemingly forgotten. A long, healthy life is all mortals dream about, but I wouldn't take a bite out of the creepy fruits to save my life.

An ice statue stands behind the tree and marks the location of a sleek glass coffin. Sarafina breezes past the roped-off path leading to the tombstone, but I pause. *By Morpheus...*

A handful of brides stop near the macabre display, but none of them dares to walk past the ropes. I catch up with them and slip inside the restricted area.

"What are you doing?" Poppy whispers.

"If they didn't want us to see her, they wouldn't have put her in a glass coffin in the middle of the gardens, no?" I answer playfully. I want to take a closer look at the dead queen, but if I'm to break the rules, I might as well not be the only one caught on the wrong side of the ropes. "Come on. Let's steal a peek."

My companions exchange nervous glances.

"You're going to get eliminated," a girl whispers, giving us a wide berth.

"Who cares? No Spring seed makes it past the first round, anyway," Poppy says as she joins me on the path.

The cheerful way she declares us out of the contest before it even starts shakes my confidence, and I promise myself to give Seth hell later for not mentioning that huge asterisk.

Daisy scoffs, her arms crossed awkwardly over her chest because of her thick fur coat.

"You chicken?" I taunt her.

The blonde digs her heels in the snow. "Not at all. But I stay away from corpses as a rule."

Aster skips to my side of the ropes. "I'm game."

Snow crunches under my boots on my way to the sepulture, Aster and Poppy quick on my trail. Under the most disturbing and crooked Hawthorn tree in history, dead in the center of the Winter King's inner gardens, Iris Lovatt lays in her glass coffin, entombed for all eternity. Her hands are clasped over her stomach, the bright red shade of her lips bringing chills to my spine.

A hiccup quakes my throat as I draw closer.

Holy shit! When Seth had told me I was a ringer for the late

Winter Queen, I'd hoped it was one of those "I knew a woman of Indian descent who looked just like you" type of scenario.

But the color of our skin is actually the one detail that's not exactly right—her being super dead and all. Well, that and her pointy ears. Aside from that, the dead queen laid to rest at the heart of the Winter gardens, wrapped in pristine white fur and laid on a bed of white feathers, could be my twin.

A sudden, cold sting creeps around my ribcage, and my abs clench. Seeing an almost perfect copy of myself in a coffin was bound to poke at old wounds, and I sink my nails in my palms, waiting for the insidious flash of pain to subside.

Acid simmers at the back of my throat as I examine the bronze plaque at the base of the ominous, see-through grave.

TRUE LOVE TRANSCENDS CROWNS, BLOOD, AND FLESH. IT DOESN'T CARE FOR COMMON SENSE AND DOESN'T PLAY BY THE RULES. LOVE HAS NO MASTERS, ONLY SLAVES.

- ELIO HADES LIGHTBRINGER

Sarafina claps her hands a few times to attract our attention, the royal chief of staff now standing inches behind the ropes. "Brides. Come with me, please. This isn't part of the tour." Her voice holds a sharp edge of reproach, but Seth bites back a smile.

Smothered giggles escape Poppy and Aster as we rejoin the ranks of the guided tour, but my tongue sticks to the roof of my mouth, parched and dry. *Did they take a close look at Iris? Aren't they going to say something?*

The sun-filled gardens suddenly look completely different. No matter how much white snow they sprinkle over the earth, this is the kingdom of death. Their king's specialty. So much death, he's drowning in it.

Wife after wife, the first one on display for everyone to see.

My father used to say that *in death, we are alone.* But this burial site screams for attention with the glass lid, the perfectly-preserved corpse, and the subtle coat of rouge on her cheeks. It's too vivid. The Winter King probably walks by every day to gaze upon a woman who looks like she's only sleeping. Like she might wake up at any moment.

A full-blown shiver quakes my body. I came here to seduce this monstrous king, but now I'm scared. *How is he going to react when he sees me? What if he wants to marry me, after all?*

Sarafina leads us through a large stone arch, where we join the crowd gathering on the other side. Thick silver ropes separate the small space in four different sections, and a single balcony towers over a sea of women.

Fifty brides... *Holy fuck.* That's a lot of giggles and manicures in one place, but we're all wearing the same cloaks and masks, so it's hard to tell any of us apart.

Seth follows Sarafina toward the balcony, but I catch up to him and grip his arm. "How did Iris die?" I whisper.

He waits for his guide to be out of earshot before he answers, "She fell."

"From the tower?"

"Yes." His dark brows pull together. "How did you know?"

I bite on my bottom lip, the sudden burst of adrenaline in my blood prompting me to run.

"Brides of Wintermere, Summerlands, Secret Springs, and the Red Forest, welcome. The Yule pageant will commence momentarily." Sarafina's gaze briefly scans the crowd before it latches on to Seth. "Fellow patrons, please join me on the balcony."

I huddle closer to the others not to draw too much attention and keep my head down, grateful for my big hood and mask. Most of my companions stretch their necks and whisper between themselves, excited to see the Winter King.

Sunlight shines through the balcony's structure, the entire thing carved out of ice. Droplets of water drip down the banisters of the two symmetrical staircases flanking both sides of the platform. The intricate transparent railings allow for the royal sponsors to get a solid grip as they head up to meet Sarafina.

A woman wearing red from head to toe climbs after Seth with light feet and unmatched grace. A blood-red hood covers her head, but a long auburn braid hangs over her shoulder, and an earth-toned tunic and sash hug her slender form. Dark marks are painted over her face, the jeweled scarf tied over her forehead masking her brows. A long, majestic katana is strapped to her back, and I press my fingertips to my empty palms.

She's a warrior.

If only I could show off my daggers as proudly as she presents her curved sword, maybe I wouldn't feel so vulnerable.

I've read about Reds, the women that populate the mysterious forest of the same name, but I've never glimpsed at one before. Their gods and customs are completely different to the rest of the Fae continent—and not well-documented. My librarian side is itching for ink and quills to take notes on the sponsor's uniform, but it is said that the secrets of the Red Forest and its inhabitants can only be written down in blood.

I'd been looking forward to visiting their lands with the Shadow King on Morheim, but I'd missed my chance because of the spider bite—and had spent the week puking my entrails out instead. My nasty scar heats up at the reminder, and I reach for it without meaning to, clasping my side with one hand.

Seth is the only male out of the four royal sponsors. Summer is also represented by a woman, though she's not as striking as the Red Fae, and Sarafina is the apparent patron for Winter brides.

A dozen cameras the size of grapefruits fly over our heads and scatter around the gardens, interrupting my train of thought. The sphere-shaped lenses look like eyes and have translucent, iridescent wings on each side. They zoom through the air with a low buzz. The first kingdoms are notorious for mixing mortal technology with magic, but I've never seen anything like this.

A middle-age looking Fae wearing a white tuxedo and holding a microphone leans against the railing. "Welcome to the Yule pageant." Blush colors his cheeks, and his bright blue eyes are about the only interesting thing about him. "Don't worry. You'll soon forget about the cameras. Not only because you'll get used to them, but also because of the clever enchantments I weaved within them." The Fae winks to the women closest to him and slicks his gray hair back over his head with a small comb.

Thank Morpheus the colonel fried chicken wannabe isn't the Winter King. If I hadn't caught a glimpse of Elio Lightbringer back in the Shadow Court's gardens, I'd be worried to see this man scour the crowd like a bird of prey scavenging for dinner. Looks shouldn't matter in my situation, but if I have to pretend to like some dangerous Fae prick, it won't hurt that he's nice to look at.

"Don't give all of our secrets away, Paul," Sarafina says, her voice higher than it was before—and full of pep.

"It's an honor to host with you again this year, Sara." Paul hikes up his sleeves and licks his lips, apparently excited to kick off the pageant. "The lucky brides who survive the first two rounds of elimination will get to tour Wintermere with us. We'll hit Snowhaven, the Frost Peaks, and Glacier's Edge before we return home to crown the winner."

"I have relatives in Snowhaven," the girl behind me whispers to her wintry friends.

Sarafina clasps her hands together. "I can't believe the wedding is only ten days away, Paul."

"Yes. The brides have a full schedule up ahead. Remember ladies... If you make it through to the top three, you'll be rewarded with one of our precious frost apples," Paul declares with an exaggerated touch of drama.

It's barely been a minute, and the showmanship is already in full swing. Somehow, the part where the winner will soon die is ignored, and all the fallacies of this "contest" are glossed over like they don't even matter.

"But we're a long way off from the top three and finding out the name of our new Queen, Sara. This is our fiftieth annual Yule pageant, so we figured the speed round should have a twist."

My fists clench at my sides. Reality TV used to be a guilty pleasure of mine, but right this second, I can't remember why.

Sarafina nods and offers the closest camera a conspiratorial smile. "Marriage has so little to do with physical appearance. This year, the first step to falling in love will be to connect with a mind—not lust for a body."

Seth turns his head toward Paul, and his serious squint sends my heart into a frenzy. *Is she saying...*

Paul wiggles his brows. "Instead of meeting every candidate face-to-face, the king will host blind dates, and the brides will only have their personalities, wits, and voices to stand out. Who will hold our king's attention long enough to advance to the next step, and who will simply be eliminated without ever laying eyes on him?"

"This is such an exciting experiment, Paul. A first impression of the heart."

My brows furrow. What fucked-up, alternate universe did I end up in?

Paul raises both arms to the sky, the sleeves of his tuxedo about two inches too short for him to look chic. "I can't wait to get started. Brides, please report to your sponsor for the schedule, and we'll see you tonight for the inauguration ball."

"Let the games begin!" Sarafina concludes the broadcast, and the cameras fly back inside a large leather-cladded chest next to the hosts.

Whispers of disappointment lament the absence of the Winter King, but adrenaline swirls in my veins. My gaze meets Seth's, and the Fae presses his lips together in an uncharacteristic pout. The whole point of me coming here was that the Winter King would see me and keep me around.

My only real chance of saving Ayaan is about to go up in smoke. *What am I supposed to do now?*

CHAPTER 8

LOVE IS BLURRY

LORI

After the welcome speech, we all walk back to the Spring quarters, and Seth takes me aside. "How did you know? About Iris?" He drags me to the corridor between his bedroom and the dressing room with a sad frown on his face and closes the door behind us. "The official investigation states that she fell down the tower by accident"—a resentful grimace twists his features—"but I just know she was pushed."

The cold tingles from before return full-force. There's something about that tower that's not right. "Pushed by whom? The king?"

He shakes his head. "I was just a kid then. I was playing with the breeze, practicing how to turn myself into a cloud, and before I knew it, Iris was dead. My mother always said that Elio wanted Iris all to himself. His paranoia that someone would steal her away prompted him to shutter her from the world. The day of her death, Elio was furious. Iris had thrown a lavish party without his assent, and they fought up on that tower, but my mother could never actually prove that he killed her. He claimed not to have pushed her, and since Fae can't lie—and Elio being the oh-so-great Winter King—no one was willing to dig deeper."

A cold shiver runs through me. "That's horrible. I'm so sorry." I rub the space between my brows and concentrate on the problem at hand. "How am I supposed to get picked during a blind date?"

Seth presses his palm to his handsome face, looking as defeated as I feel. "They fucked us, I agree."

"Can't we get an edge, here? Maybe I could watch some footage from the old pageants?"

"The previous year's games are not viewable after the fact. It'd be...awkward, to say the least. Don't worry, the candidates from Spring, Summer, and the Red Forest don't watch the Yule pageant, either, so I expect only the Winter seeds will have an edge since they all get to watch the pageant on TV."

All of my ideas run into dead ends, and my chest contracts. "Come on!" I punctuate the word with a soft punch to his breast bone. "You've been part of this circus for years, right? There must be something useful you remember about him."

Seth taps his nose in a repetitive manner, deep in thought. "Elio's a total bore. He likes poetry and sad music."

"Very helpful. Poetry and sad music... You'd make a world-class spy."

The Winter King authored a famous poetry book, so Seth's *intel* is perhaps the most well-known fact about Elio Lightbringer. My eyes narrow, all the urgency and nerves begging me to pick at the Fae prince for his flagrant ignorance. "Tell me, Seth. How far did your best protégée make it last year?"

He grits his teeth together, busted like a kid in the pantry, his hand deep in peanut butter. "Alright. My seeds never get past the first round."

"Funny how you forgot to mention that," I quip.

"We're not exactly on good terms, Elio and I. I didn't want to discourage you before we even got started, but you're a game changer, I'm sure of it."

"Not if he never sees me." I twist my hair in a bun above my head. Glossy waves and pretty make-up can't help me now.

"That's not all. I have an ace up my sleeve." Seth winces like he wasn't planning on sharing so many details. "This year, I convinced my mother to attend the Yule brunch in Snowhaven. She hasn't set foot in Wintermere in ages, so Elio will want to keep a few Spring seeds around for that not to insult her. Just make sure he remembers you, and we'll be fine."

The tight knot in my gut eases at the news. Politics could serve me well here. "Tell me more about Iris, then."

A loud knock startles us both. "Number sixteen. You're up. We have to get you ready."

The voice belongs to the Faeling, Byron, and Seth swings open the door with an asinine smile plastered on his face. "We're ready, B. Lori, here, was just powdering her nose."

"I'm not sure what good that will do." Byron marks down something on his clipboard. "Keep the hood and cloak, but you can remove the mask once you're inside the date pod, if you want. The partition walls separating the king from the brides are made of ice, making anything beyond them too blurry to see."

"It's my turn already? How long are these dates, anyway?" It's barely been half an hour since we left the courtyard.

"Up to ten minutes. The king will walk out when he's had enough, so we're lining up the contestants in advance."

"Oh, really? As long as it pleases his Majesty, " I say, unable to keep it in.

"Your quarters are the farthest away from the pods, so we have to hurry." The Faeling hikes his round glasses up his tiny nose and squints at me. "Come with me, please."

Daisy—number twenty—skips in front of me. "What were you and Seth whispering about?"

"None of your business."

Byron takes a shortcut through the maze to a large greenhouse. Triangular pieces of glass form the roof of a polygon-shaped dome. The edges of the building are made of the same material, but it's frosted over to conceal what's going on inside.

The Faeling flies up to the nearest side and presses his palm to it. The glass becomes pliable under his touch, the way a mirror would. "Here for sixteen."

"I'd wish you luck, but I don't mean it," Daisy chants behind me.

I slide through the liquid glass and tiptoe inside the makeshift room. The small space is fashioned to look exactly like a reality show, with a velvet loveseat and cushions in the middle.

Three ice walls enclose the pod, the entire room no bigger than a walk-in closet. I press my ear to the partition and slow my breathing. It's clearly meant to be soundproof, but a few muffled words echo from the pod next to me. I can't see anything beyond the wall except for two blurry shadows.

I'm next.

An eyeball-shaped camera lays on the small table next to the loveseat, and I lean forward to examine it. The ball is tucked inside a square receptacle, paper-thin wings curled around its shape. The lenses' cover mimics a closed lid pulled over a sleeping eye.

My heart booms in my chest as I consider the opaque blue ice separating the two pods again. *What am I doing here? Seth chose me because of my looks. It was a foolproof plan considering my striking resemblance to the Winter King's lost love. The king would be intrigued by his dead wife's doppelgänger, but he certainly won't care for some socially awkward orphan whose only two talents are hide-and-seek and skewering monsters.*

The camera buzzes to life on the table and blinks at me a few times. A little antenna slithers out of it, and the harsh glare coming from the sun overhead tapers down into a pleasant glow.

I have to persuade a Fae king to keep me around in less than ten minutes, or my brother will be hanged. And if I fail, his soul will be marked, collected, and sorted like nothing more than an old, useless library book by the very man on the other side of the wall.

Ten minutes to save his life.

"Hello?" the king calls to the room.

Starting now!

"Hi," I answer quickly, my eyes darting to the glass ceiling.

How should I play this? Bubbly and confident, or timid and well-read? From Seth's quick pep talk, I'm leaning toward the latter. I might not be into poetry or Fae music, but I spent my fair share of time in a library.

"What's your name?" The voice on the other side of the wall is both melodic and deep—perfectly masculine in every way, but not at all hoarse or sinister like I expected.

"Mm, Lori."

"I'm Elio."

"I know." My brain runs through different repartees so fast, second-guessing every single sentence that comes to mind, until I blurt out, "It's easy for me. There's only one guy to keep track of."

He doesn't answer or laugh—nothing.

Elio... I've never heard the name uttered without an ominous ring to it, but it's beautiful, really. Not at all fit for the King of Death.

"Elio means sun. Your parents had a fun sense of humor," I babble, unable to stand the silence any longer.

"I was born to the Sun Court. As it turns out, light and ice have much more in common than you'd think."

"I didn't know that," I say quickly. My blood runs a little hot, and I sink my nails inside my palms. How did Seth forget to mention that about him?

"Does my pedigree anger you, Lori? Do you have an axe to grind with the Sun Court?" Elio asks with humor.

"No. I just meant—my sponsor didn't mention it."

Silence, again. The unabashed glare of the eye unnerves me, and I touch the arch of my brow over the cheap plastic mask.

"You're not from Faerie, are you?" he asks.

My chest deflates, and I shake my head, grateful for the lifeline. "No, I'm from the new world."

"And why did you agree to come here?"

I hug a cushion to my lap. *It's just small talk. I can do this.* "I had to come...for my family."

"For money and long-lasting youth, right?" Elio says in a muted tone.

"Yeah," I lie.

"Don't fret, you're not the only one. You've all been enticed by the riches of my kingdom. The precious jewels from my mines and my invaluable frost apples. It's refreshing to hear you say it. I distrust the brides that proclaim to be after true love, because they certainly won't find it here."

I frown at that. "Isn't marriage supposed to be based on love?"

"Typically, yes."

"And what makes you so untypical? Besides the endless string of dead wives, that is."

The silence stretches and expands, and my heart beats in my throat. "Are you still there?"

Silence.

Fuck-fuck-fuck. "Sorry, that was rude—I just wanted to break the ice—"

A pun? Really? My brain melts from the shame, and I bury my face in the cushion not to scream.

"No, it's the truth. Never apologize for the truth," Elio whispers.

A faint *thud* on the other side of the wall goes straight to my spine, and I grab my forehead. "Hello?"

He's gone. *I've done it. I've ruined the entire mission with one stupid sentence. Why in the seven hells did I say that? The man marries—and very likely kills his wife—every year. It was incredibly stupid of me to point it out.*

Byron releases me from the ice trap, and I wait for Daisy to be done so the Faeling can escort us back together. When the blonde finally joins me on the snowy path, the Faeling buzzes forward in front of us.

"How did yours go?" she chimes in a fake, sugary tone.

I glower at the blonde, about ready to slap the satisfied smile off her smug face.

"That bad, eh?" She skips up ahead, her steps a little lighter than before. "I'm glad to hear it."

My brows raise. "I hope your date sucked as well."

We exchange a glance, and—to my extreme surprise—erupt into a fit of uncontrollable laughter. My belly clenches as I try to get a hold of myself, but the situation is just so bizarre, I can't stop.

Byron's spine stiffens, and he flies further ahead.

Daisy stops walking as she muffles an unladylike snort with her hands. "This pageant is pretty fucked up, isn't it?" she whispers.

I nod emphatically at her assessment. We're never going to be friends, but we're more alike than I thought. "Absolutely. Do you even want to marry that guy?"

Her nose wrinkles in outrage. "No. You?"

"No!" Our hilarity doubles after that, and Byron shakes his head all the way to the dorms, our reputation as ditsy, harebrained Spring seeds solidified.

There's nothing funny about my spectacular failure. I've let Ayaan, Nell, and Cece down with my big mouth, but it's better to laugh in the face of death than to admit defeat.

CHAPTER 9
FEAR THE REAPER
ELIO

"**R**eady to serve, my king," Kiro, my best lieutenant, salutes me. He's in full uniform for the soldiers' send off. The golden zipper of his sleeveless white bodysuit grazes his thick chin and marks him as a leader of the Ice City. The runes I carved into his skull burn a vibrant shade of blue on one side of his head, while long white hair covers the other.

"At ease, Kiro."

"The new recruits are all packed and ready to leave for the Ice City," he announces.

I walk through the ranks and offer a gracious nod to each of my new reapers. They all stand taller as I greet them, their chins held high.

"Congratulations. When you started this process, there were hundreds of candidates. Be proud of yourselves. You've proved your worth and taken your vows, and it's time to start your new life," I declare loudly so that the entire platoon hears. "Take a good look at your comrades, because from now on, you are family."

"Thank you, Your Majesty," a man replies. Snowflakes brand his neck, and he's got more poise than his peers. A leader in the making, perhaps.

Hands braced behind my back, I return to the front of the platoon. "Kiro will accompany you to your new home. The frost mountains are beautiful, and the Ice City is a place like no other. You will need of nothing there—but forever be set apart. The worlds need you, my reapers. You will be hated by most and cursed to the seven hells for doing people a favor. You've chosen a hard but rewarding life. Trust me, no one appreciates your sacrifice more than I do."

My reapers are my pride and joy, and yet, they don't know me. They can't. Once they move to the Ice City and get deployed throughout the worlds, they can't ever return.

They collect souls and serve the realm until they die. They don't marry or have children.

I pat Kiro's shoulder. "Help them settle in."

The bulky man clears his throat, signaling that he has something else to discuss with me.

"Yes?"

"I've received word from the Ice City, my king. The grueling haze storm on top of Frost Peaks is back, twice as big as last year. It's blocking access to the Blueridge mines."

I catch a wince from surfacing. The weather turbulence that keeps popping up all over Wintermere weighs on my mind quite a bit. "Advise the soldiers to stay outside the storm for the time being. I'll be in Frost Peaks soon enough."

"As you wish, my king." Kiro stands straight in a show of respect and obedience before turning back to his recruits. "Soldiers, put on your masks. On my command."

I leave them to their travels and return to the castle. A huge part of me wishes I could go with them. If I wasn't king... I wouldn't have to pretend to be better than them.

Sara is hyperventilating by the time I join her in the main hall, but she's earned every bit of that panicked grimace after the stupid blind date twist.

"Almost an hour late! How am I supposed to occupy fifty, half-excited, half-terrified mortals while you sulk? The entire kingdom has been looking forward to the Yule ball, as you well know. They're waiting for the results of the first round to start the music, and Paul has run out of things to say." She raises a shaky hand to her brows. "I don't think that's ever happened before."

"Settle down, Sara. I'm here."

She points her index finger at me, looking more feral than ever. "Get that jaded look off your face, or else—"

She's the only Fae that can speak to me like this, the only one allowed to act so familiar—and only when we're alone. We're the same, Sara and me. She's broken beyond repair, too.

"Here." She crams the bride list into my hands.

I force myself not to flinch, dying to ball the piece of parchment and stomp on it.

"It's only seven days, Elio. You'll get through it." She rests a hand on my arm and gives it a soft squeeze. "And the first one is almost over."

Seven days and one night...she keeps glossing over that part, but there's no use pretending with Sara. She knows I'd rather be anywhere but here.

My distaste for the whole new way she decided to torture me sharpens into anger. "But *fifty* brides? Was it really necessary? How can I hope to keep track of them all, sight unseen?"

Fifty women. Fifty pointless conversations. My brain is about to implode.

She holds my reproachful gaze. "It's the fiftieth Yule pageant in that many years. The people craved something different, flashy, and a little more modern, so we're emulating the new mortal trends."

Thick make-up covers the dark circles under her blue eyes, and her white turtleneck is meant to cover the snow flaking off her skin. Rouge brings a shade of color to her cheeks, but it's all for the cameras. Sara's blood runs about as cold as mine. And she hasn't been sleeping, either, so she tried to conceal her real mood with a little more makeup than usual.

She offers me a restless smile. "We've all grown tired of the same old routine."

Routine is safe. It allows me to go through the motions without too much hassle.

"And I'm grateful for your efforts, as always." I hand her back the list, stowing my moody thoughts and grievances away. "Whatever you decide. Keep a handful from each court not to disappoint anyone in particular. And get rid of all the Spring seeds, per usual."

She pries a new piece of parchment from her planner—a list she already prepared. "You don't even want to see their names?"

My eyes narrow. "Is that judgment in your voice?"

"You should take this process more seriously. Most of these girls have waited their whole lives to come here," she pleads. "Spring seeds included."

Sara acts as a replacement for my frozen soul. She's my moral compass—the annoying little angel standing on my shoulder.

"Fine." I scan the page quickly and skim the names. "Here. I looked. Get rid of them."

"None of them managed to grab your attention?"

A familiar name, written in a peculiar fashion, catches my eye, and I pause, surprised to see her on the list of Spring seeds. Spring brides are usually cheerful and cliché. I never would have thought that a woman as brutally honest and refreshingly sarcastic could belong to Freya.

"One stood out," I finally admit.

The thick American accent and sultry voice were certainly memorable amid a series of wide-eyed, romantic fools.

"Who?"

I tap her name. "Lori."

"Oh... How did she manage that?"

Lori made me smile, but I'm not going to freak Sara out by

mentioning it. I grab an apple from the bowl on the high table and bite into the crisp red fruit. "Don't worry, Sara. I'd never marry a dandelion fluff again."

She keeps the list right under my nose and lowers her voice. "Freya herself will attend the Yule brunch this year. It would be a bad look to eliminate all her candidates before the real challenge even starts. You can't turn your back on Spring forever."

Why not? Spring has certainly turned its back on me, and the sweetness of the apple isn't enough to erase the sour taste in my mouth.

"Keep a handful, then, not to single anyone out. As long as Seth isn't the one presenting them at the Yule brunch, we can keep a few of his fuck friends around for a few days," I say.

"So...Lori. In or out?" Sara acts aloof, but I haven't been on a first-name basis with a bride from the speed round in ages, and we both know this.

I should really eliminate any possible distraction sooner rather than later.

"In," I say instead, my brain not quite right today.

"Are you sure?"

I toss the apple core into the trash. "Yes. For now." The strange warmth at the pit of my belly doubles, and I think back to Lori's brazen comment about my dead wives.

No contestant has ever been so honest with me—not from the start. In spite of myself, I think I'm going to like her.

Paul runs in, panting, and dabs his flushed face with a handker-chief. "Are you ready? Even I can't go on speaking forever," he jokes with a big, nervous smile.

Sara quickly slips the list of Spring seeds back inside her planner. "Yes. All done."

My oldest advisor turns to me. "How did you manage to keep track of them all?"

"I didn't," I answer.

His raucous laugh creeps under my skin, and I fight off the urge to roll my eyes. He doesn't think I'm serious.

Paul's part of the old guard. When I became king, I kept him around to ensure a smooth transition from my predecessor's reign and out of friendship for his daughter, but he actually loves to host these pointless games. His obsession for the sanctity of the pageant has begun to rub off on Sara, which irks my nerves more with each passing year.

He catches his breath, even more red-faced than when he entered. "Ha, Elio. One day, when you're old and gray like me, you'll miss the way these beautiful, young women look at you."

I'm already old, but youth sticks to Fae kings longer than happiness. Paul is almost three hundred years old, and way past his prime, so I'm still a child in his mind. He's relied on his cleverness and immense knowledge to keep his job. His magic is as tepid as magic comes, and I bet my predecessor chose him for his mediocrity, paranoid as he was that someone would steal his crown.

Now that I possess the Winter crown and understand all the indelible heartache that comes with it, I'd gladly give it away, but that's not possible.

"I don't think I could miss any of this," I breathe, looking straight ahead to dodge their reactions.

"The kingdom needs this, Elio. *We* need this," Paul says.

My teeth grit together at the futile reminder. "I know."

Paul Snow is a shrewd politician. Without his love for the Yule pageant, his exhaustive knowledge of history, and the immense respect he's earned through his centuries of service to the crown, I would have to hunt a woman down and force her to marry me each year.

Me and my *endless string of dead wives* have made it hard for my soldiers to quell the sparks of rebellion that have been spreading year after year around Wintermere. Enough sparks make a flame and a strong flame brings war.

Sara clears her throat and motions for Paul to lead the way to the balcony. "It's time to shepherd the brides into the ballroom. We'll announce the names of the losers first, but you better go and change before we enter. I put your clothes in the study."

"I'll see you in there." Pretending not to notice the worried curve of Sara's mouth, I speed toward the stairs leading down to the ballroom and the adjoining study. My tongue sticks to the roof of my mouth, in dire need of some mind-erasing, numbness-inducing Nether cider.

Paul's thunderous voice reaches my ears as he steps out on the balcony, "Fantastic news! The results are in."

I skip the stairs two at a time to distance myself from the cold, miserable pressure in my gut, but alas, I carry it with me.

The Yule pageant is an age-old tradition. It keeps me from becoming a fairytale monster in the eyes of my subjects and reels in the discontented High Fae who might back a formal challenge.

Everyone loves a bittersweet exhibition of chaos, beauty, and greed, and the life-and-death stakes have only amplified the grim fascination viewers cater for my nuptials.

Sara and Paul's antics make the queen-selection process appear transparent and exciting, when it's nothing more than a sacrifice. The large rewards we offer keep the women coming, but I'm the one who has to endure the wedding night. The one who sees the fear in their eyes when death comes for them.

Keeping the kingdom safe and thriving makes all this morbid showmanship worth the hassle. In theory.

CHAPTER 10

DANCING WITH GHOSTS

LORI

The Winter ballroom is four times as big as the Shadow Court's banquet hall. Tall, checkered windows open to the gardens, and the frosted glass panes give the whole room a dramatic flair. Crystal chandeliers twinkle about our heads, and a dizzying spark of wonder steals my breath as my eyes latch onto the vaulted ceiling.

By the spindle... The fall of the Mist King.

After the Mist Wars—deadly, decades-long wars that had reduced the Fae population by half—each of the first kingdoms commissioned a mural to commemorate their victory over the scourge of the Islantide.

Sheets of precious metals have been chiseled, carved, etched, or burnished to create an incredibly detailed mosaic. My jaw hangs open, my eyes bulging from the effort to take it all in, but I could spend an entire week in this room and only grasp at a fraction of what the artist immortalized here.

While the Winter King made us revel in the wait for his royal behind, Byron instructed us to trade in the cheap plastic masks for masquerade ones, and the accessory soothes my nerves, its weight similar to the one I use to travel through the sceawere. Lost in the beauty of the mural, I graze the mask's feathery edge with trembling fingers and hold on to my hood, the thick fur threatening to slide down. My neck reprimands me for the strain, but it's just so monumental...

The mural ebbs at the edges, no trim framing the mosaic so the story can continue to be written as it unfolds. *History's never finished*, my father used to say.

"Are you a history buff, Sixteen?" Poppy asks, jolting me back to reality.

She was in the last batch of blind dates—number 48—and I haven't seen her since the welcome speech.

Aster wrinkles her nose as she searches the ceiling for an explanation. "What is that?"

Poppy quiets down and chooses her words carefully, but not the way you whisper when you don't want anyone to hear, no. The vibrant shade of her flushed cheeks and the rush in her breaths hint that whatever she's about to speak of is forbidden—or taboo. "Back then, there were not two but three types of Fae. Light Fae bloomed from the Sun, Spring, and Summer Courts. Darklings brewed from storms, winter, and shadows and out of blood-drenched, red soil." She takes a measured pause. "Last but not least—beads of mist coalesced over the tropical mountains of the Islantide. The Mist Fae worshiped Kahlee, the goddess of chaos, destruction, and transformation. They were incredibly fast learners, mind readers, and engineers that could merge disparate seeds of magic."

Aster wrinkles her nose. "But High Spring Fae can often yield darker magic."

Poppy lowers her voice even more. "I'm not talking about the way a talented High Fae can become proficient at two or three schools of magic. Not like Seth, who's an amalgam of light and dark. No, the Mist Fae created technology that allowed them to melt down magic in its purest form and forge it into jewels, bestowing immense power upon their wearers. At the height of his power, the Mist King had so many of these jewels embedded in his skin that he rivaled the Gods themselves."

"What happened to them?" Aster asks.

"All the Mist Fae were slaughtered after the war, and their jewels were supposedly destroyed. But legend says a handful managed to avoid execution and went into hiding. And now, their descendants walk among us, waiting for a chance to strike back." Poppy races through the last part for effect, her fingers extended in front of her like claws.

Daisy huffs, clearly not buying Poppy's story. "That's fantasy. Mist Fae have been extinct for centuries. The only remnants of their religion were the Tidecallers, and even they must have died out by now—"

"Mm. Ladies?" A staff member motions for us to hand off our stuffy cloaks, his arm outstretched.

While the four of us were chatting in a huddle, the other brides switched out their winter boots for heels and touched up their appearance, and we quickly do the same. The distraction leaves us at the back of the pack, the others now much closer to the stage, a sea of strangers now standing between us and the hosts.

I squint at the Fae men and women that streamed in while I was admiring the ceiling. "Who are these people?"

"About three hundred courtiers have the honor of attending the Yule ball in person to get an exclusive first-look at the contestants," Poppy says. The rumples of her blood-red gown lick the floor, her figure enhanced by the steep bustier.

I finally shrug off the heavy fur cloak, and Daisy snickers. "A wedding dress, really?"

The white dress Seth forced me into earns me frowns and grimaces from my peers. He insisted on this specific dress, the halter neckline and laced train perfectly ordinary, and I thought everyone would be wearing a similar one.

But that's not the case. No one else is wearing a vintage wedding dress, and I press my lips together.

"She's certainly bold, that one." Poppy shoots me a baring look from beneath her long lashes, her voice still full of intrigue. "I wonder if this has anything to do with her resemblance to the dead queen?"

"What are you talking about?" Daisy asks a little too loudly, the courtiers around us now ogling my dress, too.

Poppy wiggles her perfectly plucked eyebrows, her cheeks rosy and glowing. "Oh, yes. Lori here is a ringer for the dead woman we saw this morning."

Aster shakes her head. "Really? I didn't notice."

"Of course *you* didn't," Poppy says. "So, spill. Are you related to her or something?"

Before I can tell her it's none of her business, Paul taps his microphone and smiles widely at the crowd from the little stage in front of the DJ. "Esteemed guests. Lovely brides. The time has come to kick off the Yule ball—sorry again to everyone watching us at home for the delay." He slides a scroll from his jacket and raises it in the air. "I have here the names of the brides that *didn't* make the cut. If you hear yours, please exit the ballroom through the left. Members of our staff will be ready to escort you home."

My fist curls at my side.

"Heidi Clyde. Michelle Solinsky..."

Paul reads from his parchment, and whispers explode across the ballroom. It's a humiliating way to deal with eliminations. The discarded women are forced to walk off under the watchful eyes of the cameras. A recipe for drama. The names are read in no particular order, which means none of us is safe until the very end.

"And the last bride to be eliminated before the Yule ball is...My-Loc Huynh."

In the end, Daisy, Aster, Poppy, and I are all safe, along with two other Spring seeds.

Sarafina joins her fellow host on the stage. A sparkling white Charleston dress with long fringes and silver sequins hangs from her slender body, a feathery headpiece tied around her head. "Now, let's admit love isn't all that blind, and welcome the Winter King to the inauguration ball," she says on a mischievous grin.

A spotlight sparks to life to reveal the location of the Winter King. He leans casually against the wall at the back of the ballroom with his hands tucked in his tuxedo's pockets. The perfect image of jaded youth—completely different to the poised army leader I saw—but it's a dangerous illusion.

His irises shine with the resplendent glow of seawater caught in crystal, hinting at the immense power brewing beneath his royal facade. His platinum-blonde waves combine runway-chic with the nonchalance of a royal who knows he's the most powerful man alive, and the devil-may-care glint in his eyes could turn me to ice if he so desired.

The silk lapels of his navy tuxedo offer a scandalous glimpse of his naked chest, his skin white—yet not pale. It glows from within, the attractive luster interrupted only by a few blue freckles at his neck.

He pushes off the wall and approaches the small stage with the swagger of a movie star. The front of his jacket hangs open, offering a jaw-dropping view of his chiseled abs and the Fae runes tattooed over his left pectoral muscle. Darker ink stalks from the mass of intricate drawings to form the shape of an eyeless skull as the corner of Elio's mouth curls up in the shadow of a smile. "Thank you, Sara."

The boom of his chilly voice riddles my arms with goosebumps, and my gaze trips over the hem of his tailored pants to reach the ground, my cheeks too red for my taste.

Jeez... That dude definitely spends way too much time in the gym.

Sarafina beams at him with a wide, enamored smile. "The public will vote for their favorite brides all night, and tomorrow, only twenty of them will start their travels with us."

Elio offers the cameras a wink as he buttons up his jacket with long, nimble fingers. "Choose wisely, please."

My tongue sticks to the roof of my mouth, and I'm reminded why women flock to his contest every year of their own free will. It's not just about the apples, the money, or the clout. The Winter King is fucking gorgeous.

Death wrapped in wolf's clothing.

His raw charisma angers me, especially knowing how heartless and dangerous he actually is.

Elio raps his fingers on the speaker next to him. "Now... let's dance."

Music pounds through the gigantic ballroom, and nightlights freckle the dance floor.

Seth leans into my ear, speaking loudly for me to hear him over the music. "As long as he sees you, you're good. So make sure to catch his eye."

The relief at getting past the blind dates challenge is short-lived, the roil in my stomach back in full-force. "You're awfully sure of yourself. What if he sees me and doesn't care?"

"Don't worry. I'm not about to stake our victory on the whims of that ice cube. The next two rounds will be decided by the public, and if Elio loses his shit when he sees you as dramatically as I think he will, your resemblance to his dead queen will make sure that we stick around." He pushes me toward the bar. "Go and grab a drink now. And remember to look pretty."

"I hate you," I grumble.

"You're welcome."

I elbow my way across the dance floor, trying to peer over the crowd and see where the king is, but I'm shorter than most of the other guests. My tongue sticks to the roof of my mouth as I head to the bar, thirsty for some liquid courage. "A Spring tonic, please."

The entire bar is made of ice and stretches the length of the ballroom. Rows and rows of bottles add a splash of color to the set-up, the lights shining through the orange, pink, purple, blue, and green shades of hard liquor.

I play with my fingers as the barman shakes the cocktail, my stomach coiled in a hard knot.

What the fuck am I doing here? I snatch the drink from his hands after he's done and gulp it down in a few swigs. I usually steer clear of sweet drinks, but I'm not supposed to be familiar with Fae cocktails.

"Do you have anything stronger?" I ask.

"Eager to get drunk, eh?" he asks in a thick Irish accent.

"You could say that."

A small chuckle escapes him as he shakes together a shadow mule. "The wedding dress's a little much, don't ye think?"

"My sponsor's a big ass." I lick my lips and grab the classic drink from the glossy countertop—about ready to turn on my heel and storm to Seth's room for my mask so I can get the fuck out of this frozen kingdom.

The smokey, bitter aromas of the familiar drink melt on my tongue. *I can do this. For Ayaan.*

The Winter King leans on the other end of the bar and hails the barman, stealing him away, and my heart booms. No other bride has elected to get shit-faced, which leaves the counter mostly empty, but the horde of women hovering around Elio forms a shield between us.

He orders a drink and answers a few of their questions with a perfect air of boredom. The brazen way they encroach on his personal space coaxes a wince out of me. *Can't they read body language? The guy looks annoyed, not charmed.*

It's not the vibe I expected. Most men would jump at the opportunity to bed as many of these beautiful women as possible. Elio certainly didn't seem shy or introverted earlier.

I tilt my head back and gulp down the rest of the shadow mule, tethering on the edge. I've almost made up my mind to leave when his characteristic ice-blue gaze crosses mine.

The loud conversations, the raucous commotion of the dancers... everything fades under Elio's scrutiny. His ungodly eyes widen, and his brows pull together in a deeper and deeper frown.

A cold, slithering sensation laces up my spine.

The serene face of the dead woman exposed under his Hawthorn tree flashes in my mind. How shocked he must be to see a fragment of it amongst the guests—a living ghost of his beloved.

A man sits at the bar between us and blocks my line of sight, breaking the spell. Ragged breaths quake my ribcage as I grip the skirt of my dress. Magic bubbles beneath the surface of my skin, but I desperately rein in my shadows not to blow my cover and wade back into the crowd gathered on the dance floor.

I skirt around a boisterous Fae couple, my fingers clenched around the modest train of the dress. Behind them, a pair of double doors beckons.

First a sharp left to avoid a burly man.

A quick right to slip between two Winter brides.

Tiny shadows drape over my shoulders, followed by a burst of speed.

Almost there.

My pulse throbs at my temples as I dash to the exit and risk a glance behind me. From the corner of my eye, I catch a glimpse of platinum-blond hair, and my heart screeches past my feet.

Just when I think I'm going to make it out of the ballroom unscathed, a confident hand shoots out of the mass and curls around my lower arm. Thorns of ice scatter along my skin at his touch and force me to a halt, blue lines creeping over my wrist.

I stifle a gasp and spin around to face the Winter King.

With a puzzled look—perhaps the madness-induced confusion of a man who doesn't know if he's dreaming—Elio Lightbringer peels the masquerade mask off my face and lets go of me with a start.

The sting of frost melts from my arm as his lips part, and the muscles in his neck tighten in ropes of emotion, flicking in and out of view.

My neck hurts from the effort to look away, but my body is not listening to my commands and glares right back at him, the way no one should stare at a stranger. *He looks about to pass out.*

I open my mouth to speak, but the storm passing over his immortal face short-circuits my rational thoughts. For a brief moment, the ice in his eyes vanishes, revealing a deeper turmoil—an ocean of turquoise waters, endless and cold. An abyss of regrets.

His tortured gaze finally drops to my dress, and his jaw clenches. He balls his fists and scouts the ballroom for an answer, looking about ready to *murder* me.

Seth slithers to my side and offers a quick, fake-as-hell bow to the Winter King. "Ah, Elio. How do you find my favorite candidate? She's exquisite, isn't she?"

The king punches my sponsor without a shred of warning, and Seth is shoved about five feet back. The storm prince tumbles to the sleek white marble tiles with a loud *thump*, bringing an unlucky guest with him on his trajectory.

In the background, I hear the commentators reel at the violence of the blow, and the music actually fades away this time, all eyes on us. Disappointed whispers and questions buzz through the brides and courtiers.

Paul raises his voice. "By the spindle, did you all see what just happened? The king picked a fight with one of the sponsors. Who's the girl standing between them, Sara?"

"Let me see. Her name is Lori, and she's a Spring seed presented today by Seth Devine."

Paul rushes through the crowd. "Seth Devine... Why am I not surprised? But what is she wearing? A wedding dress?"

As if on cue, the fabric of my dress ices over. The Winter King holds my incensed gaze as he rips the skirt and train to shreds. The frozen silk crumbles in his grasp, and I'm left gasping for breath in my corset, unable to speak, run, or fight—a first for me.

The old-fashioned undergarments and fishnet stockings shield me from the prying lenses of the camera zooming in on my awestruck face.

The Winter King freezes all the nearby electronics like they're weeds defiling the beauty of his pristine gardens, and the eyeballs rain down in a cacophony of metallic *thuds* around us.

"I don't know who you are, where you come from, or how Seth

managed to get you here, and I don't care," he whispers in a low growl that ices the heart, his chest heaving. "You drop out, and you drop out now, or I will turn your life—or what little's left of it—into a very special kind of hell. Is that clear?"

"Crystal."

He spins on his heels and stomps beyond the roped off section, leaving the ballroom in four strides.

Paul sticks a microphone under my chin. "What did he say, Lori? What did the king say to you, and why did he punch your sponsor?" He glances away from the cameras and meets my gaze.

Sara skids to a stop behind him, her jaw hanging slightly agape.

I blink at the two Fae hosts and chew the insides of my cheeks. Stabbing one or both of them is probably a sure way to get eliminated.

"My oh my... You look just like—" Paul stops short of saying Iris's name, and silence falls over the ballroom. The two hosts exchange a worried glance.

"Don't just stand there in shock. Tell the world." Seth grips the microphone from Paul and grins from ear to ear. "Lori here is a ringer for my dear cousin Iris, is she not?"

"Where are you from, Lori?" Sara asks in a queasy, muted tone. "And where did you find that dress?"

I open my mouth to speak, to play the game, but the Winter King's horrified grimace is still imprinted in my brain.

And I did that.

The darkness in his eyes when he ripped away the skirt of my gown shivers through me once more. "I—I can't..."

"That'll be all for tonight. Excuse us," Seth pulls me toward the exit, his body shielding me from the vicious glares of my fellow contestants.

Blood returns to my cheeks and brain once we reach the gardens. My heels sink deep in the snow, the sudden pain in my calves slapping me back to reality.

I slip out of the nonsensical shoes and throw one of them at the prince's smug face. "What the fuck, Seth?"

He veers off the projectile's path with a feline smile. "Don't fret. You made an impression. That's all that matters."

I chew on that for a moment and feel my resolve sharpen. Seth is right. The Winter King's threat has reminded me of who he truly is—the King of Death. He snagged my father's soul—just as he takes all mortals—and used it to increase his own power. I can't allow myself to be swayed by his grief when he cares so little for mine.

"Seth!" Sarafina half-runs toward us, a cloak and a pair of boots bunched in her arms. She dumps the items at my feet without a single look. "What kind of sick game are you playing?"

My feet are already half frozen, and I cower inside the winter clothes with a low hum.

Sara slaps my sponsor straight across the face, and the sound echoes in the quiet gardens. "I spoke out for you, you dipshit! And you use some weak-ass enchantment to turn one of your candidates into Iris? I will kill you myself!"

"Easy, Sara." Seth backs away from her with his palms up in surrender. "She's real."

"Pfft! No way."

"See for yourself." He motions in my direction, and the pale-skinned woman walks all the way into my bubble.

Hands tucked deep in the pockets of the fur cloak, I summon my daggers, ready to fight if she strikes first.

"Well…" she licks her lips. "Just because I can't figure out how you did it doesn't mean she's real. I should throw you and your Spring seeds out tonight."

Seth's face softens the way it does when he's trying to reel me in. "The citizens of Wintermere are losing interest in the pageant. Elio's popularity with the masses has never been this low. Don't pretend this won't help your cause. The more they watch, the more they feel connected to him, the less likely it is for him to be overthrown."

"Because you have his best interest at heart, of course," Sara says on an eyeroll. "I won't join forces with you. Not at Elio's expense. A doppelgänger is one thing, but to have her wear Iris's *actual* wedding dress? That's just cruel."

Byron flies in, his wings flapping so fast, I can barely see them. "Mistress, I need you inside. *Now.*"

The guard running to catch up with him isn't a reaper, but he's wearing a similar uniform without sleeves—only gray instead of white.

Jaw clenched, Sarafina shakes her head and walks away. "Excuse me."

I dismiss my shadow daggers, the pockets of my cloak shredded to bits, and my heart in a similar state of disrepair. If I'd known, I would never have worn the damn dress. I look down at my fishnet stockings, happy to be rid of it.

"I can't believe you made me wear a dead woman's wedding gown. That's seriously fucked up."

Seth scratches the back of his neck. "I'll go back inside, but you go ahead and rest. Your early departure will only add to your mystery."

"Elio wants me to drop out. He was very clear about that," I croak.

His eyes dart to the guard before he returns to my side and lowers his voice. "He can't force you to drop out. The scene he just made assures us an easy win in the polls. People here crave drama and entertainment over a happy ending, and you are now the embodiment of both."

Arms crossed over my cloak, I scoff, and a puff of white smoke rises in the air between us. "You should have at least warned me."

Seth pats my shoulder in a soothing manner. "Don't lose sight of our mission. The end justifies the use of an old, creepy wedding gown. Trust me. We have him now."

CHAPTER 11
STORMS
ELIO

The pesky little cameras Paul tinkered with for this year's pageant emit dull electronic *beeps* as they follow me past the ropes and into my private study. I ice every single one of them and watch them shatter into pieces with a dark grin.

Byron spares them a nervous glance.

I hold out my index finger. "I don't want to hear one word about the cameras. Where is Sara?"

"She's outside, giving the dandelion fluff a piece of her mind—"

Another camera rushes in, and I blast it with an icicle, making it explode in mid-air. The metal pieces tinkle over the paved stones.

Byron's wings twitch at his back, the Faeling clearly biting his tongue.

"You're going to go back out there and tell Paul that if one more of his fucking cameras flies into *my* private space again, he can pack his bags and find himself a new job." I rake a hand through my hair, about ready to tear it off my skull. "I need to see him, and get me your mistress, too."

"At once, Your Majesty." Byron flies off.

After he's gone, I choke on a ragged breath.

What I saw out there is impossible. A fucking tear stings my cheek, and I wipe it off with a snarl. My limbs shake violently, my entire nervous system throwing a fit, and I grip the back of the velvet armchair in front of me to get a hold of myself.

Adrenaline pulses through my blood as my magic goes haywire the way it used to at the beginning of my reign, back when I was still adjusting. Ice spreads from my feet and cracks the paved stones. A pure wave of frost rolls across the study and washes off on the walls and windows. Its undertow brings my heart to a full stop, more potent than any spell—more dangerous than the darkest soul I ever hunted back when I was still part of the Sun Court.

I'm losing control, and that's not good. The magic I carry is strongest and most volatile near the solstice, and I can't afford to lose my grip on it.

Paul and Sara knock on the door a few minutes later.

"Come in," I say.

They tiptoe inside the room, taking stock of the damage. I'm the perfect picture of pissed-off royalty, but the room itself is in ruins. Tapestries peel off the frozen walls, the windows shattered, and the centennial floors cracked in many places.

A cold breeze slips past the jagged shards of the broken windows.

"I want her out. I want her out *now*," I growl to no one in particular.

"The votes already catapulted her to first place—" Paul says, but I cut him off.

"I don't care."

His eyes soften. "She looks so similar to Iris... It's only natural for you to be shaken."

Sara scoffs at his bad faith. "Similar? Come on, Paul. She's *exactly* like Iris."

"Alright, she looks exactly the same." He slicks his gray hair over his head. "But there must be a reasonable explanation."

"Blood magic?" Sara offers.

Paul chokes on her hypotheses and taps his heart with his fist, the mention of blood magic tickling his religious side. "No need to be quite so pessimistic. A good-old glamor would do the trick. We could disqualify the girl for cheating if we find out how she's doing it. A glamor of such magnitude threatens the integrity of the pageant."

I rap my fingers on the back of the frozen armchair. The piece of furniture is now entombed in ice, and if we tried to melt it down, the chair would simply crumble to pieces. *It's ruined. Like everything else I touch.*

I force my jaw to relax and inhale deeply. "Who cares if the brides are all given a fair shot? The winner is going to die, anyway."

Sara hooks a finger around her necklace. "I'll take care of it, Elio. Just be patient." A sad, lopsided smile glazes her lips. "I've got you, always."

It's probably a bad idea to dismiss my two most trusted advisors, so I give her a nod. "Deal with it, Sara."

I veer toward the stairwell heading up to the towers, but the wind picks up, and a flurry of snowflakes curls around my neck.

"An ice storm is coming." Sara shoots me a guarded look. Byron is perched on her shoulder, holding to her collar with both hands not to be blown away by the wind. "Are you sure you're okay?"

Flumes of white clouds swell in the sky, and I walk closer to the windows. Shattered glass crunches under my shoes. "I think I am."

The current of wild magic from earlier tapered down. *Did my tantrum summon this blizzard?* I sure destroyed my study, but I didn't think it went farther than that. My magic hasn't caused a destructive storm in decades.

I'm the Winter King, but ice listens to no one. The glacier that spreads the length of my kingdom is as much in control of me as I am of it. I'm merely the tip of the iceberg—a physical manifestation of its power in Faerie.

Towers of white clouds roll in over my castle, and I squint at the phenomenon. The barometric pressure slides quickly, and the inch of snow garnishing the branches of the Hawthorn is swept away by the arctic winds.

"Byron, get the guards to board out these windows," I order.

The Faeling flies off his mistress' shoulder and zooms out of the room.

I hurry back to the ballroom where Seth is flirting with a Winter bride.

She's laughing at one of his jokes, but her breath catches as she spots me, and she curtsies. "My king. It's such an honor—"

"Leave us." I give her the stink eye for her to shoo.

No matter how many girls Seth plows through, a new one is always standing in line to fawn over his basic lust magic. I rub down the space between my brows, a huge migraine suddenly playing peek-a-boo with my vision.

Seth gives a dramatic sigh. "Why did you interrupt us? She was lovely."

I grip the prince's collar and haul him to my study and away from the prying eyes of the brides and cameras. "Look here, dandelion fluff. If you're responsible for this weather—"

A wild gust of wind howls inside the room and sweeps the last few precarious, broken window shards along with it.

Seth grimaces at the incoming storm. "It's not mine. I have no idea where it's coming from," he answers quickly, not playing with words the way he usually does.

I hate the guy, but he's Fae through and through. He couldn't lie about this if his life depended on it.

I release my hold on him and turn back to Paul and Sara. "Stop the broadcast and get the brides safely to their dorms. Ring the bells. I need everyone to stay inside tonight." My brows furrow as I surveil the clouds again. "Something's coming."

CHAPTER 12
IRIS
LORI

The Winter gardens aren't crowded. No ice crusts over the shingles on top of the main tower. No walls of snow block the windows, and the thin, intricate icicles hanging from the branches of the Hawthorn twinkle in the midday light—instead of threatening to maim those who dare to stand under them.

"It's your turn, dear. Smile." A brown-eyed woman urges me along the stone runway in front of me. She looks so familiar and yet—not.

The main path is flanked by a series of smooth stone walkways leading deeper into the gardens, free of snow. I roll my shoulders back and strut forward, perfectly at ease in the tall peep-toe heels. The chiffon and sequins of my dress spark static electricity between my legs.

This dream is vivid to say the least, only... The Dreaming doesn't allow visitors in from Faerie, so this is more of a vision than a proper dream.

It looks to be Elio's first Yule pageant. The one Seth told me about. When I'd visited someone else's dream during my Shadow huntress training, I could usually act on the spot and change the course of the scenario, but not here.

A black woman holding a large fan motions for me to approach. A big, *textured wig forms a halo around her head, and a flashy jeweled topaz crown rests on top.*

The Spring Queen, no doubt.

"Winter King, I present to you my niece, Iris Lovatt," she says.

I twirl around to face the handful of reporters with a hand on my hip, my midnight-blue train scraping the stones. I smile and let them snap a few pictures, my spine straight as an arrow. Three other princesses have been presented, too, and are now standing to the side of the stage, but I barely spare them a glance.

"Thank you, Freya," Paul answers in Elio's place, using his host-extra-ordinaire tone. "Your niece is certainly the most beautiful rose."

I throw Elio a wink over my shoulder, and his throat bobs in response.

My Lori consciousness is a mere spectator to the events—quite literally stuck in someone else's high heels. The chill of winter frosts on my cheeks, but I can't hear any thoughts or feelings coming from Iris herself even though I'm inside her body.

The Elio in the vision is radically different from the one I just met. His starlight tuxedo is more traditional, with tails and a crisp, white under-shirt. He doesn't look bored or jaded—but nervous, and his lips curl in a gentle smile.

"Who would you want to meet first?" Paul asks the king, the gray-haired host not looking much younger than he does in my timeline.

"The Spring princess," Elio says too quickly, and a hint of red colors his cheeks.

I hold back a chuckle and march over to the Winter King with blazing confidence.

"Let's take a walk." I clasp his hand and pull him along toward the expansive maze behind the Hawthorn and away from the prying eyes of the paparazzi.

Elio tucks his hand in his pockets to keep me from touching him, his previous warmth replaced by a worried frown. "Why did you come, Iris?"

I nudge his side. "Aren't you glad to see me?"

"If you only came to appease your mother's ambitions, we should part as friends now. Just tell me."

We stroll past the empty area of the gardens—the exact spot where Iris's coffin is displayed in the present—and enter the network of tall cedar hedges, Paul and Freya walking ten paces behind us.

"Would I be here, if my feelings had not changed?"

Elio blinks a few times at my answer. "You—"

I skip in front of him and turn the corner. "Yes, silly. I want to marry you."

He gives chase, catching up to me in no time, and his timid smile from before grows bolder. "Why? You once said you'd never be caught dead with me."

"Oh Elio, I was so young, then. You can't hold that against me." I hook my arm in his and pull him along. "Let's lose the chaperones."

He raises a brow.

"Hurry." I kick off my heels and break into a run, zooming past a few tight corners at random.

"Iris! Wait!" Freya shouts behind us, but her command only fuels our escape.

I tag along as Iris and Elio weave through the twists and turns, each corner conquered driving us deeper into the maze.

Muffled giggles bubble out of our mouths as we reach a dead end. I push on Elio's chest until he is tucked out of view in a secluded nook of the labyrinth and glance behind me to make sure we won't be interrupted.

Our chests rise and fall as I lean closer to the Winter King, and he cups my cheek with a sigh. "This feels like a dream."

"I only need to know one thing. You know what they say of Winter and its kings... I just need to know you haven't become all dead inside. You won't hurt me, right?"

"I'd never hurt you, Iris. Never."

I stand on the tip of my toes to kiss his neck—the taste of him like shaved ice and apples—delicious, really, but Iris doesn't seem in a hurry to kiss him on the mouth and reaches for his belt buckle instead.

Elio freezes. "What are you doing?"

"You don't want our first time to be in front of my aunt and fucking Paul Snow, do you?" I say.

Iris's voice is nothing like mine, I realize. She doesn't have the same pitch, cadence, or accent, and the jaded way she breathes the words irks me.

"N-No," *he stammers.*

I slide the sequin dress' strap off my shoulders to expose my breasts. "Then make love to me now."

Oh my gods! I don't want this vision to go on, but Iris is quite in charge, here.

"We should talk this through, first," *Elio rasps, echoing my sentiment.*

"Why——" *I search his gaze, and my voice melts to a soft, brittle whisper.* "You're going to choose me, aren't you?"

"Of course!"

"Then why does it matter?" *Blistering tingles warm my palms as Iris shoves a wave of lust towards him.*

Whereas the shadows I'm used to commanding are slick and inviting —often arranged as a blanket to protect me—this new sensation registers as both sultry and destructive.

Elio looks me up and down, and a wolfish smile blooms on his lips. The air becomes charged with electricity, and his eyes no longer skirt the shape of my bare breasts as he slides a hand to the nape of my neck and reels me in. "I guess you're right."

CHAPTER 13
SOMETHING THAT FEEDS IN THE NIGHT
LORI

I wake up in a cold sweat, tangled in the bed sheets. *Holy shit!* I press a hand to my lips. The memory of the kiss Elio gave Iris in that maze is vivid and raw, and I forget where I am for a moment. Not in the maze about to have sex with a younger version of Elio, but in a dorm room full of women.

I just know it really happened. The leftover taste of magic in my mouth is too clear and powerful for it to be anything but a glimpse of the past. My mother used to get visions all the time, according to my dad. Maybe I've finally unlocked her legacy as an oracle. What if the power laid dormant, and seeing Iris's body finally unlocked it? Maybe I look like her for a reason, but that's scary as fuck.

Ice beats on the dark windows. Aster is sitting alone on the large windowsill with her duvet wrapped around her frame and a pillow propped behind her back. Her nails click along the glass as she observes the castle grounds below.

A high-pitched moan reaches my ears. I look around the room, but we're all here.

"*Argh*, there they go again," Aster whines as she tightens the duvet around her body.

My brows furrow. "Who?"

"Seth and those two dumb Winter seeds from the ball."

I press the heel of my hand to my forehead, annoyed beyond belief that Seth decided to have a threesome after the night we've had.

"You look wretched, Sixteen," Daisy chimes from the cot on my right. She rolls to her side and plays with the pink scrunchy holding her long braid in place. "Did you have a nightmare? Cause that shit's not natural."

"Of course not."

"Sure seemed like you did—"

"There's someone out there... by the entrance of the maze," Aster breathes.

Daisy frowns from her bed. "Are you nuts? Anyone standing in this storm would freeze to death in *minutes*."

Aster shoots her a nasty look. "Not the king. Or one of his reapers."

Poppy slides out of bed to check on her friend's claim, and I dangle my legs over the edge of the cot, feeling groggy and numb. My long black hair falls over my shoulder, full of knots and wavy from the sweat.

Poppy muffles a high-pitched squeal with her hand. "Aster's right. There's someone out there." She motions us forward.

Blood whooshes at my temples as I wrap a sheet around me and walk to the window. The storm allows for an intermittent and incomplete look at the entrance of the maze. The dark shapes of the cedar hedges blur in the distance, and my heart gives a big thud. The maze... I shake my head to erase the aftertaste of my vision and avert my gaze.

Daisy rolls her eyes. "There's nothing to see."

"I saw her, I swear. A woman." Aster runs to the door and wrenches it open. She tightens the duvet around her frame and walks outside to peer over the parapet. "I think she needs help."

A burst of wind swirls inside the room, and the two other girls stir in their beds. "What's going on?"

"Can someone shut the door, please?"

Daisy dashes to the open door and curls a hand around the frame. "Aster? Come back inside and close the damn door."

"She's right there!" Aster shouts over the wind.

Daisy steps out in the snow. "Aster, stop fucking around and come back. You're in your pajamas, for Eros' sake."

Poppy draws a sharp intake of breath and backs away from the windows. "Guys... Aster is going into the maze."

Without giving myself the time to think about it, I lace up my winter boots and throw my cloak on.

Ice and snow scatter in Daisy's wake as she bolts back inside, her feet and fingers red from the cold. "What's gotten into her? Seth will know what to do—" She pauses as I walk past her. "Where are you going?"

"Get Seth. I'm chasing after Aster." I pull my hood over my head and slip outside, sealing the door behind me. Aster is a privileged and pampered mortal. She won't survive alone in this storm.

Huge chunks of snow hit my face, coming from all directions at once. They frost over my eyelashes and sting my cheeks as I draw in a deep, soothing breath. I don't have much experience with Fae winter storms, but I know the night like the back of my hand.

Spiders see perfectly well in the dark.

I slide down the stairs, the boots supple and comfortable, and vanish into the shadows. Even if Poppy and Daisy are watching the entrance of the maze, they won't see me now. The woman Aster caught a glimpse of was probably harnessing a few shadows herself, which means it might be the woman I came here to find.

This morning, when we walked through the labyrinth, I couldn't tell left from right, but I know this maze, now. I'd never stepped foot in this forsaken garden before today and yet I could map it out by heart.

A powerful magic is at work here. Whatever forces sent the vision also rewrote parts of my brain, and I shake all over as I follow a fresh trail of footsteps in the snow. The King's private gardens quickly come into view, the Hawthorn's dark shape visible in the distance.

A woman stands right below it, and I pick up the pace. "Aster?"

But the silhouette in the distance isn't Aster. Long black waves peek from under the woman's hooded navy-blue cloak, and my heart slips past my feet. *Morrigan.*

Shadows creep along the hills of fresh snow, and I fashion them into a shield, slowly walking toward my mark to take a closer look and confirm her identity. I can't quite see her face, but the height and build is right.

At the bottom of the three towers, a hidden door opens to the Winter King himself. I stop abruptly, and a heap of snow gives under my feet, sucking me in. The thickness of the mound prevents me from moving without giving away my position.

The hooded woman leans into Elio and hooks her elbow around his offered arm. He steps aside in invitation, and the woman slips past him, disappearing inside the castle.

The Winter King's blue eyes pierce the darkness, and I push my magic further, piling shadows over shades, desperate for him not to see me. I count to ten in my head, Elio still glaring at the scenery like he knows something doesn't quite add up.

My chest heaves when he finally slams the door shut.

What the fuck is going on here? If Elio is getting cozy with Morrigan, why would he bother with the Yule pageant at all? Why wouldn't he just marry her?

I climb out of the snow trap and double back to find Aster. I'm halfway through the path leading to the dorms when I catch a glimpse of her heading down a deep, dark passage.

"...so freaking cold...thank you..." she says, and her lips continue to move for a moment like she's speaking to someone in front of her, but the wind drowns out the rest of her sentence.

"*Come, Lori...*" the breeze whispers.

I pause. "Aster? Aster, wait!"

She rounds a tight corner and disappears from my line of sight. I hurry over to the space she just occupied, my boots struggling to gain traction, the crust of ice beneath the fresh snow less traveled in this section of the maze.

Beyond the turn, a long, narrow corridor opens to a wide four-way node, and Aster stops. "I don't think we're going the right way," she says.

A human-shaped shadow walks in front of her, and I break into a run to catch up. "Hey!" I shout after them.

"Come."

Snow swirls in front of my face. I have no choice but to slow down and carefully press forward with my arms extended. At last, the wind changes direction and blows the snowflakes away from my eyes.

I screech to a halt.

In the middle of the empty circular passage, Aster has turned into an ice statue, her gaze angled to the sky. Dead.

A big chunk of ice near the ground acts as a doll stand, holding her upright. With blue lips and white eyes, she looks like she's been here for hours and not only a few seconds.

I backtrack, spooked, and summon my daggers to life. "Show yourself!"

Did I see the reaper come for her soul? Or catch a glimpse of her attacker as they fled? Adrenaline coils my muscles, and I raise my blades to each of the moving branches in the hedge, expecting them to reveal an ice monster—or even one of Morrigan's spiders.

Morheim has barely ended. Regular nightmares might still be prowling around Faerie, too. The strong wind whips my hair forward and blinds me again. Cold sweat ices over my brows, and I wipe it off with my impractical fur sleeves.

With a sickening *crack*, Aster's body slumps to the ground just as another icy gust hits me square in the chest. I blink away the frost and observe the four paths leading out of the node. *Fuck.*

All of them look the same, and my footprints in the snow have been erased by the storm. The hedges tower high above me, indistinguishable from one another. The map I'd unlocked from the confines of my mind vanishes, retreating back to some impregnable attic inside my brain. I don't know which way to go, anymore.

I'm lost.

The heating spell keeping the cloak and boots dry and warm tapers off, my arms and legs shaking from the cold. The chafe of snow and fear numbs my fingers, and I wonder for a moment if I'm not going to turn to ice, too.

I try to grab Aster's blanket from the ground to create a barrier over my head and block the endless onslaught of snow, but it's frozen solid.

Keep your head, Lori. This is just another hunt—only I'm hunting for the exit.

Deep breaths, in and out. In and out. Shadow magic pulses in my palms as I climb on top of the hedge in hopes of spotting the mountain range or the castle. The cedar bushes snap and crack under my weight, but I'm not called a spider for nothing. Perched over the maze, I catch a glimpse of the castle lights burning in the distance.

I'm only a few corners away from freedom, but also a few wrong turns away from death, so I double-check every single one of them. Each of my muscles screams in agony, but I won't let winter claim me. Not before I find some answers.

By the time I finally make it out, the storm is almost over, and the soft light of dawn streaks through the white sky.

"She's here!" Daisy runs over to me from her sentry position on the parapet. "Stupid girl. Running off into an ice storm like that," she scolds as she rubs some warmth and life back into me.

Sarafina emerges from the dorms, Byron perched on her shoulder. The chief of staff's thick white coat and matching ski pants capture my attention as she climbs down the stairs. *Such warmth would be divine.*

Her gaze searches the trail behind me like she expects Aster to follow in my footsteps. "Where is your friend?"

"She died. Turned into an ice statue in the blink of an eye." I watch her face, trying to see past the Fae to the woman that lies beneath. Does she really not know what's going on here? Or is she just pretending?

Sarafina turns to Byron, her hardened gaze sharp enough to break stones. "I want the maze searched and investigated. I want to know who did this."

The Faeling considers her demand with a grave nod and flies away.

A camera hovers right over Sarafina's head as she unfolds a large blanket and wraps it over my shoulders. "What's your name again?"

A cottony warmth cuddles me from all sides, and my tensed muscles sigh in relief, but I roll my eyes at the formality. Sarafina couldn't have forgotten my name already, not after the scene I had caused at the ball.

"Lori." I grunt, still shivering despite the effects of the enchanted blanket. "But you already knew that."

Her pale blue eyes snap over to me, and I get the feeling she'd strangle me if she could. "Did you see anything out in the storm?"

"I don't know what I saw. It was pitch-black outside."

I'm not supposed to see well in the dark, and I can't risk it all—gamble Ayaan's life—on a hunch. If I really saw Morrigan enter the castle, then Sarafina must be in on it. The same logic dictates that she'd know if an ice monster lurked around the Winter King's gardens. She must be pretending not to know because of the cameras.

Seth runs out of the dorms, the door left hanging open behind him as he takes the stairs two at a time. "Lori! I'm here." He wades through the thick snow separating us, sinking deeper with each step, his unzipped coat flapping in the waning breeze.

Paul steps out behind him and leans over the parapet. "Ah, the woman in question!" A flock of eyeballs buzzes in Paul's wake as he climbs down the stairs and clasps his hands. "So good to see you in one piece, Lori. You topped the public votes, but a little longer, and we would have had to leave without you. The horses and sleighs will arrive in ten minutes."

Is that what this was all about? If I hadn't been a trained Shadow huntress, I would never have found my way back in this storm, and I'd be dead or lost—eliminated from the Yule pageant.

"Aster is dead," I repeat. The trivial way they treat the news boils my blood.

"What rotten business, but the show must go on, as they say." He takes a glimpse inside his leather planner. "Rose can take her place."

"Is that all you have to say?" I croak.

Seth presses his lips together and wraps an arm around my shoulders, guiding me forward and away from the insensitive host. "Careful," he whispers in my ear. "*Accidents* happen every year. We won't get closer to the truth by throwing a fit in front of the cameras." He clears his throat and speaks louder for everyone to hear. "Come along, my flowers. We have to get ready."

Sarafina walks past us to the entrance of the labyrinth. "The storm put us behind schedule. Get her warm and hydrated, and I'll meet you out front." She tucks her hands inside her muffs and throws me a glance over her shoulder. "We should arrive in Snowhaven after sundown, right in time for the challenge."

The dubious smile on her lips doesn't bode well for me. I almost follow her back into the maze, starving for answers, but I hang on to Seth instead. The scoundrel owes me an explanation.

I use him as a crutch and let him guide me toward the dorms, my lips inches from his pointy ear. "Remember when you told me I shouldn't mind your reasons for this charade? Well, it's time to fess up, Seth. Either you tell me exactly why you enlisted me to do this, or I'm out. Why are you hunting Morrigan? Why do you need her alive?"

His lips thin, and the clench of his jaw erases all traces of cockiness or immaturity from his handsome face. He manhandles me inside the dorms, past the dressing room and into the narrow corridor leading to his private quarters. "Morrigan took my baby brother. He's been missing for two years now."

A thin sheen of sweat gathers above his brows. We exchange a heavy glance, my earlier bravado knotted in my throat as he hands me a fresh towel and pushes me toward the bathroom.

"We're the same, you and I. We're both here to save someone we love. And no matter who dies, we can't afford to fuck up."

CHAPTER 14
CARNIVAL
LORI

The *swish, swish, swish* of the sleigh's runners lull me into a soft, warm slumber. We've been divided into four groups of five, so I huddle under a heavy blanket of fur with the four remaining Spring brides. The lavish winter coats we've been given have a thick hood that acts as a pillow. They're more comfy than the cloaks from before, the fabric snug and stretchy.

"I can't believe Aster died," Rose says with a sniffle.

Her friend, a quiet bride called Flora, clasps her hand.

"We were warned about the dangers of winter." Daisy shakes her head. "She shouldn't have gone out into that storm."

Poppy scoffs, her eyes narrowing at her comrade. "So she brought it on herself? Is that it?"

"Yes. Contestants die every year, and we might be next."

I zone out the girl's argument and catch up on the sleep I missed because of the vivid dream-vision—and the dark figure lurking in the maze. Seth's revelation still buzzes in my ears, and I can't wait for us to be alone to untangle that knot of secrets.

The sunset casts pink, orange, and purple hues over the white plains by the time Snowhaven, the capital of the province of the same name, appears on the horizon. The fortified city towers in the distance, protected from the winds of the plains by a tall, circular stone wall.

The white horse pulling our sleigh slows down, and the little bells around his harness jingle at the change of pace, the thumps of his hooves on the snow spaced out and irregular. I stifle a yawn and shake out the pins and needles in my muscles.

"Look. The doors are opening," Rose whispers.

The sleighs stop in front of the city as we wait for the thick wooden doors to crack open. The sponsors are sharing a sleigh with Paul, but Elio is nowhere to be found. Uneven winds blast against the city walls, while networks of ropes and pulleys prevent the stone doors from opening too quickly or catching in the draft.

"What are those ramparts for?" Daisy asks. "Winter peeps can't be *that* motivated to keep freezing winds out."

Poppy smacks her lips together. "Winter is full of monsters. Imagine what lies out there, in the cold. You know how Faerie is. The more beautiful something looks on the outside, the deadlier it actually is."

"I thought deadly beauty was a Spring thing," Rose says.

"Poppy's right. I'd take a stroll in the Spring jungle any day before I took a peek at what lies beneath all this frost," I add, deep in thought.

The horses haul the sleighs forward and form a straight line to squeeze through the opening. The doors of the fortress close behind our convoy, and we glide toward the center of the city. I'd imagined Snowhaven to be busy and crowded, but it's a quaint village—straight from a travel brochure.

Houses nestle together, separated by streets that follow the curve of the exterior wall. Steep, snow-tipped roofs allow for most of the ice to tumble down to the ground, and white smoke clouds over an army of tall stone chimneys, their atypical length meant to protect them from being clogged in a bad snowstorm. The horses stop at the end of the snow path that leads to the center of town.

The smells of firewood, caramel popcorn, and cotton candy embalm the air, and my mouth waters. A ferris wheel gleams in the background, smack in the middle of town square. The whole block has been turned into a typical Winter carnival with booths and games peppered around the main attraction.

The hooded winter coats keep us warm as we leave the safety and comfort of the sleigh, the enchanted clothes meant to protect our bodies, fingers, and cheeks from the bite of winter. I bend down to fashion a small snowball in my hands and marvel at the sensation of the snow crunching between my fingers. I roll my wrists and check my fingertips, but sure enough, my blood vessels are not affected by the cold, like a special oil separates me from the chill.

The glittering lights hanging above the colorful carnival tents and booths shed beautiful patterns over the well-traveled snow covering the ground.

Hundreds of townspeople peruse the displays and coffee shops around the edge of the carnival—perhaps hoping to catch a peek of the brides they saw on television. Hollers and laughter resonate through the air, but none of them breaches the confines of the roped-off area.

I'm a sucker for a good carnival, and my heart hammers. I didn't think winter could hold so much beauty. Snow back home meant numb fingers, slippery roads, and brown, barren trees.

But, as Poppy had pointed out, Fae beauty can't be trusted. I've hunted many types of beasts, most of them elegant and fantastical, yet the beautiful monster that reigns over these lands is not hunted, but revered.

"Lori! Come on!" Poppy waves me over to her, and I catch up with the group.

Paul is ready with his cameras and microphones, filming our arrival. "Dear brides, welcome to Snowhaven. Now, take a good look at the girls you traveled here with."

I keep my eyes firmly planted on him, his gleeful smile crawling under my skin.

"Tonight, the king and lovely citizens of Snowhaven will see first-hand how well you can handle a little mischief. Each of you will participate in the activities, and we'll end with a special treat."

Sarafina joins her fellow host at the front, her bright smile not quite reaching her eyes. "What do we have in store for them, Paul?"

"While our guests start streaming in, the brides will get in position for the first challenge. Each group of five must now decide who to send to the dunk tank," Paul says on a chortle, apparently loving the idea of seeing us drenched to the bone. He points at the area behind the ferris wheel where a plank hovers above a rectangular tub of water. "After the plunge, just put your coats back on. They will dry you up and keep you warm."

The other spring girls all skirt away from me, and I grind my teeth together. "Fine."

Me and the unlucky contestants who lost their groups' popularity contest all hustle toward the water tank. Its walls are made of ice, and an endless current stirs the water to keep it from freezing.

A carnival attendant dressed in a blue and silver uniform and a matching bean hat is waiting for us next to the huge red button, and I blaze forward to go first, beating a Red bride to the front of the line by mere seconds.

I might as well get the humiliation over with.

The Fae attendant is tall, but his long, skinny limbs are stuck in the awkwardness of puberty as he motions for me to hang my warm coat on the rack. His round cheeks flush as I do so, his big eyes brimming with curiosity.

I fidget on the wooden stage, not used to being so shamelessly ogled by a stranger. "Hi?"

"Wow. You're even more beautiful in person," he whispers. "The mayor is campaigning hard for a Winter bride to win, but I'm rooting for you, Lori."

He gives me the go ahead to walk to the plank, but I pause. "You're rooting for me to marry the king?" I ask to make sure, stunned by the implications.

"Yes. You stood up to the king and asked *real* questions. We need a strong queen, one who can beat the odds," he says quickly, blushing a deeper shade of red before he turns to help the next bride in line.

I clench my jaw to keep my teeth from clanking and sit at the end of the plank. A crowd has formed in front of me, most of the villagers eager to get a first-row look at my memorable plunge. My legs dangle from the edge as I peek at the water. Frost creeps along the rim of the tank, and I swallow hard.

I'm already freezing, so I can't imagine how it'll feel down there.

The Red behind me keeps her arms crossed tightly over her chest. She removed her coat, too, but a blood-red silk scarf is still tied over her brows. A sharp edge shines on top of her silver ring, the odd piece of jewelry made to cut through skin. That combined with the Fae drawings branding her face, she looks quite intimidating. Her hand twitches at her side a few times like she wishes she had a blade to run me through.

A Winter bride chats happily with the attendant in the line behind her. Winter Fae don't feel the cold as we do, so I guess the exercise is meant to get a good giggle out of the foreigners' distaste for freezing water.

I crane my neck around to meet the gaze of the Summer bride at the back of the lot. She looks like she's about to faint, and I arch a brow that says, *"Sucks to be us, right?"*

She discreetly motions for me to turn back around. On the other side of the fence preventing onlookers from crowding the shooting area of the dunk tank, a different line has formed for the snowballs meant to strike me down.

Daisy beams from the front of the line, waving cheekily at me. My best frenemy showcases the snowball with a devilish grin. Her pink nails dig into the surface as she squeezes it, ready to take her best shot, but the king slices through the crowd to stop her and interrupts her movement at the last possible second.

What the—

Elio's arrival sparks a wave of audible gossip in the crowd, the shortest courtiers stretching to their tiptoes. Daisy and Elio are too far away for me to hear their conversation, but I'm good at lip reading.

He leans toward her with a smile and opens his palm. "Can I?"

Daisy offers him a small, delighted bow before passing him the snowball. "Of course."

They both turn in my direction with their eyes narrowed. I'm not sure which one is looking forward to my fall the most, but the king's ball is swooped away by the wind. It careens off to the side and away from the bullseye. A smirk glazes my lips, and his failure emboldens me.

I cup my hands in front of my mouth to amplify my voice. "What was that? You throw like a little girl."

Elio laughs and shouts loud enough for me to hear, "Seth. I don't know where you are, but you fuck with my ball one more time, and I'll have them throw you out of my city." An evil glint burns deep in his blue eyes as he summons a new snowball to his palm.

I search for Seth in the crowd but find a familiar midnight-blue cape instead. The woman I saw with Elio in the garden last night is here, blending in with the crowd. A big hood still masks her features, and I stretch my neck to see better.

Next thing I know, my breath is knocked out of me by the coldest water I've ever felt. By Morpheus and his darkest impulses! People who choose to do this for fun at the spa are absolute *lunatics*. My skin stings all over, and my pulse swirls. The pain takes me right back to the Shadow Court and the venomous spider bite that almost killed me.

Water seeps inside my ears and mouth like spider silk, and my eyes snap open. The blurry white and blue scenery becomes muddier as I spring up from the bottom of the tank and shoot upwards, but instead of breaking the surface, I slam my head. Hard.

"Careful," the ice slurs. "He's coming."

A painful boom in my skull dizzies me, but I extend my arms to the sky and bump solid ice. Despite the small size of the pool, I can't find the surface.

I slap the thick frozen wall above my head to no end, quite literally entombed. My lungs burn, and the hurtful boom in my chest tells me I need air, and soon.

My long dark hair snakes at the edge of my vision, and when I look up, I see a younger version of the Winter King gazing down at me through the ice. A soft smile glazes his lips as the lack of oxygen eddies my vision.

There is no air in this watery grave. Nowhere left to run. Only ice, and the promise of the cold, sweet embrace of death.

I'm drowning.

CHAPTER 15
KISS THE GIRLS
LORI

Death is nothing like I'd imagined. Blurry and cold, without a big light to walk toward or shiny golden gates to greet me. Definitely no fires of hell, either.

I'm numb all over, and my eyes are shut in acceptance when a thunderous sound echoes in my water-filled ears.

Boom. Boom. Crack.

Before I can form a conscious thought, unfamiliar hands skim my shoulders, trying and failing to get a grip. Someone on the other side of the ice is obviously trying to come to my rescue. So annoying... Can't they let a girl rest in peace?

A wall of bubbles blurs my vision as someone jumps into the pool beside me. A strong pair of arms wrenches me out of the tank, shattering the silence. I'm not dead, and the realization comes with a butt-load of pain.

Elio's pupils are dilated, his irises all black as he hauls me out of the pool, supporting my entire weight. Water drips from his fancy black wool coat, his hair soaked and disheveled. I suck in air, water still lodged in my throat, and the sudden, ungraceful gurgle jolts me out of my hypoxia-induced trance.

Elio's coiled arms relax, and he shoots me the nastiest glare before his lids flutter shut. With a frustrated groan, he dumps me back inside the tank and climbs out.

A woman jumps in behind me and grabs my arm, and I use her as a crutch to grip the ice rim. A series of coughs rocks my body as I spring over it, tumbling stomach-first into the snow. I spurt out another mouthful of water, about to choke on the taste of my own fear. My body gives wild, violent shakes as the Winter bride that came to my aid skips out of the pool and twists the water out of her hair.

"Is she alright?" a voice asks.

The woman taps my back forcefully, pulling me out of the haze. "Are you okay, dandelion fluff?"

The Red that was standing behind me on the plank rolls her eyes. "Don't bother, Wendy. She only pretended to drown to get more screen time."

Her arms are still wrapped around her chest, and I realize merely seconds have passed since the Winter King's snowball hit the button. My skin stings from the cold, a circle of women gazing down at me from all sides.

"Look at her. She's not faking it," Daisy says. "Besides... how do you explain the ice, dumb nut?"

I rub a drop of saliva from my blue lips. "I'm okay. I'm okay."

Wendy claps her hands and shoos off the crowd. "Give her some air, people."

"Thank you," I croak.

"Don't think we're friends because I wouldn't let you get all the attention," she whispers under her breath.

The cameras buzz closer, and Paul sticks a microphone close to her face. "Is Lori alright?"

"Oh, yes. She's fine, now," the Winter bride says dismissively, combing her fingers through her long black mane.

"What's your name?"

"Wendy Frost."

Her surname rings a bell, and I check her ears. She's Fae... I didn't know Fae were allowed to enter the contest.

"Frost... My oh my, we have a legacy candidate over here. The only Fae on the roster, I think."

"You're right, Paul, but I just don't see why all the fun should be left to the mortals."

The host chuckles at that and asks Wendy to talk more about herself, but I zone out the rest of their conversation.

Seth dumps my coat back over my shoulders. "Are you okay? What the hell happened?"

The coat heats me up and absorbs the moisture from my skin, and I hold the lapels tightly around my frame, still shivering. "I'll live," I grumble.

Seth and the Spring brides usher me away to a secluded spot behind the dunk tank. Poppy sticks a hot mug of coffee under my nose. Steam rises from the black liquid, and I sip on it slowly, each swig more delicious than the last. My fingers and toes are itchy as hell, but a bit of life returns to my core.

"Wow. That Wendy is even more of a camera whore than you are," Daisy says, the Winter bride still deep in conversation with Paul. "You think she planned this? To profit from your clout?"

Seth's brows furrow. "What do you mean?"

Daisy huffs like she's disappointed in him. "Grown women don't often drown in kiddy-size pools. Someone casted a pretty powerful spell over that tank."

While Daisy's hypothesis makes sense, I can't shake the intuition that the king is somehow responsible for what just happened; not just some ambitious, ruthless competitor.

"What about Elio?" I ask with a grimace. "Ice is his thing, right?"

"He pummeled through it with his bare hands. I don't see why he would have bothered to rescue you if he was the one trying to kill you," she whispers back.

I saw him so clearly. Standing above the ice, watching me

drown... "Maybe he thought I was already dead and wanted to avoid suspicion."

It's not such a crazy theory. I am more resilient and made of sturdier magic than the Spring seed I pretend to be, but I can't let Daisy know about that.

Sarafina disperses the crowd still gathered by the fence. "Alright. The tank is closed for the day. Let her warm up for a bit." She calls Seth and the brides away for the next challenge, the teams once again having to select a sacrificial lamb for another humiliating game, and I wait until I'm alone to approach the dunk tank.

Daisy's right. We're all vying for a bushel of blue apples and a crown nobody survives, but someone must be more desperate to win than I'd originally thought possible.

Rose becomes fodder for the dart game, and so the next hour goes, each task sillier than the last. Finally, the last member of each group, the one who never got picked by her peers to suffer the whims of the hosts, gets a turn around the ferris wheel with the king. But there's no swinging gondolas in the cards for me. The thick, enchanted winter coat dries my clothes, and by the time everyone gathers back in the middle of the central plaza, I almost feel normal again.

Byron zooms toward Sarafina with a silk bag in his hands, and the woman claps her hands to get our attention. "Alright. Now that you've all had your fun, we're ready to announce the carnival's elimination challenge. Please rejoin your starting groups."

Here we go again... I catch up with the girls and glare at the humongous teddy bear in Daisy's arms. Of course, she had to win the ring toss challenge.

"Brides, welcome to the Snowhaven's carnival kissing booth," Paul announces.

Excited squeals rise from the audience, but my stomach sinks.

"A kissing booth? Seriously?" Daisy snickers.

"I'm with you." I slither between Poppy and Rose to get a better look at what's going on.

Cameras buzz in the four corners of the covered, open-air theater, poised to capture the next challenge from every angle to satisfy the public's creepy fascination with social disasters.

Sarafina waits for the burst of whispers and nervous giggles to break before she continues with the rules. "Each of you will share a kiss with the king, and the viewers will vote for their favorite one."

My teeth grit together. I mean—I expected a challenge of the sort —just not so soon, I guess. The Winter King would rather bite me than kiss me, so whatever happens next might ruin my chances to win over the public.

"Don't think your previous encounters with the king will help you here. He's going to be blindfolded and bound, so only the taste of your lips counts," Paul adds.

Sarafina frowns at that, her gaze flying to Paul, but she quickly schools her expression back to neutral. "What a fun twist! A kiss for each bride, and blindfolded at that. What do you think is about to happen, Paul?"

Paul wiggles his bushy gray brows. "Whatever happens, you can't accuse the king of playing favorites, that's for sure." He takes a dramatic pause before looking at the cameras. "The twelve women with the least votes will leave the competition *tonight*."

Sarafina chuckles. "Oh, I'm all for that, Paul. Twenty brides is still a ridiculous number to deal with."

"Let's see who can tempt our king into kissing them back, and who will have to say goodbye to him—and their dream of ever tasting a frost apple." Paul rolls up his sleeves and loosens his tie like he's about to march into a fight ring. "Here he is. The king is walking on stage as we speak, so if you're cooking dinner or taking care of your little ones, this is your last warning."

Elio walks onto the stage, indeed. With a rogue grin, he slips his feet out of his boots, tossing them one after the other over the edge. Barefoot on the wooden stage, his opened jacket showcasing his damn abs, he looks too enticing. But it's nothing but a performance.

A spark of disdain curls his top lip as Sarafina ties the blindfold around his head. "Don't cheat," she says playfully.

Elio offers the crowd a fake smile in response. "I wouldn't dream of it."

The women around me laugh. Sarafina and Elio certainly make a lovable pair. *Maybe they should get married instead.*

We all draw a number from a velvet pouch. Number 18. *Eek.*

Twenty kisses. Twenty young women standing in line to impress a cold, soulless king. It's not right.

I'm last of the Spring group. The quiet one is going right before me, while Poppy, Rose, and Daisy are in the middle of the pack.

I let my eyes glaze over and concentrate on anything besides the other girls kissing the Winter King. There's nothing I can learn from their successes or mistakes, and if I am to be filmed and eliminated for being a bad kisser—so be it.

But quickly, a pattern emerges. Elio holds himself away from Poppy and Rose, giving them a boring peck on the lips and a quick boot. Meanwhile, the candidates from Wintermere and the Red Forest do significantly better, like the king can easily tell us apart.

Still... the tug of envy in my gut is annoying as hell, and the ball in my throat throbs when Daisy pushes her tongue inside his mouth. Elio reciprocates the kiss for half a second before he pulls away.

A satisfied smile stretches Daisy's lips, and she blows the cameras a kiss as she hops off the stage. That girl knows her stuff.

I inch forward again, a handful of women still in front of me.

Wendy manages to keep her kiss going for a good minute, and the fire in my heart swells. I start unlacing my boots and slip out of them, looking anywhere but at Elio.

Two to go.

I peel the magic coat off and toss it to the ground. My damp hair frosts over, and I slick it behind my ears.

It's barely below freezing. I can do this.

If I'm to kiss the Winter King in front of his whole court, I'm not going to let some spell shield me from his magic and him from mine.

I'm going all in. Who knows, maybe my stripping session will garner a few votes.

I don't have to be first, just high enough in the ranks to stay.

Sarafina scowls but motions me forward to the line of tape on the ground.

The quiet Spring girl in front of me, Flora, walks off the stage after a lackluster kiss. She presses a hand to her mouth to stifle a cry, and my eyes narrow. *That fucker. He's playing with us.*

Cold air seeps inside my pores, but I rub the chill of my arms as the cameras adjust their lenses. I squint at the blindfold, but it looks legit, and Sarafina nods to give me the go-ahead. I tiptoe over to Elio, light as a feather without the heavy coat and boots. It makes me feel more like myself—a huntress.

Elio is awfully tall, his dark tattoos on full display. The skull-like shape I caught a glimpse of yesterday isn't visible now, the luster of the black ink only revealing the shape of the Fae runes.

Many girls have copped a feel at this point, but I climb up the defined muscles of his stomach to his ribs with spider fingers, up and up until I reach his full lips. He frowns at that, like he's suddenly very uncomfortable.

Taking this as my last chance to act, I throw all caution to the freezing wind blowing across the square and press my mouth to his.

CHAPTER 16
LOVE IS MADNESS
ELIO

Kissing an endless string of beautiful girls is tedious. The kissing booth part of the carnival is broadcasted live, and the votes are tallied in real time. The *ohh*'s, *eek*'s, and *yikes*' of the spectators drill through my skull, and the blindfold digs into my forehead.

Sara's tight knot spells out exactly how cross she is with me after my lack-luster performance in the ferris wheel. I can't go on with this charade without her support, and if I don't want to come home to her resignation letter, I have to give the public a few swoon-worthy kisses. Nothing too hard to fake.

But I can't take the chance not to eliminate Iris's macabre twin, so I'll just take all the Spring seeds out in one sweep. It was foolish to let them get this far to appease Freya. It's not like we could ever get past our mutual hatred, not after the hell she put me through.

The kissing booth offers a rare opportunity for me to control the public vote. Spring brides are easy to spot. The overbearing aromas of roses, lilacs, or peonies make me cringe with disgust whenever they draw near. Anything that resembles Iris's smell is sure to trigger my damn brain.

But twenty kisses is a ridiculous number to keep track of. By the halfway point, I've only pecked two Spring brides on the lips and sent them on their way. There's still three to go, and I'm losing patience.

A woman feathers closer, and I take a good sniff. The cherry blossom smell comes on quite strong as she slips her tongue inside my mouth. The taste of her is so potent and unexpected that I freeze, taking a second too long to pull away.

I flex my fists. *I bet it was the evil twin. Damn her.*

There's still two Spring seeds left to eliminate.

A Winter seed approaches me next, and I linger inside the familiar scent of pine needles and snowflakes. I drag out the kiss to give myself a chance to regroup. A firefly presses her body into mine next, her breasts all but crushed into my naked chest.

"Ready to serve, my king," she says in a sultry tone, and I let her feel me up to her heart's content as she kisses the base of my ear.

Points for originality, that's for sure.

The next woman is a Spring thing, and I hold myself away, counting down to ten. The strangled cry that escapes her fills me with a prickly sense of pride. Only one Spring seed to go.

The next bride inches closer, and her scent is both airy, fresh, and smokey—like rain falling over a funeral pyre. I inch closer and catch myself sighing, intrigued by the unfamiliar bite of her magic. An exceptional Winter seed, surely, and I smother the alarm bells going off in my brain. This woman can't be a Spring seed, so I might as well kiss her back.

She grazes the ridges of my abs and skips up my chest one rib at a time with her fingers, unspooling a loose string inside me.

Her taste is even better—all cinders and snowdrops. Her kiss drags me into a mudslide of lips and rushed breaths. Before long, I'm drowning in her and stretch my neck to deepen the kiss, but she teases me by remaining slightly out of reach.

The silk tied around my wrists bites into my flesh as I try to reach for her.

Damn scarf...

Just as I'm about to destroy it with a flare of ice, the bothersome binding vanishes. *Yes.*

I cup my partner's neck and hold her to me. My other hand slips below the hem of her shirt to the small of her back, her skin as smooth as a cloak of snow under a bright moon. A low rumble of victory quakes me. She's at my mercy, now.

Small and perfect in my arms.

All I can think about is not letting this woman—this feeling— slip through my fingers. I dig a hand into her frosty locks and tug, jerking her head back to make space for my hungry mouth. I kiss her with so much abandon that I forget about the Spring seeds, the kissing booth—even the spectators. I'm no longer performing for Sara and the cameras, and the rhythm of our lips and tongues creates a beautiful sheet of music. Whoever she is, I never want to let go.

Magic claws its way through me, scratching fiery lines into my frozen heart and dipping down to my navel before slithering lower. It's not cold as the ice in my veins or bittersweet as the light I have forsaken. This magic is new to me, yet so ancient I can't fathom where it comes from. A fuse that lied in wait for this moment. For this kiss.

Our tongues battle for dominance, and the delicious tug-of-war triggers a primeval trap laid by the gods themselves, if the flavor of the magic is any indication.

A kiss that never should have been.

A verse that can't be unwritten.

I'm a beast, drinking her in. I want to sink my claws in her and drag her to my lair without looking back.

A gasp rushes up my neck, full of warmth. Too warm for a Winter seed.

A Red seed, then? How interesting. Reds usually taste of blood and tears—a leftover sting from their dark, forsaken gods.

"Elio," Sara warns.

My partner wriggles in my grip, fighting to break free. *Oh no, you don't...* I catch her jaw and hold her close, my other arm ensnared around her small waist, but she pushes on my chest with impressive zeal.

Some part of my brain stirs to life, and I let go of my temptress. The pressure of her hands on my chest relents, and her heat leaves me. My soul howls at the loss as I tear off the blindfold.

The clear gray eyes and trembling chin of Iris's doppelgänger fill me with dread, but a tiny part of my soul is not surprised in the least. It had to be her.

Only a ghost could ever feel so perfect. So...mine.

The beast nestled in my ribcage snarls, roaring at me to act.

Fight. Take back what's mine. Claim her now, and kill everyone who might interfere.

The beast is strong, but I'm still its master and rule it with all my might. If the Winter crown taught me one thing, it's that all human urges can be denied. No matter the height of the flames, our strongest, most vibrant desires can always be snuffed out. Whether by duty, grief, or despair, and at the end, by death.

No matter what, fire always runs out of fuel. In matters of flesh, blood, and bones, only ice remains unyielding.

"By the spindle... I think we have a winner." Paul's voice shatters the bubble we were suspended in, and Lori runs off the stage as though she wants to taunt my beast out to play.

"There's nothing that could beat that," Paul adds on a low whistle.

Sara is speechless, and the buzz of the cameras is the only sound audible as we watch Lori run across the town square. The crowd parts to let her pass, and I force myself to stay rooted on stage and not immediately give chase. I can't storm out of yet another part of this contest without an explanation. Whatever twisted magic is at work—my body is wired to respond to this copycat, and I bend down to retrieve the red piece of silk that should have kept my beast in check.

"I must not have tied it right," Sara says on a frown, but I shake my head.

"You tied it just fine." The knot and bow in the red scarf is still perfectly shaped, and a smirk tugs on my lips. "It was sliced through."

The two leftover candidates observe me with wide eyes, and I offer them an apologetic shrug. "Tough luck, ladies." I peck both of them on the lips, my beast rattling inside its cage. "Shut it down, Sara."

While the cameras fly back to Paul, I close my eyes and hone in on my prey. Her magic leaves delicious breadcrumbs of darkness in her wake. Even blind, I could find her now, my powers completely attuned to hers. The glaring difference between her and Iris is almost too obvious.

She's no Spring seed, after all.

No light Fae could ever taste so good. No weed could ever ensnare me so tight.

She's a darkling—an absolutely perfect shadow thing. Not a rose, but a spider. It's laughable to think I could ever taste her lips without figuring it out, and a hot sense of relief washes over me. She doesn't belong here—which means I won't have to endure her presence any longer. I could throw her in a dungeon for illegally entering the pageant, or ban her from Faerie forever, and no one would dare to protest.

I wait for the crowd to disperse and search the carnival grounds. My gaze immediately lands on the industrial wagon behind the ferris wheel. *There she is.*

Magic or no magic, I'm still in charge. The gods can choke on their well-laid plans, because I'm not going to give in to their rather rude, beastly demands. I won't lose my head because of one kiss. Instead, I'm going to figure out exactly how Lori managed to mimic Iris's looks and why Seth hired her, and everything will be right again. Sara and Paul follow me to the entrance of the hall of mirrors, Seth quick on their heels.

"No one comes in until I come out." I turn to Paul. "Make sure Seth gets comfortable in his room for a few hours. I want him to stay there until I say so."

He nods and doubles back to block Seth's path. The prince becomes quite agitated as Paul and the guards escort him off to the Snowhaven Inn, but I don't spare him another thought, turning away from his vehement demands.

Sara lowers her voice. "Are you going to kill her?"

I consider her question for a moment. "I don't know, yet." With that, I grip the handle and jump into the carnival wagon.

Darkness shrouds the hall of mirrors, and my little spider slips from one shadow to the next, intangible as smoke. A normal Winter King would be powerless against that type of magic, but I've been raised in the chasm between light and dark. I know how to catch a beautiful shadow and crush it under the sun.

I call forth a spark of sunshine and bounce it off my knuckles. The gesture feels as natural as breathing, but also stiff and unrehearsed. Rusted from years and years of disuse. I almost never summon this light I once believed to be my birthright, the memories cradled inside its soft glow too painful to bear. But all self-made rules have exceptions.

With a loose grin, I let what little light is left inside the wagon pierce through me, becoming invisible, too.

The itsy bitsy spider crawled up the water spout.
Down came the rain, and washed the spider out.

CHAPTER 17

ITSY BITSY SPIDER

LORI

The only place I could think of to escape was the hall of mirrors. Mirrors are my friends. Each of them is a way home, but not without my mask, and the silver key in my pocket is a very poor replacement for it. Elio is here with me. His bite of power drums through the wagon in lush, drugging waves, but for some reason, I can't see him.

"I want to talk." I say quietly enough not to reveal my exact position.

"You're not a Spring seed, are you?"

The way his voice raises at the end feels forced. He already knows, and he's trying to catch me in a lie.

"I'm a shadow," I admit, trying to pinpoint his location. In the space between light and dark—where shadows flourish, I should have an advantage. It's my home, but he eludes me.

"Looks like Seth hired himself an assassin. Is that why you look like her? I knew it had to be a glamor—" He scoffs, mostly to himself. "Were you hoping to get me alone? Slice my throat? Don't bother because it wouldn't work."

"I'm no assassin, and I was born this way—no glamor needed."

"Prove it."

Spears of ice shoot out of the wagon's floor, and a blinding sunshine blares through the claustrophobic space. Two bright halos brand my retinas, and I rush between the shiny shards, disoriented. My grip tightens over the hilts of my daggers, but they're fractionated and incomplete. *Shit.*

Elio extinguishes my shadows one by one with his light, leaving me without a shield or weapons to defend myself. I dash toward the closest pane of glass, about ready to risk it all and enter the sceawere without my mask, but frost covers the mirrors. The thin film of ice blurs my reflection and makes it impervious to my magic, blocking my escape.

I collide with the mirror face-first.

Elio cages me in between the smooth glass and the hard planes of his chest—one I had explored and prodded at with hungry fingers mere minutes ago. "I've got you, now."

Colors fly behind my closed lids, his body crushing me like a wall of ice. His hands are locked on my shoulders—the same hands he'd used to caress my back and hold me captive as he'd ruined me with his mouth for the whole kingdom to see. He's not yet smothering the life out of me, but his confident hold is enough to steal my breath and spells out in no uncertain terms that I still live only because he wishes it to be so.

The icy mirror chafes my cheek as he slides a thigh between my legs and paws at my waist. The lack of restraint—or even the slightest hesitation—in his movements feels blasphemous, Elio acting as though he took ownership of my body with one kiss and is now merely mapping out his rightful property.

"What are you doing? Don't touch me!" I snarl, the property in question having an entirely inappropriate reaction to his flag-planting antics. The sudden heat in my belly leaves me more confused than when I was on the cusp of drowning, and I blush a thousand shades of *fucked up.*

His frosty breath stings the shell of my ear. "Either I check you for active glamors, or I kill you right here and now. Your choice, little spider."

He looks ready to skewer me on ice if I so much as open my mouth again, and I offer him a tight nod.

"Wise choice." His spears retreat, and he draws back a few inches. "Both palms in front of you, don't move, and maybe, if I don't find anything, I'll give you a chance to explain yourself."

A hoarse sigh rocks me as I flatten both of my palms to the frozen mirror, and Elio digs his hands inside my pockets.

"What's this?" He dangles the silver key in front of my eyes.

"It's for my mask. I left it with Seth."

"Pretty stupid of you." With an unkind chuckle, he tears off my shirt and picks the leftover shreds off my shivering frame.

After he's done with the top, he dips his fingers below the hem of my black leggings to pull them off. My stupid body bends to help him along, my skin feverish as I step out of the leggings one foot at a time, my black underwear the only barrier left to shield me from his gaze.

Why is my body reacting this way, when I should want to kick his teeth in for what he's doing? Why are my breaths so damn shallow, and why oh why are my breasts so heavy and sensitive? He's hard-core frisking me. This is not sexual. This is not sexual.

But I'm delusional, because it's absolutely sexual.

My reflection in the mirror to my left is one of pure submission, and my gut cramps. "Enjoying the view, ice prick?"

"Not particularly," he barks in response. "I'm busy."

The calluses of his hands trace every single inch of my naked back slowly and methodically. He inspects every groove like he's afraid I've hidden the runes under an invisibility enchantment of some kind, and I shiver at the pressure. He's very careful not to bruise me, but his touch is colder and heavier than strictly necessary. The bastard wants me to feel small and under his control, but the rather intimate search only spurs the fever along. Hell, the touch of his smooth, large hands spreads the disease from my treacherous body to my intoxicated brain.

He's got very graceful fingers, long and nimble. The girls were saying how he loves to play the piano—I bet he's good at it, too.

No! Nope. Ugh-Ugh. Stop thinking about his pianist hands, I try to reason with myself, but the strange warmth in my belly is intent on dragging my mind deeper and deeper down the gutter. From his expert musician hands, to his rock-hard abs, to the long, steely ridge of his erection pressing against my thigh, earlier.

The fever, and the magic behind it, is too powerful to resist. What started as a spark of madness back on stage—with a kiss no one would argue was the best damn first kiss a man and a woman ever shared in front of an audience—has caught fire.

"Stop looking at me like that," Elio barks darkly, no longer meeting my gaze in the mirror. After he's done with my back, he rakes his icy fingers through my hair and gives it a rough pull to check my skull.

I swallow back a whimper. "Careful with the hair."

He twists it around his hand and tugs harder in response, jerking my head back. "Where did you hide the runes?"

"I told you," I scold him. "You're searching for something that doesn't exist."

"We'll see."

When he's confident there's nothing written on my scalp, he traces new lines over my backside, all the way down to my heels. Jolts of electricity scatter through my body, but he hurries along my curves like he's intimidated by them. Or rather...distracted?

I watch him in the mirror, and he pauses for a moment, his bottom lip tucked between his teeth like he's not sure what to do. He extends two fingers toward my spine like he's yearning to touch it but stops himself at the last second.

He growls when he catches me looking.

"You're certainly enjoying the view *now*..." I trail off.

"Spin around."

I swallow hard, but he doesn't ogle or leer at my chest as I obey. The earthy, fresh scent of him drills into me again—pine needles, dewdrops, and apples—so perfect I could scream.

His eyes fall to my ribs, and he pauses. "What's this?" he grazes the swollen spider bite, and the small touch causes my abs to clench and my nipples to harden.

"A scar."

"That's more than a scar. You were wounded, and badly at that." His blue eyes pulse with anger. "You almost died."

"I know," I answer quietly.

I can't tell if he's mad that I escaped death or what, but his hand shakes. He scans every inch of my arms to the very tip of my nails and applies the same process to my face and chest.

"A glamor rune could be as small as the tip of a signet ring," he breathes. "You must have hidden it well."

He sounds so certain that I'm lying, but his hypothesis that I could have hidden the runes anywhere on my skin is flawed. Only a fucked up witch would carve glamor runes into her *breasts*. Gods!

When his gaze finally falls to my dark, erect peaks, his cheeks become slightly hollowed out, and he pauses.

His throat bobs, the pressure of his fingertips more gentle than it was when he first started. He bites his bottom lip again and glares at my breasts like they exist solely to torture him. Like he's furious with me for having them in the first place. My damn belly squeezes in anticipation without a single consideration for common sense. I want him to stop playing chicken and fucking *touch them* already. He's clearly thinking about it, the bulge in his pants becoming more obvious by the second.

The fever's getting to him, too.

I'd feel thwarted if it didn't. No one wants to burn alive alone. When ice itself is ablaze, you know that the flames were quite unstoppable.

I bite back a moan as he finally, *finally* ghosts his index and middle fingers across my chest.

"You're totally enjoying this," I say in a scalding tone.

The corners of his mouth twitch. "So are you." He punctuates his statement with a sharp squeeze of my left breast, and I moan in a totally *fuck, yes* and not at all *get off me* way. My mouth hangs open at his boldness, and I want to curse him to the seven hells, but the fire is still raging.

Are we going to continue to pretend this isn't actually happening?

Even if he followed a strict process, never lingering too long in one place, his breaths have grown shallower, and his glacial blue eyes are now pulsing with something dark and foreign.

When he curses under his breath and falls to his knees in front of me, I stiffen from head to toe. "You're not serious—"

"Either I check every inch, or I shouldn't have bothered at all."

He seems about as angry with himself for not thinking it through as he is with me. His fingertips slip under the lace of my thong, and I mold my back to the mirror, my legs about useless at this point.

He might kill you after he's done. Focus on that.

But the reaper king is on his knees in front of me... No matter how much I try to rationalize it, he's still the most powerful Fae in existence. His hair shines in the dark, and the stiffness of his shoulders does nothing to calm my nerves. The coiled muscles of his abdomen move as he breathes, and the slope of his neck is peppered with snowflakes. All I can think about is licking them off his skin.

Burn them.

Burn him. Make him see *you.*

Damn fever.

Never mind the feel of his cold, blistering touch. My entire body shakes, and I force myself to close my eyes.

But it doesn't help.

With or without the fever, his insidious lure is made to seduce mortals even though we know better. Power electrifies the air the same way it does after I kill a nightmare, but instead of melding into me, the restless energy glides along my skin, hovering like it doesn't quite know where to go.

Long fingers trace my inner thighs in search of runes as Elio clicks his tongue. "Do you fear me, little spider?"

"Yes."

He caresses my legs up and down, all the way to my feet and back. "Is that why you're trembling?"

I shake my head no, staring up at the ceiling. His touch grows even softer, and goosebumps riddle my neck. *This is beyond embarrassing.*

"I hate you, and yet..." He slips a hand outside his strict search area to the flesh of my thigh. His nose ghosts along my leg, and he inhales deeply. "You smell...perfect. What's your real name?"

"Lori," I cry out, my eyes darting down to Elio.

He digs his nails in my skin. "Your entire name."

Giving him my entire name means that he'll own me from this day forward, and yet I can't refuse him. I feel like I'm being sucked in by his gravity. I want him to *see* me. I *need* him to know who I am. "Lorisha Pari Singh."

"Do you want me to touch you, Lori?" A carnal promise burns within his hardened gaze, and the hunter inside me bristles.

Luring in the most beautiful, dangerous predator in Faerie is no small feat, but a beast caught in a snare is much more dangerous than a free one. He could kill me before I tamed him.

"Fuck." I slap the mirror behind me with my open palm, the truth about as shameful as his behavior. "Yes."

The tips of his fingers glide under the flimsy lace, and I fail to stifle a gasp as he brushes my sex.

"Why are you so wet? Are you so turned on by death that you can't recognize what's bad for you, little spider?" he says on a hiss, like this is all my fault.

"That kiss..." I rationalize, the feel of his hand fucking incredible. My whole body is knotted and curled, begging for this Fae king to take whatever he needs and destroy me. "It unleashed some kind of old magic."

"*Powerful* old magic," he confirms on a defeated growl. "Tell me what you want." His words are gruff and yet soft, like we're both dangling from the same thread of insanity. "Or better yet, tell me to stop. I can't see straight when you're near, but I'd never force myself on you. Say the word, and I'm gone."

My heart stumbles. "Is that what *you* want?"

His aren't the lazy touches of a casual lover, and I gasp when he tears the lace off and kisses the soft skin underneath with reverence. "What I want is to lick every inch of you, if you'll let me."

The sharp craving between my legs expands like a dark hole that could never, ever be filled.

"Yes." My lids flutter, and I take solace in the knowledge that, even though some higher power is really in charge, I could have said *no*. "I need you."

The brazen touch of his hand plagues me with self-loathing, but it's the first flick of his tongue over my drenched folds that almost kills me. It's too cold, and yet... I've never thought of ice as sexy, but every lick soothes the inferno in my belly. Each brush is divine, and I feel like I will burst into flames if he stops.

His ice is *burning* me, and yet... "Oh please, please, *please*," I moan, horrified to hear the words out loud. I'm so fucking sensitive; I can't deal.

"You taste better than Feyfire wine," he growls, the heaviness of his breath on my clit almost enough to send me over the edge. "Better than life."

He hikes my leg over his shoulder, the new angle allowing his tongue to rub deep, and I reach down to pull on his blond locks.

Elio simply *devours* me, branding me with his hands and mouth and coaxing sounds out of me I've never heard before. Dark embers of magic rise into the air, and I arch my back, ready to die at his command. He presses the tip of his tongue where my will is most fragile, the rub of his fingers now hard and unrelenting.

"Come for me, little spider. Come for your king."

My body doesn't care about his earlier threats, and the pleasure both stings and soothes, like snow melting on my tongue. Wicked tremors shake my legs, and I hate myself, but it's the best orgasm of my life. It lasts for *minutes*, the Winter King's face buried between my legs.

"You belong to winter, now, Lorisha Pari Singh." He glides up to stand and wraps a hand in my hair. "Why does Seth want to kill me? Does he really think he would last a week as the reaper king?" A dry snort rakes his throat. "Does he truly believe death would come so easy to me?"

"I'm *not* an assassin."

He places an open-mouthed kiss on my temple. "So you said, but I don't believe you."

Ragged pants quake my chest. Are we lovers or enemies? Is he going to kill me or fuck me?

He loosens the knot of his lace-up pants, his current actions pointing to the latter. He's only attracted to me because of his dead wife, and yet...

"How did you know who I was earlier?" I'm panting and furious and fucking *mad*.

"I didn't. Not until it was too late. Hell, I *prayed* it wasn't you—"

How dare he pray for another when the Flame weaved him such a gift? Burn him.

"—but here we are." He pulls himself out of his pants and strokes his cock up and down.

By the spindle and all the dark Fae Gods... Long fingers. Tall. I shouldn't be surprised.

"Then why would you kiss me like that?" I croak.

He raises a brow that tells me to evaluate my own choices before judging his and leans in to suck my earlobe into his mouth. "Why are you letting me fuck you?"

"I'm not—"

But I am. I'm not fighting him at all—hell, I'm so fucking ready. My right thigh is already hooked around his waist. "It's the fever."

Burn. Burn. Burn.

He places a hot kiss to the valley between my breasts. "You know who else was supposedly overcome by a *fever*? The Summer King before he killed all those innocent Mist Fae civilians. It was the *will of the gods,* he'd said."

"We're about to have sex, not commit unspeakable murders."

He grins at my response, the Winter King actually amused. "You have a point.

He kneads my breasts with both hands, twisting, flicking, and teasing, and I push against them even harder, greedy for more. I've never felt this urgency before, such a raw need to be claimed by a man.

"We're going to give in to this magic. Once. Because our bodies need it. But that's all it's ever going to be." Shards of ice magic drift in his eyes. "A moment of weakness."

I nod too many times. "Yes. Just once." The pulse of magic in the room is so powerful, I just know I will wither and die if he walks away.

He picks me up and pins me to the mirror at my back. "Can you feel it?"

"Yes," I gasp as the wide tip of him lines up with my entrance.

"Did you cast a spell on me, little spider?" he asks. "Did you sell your blood and soul to some forsaken god so he'd change your appearance and enchant me?" He gives me an inch, when I need so much more. "Did you plan this, somehow?"

"No. I swear."

His eyes flash with a sense of acceptance. "I believe that at least. Will you let me have all of you, even if it's just for one delirious moment?"

"Take me. Take me and make me scream your name, King of Death. Make it so I never forget how sweet it tastes."

He plants a soft kiss on my lips and thrusts so deep inside me that my head hits the glass. We're both speechless for a moment, our opened mouths resting against one another. He stretches me, cold and yet warm at the same time. Rock hard, and so, so big.

"You're...perfect."

Finally.

The fever recedes, content with its work, and leaves us to face the consequences of our actions. I twist my fingers in his hair and inhale deep. "Oh, fuck!"

Elio remains unnaturally still, supporting my entire weight. "Do you want to stop?"

I squeeze my walls around him, wishing I could keep him there forever. "No!" I feel torn about this, but fuck it, it's the best sex of my life. There'll be time to curse myself and feel guilty later.

He draws in a sharp breath, his hand shaking as he caresses the slope of my neck. "Thank the Blessed Flame."

"What's th—"

Elio's lips are firm and unapologetic as he starts to move, and I taste myself on his tongue, my half-formed question forgotten. It's the most intense sensation, like my skin, body, and soul have been starving for years, waiting for him.

When he speaks again, his voice is quieter—almost pleading. "You ignored me last time, but you will throw the next round and go home, yes? If you don't obey...you'll find out exactly how cold the mountains can get when you disobey the Winter King." He thrusts deeper inside me with each sentence. "Am I being clear, now?"

"Yes."

His abs roll, and he hits the sweet spot inside me *just so*, like he wants me to melt him as much as I need him to crush me. "And you'll go away. Forever."

"I'll do whatever you want. Just don't stop. Never stop." I wrap my arms around his neck and kiss him hard.

Elio Hades Lightbringer is a devil, and as he fucks me for the first and last time, I can't help but wish I was his evil queen.

I suck the snowflakes from his skin one by one, and his groans of pleasure fill me with pride. My legs are wrapped tightly around him, and I cry out, another orgasm threatening to shatter me.

"Shush, or the whole town will hear you..." He smothers my

sounds with his hand. "Fuck. You feel too good. I'm tempted to play with you all night."

I smile against his palm, and for a moment, everything is perfect. I forget that we hate each other and live for his next demanding thrust—his next growly praise. Under his touch, I live for him and him alone, and it's no longer the fever talking.

He stops, leaving me tethering over the edge. "Beg me for your release, little spider. Let me see the anguish on your face." He brushes my hair away from my eyes with maddening care. "I'll never touch you again after today and marry any of them but you. Are you hearing me?" The loving way he breathes the words is a stark contrast to their meaning.

He squeezes my breasts in turn, demanding an answer.

"Yes! You sly fucker, I hear you." I rock my hips, desperate for him to finish what he started. "I need you to fuck me so hard that I'll still feel you long after you're gone."

He wraps a hand in my hair and kisses the hollow of my neck. "Why did you have to go and say something so perfect? Now, I want to chain you to my bed so I can spend *weeks* inside of you."

"Do it!" I taunt him.

The Winter King slams his hips forward, over and over again, and the climax comes about as violently as the sex. I sink my nails into his neck, the clench in my belly sharp and delicious.

My pulse swirls as he holds himself up against the mirror, following me right over the cliff of this suffocating, destructive lust. The glass cracks under his palm, and all the mirrors in the wagon burst in unison as he shakes from the aftershocks of his orgasm.

Broken pieces scatter to the floor.

My feet search for solid ground, my bones soft, and my muscles weak. Tears streak my cheeks. I've never felt so perfect...or so cold. The ecstasy leaves my body, replaced by a gripping sense of emptiness. A piece of broken glass cuts the flesh of my big toe, but I can barely feel it.

Morpheus help me. I craved this more than I've ever craved

anything in this life. I let the King of Death, the reaper king and collector of souls, the man who dispenses grief left and right like it's nothing, touch my soul. And I loved it.

Shame licks my insides, almost as hot and debilitating as the fever was. I could cower inside a "magic made me do it" narrative and absolve myself from blame, but I know I could have stopped it. Morpheus knows Elio gave me plenty of chances.

I wanted it to happen. I wanted *him*.

This man is most likely plotting with the woman who almost destroyed my family. He took my friends' souls, my parent's souls, and every other soul he damn-well pleases. And yet here I am, quivering in his arms.

Another voice inside me argues that it was worth it, but I can't afford to trust that voice anymore. It just made me do something incredibly selfish.

Elio hides his face in my neck and groans like he doesn't want to confront what he's just done, either. He certainly didn't want to have to look at himself in a mirror, because he destroyed them all.

He rests his forehead on mine and drinks the tears from my cheek with care. "It's alright, little spider. It'll be our secret."

CHAPTER 18

KISS. MARRY. KILL.

ELIO

My bare feet hit the ground outside the wagon with a soft *thump*, and Sara peels herself from the ground. The wet trail of salt on her cheeks tells me she's been crying, but her voice is steady when she asks, "Is she dead?"

Sara fully expects to bury another body today, and I can't pretend to be insulted by her assumption. Spies, snakes, and liars don't survive for long in my court, and I'm more than comfortable serving as both jury and executioner when the time comes for traitors to be dealt with. But the usual criminals don't quicken my heartbeat or turn my brain to a puddle...

I search the square, but there's only us. "She's alive," I croak.

Freshly fucked, but alive. Did that even happen? The little shards of broken glass embedded in my palms confirm that it wasn't all a fever dream, and I button up my jacket. I should have given it to Lori as a replacement for her shredded shirt, but I couldn't stand the thought of her ogling the distinct scars on my back.

What in the seven hells happened in there? I was so sure she was using magic to alter her appearance that I ended up kneeling in front of *her*. I lost my grip, I—

I was cruel, I was crude, I used her body for my pleasure and unveiled parts of me that had been locked away for decades. Broken, secret parts. I went back on my promise not to yield to the beast's demands. It slithered away as I entered her, and yet the blackest shards of my soul yearned to touch her and make her mine anyway. I still can't believe how much she got off on my filthy mouth, each devious word causing her walls to tighten around my cock.

Stop thinking about it.

I pinch the bridge of my nose, at war with myself. "I need you to take her to your room."

"My room?"

"She needs a shower before we return her to Seth." I'd briefly hoped to keep the sex secret from everyone else, but I'd rather tell Sara than let Lori's scent announce what we did to the whole Fae population. "You can say we inspected her for enchantments and glamors and found nothing out of place."

"Elio—"

"I know. I betrayed the sanctity of the pageant again."

"Who cares about the pageant? What about her? Elio, tell me you didn't force yourself on that girl—" Sara chokes on a sob.

Now, I'm insulted.

"Of course not!" The disbelief in her eyes cuts to the bone, and I cup my best friend's cheek. "Have I changed so much that you would accuse me of that?" I say quietly enough for Lori not to hear.

Her voice rises a few octaves. "You're so...withdrawn." Her throat bobs, and she shakes her head, looking to the sky so the tears in her eyes don't spill over. "I swear, sometimes I look at you and I'm not even sure if the Elio I knew is still in there—" she taps my chest with her index and middle fingers, and I want to comfort her, but she's right.

The Elio she used to know is gone, and no matter how much it pains me to disappoint her, he's never coming back.

My demon slithers out of the wagon behind me, interrupting my quiet moment with Sara. "Please, take your time to gossip about this. I'm only freezing in here," she says.

My spine stiffens, and I look everywhere but at her, clamping my mouth shut.

Sara's brow lifts in surprise as she throws her coat over Lori's frame. "Come on, Sixteen. I'll take you to my room."

The women walk off toward Sara's temporary apartments in Snowhaven Inn. The other contestants are all huddled up inside their big tent, and the town's people were instructed to go home, so no one else should have caught a glimpse of us.

I wait for a minute or two before following in their footsteps to reach the royal suite on the third floor, but Lori's scent lures me toward Sara's room, and I rest my head on the door, about ready to trample it down.

I've got half a mind to find my demon in Sara's shower and taste her again... Fuck, I need a shower, too, and a very cold one at that.

I hurry to my bathroom and lock the door behind me as though something as trivial as a piece of wood could actually prevent me from feeling her, one story below, her presence so vivid I can hear her breathe when I close my eyes. I feel the hot water gliding down her skin, and imagine her parted lips as she drags the soap across her stomach to the space between her thighs, desperate to wash me off her.

My soul is in shambles, and she's got the pieces.

But no matter how much I wish I could heal, how much I desire a fresh start, I know I will never be happy. And it's alright, because I don't deserve to be. No matter how badly the gods want Lori to be my next wife, the curse condemned me to never love again, and I would never sentence her to a loveless marriage followed by certain death.

Never.

The modern fixtures they installed in the inn for the tourists take me back to my time at the Royal Academy. With an annoyed huff, I turn off the knobs offering various fragrances of scented water and disable the rain shower jets above my head, looking for nothing more than cold water to drown out the chaos in my brain and distract me from the eerie link I still share with Lori.

The water turns on, but I hiss at the spray, the cold jets stinging my skin. A big frown twists my face as I raise the water temperature to lukewarm, and a full-bodied shiver rakes through me. I haven't tolerated warm water in years, but somehow, it's still not enough.

I grip the handle of the knob and tentatively twist it toward the engraved "hot" in the brass plate. Pushing well past discomfort, I crank up the temperature until it starts to hurt.

Steam fogs the glass as I let the water burn my skin for a second.

For some reason, my heart is beating faster in my chest than it has in a long time. The events of the night melted a bit of the frost that's been waging war on my body for years, and that's scary as fuck.

But I won't let some old, powerful spell control my destiny. Who cares if some otherworldly force wishes for us to mate? I'm not going to let the spindle of the gods have the last word on whom I fuck, marry, and kill.

Iris stole parts of the old Elio forever. I can't let Lori play with the broken pieces and ruin what's left of him.

I need her gone as soon as possible.

CHAPTER 19
ANOTHER DEAL
LORI

Afluffy white robe hugs my curves, and the pleasant sting of the warm water still tingles on my skin. Sarafina lent me underwear and socks, too, and everything fits just right. I slip them on before joining her in the bedroom, making sure my silver key is safely tucked inside the pocket.

Her private space is not big, but it has a bathroom, a bed, and a large fireplace. Loud music and laughter rise between the floor-boards from the first floor of the inn, and the windows offer a frosted view of the empty street below.

"Thank you."

"You're welcome. Tea?" She hands me a mug of contraceptive tea, and the familiar, purple-colored liquid flips my stomach.

A languid ache takes hold of my body. I can't believe the last few hours really happened, and now that I've washed Elio's scent off me, I can't wrap my mind around any of it. All the adrenaline fizzles out, leaving me exhausted and famished—and deliciously sore, though I'm doing my best not to think about it.

Sarafina watches me with her arms crossed as I down the entire mug. When I'm done, I set it on the dresser and move to walk past her, but she puts herself in my way. "Before you go, I need to check you for active enchantments."

A wry grin curls my lips. "Your king has already inspected me."

"I'd rather make sure. He seemed awfully distracted."

Sarafina hikes the sleeve of the robe up my arm, and she's a champion of modesty compared to Elio. She inspects me section by section and avoids my private parts, probably confident that her boss paid enough attention to them. I come out of the second search feeling slightly more like myself, but the woman in front of me looks rattled to say the least.

She fetches a sewing pin and holds it out to me. "Prick your finger."

My jaw clenches. "I'm not a fan of blood magic—"

"Neither am I. Just do it."

I coax a drop of blood from my fingertip and Sarafina guides my hand to the hollow of my neck and draws the Fae rune for "heart" in blood over my skin. She punctuates the drawing with the rune for "Truth", and air rushes out of my lungs.

Magic envelops me from all sides, but it quickly draws back, and Sarafina gives a big sigh. "Alright. You're a true doppelganger." She crosses her arms around her small frame and taps her foot to the ground. "Why do you look like Iris?"

"I have no idea," I answer truthfully, acting a little more aloof than strictly necessary.

She clicks her tongue. "Don't play with him. He deserves more than that."

The way Elio looked at her earlier—with so much tenderness— haunts me. That combined with the obvious love in Sarafina's voice just now... I'm almost sure they're together. I roll my shoulders back, trying to summon some much needed anger.

If I'm right, Elio cheated on his girlfriend and enrolled her to take care of me, but the possibility only fills me with misery.

I clear my throat. "You seem to be quite taken by him. If you like him so much, why hold a pageant to find him a wife? Why not just marry him yourself and spare us all this charade?"

She laughs at that, all smiles, and her reaction throws me for a loop. "You're jealous?"

"No," I huff.

"You should have seen your eyes just now. Don't worry, Sixteen. I'd be more inclined to fall for you rather than Elio." She presses her lips together to stifle another giggle, and her eyes flick to the sash of my robe suggestively.

"Oh! When I came out of the wagon, you were crying, and he was whispering in your ear, so I thought—" I blurt out.

She lets out a cheerful snort and shakes her head again. "I was crying because I thought he'd killed you, and that would have wrecked him for *months*. Come on now," she motions for me to follow her into the next room. "You deserve some food for making me laugh."

Bread, charcuteries, and cheese have been laid out in a buffet fashion next to a big table, but the dining room is empty and quiet.

Sarafina tiptoes over to the doors on the other side of the room and twists the locks. "Here. Paul won't disturb us, now. We wouldn't want him to think that the two of us are sneaking around."

My stomach rumbles, and I bee-line for the buffet. Feeling foolish for my earlier fumble, I snatch humongous pieces of bread and cheese from the plate and smash them together. A low hum escapes my throat as I take a bite out of the divine, sweet and salty makeshift sandwich.

"Easy there, ogre. I'm hungry, too." Sarafina breaks a piece off of the loaf and dumps it onto a plate. She looks pensive as she sits in the seat across from me and munches on the bread. "Why are you here, really? To kill him? Steal from him?"

I swallow down another bite before I answer, "Not at all. I'm no assassin or thief. I'm a true Shadow huntress."

"Let's say you're telling the truth, and that you work for the Shadow King. Why did he send you here? And if you're truly one of his, why weren't you part of his court on Morheim? It's not like he's got hunters to spare."

"I was too hurt to come along on Morheim."

Sara's eyes fall to my ribs. "That I believe."

My mouth still full, I follow her gaze to my covered ribs and growl. Can every single Fae in existence sense the damn venom embedded in my bones?

"I'm here to pick up the trail of a woman called Morrigan. She's been through here recently," I sum up, leaving out a few important details, but with enough truth to test my interrogator. "And the Shadow King wants her alive."

Sarafina pushes her plate aside. "What did you truly see in the maze, when your Spring friend died?"

"I saw Aster speaking with someone—she'd said earlier that a woman needed help by the maze, but all I could make out in the storm was a dark silhouette. I thought it might be Morrigan and followed."

Sarafina sits back in her chair. "Alright. I don't know anyone by that name, but I'll verify your story at the Yule brunch tomorrow. If the Shadow King vies for you, I'm tempted to keep you around. Us darklings need to stick together in these uncertain times."

I'm grateful for her use of the word *us*. Fae seldom consider mortals their equals, but I shake my head. Her plan clearly ignores the most obvious hurdle. "Ugh-ugh. Elio told me in no uncertain terms that he never wanted to lay eyes on me again."

Sarafina flattens both palms to the table, and a flurry of snowflakes scatter in the air above her knuckles. Magic creeps through the room, frosting the windows through and through, along with the doorknobs and the gaps between the solid wooden doors and the floorboards. An eerie silence takes over, the bustle of the tavern below us vanishing in a flash.

"What—"

Sarafina holds up one finger for me to wait and nods after a few seconds. "No one could possibly hear us now." She straightens her spine and links her fingers over the table. "I won't waste your time, Lori, and take a leap of faith. As a spider, you're not loyal to the first kingdoms, which allows me to be candid.

"Something is very wrong with the magic of this realm. Unpredictable ice storms have disrupted the activities in the mines, and snow is melting in places it shouldn't. I've only picked up a few pieces of the puzzle so far, but I think something big is going to happen before the pageant is over.

"If someone wants to move against the Winter King, it'll happen before the solstice. I know your kingdom has faced similar challenges, so it wouldn't hurt to keep you around—as long as you didn't press your advantage with Elio."

"And what would I have to do?"

"Just keep an eye out for anything out of the ordinary. It would give you an opportunity to hunt for your mark in the next two provinces, and I would have eyes and ears on the ground, along with a competent fighter to protect the brides if something happens. Whoever killed your friend Aster is still on the loose, and I'm sure Seth told you what happened in the maze was not an isolated incident. Things of the sort happen every year during the pageant, and I'm sick of it."

My mind flashes to the gorgeous, ethereal warrior accompanying the Red brides. "Why don't you ask the Reds for help? They look deadly as fuck."

"Reds don't fight for anyone but themselves," she says with a decisive slice of the head. "The next challenge will be a survivor-type situation. Are you up for it, Sixteen?"

"Call me Lori."

The corners of her mouth quirk. "Very well. But only if you call me Sara."

I chew on my bottom lip.

I don't know if I can trust any of these Fae, but Sara's concerns sound valid and genuine. If some scourge or curse is spreading across the Fae Continent, I'm all for stopping it before it reaches the Shadowlands.

"Can I tell Seth?" I ask.

I can't jeopardize my chances to save Ayaan, but what Sarafina is offering would allow me to stay in the pageant and fulfill my duty to the prince as well.

She wraps her arms around her body at that. "Are you sleeping with him, too?"

"No, but I trust him. You don't think he's involved in whatever's coming, do you?"

She rakes a black nail across a knot in the wood table. "Seth isn't cut out for the Winter crown, and he knows that. I don't see what other angle he could have to conspire against us." Her lips are still pursed, but she finally leans forward with a quick nod. "Very well, then. But if we are to trade information, I'm going to need some transparency from you both. Byron will have a long chat with Seth in the morning to lay out strict ground rules, and if everything works out, I will smooth things over with the king."

She appears confident in her ability to sway Elio into letting me stay, and my stomach flip-flops. A part of me was relieved to be out of the pageant and free to leave Wintermere. *If I stay, what happened earlier will happen again...* but I swat the intrusive thought away and vanquish the little voice in my head that pleads for me to run.

The ice cutting Sara and I off from the rest of the world melts a little, the windows returning to their original tint.

I almost mention the hooded woman I saw meeting with Elio in the gardens, but if the Winter King is in leagues with Morrigan without Sara's knowledge, she won't believe me. Worse, she might ask him about it. Until I know more, I need to keep this close to the vest.

"Alright, I'm in." I move to stand. "Where is Seth?"

Sara escorts me to the exit. "In one of the rooms below, but he's not alone." She swings open the door. "The brides are expected to sleep in the big tent outside. Tell them that you've been interrogated by me because of your resemblance to Iris, and make no mention of Elio. I'll be your alibi."

The Inn's tavern is still loud and cheerful as I wrap myself in shadows, and I make my way down the hallway, pressing my ear to each of the doors to find Seth's bedroom. Heated moans blaring from behind the first door around the corner clue me in that Seth is indeed not alone, and I knock on the wood with a wry grin.

The moans stop abruptly, and a storm of curses echoes inside the prince's bedroom.

"Are you really going to open the door?" a familiar voice asks, and I arch a brow.

Poppy? Really?

She probably figured she'd be out of the competition because of Elio's attempt to disqualify all the Spring seeds, and I don't blame her for making the most of the experience.

"It could be important," Seth answers, not sounding half as sorry as he should. "Just be patient."

If I was the woman in bed with him, I'd be tempted to slap his princely face.

The Fae cracks open the door, naked, and I catch a glimpse of Poppy holding the covers to her chest on the bed. The brunette looks absolutely scandalized, but I don't allow her to see me and engulf Seth in my shadows instead.

"Hey, partner," I press my lips together to hide my big, goofy smile.

I can't believe his lure affected me so much when we first met. He's just a man, and his lust magic pales in comparison to Elio's life-shattering thrall. Still, the naked storm prince is easy on the eyes.

"I need a moment, and it can't wait," I say in my best, all-business, corporate voice.

He rakes his hand through his dark hair and groans. "Give me a minute."

"Just one? I thought better of you."

He cracks a smile and doubles-back to wrap a silk black robe around his body before joining me outside his door. "Where were you? I was worried."

"Not so worried that you came looking for me." I raise a brow that commands him to cut the bullshit.

A sheepish pout twists his lips. "I'm sorry. Guards corralled me in here right after you ran off. There was nothing I could do without raising some serious hell and blowing your cover."

"Well... Consider my cover blown where Elio and Sara are concerned."

Seth's gaze falls to the sash of my robe. "What are you wearing?"

I cross my arms over my chest and fight off the urge to roll my eyes. "You first. How is your brother mixed up in this?"

He rubs the arch of his brow. "I wasn't supposed to tell anyone, but my youngest half-brother, Luther, is missing. He's the most powerful and versatile storm Fae in centuries. He has both storm and shadow magic in spades, so my father didn't want to introduce him to the other courts until it was time to enroll him in the Royal Academy. But somehow, our enemies found out, and Morrigan kidnapped him."

My mind spins at the possible implications. "Morrigan weaved hundreds of Dreamcatcher spiders to attack the Shadow Court. Obviously, she couldn't have done this using her magic alone. Do you think she could have used your brother's magic?"

The hard line of his jaw spells volumes. "Maybe. Luther's powers are immense, and I think Morrigan is working with dangerous rebels to try and steal them. I've heard rumblings about revolutionists— Fae and mortal alike—using illegal technology to boost their power. That's how I ended up chatting with your brother in the first place. A mortal that confessed to carving a forbidden arrow on his own... I had to verify the story myself."

My pulse swirls at that new tidbit of information. "He *confessed*?"

"I'm afraid so. When I read his file, it said that his sister was training as a Shadow huntress, so I connected the dots."

"Do you trust Sarafina?" I ask point-blank, stowing all my doubts about Ayaan for later. Whatever Seth believes, I know my little fox of a brother isn't dumb enough to admit to a crime punishable by death...

Seth frowns at that, my swift change of subject probably making me appear as unstable as I feel. "As much as I can trust a snowflake, why?"

"Put on your listening ears. I've got a *ton* to tell you."

I cradle us in shadows to prevent anyone from overhearing and catch Seth up on the situation. But I leave out the part where I had sex with the Winter King. Seems hardly relevant, now.

I GET TO THE TENT HALF AN HOUR LATER AND LEAVE MY SHADOW CLOAK AT the door.

A loud, disappointed groan rises from the cots near the entrance where the reds huddle together. The Red from the carnival alerts her friends of my arrival, the women apparently taking shifts to guard the entrance of the tent.

I search the space for the Spring seeds and find them huddled in the back with the Summer fireflies while the Winter brides claimed the rest of the tent for themselves. They make about half our numbers by now.

Wendy Frost, the Winter bride who rescued me from the pool— or maybe entombed me in there in the first place—greets me with both hands on her hips and puts herself in my way. "We thought you were out, Sixteen. What happened to you?" She eyes the robe wrapped around my body with her top lip curled in disgust.

"Let her through. It's none of your business," Daisy shouts at her back, leaving her section of the tent to join us.

Wendy flashes me her straight, white teeth. "Weeds stick together, I see."

Daisy balls her fists at the jab, the blonde more feisty than I've ever seen her. "Who are you calling a weed, pointy ears?"

Wendy offers a dismissive wave in response. "All Spring seeds are weeds to me."

"And all snowflakes melt in spring, dear," Daisy shoots back.

I slip toward the cots, Daisy quick on my heels, and observe Wendy from the corner of my eyes. The Winter Fae is whispering with the Reds by the entrance of the tent.

I grin. "You really pissed her off."

Daisy's eyes shine in the dark. "That Fae bugs me more than you do, which is saying something."

She's by far my favorite. The enemy of my enemy makes a great shield, and the thorniest flower in the garden is the perfect spot for a spider to hide.

CHAPTER 20
SIPPING ON REGRETS
LORI

Excited squeals and bitter sobs pull me from my slumber the next morning. I need a moment to gather my thoughts, the small of my back tingling as though a hand has just been resting there.

Elio's hand.

For some unfathomable reason, I feel him behind me, hovering between oblivion and consciousness with nothing but a silk sheet wrapped around his midriff, but as soon as I try to focus on the strange tether, it crumbles to dust like it was never there at all.

"By Eros, guys! The results are in," Poppy announces from the thin mattress next to me, scurrying to her feet. She must have sneaked back inside the tent during the night.

The pep in her voice makes me want to curl into a ball and never wake up, and I bury my face deep in the pillow.

Daisy snatches the end of my sleeping bag and slides it off the camp bed. "Get up, Lori. It's time to find out exactly how much damage you've done to this competition."

The cold breeze raises all my hairs to attention, and I sit up, rubbing the sleep off my face. "What now?"

Murmurs and glares follow me to the tent flap.

Outside, in the sunny, breezy winter morning, Paul has set up the hosts' booth between our tent and the Snowhaven Inn. Microphones amplify his relentless chatter, and my stomach twists up in knots at the prospect of hearing his commentary on the kiss I shared with Elio.

Gods. As long as he hasn't figured out what happened *after...*

"Here they are. The eight lucky women who best kissed our King will be collecting their invitation to the Yule brunch in a few seconds," Paul says, his clear-cut voice carrying on the wind.

Before my unexpected performance, they were supposed to tally the votes in real time, so I figure the public has already been informed of the winners and losers. Fancy envelopes are laid down on a table right outside the tent.

Paul shoots us a glance over his shoulder, his usual white tuxedo spruced up with a sequined white tie. His gray hair is a little messier than usual, a few strands flying in the stiff breeze. "The brides are now searching for their names on the invitations. For most of them, the journey is over, but I'm sure the stir caused by the kiss-that-ended-it-all made their night interesting."

Sara joins his side. "Our viewers were pretty clear on their favorites. Only two brides really came out on top from this stop in Snowhaven, Paul."

"No surprise there, Sara. The public is really leaning into the rivalry between their kin, Wendy Frost—the only Fae to sign up for this competition in years—and the woman that has been on every-one's lips since her first appearance, Lori Lovegood."

"Yes. Wendy and Lori are truly this year's darlings. Wintermere will be heartbroken if—Thanatos forbid—both of them don't make it to the final round, Paul. The challenge that comes directly after the Yule Brunch is always grueling, and neither the king nor our viewers will be able to influence the outcome."

I tiptoe closer to the envelopes and pick up the one with my name on it. A heavy weight settles in my stomach.

"Let's observe our eight finalists for a minute longer before we peek inside the inn where the royals are about to arrive. Freya Heart herself is attending, and unless you're living under a troll bridge, you know how rare that is."

Paul turns off his mic and chats quietly with Sara before they stroll over to the entrance of Snowhaven Inn together.

The camera above my head angles itself to catch my reaction, and I hold the envelope in front of my face to mask a cringe as it canvases the crowd, capturing footage from the elimination. A sigh escapes my lips as I pry open the envelope. The thick silver and white invitation card inside feels heavy in my hands. The meticulous calligraphy congratulates me on a job well done and marks me as one of the eight brides still in the running to become queen.

Rose's sad hiccups remind me that it was all too real for her, and a twinge of guilt squeezes my windpipe.

I'm part of the pageant's schemes now. A sanctioned spy.

A camera zooms in on her disappointment, and I can't resist the urge to glare at it.

Poppy pats her disgruntled friend on the back. "Come on, now. We did our best."

All the sex she had with Seth probably helped to ease her own sorrows at being eliminated.

Daisy, however, did receive an invitation and flips it back and forth in her hands as though she's looking for a secret code. "What do you think the next challenge will be?"

Wendy, two of her wintry friends, and three of the most dangerous-looking Reds are still in the running. Summer brides are out of the contest altogether.

Byron flies over to us. "Brides, please change into your provided uniforms and join me outside. Do not worry about shoes, make-up, or accessories. The next challenge calls for no artifice at all. And if you didn't receive an invitation, just wait. I'll be ready to take you home soon."

Sniffles and sobs mingle with nervous giggles and relieved

smiles. While some of the eliminated brides are sad to go home, others are not, and I double back inside the tent with Daisy on my heels. The cameras remain outside, giving us a moment to breathe.

While we were fetching the invitations, folded uniforms were laid out on the finalists' cots, and I unravel the silk bow on top of mine with a trembling hand.

Another white dress. Great.

Only...this one isn't fit for a wedding as it's barely thick enough not to be see-through. I shrug my robe off and slip the airy piece of silk over my head. Magic coats me from all sides as soon as the fabric glides down the length of my body, and the underwear and socks Sara lent me last night flake off into nothingness. My hair band vanishes, too, the accessory's sudden disappearance sending my long black hair cascading over my shoulder.

My socks, underwear, and missing hair tie reappear on the bed a moment later, folded and clean—along with my small silver key.

What the fuck?

My grandmother could do a week's worth of laundry in mere minutes, but this is something else.

"Your sponsors will bring your things along to our next pit stop, so you don't have to worry about losing them," Byron adds.

The white dress is as plain and simple as can be, but I feel completely protected from the cold. I slip on the matching long-sleeved jacket that completes the outfit, its hem finishing up at my waist, and peek at the other brides.

Daisy's make-up has been erased by the spell, her glossy straight hair now naturally wavy. The Winter brides' elaborate updos and braids were unraveled, too.

The Red brides gasp and reach for their brows, but the rules apparently apply to all. Without their jeweled scarves, sharp rings, and blood-red hoods, they don't look so intimidating. But the fiery tints of their auburn and red manes still set them apart.

With our hair down, bare feet, and no makeup to speak of, we look like a bunch of virginal princesses. My teeth grind as we form a single file and follow Byron to the first floor of the Snowhaven Inn where the brunch is taking place.

The large room has been decorated to fit the needs of a king—or several kings and queens, in this particular case. Silver and platinum abstract centerpieces garnish the long table, and gold cutlery shines under the light of the floating bronze chandeliers. White poinsettias, snowdrops, and Christmas roses hang in thick garlands above our heads, embalming the air with a honeyed and floral scent.

Sunshine streams through the bay windows and wraps the whole room in a golden glow, twinkles of white snow hugging the windowsills. The flying eyeballs send vibrations through the air, and my huntress senses allow me to pinpoint their location, but a magic cloak currently hides them from view.

My breath catches in my throat when I see Elio. The shape of his shoulders under his navy blazer takes me right back to the hall of mirrors. To his soft blond locks in my grip, and the greed in his ice-blue eyes.

To his hungry, almost vicious kiss owning every intimate part of me...

He sits at one end of the table with three place settings on each side of him. Only six monarchs are present out of seven, leaving one of the six guest seats vacant. Elio's father, Ethan Lightbringer, is apparently not attending.

I've never felt so much power in one place, and we're clearly not expected to join them. My skin tingles under their scrutiny, and I resist the urge to throw Damian a small wave. The Shadow King is sitting between Freya and Thera, the queens of Spring and Summer. Seth was banished to a small table in the back and away from his royal parents, his father Thorald Storm sitting across from Damian.

The Storm King has a jackal tattooed on his neck, his white beard and hair clashing with his stormy aura. A thundercloud sticks to his shoulder and blurs the shape of his body.

My throat shrinks, but I hold my head high. I thought we'd have a meal, too—not be paraded around like chattel up for auction.

Elio's chair creaks as he stands. "Welcome to the Yule brunch, cousins." He raises his champagne flute in the air. "I thank you for your generous bounty."

Elio is not related by blood to every monarch of Faerie, but *cousin* is a word often used by the Fae to address a peer of equal power and not blood relation.

His gaze skids over me, his deep, leveled voice sparking goose-bumps on my neck. I don't have to look down to know my nipples are showing through the damn dress, but the bastard doesn't spare me a full glance.

"Per tradition, the next challenge will be harsh, but the Frost Peaks have a way of weeding out the weak," Elio muses.

The royals raise their glasses in the air.

Elio sits back down, and the tensed way he grips the armrests of his chair is the only clue that he saw me at all. I wait for him to slip up and steal a glance at me, but he doesn't. Instead, he sparks up a conversation with the Red Queen sitting to his right. Nothing in his behavior hints at the secret we share, and my toes curl over sleek hardwood floors.

I'm number sixteen. Nothing more.

If I tricked myself into believing we'd shared a moment back in the hall of mirrors, and that a tiny, minuscule part of him actually didn't want me to leave, it's my own damn fault.

Whereas Elio treats me like I'm invisible, the Spring Queen, Freya, drills holes in my skull with her deep brown eyes. I bet she's wondering why I look so much like her niece. Normally, I'd feel sympathetic, but it's hard to feel anything but hatred toward the woman who condemned my brother to death.

Damian adjusts his napkin over his lap and utters a few words in her ear. Freya immediately stops staring and shakes her head, fanning herself dramatically.

The brides curtsy, and I imitate them. My court etiquette isn't quite as polished as theirs, and Damian conceals a smile with his gloved hand.

"Now, follow me," Sara commands, ready to escort us to the next challenge, no doubt.

Daisy leans closer, walking right behind me. "We have to talk."

"I need to pee, first," I lie.

The bathrooms are at the back of the inn, and I quickly make my way toward the ladies' room. As soon as I'm out of view from the brides, I wrap myself in shadows and wait.

As I expected, Damian had the same idea. He quickly joins me at the end of the corridor, and the shadows around us swell, cloaking us in a darkness so deep, I bet none of the other royals could see through it.

"We can't speak for long, or someone will notice that I'm gone," he says.

The Shadow King isn't wearing his mask, and it's weird to see him whole. But I have a bone to pick with him and point my index finger at his face. "Why didn't you tell me about my striking resemblance to Elio's first wife? You knew her, yes?"

A sad smile curls down his lips, and he looks a little more like the haunted man I used to know. "Yes."

My brows pull together, my trust in my sovereign and friend shaken. "So, from the first moment you saw me, you knew."

"I wouldn't have wished for you two to meet. Ever. Some scars are better left undisturbed." He scratches the back of his neck. "I did try to figure out how it was possible, but I never found any tangible lead."

"What really happened to her? Were you there the day she died?" I whisper, even though no one can hear us.

"I wasn't. By then I was already cursed and avoided social gatherings at all costs." He frowns, the straight line of his brow interrupted only by a faint scar. "I heard that one of the brides was killed back at the castle."

"Yes, she turned to solid ice."

His fists curl and uncurl at his sides. "Damn it, Lori. I'm not in charge here. I can't protect you."

"Don't fret. Your *buddy* Elio isn't that dangerous." I emphasize the word, the sting of his lie by omission still raw.

A heavy sigh whistles out of his lungs. "Don't say it like that. Elio and I haven't been *friends* in a long time. You need to be careful with him."

Seth barrels down the corridor, his purple gaze searching the space in front of him like he can't see us but is pretty certain that we're close. He walks right past us and peeks inside the men's room, and the women's. "Are you guys having a secret bathroom meeting without me?"

Damian brings him into the conversation, and Seth jolts in surprise. "Jeez. That's a strong cloak of shadow you got there, D. I must have walked right past you." He rubs down his chin to mask a cringe, clearly spooked. "The others have remarked on your absence."

"Are you sure you don't want to come home with me, Lori?" Damian offers.

I nod with unwavering confidence. "Tell Nell I'm doing great. I'm going to get answers."

Damian glowers at my sponsor, his fists balled at his sides. "If something happens to her, I'll hold you personally responsible." The Shadow King reluctantly spins on his heel, his eyes glued to Seth for a breath before he returns to the dining room, a patchwork of serpentine shadows hanging over his shoulders like a cape.

Seth arches a brow at Damian's retreating back. "Wow. He's grumpy today." He stretches gingerly, clearly relieved to be rid of the Shadow King as he looks me up and down. "Are you alright? You look a little pale."

"Do you know what the next challenge will be?" I ask quickly, pushing aside my fears and doubts in favor of more pressing matters.

"No, but it's supposed to be brutal."

My fingers curl around the flimsy edge of silk above my knee. "I'm ready."

When I get back to the tent, the flaps seal behind me, and the girls all turn in my direction.

"What?"

"We're all here, now. Read the card," a Winter bride barks.

Wendy picks up the white, embossed invitation in the middle of the table and reads it aloud. "If you want to participate in the next challenge, you've got to renew your commitment to the Winter Court. There's only eight of you, now. The winner of the pageant will marry the king and become queen. You might have come for fame, money, power, or immortality, but think long and hard about the consequences of your decision. If, and only if, you're ready to continue, gulp down the blue elixir. If you wish to leave, you'll be escorted back to the new world at once, never to return to Faerie."

That's a huge drawback. Most of the seeds here expect to work for the Spring Court if not chosen, the way I serve the Shadow King. Being exiled from Faerie forever is not an out many would choose, but I guess it's still an out.

A new card appears on the table, and Daisy snatches it before the Winter brides can react. She licks her lips, the white, rectangular piece of paper fluttering in her grip. "Beware the dangers of the mountains. And each other. The ones who make it to the battlements of the Ice City before dawn will accompany the king on the last part of his journey before our return to court. The others"—her brows pull together—"will be left behind."

"Left behind as in *go home,* or left behind to freeze to death?" A Red asks.

Daisy grunts. "That's the beauty of this competition, isn't it? The mystery."

The tiny blue vials contain about an ounce of liquid.

"What happens if we drink two? I'd happily keep that one out of the running," Wendy says, but the veil of magic keeping us from seeing the cameras thins at her suggestion, and a forced chuckle dribbles out of her mouth. "Just kidding, of course."

I offer her a wry grin and pick up one vial from the rack. "Cheers!" Tipping my head back, I swallow its contents without hesitation.

Almost as soon as the exaggerated "ha" leaves my lips, everything turns to shadows.

CHAPTER 21
FLICKERING AMBER
ELIO

U p on the cliffs, the sacred city of the reapers towers above us.

"The Ice City was carved right out of the ridge of the extinct Birthstone's caldera, the volcano that shaped the entire Fae continent. We can glimpse at its beauty from down here," I explain.

I've never allowed the other monarchs so close to the root of my power. The safety and peace of my reapers is more important than PR opportunities, but I need to wow them today. Rumors reached my ears during brunch that my attempts to conceal the unruly weather that plagues my lands haven't gone unnoticed.

I have to send my brethren home with a sense of awe if I am to erase the impression that my control over the glacier that runs underneath the snow is—for lack of a better word—melting.

"It's magnificent," Thera says. The Summer Queen's eyes water. In all my years as Winter King, I've never seen her show emotion, and the sight throws me for a loop.

The leaders and citizens of the other realms—and especially the light Fae—hate me because of what I stand for. Even immortals fear death. Sicknesses and old age can't claim them, but a rowan spear to the heart pretty much cancels any of them in the blink of an eye.

But not me, of course. For me, death will not come so easy.

The political game of "look how pretty my reaper city looks from afar" is getting old quick, and I can barely hide the jitters. The large meal I had back in Snowhaven sits heavy in my stomach. It's been years since I worked up such a genuine appetite, but I was simply famished.

Thera inches closer, the wrinkles at the corner of her eyes deepening. The Summer Queen's auburn hair is pulled tight away from her face and tucked in a bun behind her head. Round, rosy cheeks contribute to hide her true age, but she's paler than usual. Her ruby and amber crown rumbles with constant, barely-contained flames, but the fire burning inside the Summer crown is not as steady or powerful as it once was. "Would you give me a frost apple if I vowed that no one else would ever find out?" she whispers with an affable smile.

Her body language remains a picture of ease for the others' benefit, despite the unusual—and frankly troubling—request.

My Hawthorn only produces three to four apples each year, which makes them particularly rare, and while the use of those apples falls into my per-view, the official channels for other monarchs to procure one can be incredibly complicated and tedious, the wait list already spanning across decades.

They are only supposed to be requested by a reigning royal to grant immortality to their half-Fae, mortal children—or the rare mortal spouse. Some try to skirt the rules for a particularly beloved lover, but that's clearly not the case here. I consider Thera in a new light. The sickly tint of her skin, along with the words she used, hint at her secret.

A frost apple loses its properties when cooked or enchanted to look like anything else, so if she's promising that no one else would find out, it means she needs it for herself.

I give her a discreet incline of the head. Thera's been queen for centuries, and I won't insult her by prying into her health or asking why she doesn't want anyone to know she's sick.

"Thank you, Elio. I won't forget this." The emotion in her voice contrasts with her breezy, casual behavior as she moves to leave.

"Brr. I'm freezing," Freya whines.

My royal peers all thank me for my hospitality before stepping out through the travel mirror I had installed for this specific trip, but Damian hangs back.

I raise a brow at the Shadow King. I haven't seen him without his clawed black and white mask in decades. "You look better, my friend."

"I am. You know you can count on my support, right?"

I observe him for a moment and ponder the possibility of mentioning Lori's heritage. He could help me get rid of her by offering her a place in his court, where she belongs. But I can't bring myself to snitch on her. Shadow seeds often wash out during training.

Asking her to leave Wintermere is one thing. Alerting Damian to her existence so that he can possibly strip her of her magic...is another.

"Your support?" I say instead.

He arches his scarred brow. "Elio, you can trust me. I can still trust you, right?"

Just asking the question makes it clear that he doesn't. Damian is about the only ruler I trust not to move against me, but he's always speaking in riddles. Once, we were much closer, but he locked himself in a prison of secrets long before I became king.

"Of course. I'm glad to see you in good shape again," I say in lieu of goodbye, burying my hands in my jacket's pockets.

I'm not in the mood for games. My lieutenant Kiro is waiting for me to inspect the sleet storm that blocks the entrance to the Frost Peaks mines. I walk down the snowy hill to Sara who's overseeing the next challenge.

The unconscious brides are being carefully transported to the starting point of the mountain trek.

My friend tucks her short blond hair behind her ears at my approach, shifting her weight from one foot to the other. "Everything good with your guests?"

"Yes." I search the sleighs for one bride in particular, almost convinced I won't find her. "How many of them dropped out?"

"They all drank the potion," Sara squeaks.

My pulse flutters. "All?"

Her blue eyes dart to the ground between us. "Yes. Even Lori."

My fists curl. She promised she'd leave... Lori might have been a little desperate when she vowed to obey, but she still promised not to go through with the rest of the pageant. And I wasn't kidding when I told her Winter would make her life hell for ignoring my command.

Strange and powerful forces rule over the mountains. *She could die out there...*

I shake out the urge to scream and ball my fists at my sides. Lori broke her promise to me. She made her choice.

"Make sure she doesn't make it to the Ice City in time to win," I breathe.

Sara glances up from her clipboard. "But—"

"I don't want to hear it. Make sure she goes *home* this time. Before something worse happens."

Sara grumbles an almost unintelligible and completely insolent, "at your command, my liege" before crossing her arms over her chest. "Did you see how Freya stared at her? She clearly had never seen her before today, but she didn't ask to speak with her, either."

"If she'd asked, she would have had to admit publicly that she didn't know why a carbon-copy of her niece was walking around Faerie. She's probably waiting for Lori to be eliminated before she sends her cupids to drag her and Seth to the Secret Springs by the ears..." I shake my head, trying to quell the unpleasant twinge in my stomach at the thought of letting Freya interrogate Lori. It beats dying in the mountains, but not by much.

"Kiro's waiting. I have to go." I toss a tired glance at Seth and the other sponsors, silently pleading with Sara to keep an eye on them, too.

She nods and motions for me to go on with my day. "Don't worry. I won't let Seth out of my sight."

"At ease, servant," I say, retaliating for her earlier sarcasm with a wink. Her annoyed eye-roll coaxes a smile from me. "Oh, I almost forgot. Please arrange for Thera to get a fruit basket. Quietly."

Sara raises a pointed brow, fully aware of what I actually meant. "Alright."

I plaster my platinum mask over my face and walk through the mirror.

The Ice City is easily accessible through the sceawere to those who know the special runes marking its location and carry enough frost in their veins. Kiro is already waiting for me in the battlement's war room at the foot of the fortress, and I shrug off the brunch's flashy and overly chic apparel in favor of a lightweight and supple windbreaker. "Are you ready?" I ask.

"Yes, my king. I brought five newly anointed but capable soldiers along to back us up. They're all looking forward to catching a glimpse of Mistress, if we're lucky," he says.

A wide smile pierces my scowl. "She's been sleeping since summer. She's bound to wake up soon." Just the thought of seeing Mistress sends a jolt of excitement up my spine.

My boots crunch in the heavy snow as I lead the small squadron out of the Ice City battlements and up toward the coldest, wildest, and most beautiful mountains in the realm. The sceawere cannot reach such primeval places, so we breed wolves to pull us up on sleighs.

The hours-long ride up to the mines is the perfect outlet for all my pent-up frustrations, and the weather is perfect for it. Out west, the sun burns on the horizon, the short day almost over.

Kiro sticks close to my side as we reach the top of the extinct volcano's rim, the lights of the Ice City shining at our backs.

In spite of myself, I wonder how Sara will carry out my orders. The baring, incensed gaze Lori threw my way over the brunch table still heats my chest, and I pick up the pace.

The brides' challenge starts close to the volcano's caldera, so I could cross paths with her on my way back... I shake my head at the intrusive thought, trying to push all notion of Lori or the Yule pageant out of my mind.

The storm that curses the Frost Peaks mines with the most inclement weather in centuries needs to be dealt with. My expedition has nothing to do with Lori, I remind myself.

I'll never see her again, so I better concentrate on the task ahead, and the prospect of seeing Mistress again.

CHAPTER 22
MADE TO BE BROKEN
LORI

Phantasms push and pull at my soul until I float into another nugget of the past. I am right back at the Yule brunch, but this time, I'm sitting beside Elio as his future queen. The big fat diamond on my ring finger paints a clear picture.

Iris had attended the Yule brunch as Elio's fiancée—not some piece of meat to be paraded around—and my Lori consciousness hisses and snarls at the knowledge.

My manicured nails click along the body of a crystal flute as the guests stream in. Garlands of white roses and irises sag above our heads, braided and weaved, and the guests wear old-fashioned gowns. But otherwise, the Snowhaven Tavern looks about the same.

The Shadow King's full-face golden mask confirms my suspicions that this is a true vision, and not merely a half-assed fabrication of my overactive brain.

To my left, Elio leans in so close that I can count his eyelashes. "Ugh. My father sent my brother in his place."

I take a sip of wine, Iris's body completely unperturbed by the Winter King's closeness when I'm simply burning inside. "I thought you'd be thrilled not to see him," I say.

"I am. I'm just..." Elio shoots me a sideways glance. "Have you seen Ezra since the academy?"

I hold his ice-blue gaze. "No? Why?"

"Never mind."

While Iris and Elio look at each other for the longest time, my consciousness drifts. I study the ice-flecked shadows in his blue eyes, pretty sure I'll never get to examine them so closely in real life.

I finally shake my head and drop my cloth napkin over my untouched meal. "Excuse me."

The heavy mahogany chair doesn't make a sound as I slide it back. The lightweight fabric of my red dress moves along with me, earning me quite a few appraising glances from the males in the hall—staff and kings alike.

Their stares crawl along my naked back, and my Lori awareness stirs again. The way Iris walks draws more attention to her in this moment than I have in my whole life. My heart is beating faster than it has before, and the way Iris straightens her spine and stares at herself in the mirror of the bathroom clues me in that she is shaken.

She fixes up her face and hair with an expert hand, putting on a fresh coat of lipstick and eyeshadow.

A man with golden hair corners me on my way out of the ladies' room. Even though he does not exude the same energy at all, I can easily recognize Elio's brother. He is taller by an inch and broader in the shoulders, but equally handsome—if a tad dissolute. His tie is undone, hanging loosely between the lapels of his white dinner jacket, which features a sharply cut, double-breasted design. The jacket is paired with a matching waistcoat and high-waisted trousers, completing the classic evening ensemble. His long platinum locks are slicked back meticulously, adding to the refined yet disheveled appearance.

A halo of light hugs his tanned skin, the phenomenon slightly more pronounced over his head and shoulders, and the ethereal glow gives his whole body an edge of religious fantasy.

A huff whizzes out of my lungs as I try to walk around him, Iris's eyes purposefully not settling on his face like she wants to avoid his scrutiny at *all cost. But the angelic man braces his hand against the wall, blocking our escape.*

Iris's pulse swirls, leaving us both breathless.

Elio's brother reaches for my waist and leans into my ear. "You look ravishing, my flower." The greeting is warm and heavy with meaning, riddling me with goosebumps.

I sidestep away from him, almost violently, the body I'm currently inhabiting desperate not to brush this man's skin. "Careful."

The devil-may-care smirk vanishes from his features. "You're serious about this?"

I raise my ring finger in his face. "I'm wearing a ring, aren't I?"

An unkind chortle quakes the man's chest. "I wondered if it wasn't your way of punishing me for what I said the last time we saw each other."

"I haven't thought about you in years, Ezra." My hips sway as I walk away from him.

"Iris!" he hisses after me.

A big smile appears on my face, and my neck hurts from the effort not to glance back at him, but I strut off without acknowledging him further.

Elio is waiting for me at the end of the corridor and my chest expands, blood gathering at my ears.

"What did he want?" Elio glowers at his brother before catching my hands in his.

I lean into my fiancé and pick a piece of lint off his collar. "Oh, you know Ezra. He wants to be the center of attention, as always."

"Did something happen between you two back at the academy?" Elio whispers on our way back to our table.

My face creases into a million lines. "Happen like... romance? Me and Ezra? Never! Why would you ask that?"

"I don't know. He seemed only too happy to imply that he knew you... intimately."

I blink a few times, still holding my fiancé's gaze. "Well, I can't help that."

Elio clears his throat, and his eyes find mine again. The bend of his brows is a little more pronounced—perhaps betraying a hint of doubt. "Did you two ever have sex?"

"No! And I can't believe you would double-check my words like that, Elio Lightbringer. When I said no romance, I meant it. I wasn't merely playing on words," I scold him, the pressure in my chest nearly unbearable.

"You're right. I'm sorry," Elio says, leaning away from me and shaking his head. "Ezra and I haven't really talked. Not since..." He becomes engrossed in a notch of wood on the mahogany table. "You know."

A wild bite of power rolls off him, his skin suddenly a lot paler, and a hint of frost spreads to his neck.

"I'm so sorry about what happened, Elio."

"I know you are." He wraps my hand in his. "Iris, I'm not a fool. This is a marriage of convenience for you, but my feelings haven't changed since school. Do you think you could grow to love me in time?"

I cup his cheek, the tension between my ribs easing. "Without a doubt."

He offers me a small, secret smile. "Never mind Ezra—or my father. They can't hurt us, now." He grips my hand, eyes full of devotion and love. "You and I, we'll be happy. I promise."

I stand on my tiptoes to kiss him, and as our lips brush, the scene melts into darkness.

CHAPTER 23
SOMETHING THAT BITES IN THE DARK

LORI

The kiss catapults me back to the present and into my rightful body, just as it did the last time. I'm already growing accustomed to the sluggish ache in my bones that accompanies my forays into Iris's past and feel more certain than ever that it's real.

I'm not only identical to Iris, but also forced to relive specific events of her life.

A big question mark sticks to my face. Iris is Fae, so she couldn't have lied to Elio, and yet, nothing about the way his brother interacted with her—or her with him—sets me at ease.

I gasp out and try to press a hand over my frazzled heart, but I'm... stuck.

The chafe of rope digging in my skin pulls me out of my musings about the vivid scenario I've just witnessed. My wrists are tied behind my back—a terrible feeling I'm all too familiar with.

Daisy's voice comes into focus. "Be cool. I'm not with her. She took my sister's place. I hate the girl. Let me come with you." The thick fear breaking her usual snark sends a wave of adrenaline through me.

"Nope," Wendy answers.

I blink. The striking freckles from one of the Reds are inches from my face, but the woman lets go of me with a start. "Wendy. She's conscious."

"Good thing we didn't dawdle," Wendy says with a satisfied nod. "Here. The weeds will be gone for good."

I force my eyes to remain half closed and keep my posture groggy, taking stock of the situation. Two long imprints in the snow and the footsteps surrounding it tell a straightforward story. Daisy and I have been dragged from the center of the clearing to the trees and tied there with a few scraps of rope.

One single row of maple trees creates a perfect circle around a tall podium with a glass cloche. Beyond them, thick evergreen trees flourish. Pines, spruces, firs, and junipers create a canopy of needles and scale-like leaves. Both of my wrists are pressed flush against the rough bark of the pine tree at my back, but Daisy has still got one hand free, her restraints loose and tied hurriedly like she put up a fight. "Take me with you. I'm not a threat," she pleads.

Wendy looks down her nose at the Spring seed. "I don't want any flowers—except for the torn-off rose petals that'll pave the way at my wedding."

Sarafina mentioned *Survivor*, but this is more like *Naked and Afraid*. True, the cold doesn't affect us, but we're still a bunch of girls in the middle of a moonlit forest, barefoot and without food. It's every woman for herself, and Wendy and her two Winter friends apparently teamed up with the Reds to take me out.

I fake a nonchalant yawn. "You shouldn't count on it, Frost." I offer her my best asinine smile and look at every single one of the Reds in turn. "Do you really think your deadly little pals won't turn on you? If I were them, I'd get rid of you as soon as possible."

"They can't find their way in a snowstorm without me," Wendy replies.

"What about when the Ice City becomes visible in the distance? Will you still trust them then?" I taunt her.

She inches closer to ram a snowball in my eyes and mouth, and I take advantage of her mistake to trip her up. Just as I'm about to kick her shin and hopefully snap her leg into two separate parts, her allies drag her out of the fray by the shoulders.

"You little snake! You're dead now," Wendy says before she spits on my bare legs.

"Don't push me, Frost. I'm tied to a tree in a flimsy cotton white dress—and growing increasingly pissed."

"What are you going to do? Throw roses at me?"

The brides chuckle between themselves as they leave, confident that two Spring seeds couldn't possibly get out of this without help, and my eyes narrow. No more Miss Nice-Flower. They're going to feel the wrath of a Shadow huntress before the day is over.

The cameras follow the other brides but for one, clearly not expecting much action from us.

Daisy tugs at her restraints like a wild stallion. "Enjoyed your nap? If you had deigned to wake up at the same time as everyone else, we wouldn't be stuck here!"

I keep my cool and observe our surroundings. "Settle down and keep your energy. You're going to need it."

"We're not going anywhere anytime soon, Sixteen."

The trees' branches are heavy with snow. Silvery patterns glimmer over the white powdery blanket covering the clearing, and the forest is quiet. Calm. A cold immensity that slows down the very beats of my heart and allows me to hold the panic at bay.

A rustling sound from the juniper closest to me sparks a fresh trail of goosebumps along my neck, and Daisy draws a sharp intake of breath. "What was *that*?"

"Shush." I canvas the area for signs of life.

The foliage moves. The overlapping scales of the juniper are arranged in whorls along the branches, giving the tree a dense, feathery appearance, and I spot a white animal hiding inside.

Tiny black eyes meet mine, but it's the shape of the weasel's mouth that really gets my blood going. Instead of a run-of-the-mill carnivorous snow weasel, the creature has a long, tubular mouth that extends in my direction. A circle of tiny teeth shaped like a leech's sucker adorn the extremity.

It emits a small, high-pitched noise, and a chorus of answering calls echoes through the vegetation.

"Tell me what's going on," Daisy says on a rushed breath.

Never looking away from the creature, I point at the eyeball camera. "When I say *go*, you'll throw a snowball directly into that eye."

She frowns at my demand. "Why?"

"Would you rather find out what these weasels intend to do to us with their mouths? Because I'm sure neither of us would enjoy sharing a smooch."

Arms shaking, Daisy fashions a snowball with her free hand.

"Go!"

Right as her projectile hits the lens, I summon a shadow dagger to cut off my bindings and free my hands, immediately letting it fade again, just like I did during the kissing contest when I cut the scarf shackling Elio.

The memory brings acid to my mouth as I untangle myself from the leather straps and stand. I'm still unsure what possessed me to do such a thing, but if I'm honest, I can't bring myself to regret it.

The eyeball camera blinks a few times to clear its lens before it settles down again, hovering a little closer to us. Half a dozen weasels scurry along the lower branches and exchange a few warning cries before turning their eyes to Daisy, slowly creeping closer and closer to her.

I raise a brow at my tied-up comrade. "Can I trust you?"

"No, but I won't stab you in the back with an icicle. That I can promise." Her throat bobs, her wide eyes scanning the clearing like she can't quite believe what just happened. "Those bitches left us here to die. I want to beat them, and I'm not stupid enough to think I can find my way through this forest without you."

Daisy stands barefoot, ankle-deep in the snow, her feet and legs reddened by the cold. I've never seen her look so small. The silk dress meant to protect her from the cold has a small, uneven tear at the hem. It's clear that it wasn't deliberately made by one of the girls. Without the magical garment's protection, she'll freeze to death before we even have a chance to find our way to the Ice City.

"How bad is it? Can you fix it?" I ask.

Over the last few days, I've watched the Spring seeds fix small imperfections in their dresses, hair, and makeup. "Yes, it's something we can all do, and you would know that if you were truly a Spring seed. But I'll need both hands."

I untie her bindings, and her keen blue eyes never leave mine as she measures my reaction. The camera emits a series of electronic sounds and glides closer, probably desperate to pick up our quiet conversation.

"I knew *I* could fix it. I just wasn't sure *you* could," I add with a wry smile.

Daisy covers the tear in her dress with both hands and mends it with her magic. Her long blonde hair drapes over her shoulder as she squints at me. "Nice recovery, Sixteen, but I don't believe you. No offense, but a Spring seed would never"—she gestures to me up and down with her palm face up—"endure *this*."

I roll my eyes, her fishing expedition into my true identity falling flat. She wants to goad me into revealing more than I have to, and I won't give her the satisfaction.

The weasels move like eels through the snow, creeping closer and closer to us. We hurry to the podium in the center of the meadow, away from our white-furred visitors and peer through the glass cloche. A red and green apple, a mirror, and a crown of thorns are tucked inside.

"What's all this for? The other girls were whispering about it before you woke up." Daisy curls her hand over the round knob located at the top of the cloche.

I rush to stop her, covering the entire dome with my hand and preventing her from lifting it. "Don't!"

She eyes me sideways. "Why?"

"I've read about this. In a fairytale."

A forced chuckle quakes her breath. "A *nice* fairytale, I hope?"

"There's no such thing," I mumble, slowly peeling my palm away from the glass.

Daisy uncurls her hand from the knob, but the rim of the cloche glides along the marble base of the podium and bumps against the apple. Long shadows stretch from the barren maple trees, their trunks and branches casting tall, gnarled silhouettes toward the center of the clearing.

The weasels pause as a strong breeze beats my hair forward.

"Run."

"Did you hear that?" I ask Daisy.

"Hear what?"

One weasel stands on its hind legs, its nose twitching with a series of rapid sniffs before it jumps back into the juniper hedge with a loud squeak. The other critters quickly retreat into the protection of the forest.

I turn around just in time to see a naked, gangly ice giant, twice our size, ambling toward us. His long arms swing at his sides, nearly brushing the ground, and sharp claws extend from his hands.

The moon shines brightly behind him, and the shape of his heart is visible through his quasi-translucent body. The crooked organ displays the smooth, white face of a sad, tortured man.

CHAPTER 24
APPLES, MIRRORS, AND CROWNS
LORI

The eyes of the face-shaped heart bore into me, and my skin tingles all over. His mouth is curled downward, his brows drawn into a painful frown, while high cheekbones and an elegant jawline glare at me through the ice.

Tears blur my vision and freeze as soon as they touch my cheeks. I angle my jaw to the side, unable to endure the direct gaze of the giant's heart.

The creature's spiky white hair and pointy nose look sharp enough to spear through flesh, and his bite of power ripples across my skin. This creature is ancient. It was born long before any of the royal Fae we met this morning, and will live long after they're gone.

Whatever it is...is permanent.

"I am Chenu." The raspy tenor voice comes out rough and dry, like stone grounding on stone, and gives the impression it hasn't been used in decades. "What would you offer me in exchange for your soul? An apple, a mirror, or a crown?"

I close my eyes for an instant. My mother's voice echoes in my ears, and my mind drifts back to the yellow-painted walls of my childhood home. My fingertips tingle at the vivid memory of the textured illustrations glazing the pages of her old book full of bedtime stories.

"You were a man, once. A powerful oracle," I blurt out, remembering the pretty patterns of my frosted bedroom window. "But you ate your brother to survive out in the cold."

The Chenu gives a small incline of the head. "Men eat men in the cold embrace of hatred, ambition, or desperation. I was not the first nor the last."

I run through the items lying under the glass cloche.

A mirror would reveal how far he's fallen, how little of the man he once was remains. But it also serves as a doorway to other worlds —a means of escape. It's too small to squeeze through, but it might represent freedom. I'm fairly certain that the crown of thorns wouldn't fit over Chenu's disheveled hair, but circles symbolize the cyclicality of life: birth, death, and rebirth. The apple, a symbol of knowledge, immortality, and temptation, also represents love, beauty, and wisdom.

It's also entirely possible that the riddle forgoes another secret option I'm unaware of.

Chenu's vibrant eyes fall to my side, his hardened irises sparkling in the night. "You've been a hair away from death."

The spider bite throbs under his scrutiny. "I have."

"What would you offer me in exchange for your soul? An apple, a mirror, or a crown?" he repeats patiently, a dreamy smile stretching his cracked blue lips.

I could try to kill him, but not without revealing my identity or risking a fight I might not win. Violence should be my last resort here.

"If we answer correctly, you will let us pass?" Daisy asks.

Chenu raises a long claw toward Daisy. "Why should I *let you* do anything? You do not truly crave the price at stake and you..." He extends and flexes his hand in my direction. "The immortality you seek will not satisfy your hunger. A mortal man and a tree grow until they get old. An immortal festers in his own hubris, unaware of the one thing no one should take for granted."

I arch a brow. "And what exactly is that? Life?"

If I make him talk, he might drop hints at the solution to his riddle.

He shakes his head, chunks of ice detaching from his hair and falling to the ground. "All life starts and ends at the whims of the spindle of the gods. Thousands of creatures are born and die every day, without fail. In itself, life is not righteous nor worth protecting, and death is not the enemy, but a certainty. I live, and yet I suck souls out of imprudent girls and murderers alike. Why shouldn't I eat you, too?"

A full-blown shiver rattles me to my core. Blood-sucking weasels were bad enough. I do not want my soul to be munched on and swallowed by this damned ice creature.

"What would you offer me in exchange for your soul? An apple, a mirror, or a crown?"

His voice is sharper, and I know he won't ask again.

I live, and yet I suck souls out of imprudent girls and murderers alike...

I reach inside the glass dome and pick up the apple, quickly tossing it at Chenu. "An apple. So that you would know right from wrong."

The ice giant bites down on the plum red flesh of the fruit and transforms into a man in front of our eyes. He's perfectly naked and beautiful, his jaw matching the shape of the previously frowning heart. "I see you now. You are the one who comes as two. You will make a fine queen."

His piercing gaze causes my teeth to chatter and my arms to shake as he raises two fingers to the trail. "You should hurry along if you want to save the midnight sun."

I follow his gaze, a ball-shaped cloud visible in the distance. "Midnight Sun? You mean Elio?"

Daisy hooks her elbow in mine and tugs me along the path. "The scary monster-man told us to go, Sixteen. Let's go!"

The strength of the pull almost knocks me off balance, and I follow her lead, my extremities still numb from the pressure of Chenu's gaze and the sizzle of his enigmatic smile. *It's like he could see my entire future...*

Daisy gives him a wide berth, and her chest heaves as he lets us walk past him. "Come on! Let's catch up with the others before we lose their trail or another creepy fairytale creature comes for us."

I crane my neck around to catch one last glimpse of him, but Chenu is gone, vanished into a cloud of snowflakes.

THE HUGE, SILVERY MOON AND AN ABUNDANCE OF STARS ILLUMINATE THE snowy forest, and the absence of clouds makes it easy to follow Wendy's trail. The Winter Fae is best equipped to find her way in this white immensity, and her mortal friends follow her lead. Six pairs of footsteps are visible in the fresh snow as Daisy and I walk carefully behind them and slow down whenever I catch their voices on the wind.

Luckily, I've got a better ear than all of them, and the mountain breeze hits us square in the face, keeping our hushed conversations from carrying forward.

Walking in fresh snow is tiring to say the least, but the dresses keep us warm, and the lonely eyeball camera doesn't fly higher than our heads as though it understands our need for stealth.

After about an hour, the trail in front of us switches from the clear footsteps in the snow to a well-traveled trail flanked by a steep rocky cliff. The imprints of sleigh runners, foot traffic, and paws make the terrain easier to navigate, but Wendy and her team are nowhere to be found.

Daisy braces her hands on her thighs, sweaty and breathless, and I motion for her to stay quiet. "Those prints are too big for sleigh dogs."

She bends down to touch the closest set of animal prints. "That's an understatement."

We continue forward and reach a crossroads. The path to our right ascends the mountain, while the path to our left heads downhill, revealing a gap in the rocks that offers an unobstructed view of the valley below. The spectacular oval shape of the crater makes it clear that this entire mountain range was once an active volcano.

"We were walking along the rim of a huge caldera," I say.

A narrow path heads down to the crater's center, at least four or five miles down.

Far off in the distance, the lights of the Ice City flicker in the night. The fortress of death emits a warm orange glow, its walls snuggled up to the crater's steep cliffs.

Screams and shouts echo in from the narrow path leading down to the Ice City, and the shrill edge of the voices quickens my pulse as I peer over the ledge.

About half a mile down the winding path, three sleds pulled by enormous black-and-blue wolves have stopped to greet our fellow competitors. Humanoid figures stand on the footboards behind each sleigh, and I gawk as one of the horned silhouettes steps toward Wendy. The monster slams a long stick that shines with a yellow glow into her chest, and the Winter Fae falls prone to the ground, the motion knocking her out in an instant. Her two friends quickly suffer the same fate.

The Reds crouch with their hands extended forward to retaliate against their attackers, but they're unarmed and outnumbered four to one. They manage to escape the first couple of blows coming at them, but even with their impressive hand-to-hand combat skills, the creatures make quick work of them.

A long set of white horns spirals upward from the monsters' foreheads, making them about seven feet tall in total, but their leather boots and knee patches look as mundane as they come.

"What are these monsters?" Daisy gasps.

"Not monsters. People," I correct her, slowly coming to terms with the truth myself. The men's helmets are mounted with intimidating horns, but it's a uniform. Human hands tie up the girls' wrists and pack them in the front of their sleighs like luggage.

A bit of color returns to Daisy's cheeks as we both retreat from the ledge and back onto the trail. "Are we supposed to walk around them? What kind of challenge is this? Even the Reds were powerless against them."

"I don't think they're part of the challenge." The bite of power rolling off of them is odd, and what would be the point?

"I'm no good at throwing roses, Sixteen. So unless you want me to seduce them into letting us pass—"

"Look there. Another camera," a man shouts over the wind, pointing to the eyeball hovering above our heads. His voice is powerful and slightly accented, close to a Celtic accent, but I can't place the exact provenance.

The sleighs glide swiftly toward us, and I press Daisy against the rock cliff behind us. Her mouth hangs open in a silent gasp as I cloak us both in shadows. The ice wolves race past, their drivers clad in thick leather gear and gray scarves.

One of them shoots an arrow at the camera, and it falls to the ground in front of our feet with a *tok*.

"I'll get the Spring seeds and meet you back at the mine," the archer says, then separates from the group, heading toward the challenge's starting point.

The others quickly steer their beasts up the mountain. Up close, the massive wolves stir a deep unease in the pit of my stomach.

Daisy's eyes widen, her ire melting in favor of muted fear. "You're a *spider*?" she whispers like the word is blasphemy.

"Yep." It's useless to deny it now, and I summon my shadow blades to life. "We should follow them."

"Why? The Ice City is all the way down there."

I squint at the nefarious storm sticking to the top of the tallest peak. Something's not right, and my blood races. "Elio's up there."

Daisy braces her hands on her hips. "And how would you know that?"

Blood floods my cheeks, but my voice cracks with fear as I say, "I can feel him."

CHAPTER 25

IMMIGRANT SONG

ELIO

O ur ascent is quick and easy until the main trail ventures into dragon territory. Dragons and wolves don't mix, and their presence is likely to spook Mistress, so we leave one man with the sleighs and continue on foot. The animals were overdue for a well-deserved rest anyway.

The ice storms that drove the miners away and blocked access to the mines have scattered murky clouds over the top of Bluenest Ridge—and only Bluenest Ridge.

"It's been here for weeks, and it hasn't moved or dissipated in days, not since we sent the first platoon to investigate," Kiro says.

"You were right. It's not a natural storm." This isn't an outbreak of dragon pox or a conflict between mountain gnolls. "Whoever summoned this storm here did so at great personal cost."

The closer we get, the air thickens with humidity, and the sudden rise in temperature sends a shiver of warning up my spine. Altitude isn't supposed to be associated with warmer weather.

We finally reach the edge of the phenomenon, and I raise a hand to the clear-cut blizzard. Everything beyond the veil of sleet is heavily obscured.

I kneel down to touch the snow, extending my powers to the rock bed below it and the sacred glacier underneath. The answering shiver quakes my entire body as I draw a series of runes over the ice with my powers, trying to discern the source of the magic. "By my estimation, the storm is no more than two miles wide, and though it's been made to look harmless and natural from a distance, the core of it is perfectly circular, radiating outward from the entrance of the mine." I give my soldiers a serious nod. "Spread out and keep a cool head."

The reapers stand a little taller, and we all summon our ice blades to life. I canvas the cliffs for snipers or sentries but find nothing out of the ordinary.

Magic crackles in the air as I lead the way into the sphere of clouds and ice. The inclement weather immediately in front and behind me melts into a thin mist. A soundless alarm sends vibrations through the ether, stretching like a spiderweb before breaking as I advance.

"Whoever crafted this storm made sure to be notified if someone prodded at it." I quicken my pace and exchange a knowing glance with my lieutenant. "They know we're here."

The sleet stops abruptly half a mile in, leaving the center untouched and merely cloudy. The snow beneath my feet becomes denser due to the warmer temperature, and the sound of our footsteps shifts from a soft *swish* to a steady *crunch*.

I remove my hood and squint at a rock cliff in the distance.

Spiders crawl around the outskirts of the ice bridge that crosses the chasm to the mine. The imprints of their claws in the snow are not as pronounced as they would be if the monsters were entirely made of flesh, and their bodies glimmer with a nefarious twinkle of magic. They're nightmares, and fancy ones at that.

With Morheim behind us, the only explanation for this invasion is that Morrigan, the phantom queen, has taken refuge on my lands. But that particular spider, however formidable she is, couldn't have summoned this winter storm to keep herself hidden. She's not alone.

My mind flashes to Lori, and icicles prickle my heart. *I should have known that a Shadow seed couldn't have wandered into my lap by accident.*

Ice spreads forward beneath my feet as I survey the damage.

Under the breach in the rocks that marks the mine's entrance, Mistress—the most gentle and beautiful ice dragon to ever guard the Frost Peaks—is sleeping. Yet her usually pristine white mane is marred with bloody streaks, and her massive body—three times the size of a Percheron horse—is pinned to the rock bed with ice picks and wide metallic nets.

A cluster of her scales have been cut off and harvested, leaving sores the size of my hands in her sides. Fury pulses through my veins. Who would dare capture and harm such a sacred creature, especially on my lands? Magic roars in my blood, demanding revenge.

How did I not notice that my kingdom had been invaded? They must have been running this operation for months—right under my nose.

Over the hill to my right, a tall, masculine silhouette catches my attention, and my pulse quickens. My enemy wears a gray mask and matching winter gear that looks straight out of a fairytale, with a ghostly, otherworldly cut and a design that eschews zippers and modern features. The edges of the fabric wisp as if tailored from a piece of cloud, and the lower half of his face is covered by a triangular metal plate reminiscent of a muzzle. This contraption conceals his mouth and part of his nose perfectly, while a long cape billows behind him.

The storm subsides, the mist sucked up and swallowed into his gravity, imbuing him with power. It would take an enormous amount of magic for any Fae to craft a storm of this magnitude—let alone keep it going for *weeks.*

Whoever he is, he's not your run-of-the-mill pretender.

I squint at the ice wolves standing on each side of him. A thread of shadows burns inside them, and a foreboding sense of doom settles in my chest. The melting snow, the uneven storms, and now this disgusting violation of the most sacred creature in Wintermere... I can't pretend it isn't real. The Tidecallers have returned.

"What should we do, Your Majesty?" Kiro asks.

I tighten my hold on the hilt of my ice sword. "Kill the soldiers and nightmares, but leave their leader to me."

My reapers lunge into the fray. Spiders, wolves, and their handlers defend the entrance to the mine. Their striking helmets are adorned with two curved horns harvested from Bloodcrest or Razorback Maulers—carnivorous whales that populate our seas. These beasts are as dangerous and deadly as the Dark Sea sirens, and they're incredibly hard to kill. The look is straight out of the history books I've read on the Islantide, confirming my suspicions.

The Tidecallers—Fae vikings of the sea and sky, bent on bringing destruction and chaos to our world—have used my lands and the power of my glacier as a stepping stone to harvest and forge stolen magic into weapons of war.

My arms shake at the thought.

The men wield two double-bit axes with short handles and heavily curved blades. They're about as tall as I am but built like polar bears. I strike the ground at my feet, causing the snow to ice over beneath the soles of their boots and forcing them to slow down.

The soldiers grunt in response and slam their cleats into the ice to stay upright.

Four sleighs glide across the bridge leading out of the mine, heading toward the far side of the mountain. Burlap sacks and a trove of precious metal and dragon scales are loaded inside them. Kiro throws his axe at the back of one of the escapees and runs toward the sleigh. The driver drops to the ground, but the wolves don't stop running. If I'm reading this correctly, the beasts are not controlled by the drivers but by the will of the man in front of me.

Leaving my reapers to fight the underlings, I return my attention to the phantom standing on top of the hill and squint, trying to see past the unusual attire to the man underneath.

"Who are you?" I shout.

The hooded figure gives me a lazy shrug in response, not uttering a word as he marches forward. I know every powerful Fae on the continent, so this man must be from the Islantide, the infamous island off the coast of Storm's End. Tidecallers haven't crossed the Breach in centuries—well before I was born.

Thunder crashes down the mountain as our swords collide. His long, one-handed blade shimmers with a hint of purple fire, and lightning bolts zigzag along the hilt as we parry and strike in turn. His blows carry serious power and blunt force, yet his attacks betray an undercurrent of impatience. He acts as though any outcome other than a swift, decisive victory is beneath him. While his skills are impressive, my approach to combat is more nuanced.

In the face of a worthy opponent, caution is always the best approach—a lesson the warrior in front of me clearly never learned. His lack of restraint prompts me to circle around him, buying time and delaying the inevitable.

He tilts his head to the side before lunging forward, and the tell allows me to sidestep and drive my elbow into his back. The blow sends him face-first into the snow, but he rolls out of reach of my sword with impressive speed.

A pack of wolves roars in my direction. The beasts encircle me, baring their long, icy teeth, their massive paws digging into the snow. Dark energy swirls within them, as if each wolf is a storm of ice and lightning bottled within a living, breathing carnivore.

One of the large beasts lunges at me with reckless abandon. I drive my blade into its belly, and it disintegrates into dark flakes of magic. The remnants of the beastly construct zoom toward my opponent, the bite of his magic intensifying upon contact.

Killing them won't help. To the contrary, each vanishing beast only makes their master stronger. My enemy takes advantage of the wolf's attack to rise to his feet again. He advances upon me with an iron grip on his sharp, forsaken blade.

His next attack is so quick, the blade nicks my side, and I reel at the red splash tainting my windbreaker. The sting of pain barely registers as warm blood runs down the fabric and pools at my hip. I haven't bled since I became king.

Cuts and scrapes only draw frost and ice from my veins. I can't be killed by ice, fire, shadows, light, blood, lust, or lightning, but maybe I can be struck down by this volatile blend of magic.

A part of me is in awe that this man might actually be able to kill me, but I will fight back with every ounce of humanity I have left.

For all these years, I prayed for a swift release, a way to escape my pain. But now, faced with the possibility of death... I've had it all wrong. I may have allowed myself to become numb to the core, but I crave more than this cold, lonely fate.

It's unfortunate that it took a fight to the death for me to realize just how much I want to live.

CHAPTER 26
MIDNIGHT SUN
LORI

Daisy and I are halfway up the mountain when the snowstorm is blown away by a warm, unnatural wind. The sudden change reveals a dark figure standing on top of the hill, and I rush along the steep path to see better. A dark gray hood and cape cover the tall, imposing man.

While the magic rushing off the Chenu tasted of permanence, this new phantom reeks of passion and revenge. His cape flies in the breeze, but his laser-like focus is entirely directed to the area concealed by the large rock cleft in the mountain. His energy drums through the air in wild, uneven waves.

The mask that covers his face is bigger and thicker than the ones I'm used to. The sharp angles of the geodesic shape are reminiscent of a stone that has been beaten into submission, and a thick metal muzzle covers the man's mouth and the tip of his nose. Vertical holes crack the terrible accessory right over the space where the man's lips should be, but if it wasn't for his black leather gloves and boots, I wouldn't believe he was human at all.

Black and white clouds roll above our heads and bring all my hairs up to attention. I hurry closer, the dramatic opening in the rock cliffs no doubt leading to the precious Frost Peak mines I've read so much about.

In front of the powerful stranger stands Elio. The Winter King digs the balls of his feet in the snow and raises his two-handed sword. Blood taints his coat, and my heart hammers.

Behind him, the fight between the reapers and the horned soldiers is in full swing. A dozen spiders are scattered among them, and I freeze. Acid rises in my mouth as I blink a few times, lost in a haze. My lips are cold, and I can't focus on anything other than the sharp pain in my side—not the metallic net holding a huge white dragon pinned to the ground, or the sleighs streaming out of the mines.

One of them must contain the brides they kidnapped earlier, but my eyes are glued to Elio and his opponent.

The wind churns into a tempest, blurring the edges of the Gray Man. A thunderous echo shakes the mountains as their blades clash.

Enormous wolves circle the pair. The clouds swirl in a cyclone above them, and the center of this swirling vortex dips downward to pat the Gray Man on the back. He marches forward, his footsteps sending ripples across the snowy hill as if it were made of liquid instead of ice.

An intense burst of light blinds me momentarily, revealing Elio now enveloped in radiant sunshine. The wolves howl and flee in a panic, their peculiar forms disintegrating into nothingness as golden sunbeams pierce their hides, melting them from the inside out.

I hold my breath, but the Gray Man isn't bothered in the least. The ashes of the wolves zoom toward him, and he absorbs their power. With his weapon drawn, the Gray Man blazes forward, ready to strike down the Winter King.

The sunlight tapers off as Elio veers off the path of the blade. The tip of the sword slashes the side of his chest, his opponent poised to strike again.

Two bright orbs are imprinted deep in my retinas, but there's no time to waste. Shadows keep me hidden from view and muffle the crunches of my footsteps in the snow as I flank the Gray Man.

The thunder above us drowns out the rest of my sounds, and I build enough momentum to slide feet-first toward him, the icy terrain diminishing the friction and facilitating my otherwise difficult approach. The dauntless move allows me to sink one shadow dagger into his side.

Hot blood streams over my palm, slick and red. My prey roars as I dart out of reach, my weapon dissolving into embers of shadow magic. The Gray Man's multifaceted sword arcs through the air before cleaving into the snow precisely where I had just stood.

The mountain begins to shake, knocking us off balance as the rock bed beneath our feet cracks. A massive earthquake splits the ground, creating a chasm that separates me from the two men. The terrain around us is torn into three distinct sections, like slices of a pie. The rest of the plain is in ruins, with only a narrow bridge remaining to connect the trail down the mountain to the mine.

Elio and the Gray Man grip their respective injuries, panting hard.

The Gray Man lets his sword vanish into thin air, and he glares at me from behind his mask before gazing down at the wide crack separating us. The deep abyss is three times as wide as the fissure keeping me from Elio, but I have no doubt he could cross it if he wanted.

He removes one of his old-fashioned black leather gloves, revealing a series of runes and glittering stones embedded in his knuckles. His shoulders twitch as he quietly laughs, rubbing his bare hand over his wound and coating it with his own blood.

The red liquid drizzles down his arm as he extends his hand toward the sky, summoning the clouds above. A long white column descends from the heavens, enveloping him completely before dissipating and leaving nothing behind.

I leap over the narrow crack separating me from Elio. The Winter King is kneeling in the snow, his back hunched. Dark burgundy blood stains the ground at his feet.

"Are you okay?" I ask.

"I should have known you'd be involved in this," he grunts back.

"I just saved your life. A heartfelt *thank you* is in order." I grab his elbow to help him up.

He rises to his feet, but the tip of an ice shiv presses into the hollow of my neck. "And you just happened to be at the right place at the right time? It's too convenient. Give me one reason not to kill you."

Elio's platinum mask prevents me from seeing his eyes, and I shake from head to toe. "I'm not with him. I'm with you," I breathe.

"Or you've been lying through your teeth all this time."

"You have pretty fucked up trust issues, you know? I've told you a million times. I'm not here to kill you or help anyone steal your crown. If you still don't trust me after what I just did, then by all means—" I press my neck further into his blade, ignoring the sting of pain.

He lets the ice shiv fall to the ground, harsh breaths rushing from his lungs as he curls a hand around the back of my head. His lips brush against mine, and a pained, half-mad chuckle bubbles from his throat. "Thank you."

Elio kisses me hard under the endless blue sky, the frosty taste of his blood sweet on my tongue.

CHAPTER 27
AVALANCHE
LORI

The remaining enemy soldiers scatter. The horned warriors jump on the back of their sleighs and steer their wolves forward right along the ice bridge, heading toward Daisy. I move to chase after them, but Elio wraps a hand around my upper arm and points to the peak.

Three white flumes of snow are visible far in the distance, near the top of the mountain. The deafening thunder signals the start of an avalanche. The leather-clad sleigh drivers speed down the bridge leading off the snowy mountain and disappear between the trees.

"Nothing can stop an avalanche of this magnitude once it's started. Not even me. We have to take refuge in the mine," Elio says.

"If it wasn't for the stupid barefoot-in-the-snow challenge, all the girls would be safe. This is on you." I shake him off and turn to face the sleigh's escape path, searching for Daisy, but she's no longer there. *Fuck!* The soldiers must have passed her by and captured her. "We have to stop them and save Daisy!"

The mountain continues to tremor beneath our feet as Elio marches over to the captive white dragon. "That bridge will shatter before you can cross it."

The unstable ice bridge veers toward the trail Daisy and I had hiked earlier, leading away from the mine. Beyond it, deep imprints from the sleigh runners weave between the trees, marking the soldiers' escape route. I head toward the forest.

"Winter is going to swallow you whole!" Elio shouts.

"I can't just let her die!" I answer without looking back.

My legs burn as I run. The ice bridge hugs the side of a steep cliff, but before I can reach solid ground, deep cracks spread around me, and the ice creaks as it breaks apart.

The bridge crumbles beneath me. I bend my knees and dig the balls of my feet into the snow, but there's nowhere left to run. The last inch of crust finally gives way, and I plunge, feet first, toward the black abyss below.

This is the end. I couldn't run fast enough. Not today.

It takes me a moment to realize I'm not falling. Not impaled on the ice shards I'm sure to find at the bottom. My feet dangle above the chasm, and a hard hand grips the flesh of my upper arm.

Elio's nostrils flare as he pulls me to solid ground and snakes an arm around my waist, crushing me to him. A new ice bridge has formed to replace the broken one, the fresh ice sturdy and smooth.

The Winter King's brows pull together like he can't quite believe what he's done, before his gaze settles on the forest behind me. "Let's find her."

"Okay." The solid hold doesn't relent as he tucks his index finger and thumb between his lips and whistles.

The ice dragon has been freed and lands beside us. A loud huff escapes its snout, its nostrils flaring as it leans in to sniff Elio. Smoke billows from its nose, forming a murky veil between us. Intricate white antlers extend from its head, but their bases appear to have been prodded and cut, as though someone tried to saw them off. Scales are also missing from its side.

Poor beast.

Elio raises a hand to the formidable creature. "Easy, Mistress. I know you're hurt, my friend, but I need to ask too much of you."

The dragon blinks and extends its neck in greeting, its nose nudging Elio's uninjured side before its reptilian gaze shifts to me.

"This is Lori. We kind of like her, so we can't eat her—at least not yet." A smile escapes Elio as the beast nuzzles his outstretched hand, and he caresses it with a loving whisper, "Good girl."

Shivers rock my body when the majestic creature bows its head. Elio proceeds to boost me up onto the back of his ice dragon like it's the most natural thing to do, and I grab a fist of the beast's long white mane not to topple right over to the other side.

The shape of the dragon's back allows for my thighs to hold on to each side of its spine, but without a saddle or stirrups, I can't imagine how I'm supposed to remain in place when it flies.

My eyes bulge, the blood draining from my knuckles and face, my mind screaming at me to *get the fuck off this dragon.*

"You don't ride," Elio says as he climbs behind me.

"I ride *horses.*"

And sparingly.

"You're shaking."

No measure of urgency can justify this folly. "I need to get off—"

"Shush. It's just like riding a horse. Trust me." Elio adjusts his position with ease and tightens an arm around my waist. He nestles me in the space between his thighs, closer, closer, closer...

A hiccup of surprise quakes me at how warm he feels. The king of ice isn't quite as cold as he was the other day in the wagon, and I barely resist the urge to relax against him.

He reaches for the dragon's mane with both hands, caging me in. The hard planes of his chest are pressed flush against my back and swell with each breath—every thunderous beat of his heart racing even harder than my own.

I scream as the dragon extends its wings and jumps straight off the cliff. My lids screw shut, and my body instinctively cowers inside Elio's embrace without an ounce of shame. The scenery blurs, and black spots dance in front of my eyes.

Tumbling down an ice dragon's back sounds just like the kind of *accident* that could happen to a bride.

"Breathe, little spider," Elio says, the smile in his voice audible. "I've got you."

That fucker sounds perfectly amused... My mind spins as I try to get a hold of myself.

Elio's hot breath sears the shell of my ear. "At this rate, the sleighs are going to tumble straight off the mountain."

I snap my eyes open, my hunter's instincts kicking into gear. The sleighs are racing downhill, the avalanche gaining ground every second. "That one isn't carrying a heavy load. Daisy must be on it, and maybe the other girls, too." I point to the last of the three sleighs. The precious metal and dragon scales give the other sleighs more momentum and less precision than the one carrying the prisoners. Hopefully.

The path leading down the mountain will be overrun by the avalanche in minutes, and the Tidecallers and their sleighs will be swept right off the rocky cliffs.

Elio conjures a chain of ice with his magic. The solid links glisten in the early light of dawn as they wind around the dragon's chest, forming a secure anchor around its neck and front limbs.

No, no, no, no, no.

Elio guides my hands to the dragon's mane. "Hold on tight. And whatever you do, stay on the dragon."

With that, Elio grabs the free end of the chain and leaps from his mount, swinging from the dragon like a furious pendulum. He impales a soldier below, causing the enemy driver to topple off. Elio then lands on the sleigh, takes the driver's place, and yanks the tarp off the cargo.

It's the right sleigh. Daisy's hair is visible, but she's either tied up or unconscious because she's not moving. Elio steers the wolves to a complete stop, the animals obedient even though they are about to be swallowed whole.

He ties the chain to the sleigh and signals to his dragon with a sharp whistle. The beast perches atop the tallest nearby pine, about halfway up the tree. I hear its jagged claws splintering the bark, the sound harsh and unsettling as the tree shudders under the dragon's weight. My feet slip from the spikes on its side, and the fine hair of the dragon's mane digs into my hands, my legs dangling above the approaching storm.

I hang from the dragon's neck, the nearly vertical angle making my muscles scream in agony, but I manage to hang on. The quietness I find whenever I hunt engulfs me, my shadows pulsing over my skin as I force my thighs back around the beast's body and squeeze, relieving part of the strain on my arms.

The dragon clings to the thick conifer's trunk with its talons, the ice chain Elio fashioned wrapped tightly around its thorax. The avalanche roars past the edge of the cliffs in powerful torrents, ready to take its passengers straight to the gods. Clouds of snow and white smoke swirl around me, and flakes of ice stick to my lashes, blurring my vision.

Trees crack and bend under the force of the avalanche, the pine we landed on resisting the onslaught of ice—for now. The rolling thunder tapers down, and my vision clears a little, allowing me to see further down than before.

I search for Elio in the chaos and find him dangling from the curve of the sleigh's front bow, his hands gripping the wooden arch of the shaft. His feet are stuck in the current of the avalanche, its unstoppable pull dragging him down. A pain-filled grimace twists his lips, and his biceps strain with the effort to keep himself above the fray.

He's not going to last much longer.

I carefully slide down the dragon's back and past its backside, holding on to the ice chain, until my feet find footing on the sleigh's steering shaft.

"Get back up there," Elio grits through his teeth, his eyes dark and full of reproach.

"Hang on. I'm coming."

"It's almost over. Just stay put." His eyes dart to the snow below him and back to me, a shard of danger or wrath or perhaps even capitulation gleaming inside of them. Like he might just...give up.

"Don't you dare let go, or I swear, I will plunge in after you!" I shout, terrified by the keen pulse of shadow in his gaze.

I wrap one leg around the chain and hook my other foot in the narrow space between the two wood panes that form the handle of the steering shaft, slowly leaning over the bow until I glide down to the front of the sleigh. A strap of my dress gets stuck and tears right off, but I finally manage to extend my hands toward Elio, quite literally hanging upside down. "Here!"

His lids screw shut. A grunt tears out of his throat as he releases one hand from the sleigh's curved extremity to reach for mine. His hard, steady grip fills me with a blinding sense of relief.

My arms burn as Elio pulls himself up, but I don't dare to relax my muscles until both his feet are secured on the front shaft bow.

He stands tall, trembling all over. "You silly spider. Why would you risk your life like that? All the ice in the worlds couldn't kill me—"

I wrap my arms tightly around his midriff, burying my face in his stomach. His proximity wards off the chill, offering a welcome shield against the cold. "Stop complaining. You're safe now."

A deep, crystal-clear *crack* echoes near my ears as the tree's trunk succumbs to the dragon's weight. The beast flaps its wings, sending a frigid gust that numbs my fingers and toes. The ice chain wrapped around my thigh tugs painfully, and I release my grip on Elio to avoid being torn apart as it wrenches me upward.

For a moment, it feels like I'm flying—but I'm not. I'm plummeting head first toward the ground, and the tide of the avalanche sweeps me into a dark void. Snow swallows me from all sides, as soft and suffocating as spider silk, filling my ears, nose, and mouth until I can't breathe.

CHAPTER 28
FROZEN
ELIO

Water slips inside my mouth, and I cough it out, slowly stirring back to life. I'm surrounded by a warmth I haven't known in decades. Rocks dig into my back and hip, and my lids flutter. White and teal stalactites hang above my head and reveal my location. I'm in the heart of the Ice City, immersed in the magical hot springs beneath the mountain. Its powers have already repaired most of the damage I suffered during my fall. Sara must have found me at the foot of the Blueridge cliffs and decided to use desperate measures to patch me back together.

She shouldn't have bothered. Maybe I should look how I feel and become as monstrous on the outside as I am on the inside.

"Good morning."

The water sloshes around me as I struggle to sit up. *Lori. She's alive.* Sara's swift and thorough rescue isn't so disappointing after all.

"Or evening? Or night? I can't tell," Lori adds. She waves her arms in the water and rests her head against the natural stones lining the rim of the basin.

"It's night. We've probably been in here for a day—maybe

longer," I say, my magic always in tune with the sun. "How long have you been awake?"

"About twenty minutes. Why?" Her eyes wrinkle at the corners. "Are you worried that I casted some dark spell on you while you were sleeping?"

She sounds way too amused for my taste, and my brows pull together. After the tree cracked, I pushed and pulled and used every single ounce of magic I had left to find Lori in the avalanche. I waded through tons of crushed ice and branches until I washed over the cliffs and fell to the valley below, the impact breaking about every single bone in my body. I passed out from the debilitating pain and figured Lori had about no chance of survival.

I rub the water from my eyes, frozen in place. Why the fuck did Sara bring us here *together*? There's at least a dozen basins in the caves. I should leave, but the magic water is still working the knots out of my stiff muscles and healing the deep cut in my side.

Despite the lingering pain, I haven't felt so alive in decades. The scent of lemongrass and rock salts mingles with the humid air of the hot springs, infused with a mystical quality.

I scan the cavern for signs of life, but we're alone.

Where are those annoying little eyeballs when I need them? If cameras were around, I wouldn't dare to touch her. The spring's water is murky, full of glacier sediment, but I can still make out the alluring shape of Lori's breasts under the surface. Her long black hair is all wet and beautiful, a few strands sticking to her shoulders and neck.

I've got to find something to talk about, and soon.

"How are you even alive?" I croak, the question rough and unrefined.

Lori's clear gray eyes pierce the darkness, her brows pulled together. "Don't sound so disappointed."

"I'm not. Just surprised." I clear my airways again. "Are you alright?"

She immerses herself completely with a low sigh and emerges a few seconds later. "Yes, but I really thought I was done for..." She draws concentric circles in the water, her gaze fixed on the patterns formed by the shifting sediment. "I was sure death had finally come for me this time."

She says *death*, but she means *me*. Like so many others before her, she believes I've got the final say in all of this, and her eyes flick up to meet mine.

"And you're surprised, so sparing me wasn't your doing..." The veiled betrayal in her voice rakes my insides. "Would you have collected my soul yourself, if I had died?"

"No."

She arches a brow, her eyes narrow and unyielding. "So I'm not worthy of the reaper king?"

"Your worth has nothing to do with it."

"You leave the dirty work to your minions, then?"

Maybe an argument is exactly what I need to stop staring at her. "Usually, yes," I answer in jest, leaning in to her prejudice. "The few odd souls that call to me are typically those of Fae monarchs, but I could make an exception for you. In fact, I have some free time later today."

Her mouth hangs open for a second. "I didn't mean— How can you speak so plainly about death?"

"Our entire lives are about rushing from place to place until we get enough wisdom to slow down. Death is the final destination where we finally stop running. Without it, there'd be no life."

"That's easy for you to say. You're the reaper king." She chews on her bottom lip for a moment before her eyes bore into me once more. "So it's true? You can't die?"

Sadness laces her words, like my title and immortality create a chasm between us that could never be crossed.

"I can't be *killed*, but I'll still die someday, crushed under the weight of a magic I can't bear to carry anymore," I explain. "Which makes what you did on that dragon incredibly useless."

"So you would have survived? Entombed in the snow?"

"Yes. But ice takes without giving back. If Sara hadn't found me in time, I would have left the rest of my humanity out there."

She pushes off the wall and inches forward until she's right in front of me, in the deepest part of the pool. "What does that mean? Would you have become an ice giant like Chenu?"

My ears perk up. "You met Chenu?"

She nods. "What is he, exactly?" Water licks her chin, her head bobbing up and down because she's not tall enough to touch the bottom. I bury my hands in the thick coat of sediment filling the space between the rocks not to reach out and pick her up. *She'd wrap those smooth, sexy legs around my midriff...*

Don't go there.

Just keep talking. It's easier when you talk.

"Some souls aren't collected in time, or they run from the reapers and become lost. When that happens, it's the Sun Court's job to guide them toward the light. The soul catchers have until Alaveen, the festival of light, to bottle up the lost souls in lanterns and send them to the gods," I explain. "The Sun Court boasts that it always catches them all, but that's simply not true. A soul that remains earth-bound beyond Alaveen...darkens. If it was mortal, it wanders the world of the living, invisible, until it fades away, but a few immortal souls haunting the Fae continent have grown powerful and deadly. The most famous of such spirits is the Dark One. I'm sure you've heard of it."

She inches closer and stands on the tip of her toes to reach the bottom of the basin. "The evil spirit that haunts Lorntre Hollow was once flesh and bones?"

"Yes. The blackest thorn in my father's immaculate reputation. The Dark One has grown so powerful that even the King of Light can't destroy him. As for Chenu, he served my predecessor for centuries as a powerful oracle. But kings hate to be told the truth about their futures, and so the old Winter King banished him and his brother to the mountains..."

"We all know how that turned out," Lori cracks, Chenu's infamous bout of cannibalism a punchline of every worthwhile Fae campfire story.

The corner of my mouth quirks. "He's been haunting the Frost Peaks ever since, but he doesn't have enough malice in him to feed on souls beyond the occasional meal he needs to survive. His meager appetite has allowed him to evade the Sun Court's catchers for centuries."

"Why do the stories hide the fact that he used to be a lost soul?" she asks.

"Can you imagine what would happen if all the immortals in this realm knew it was possible to cheat death? Spirits like Chenu and the Dark One are the exception, and it needs to stay that way. Lost souls threaten the balance between life and death, and the very survival of our magic. The more lost souls there are in any given year, the more droughts are born into the Fae population, and for each soul we do not return to the gods as we should, a hundred seeds wither and die in the womb."

"That's a terrifying thought…" Her eyes narrow. "What about the Gray Man?"

My mind flashes to the wispy gray cloak of my faceless assailant. *The Gray Man* is certainly a good nickname for him. "Despite his appearance, the man we saw on the mountain was made of flesh, blood, and bones, I assure you."

"He bled and felt pain alright…" she trails off in a whisper. "You say you can't die, but you looked truly shaken up on that mountain." She points to my side, and her emphatic movement sends ripples over the water. "Could he have killed you with his eerie sword?"

"Possibly."

Her lips purse in a grimace. "And the reapers? Do they die naturally, or are they wired more like you?"

"Reapers give up their lives and souls to the cause. Within the limits of the Ice City, the oldest of them have lost everything that made them human. They're not meant to be seen by the living and become mere skeletons that grind the days away until they crumble to dust." I press my lips together for a moment before adding, "I'll turn into an ugly skeleton, too, at some point. It's already started." I graze the snow-flecked blue freckles near my collarbone to show off the first signs of my transformation.

"You've got snowflakes on your neck. I'd hardly call that ugly." She swims forward to the shallows, and I follow her gaze to the distinctive freckles.

"My skin is changing. Eventually, I'll start losing my hair."

She extends a hand toward my wet blond hair. My breath catches in my throat as she hooks her finger around one lock. "Not that hair?" Her other hand rests near my right thigh, her perfect body still submerged in the water, and my dick stirs.

"Of all the things we've discussed, the idea of me bald is what shocks you?" My chuckle comes out darker than I'd intended, and I smooth it over with a hint of a smile.

"You've got great hair." She combs it back behind my ear, and I blink, taken aback by the ease and warmth of the gesture.

"You're half Fae, then?"

Her lips purse in the semblance of a grimace, but it quickly vanishes in favor of a careful, neutral expression. "How do you figure that?"

"You seem to know more about Faerie than most of the other brides." I watch her reaction, still wondering exactly how Seth stumbled upon a Shadow seed that looks exactly like my dead wife.

I can't explain why Lori looks the way she does, and it would be naive to let my guard down until I understand the reason.

"My grandmother was Fae," she admits.

I arch a brow, wondering if I can trust anything she tells me. "A Shadow Fae?"

"A Spring Fae, actually."

"What about your parents?"

"My mum was a Spring seed. My father...was normal." Her gaze darts to the side.

I know grief like the back of my hand, and while most of my

peers would apologize for bringing up her dead parents, the fact that she suffered such a great loss at her age actually makes me feel closer to her.

It also explains her visceral reaction to some of my comments.

"Were you very young when they died?"

"Too young, but I managed," she says, her voice tinged with quiet sadness. "The worst part was being separated from my brother by the new world's deranged foster system. For years, I was alone."

"I've been alone since I inherited the Winter crown," I reply, my voice carrying a deep sense of resignation.

She nods slowly. "In death, we are alone."

If I didn't know Iris's entire family tree, I might be tempted to delve into Lori's parentage, but the downward curve of her mouth and the coldness creeping into my heart compel me to change the subject.

Who cares if she's a long-lost blood relative of Iris? It wouldn't change anything.

"Would you come with me? If I collected your soul myself? Or would you try and cheat death, little spider?" I croak, dipping my head down.

Our noses bump, and she cups my cheek as if she's about to kiss me. Yet, at the last possible second, she pulls away, submerging herself up to her chin in the pool. "I'd run from you. As fast as I possibly could."

Water glides down my shoulders as I lean forward. "I'd chase you."

"I'm fast." Her raincloud eyes shine in the dark. "Maybe even faster than you."

The defiance in her voice shivers through me. *Oh...fuck it.*

I dash forward to grip her arm, but she slinks away from me, retreating toward the center of the basin. My hand grasps at air, my brows pulling together at the speed with which she moved.

"Told you so."

The sizzle in her impetuous gaze goes directly to my cock, and my heart beats in my throat as I give chase, sinking inside the hot spring until only my head pokes out of the surface. We play cat and mouse around the small natural pool, Lori always staying one step ahead. My ice magic is too dangerous to use inside the healing springs—not if I don't want to ruin their properties for centuries to come.

She splashes water in my eyes with the heel of her palm, and the giggle that escapes her as I rub my face off with a dignified huff wrecks me. Still laughing, she lets me catch her.

My chest heaves in victory as I wrap my arms around her slippery form, caging her in. Smooth, wet skin glides against mine.

"You should see your face. It's like you've never played tag in the water before," she says.

Every movement makes her breasts brush deliciously against my torso, and a dark chuckle rumbles through my body. "I didn't have that kind of childhood, I'm afraid."

Her scent tickles my nose, a subtle aroma both elusive and dark, as if she's part human, part shadow. Goosebumps rise on her skin as I drag her back to the shallows, settling her gently onto my lap.

The sight of her chest—bare and wet—destroys the rest of my good intentions.

With a defeated sigh, she presses her forehead to mine. "I thought you never wanted to touch me again."

The broken promise riddles me with doubts and self-loathing, but I need this. "I changed my mind." I trace her back, mesmerized by the shape of her spine.

Her mouth finds mine, warm from the springs and yet tormented, like she battles the same demons I do. She tastes like the embers of the fire that blazes inside of her, and I long for her to burn me the way she did in the hall of mirrors.

This...intimacy could choke me. I'd rather turn it into sex. Sex, I know how to navigate. I can make her feel good.

I spread her thighs so she's straddling me and caress the valley between her breasts up and down. "As long as we're here and naked... Might as well make the most of it."

She lets out a low, frustrated grunt. "I almost died of frostbite. I'm not in the mood."

I caress the underside of her breasts in turn. Her nipples are taut and dark, begging to be kissed. "No?"

Like all mortals, she lies. She lies and never stops to think of the damage it does around her, and I can't forgive her for that. We're no longer strangers or enemies, but we could never become more than we are now, reluctant allies who lust for each other because of some annoyingly persistent magic. There are a million reasons for me to stop this from happening again.

She shouldn't even be here, all mortals are banned from the Ice City.

She risked her life to save mine.

She looks exactly like my dead wife.

She's a spider, and I still don't know what she's after.

No matter what, I can't marry her.

I don't deserve this.

Some of these reasons sting more than others. A few have become so deeply ingrained in my soul, they might as well be part of my flesh. Yet none seem sufficient to rob me from hearing Lori cry out my name in pleasure. We've already crossed the line once; a second faux pas won't change the fact that I have to marry any one of them but her.

It might make it harder to walk away, a small voice whispers in the back of my mind. *Walk away now before you start to care.*

Our gazes lock, and Lori tightens her hold on my neck like she sensed my hesitation. Her eyes are so expressive and wide and open... I want to learn their language. Her fingers travel to my shoulder, her thumb resting in the small dip beneath my collarbone. Whether she intends to pull me closer or push me away, I can't tell.

We're tethering on the edge of a precipice so deep I fear we'll never reach the ground.

I'm terrified that if we tip over, we'll just fall and fall and fall. Fall so thoroughly and for so long that we'll start to think we can fly.

But death will be waiting. Death is patient, if not merciful.

Walk away now. Walk away while you still have the chance, or it'll hurt more when you do. Your duty is to the kingdom. To the souls. You can't falter now.

You can't change your destiny, Elio. You still have to marry someone else.

Fuck someone else.

And condemn her to die.

Break Lori's heart now so you don't have to do it later. If not for your sake, then for hers.

The small voice goes mute as she bends down to kiss me again, her nails digging into my upper back to claw me closer. Nudging me over the edge.

I find her soft heat under the water and drag a finger across her folds. She's slick and ready, and my cock throbs.

"You're in the mood, I think." I start a slow rub, teasing her.

She tucks her lip between her teeth. "Mm... You're too good at that."

"Want me to stop?"

"Nope." She traces my skull tattoo before snaking a hand down to my erection.

My abs clench, the tension in my groin almost painful. "Not yet. I want to hear you beg, first."

You're a selfish, unworthy bastard, the little voice coos.

Lori's thighs are perfectly spread out in this position, and I draw slow, sluggish circles between her legs until she pants. I drink in the sight of her round, exquisite breasts. Small beauty marks darken her left aureole and run all the way down to her navel. The marks are all hers, and I can't stop looking at them, wishing I could map them out on parchment.

She has more muscles than Iris did, her body shape completely different, despite the similarities. The differences only feed my need to claim her, and I swipe my thumb across her clit. "Promise me you will never risk your life for me again."

"Oh!" Her sharp nails sink into my shoulder again as she holds on to me. "You like to steal promises from me when I'm distracted. You're...evil."

"Promise me."

"No."

"Promise me, or I'll spread you down by the edge of this pool and lick every inch of you without ever making you come. I'll take my pleasure between your gorgeous breasts first—" I twist her nipples between my index finger and thumb in turn, coaxing a mewl out of her.

"And then in your mouth." I slide a finger into her mouth, and she hums, closing her lips around it and sucking every drop of her arousal mixed with the mineral water. "I will take everything there is to take and give nothing back. I warn you."

She smiles like my threats are fucking music to her ears. "Bite me."

I suck a bruise on her shoulder and push my teeth into her skin, and she quakes in my arms.

"Promise me."

"Fine I promise—"

So easy... I sink one finger into her, then another, curling them to reach the apex of her need, and her hips buck as she writhes against me.

"—that I will only risk my life for you when you're actually in danger."

Cheater.

Before I can move, the evidence of her climax coats my fingers from all sides, her walls clinging to them with wild, powerful squeezes as she rides out the high.

So fucking wet and ready. I will punish her for this treachery and make her scream so loud, the walls of the Ice City will crack.

I rein in my impatience and give her some time to catch her

breath. Shivering, she runs a hand down my shoulder blade and traces one of the two deep scars that runs to the middle of my back. Luckily, the wretched mark above my left buttock is still hidden by the water, but *fuck*.

Lori's face wrinkles into a worried frown. "Your scars. Let me see them." Without waiting for an answer, she peers over my shoulder, and the movement causes her breasts to dangle an inch from my face, so I suck one nipple inside my mouth.

She chokes at the caress. "Wait."

"I've learned from a very early age that one should never cry over clipped wings. It won't grow them back." I rub myself against her inner thigh. "I want to fuck. *Now*."

"We can fuck *after* you've answered my questions." The energy in the room changes, her hooded eyes full of rage…and fear. She looks about to burst into tears, and that seriously hinders my priorities.

I force a breath down my throat, my cock so stiff and painful, my vision blurs when she adjusts her position on my lap.

She's obviously no longer in a *take me now* mood, but furious. The black flames of her wrath cast shadows along her shoulders and suck a bit of light out of the room itself, but for once, her ire isn't directed at me. "Who cut them off?"

Her jaw ticks, and I know she won't back down until I've answered the question. I bury my face in her hair to avoid seeing the pity that's sure to ride on the carriage of her anger. Pity is not the emotion I want to see in a woman's gaze before I fuck her.

"My father. He didn't feel I was worthy of them after I left the Sun Court." I encircle her waist to keep her close.

I do not want to disclose my secrets to a woman I know almost nothing about, but the feeling of her in my arms is so natural, so *right*, that I can't help myself. And besides, this is hardly my darkest secret.

"And in spite of that, you've kept all the gifts you were born with? Even after taking on the Winter crown?"

"I did. It drove my father crazy, but even clipping my wings wasn't enough to destroy the seed of light burning inside me."

She draws back an inch. "And there's nothing that can be done? No spell or..." she trails off as she reads the answer on my face, and cradles my head in her hands. "I'm so sor—"

I peck her lips. "Shh. It's alright. Everyone's got scars. Unsalvageable broken parts. Indelible trauma that's altered them forever. I just have to wear some of mine on the outside."

And I can't fly. Not now. Not ever. If I tried, I would just crash and break something more. Until there's nothing left of me to break.

"Back in the hall of mirrors, you mentioned a Blessed Flame?" She twists her fingers in my hair, and I chuckle at the reminder, grateful for the shift in subject.

"A pesky leftover of my old religion."

"Tell me about it."

"Light Fae believe the threads forming the tapestry of the gods are sometimes burned at the ends to prevent their will from fraying. That some destinies are too important to be left to chance, and that the Flame is then used to strengthen the pattern. It is said that the Flame of Fate can also be used to burn stray threads that do not serve the gods' interest. Some of us believe it's actually used to erase their *mistakes*, but others think that the idea of our gods making mistakes is heresy."

Her thumb caresses the column of my throat, and I tip my head back to rest on the edge of the pool, enjoying each twisted, sinuous line she traces on her way down to my stomach. She takes her sweet time, rekindling the fire in my groin until I'm panting.

"And what camp are you?" she asks.

I bite my bottom lip. "I'd rather not say."

"Tell me anyway." She dips her hands to my aching Faehood, her small hand teasing the length of it from root to tip, and I hiss.

"Everyone makes mistakes."

"Even you?"

"*Especially* me," I rasp, my lids fluttering.

She places a soft kiss on my neck. "What kind of mistakes?"

"The kind that are so tantalizing that I'd tear out my soul if it meant I did not have to give them up."

She stops her glorious exploration, and my eyes snap open. With both hands on my shoulders, she leans back. "Is that what I am? A mistake?"

I shift forward and grab her waist to prevent her escape, digging my fingertips into the flesh of her ass. "A ravishing, sumptuous mistake."

This indulgence is only meant to soothe the ache in my bones, and me, hers.

Nothing more. She can't be more.

She crosses her arms over her breasts, shielding them from my view, clearly torn as to what to do next. "Keep talking."

I trace the black and red scar that licks her hipbone all the way to her rib. "As long as we're threading painful territory..." The wound hasn't changed at all since I last saw it, despite the fact that Lori has just been swimming in the purest, most-effective healing spring in existence.

A terrible pressure squeezes my ribcage. "What kind of venom was it?"

She trembles in my arms. "A dreamcatcher spider. Like the ones we saw up on the mountains."

Two half-crescent tears form a long line in her side, and the pattern showcases exactly how the fangs of the spider tore through her. My jaw clenches. The venom inside that wound is counting down the days until it spreads. I can almost see the taint of dark magic swirling beneath the skin, biding its time.

By Thanatos... I will nail every last one of these spiders to my ice wall before the month is over.

"A frost apple would cure you... Is this why you agreed to do the pageant?" I ask, putting my guard back up. No matter how fierce or beautiful she is, I can't forget she conspired with Seth to deceive me.

A tremor rocks her from head to navel. "No. I didn't even know a frost apple would work on this venom."

"So you came to help Seth steal my crown and yet risked your life to save me? I don't get you, Lori." I wrap my hand in her hair, ready to make her mine again, if only for a little while.

She slaps my chest. "For the last time, Seth and I couldn't care less about your crown. We're here to find Morrigan. She attacked the Shadow Court during Morheim, and we need to capture her, not kill her."

My grip on her hair waivers. *The Shadow Court...* "You're one of Damian's spiders?"

"I prefer the term *unpaid employee*."

Oh for Thanatos' sake!

I've had sex with this woman—even considered killing her a few times—and she's a full-fledged Shadow huntress acting in her king's name? "You should have told me that before." I slide her off me and jump out of the pool.

You're a selfish, dumb bastard. She was never yours to save. Or to destroy.

Water streams down my body and splashes the floor of the cave as I beeline for the white towels Sara left for us, but Lori chases after me.

"I've caught a few glimpses of a woman with black hair wearing a dark hood. She came to meet you at the castle and observed the carnival from a distance, yet she kept her face hidden." Lori tilts her chin up, and a spark of thunder ignites behind the clouds in her eyes "She might have fooled you into thinking she was someone else, but I'm here to bring that traitor to justice."

I grab a towel and press it over my raging erection. Lori's accusation slowly sinks in, and my temper flares. *Of all things, she thinks I'm too naïve to recognize my own cousin? What a joke!*

"Morrigan Quinn stabbed my mentor and friend through the heart right in front of me in the middle of dinner. I think I can recognize her without your help." I throw her the extra towel, desperate to erase her body from my sight. "Come on. I will take you to her. Your *traitor.*"

CHAPTER 29
HEAVEN'S DOOR
LORI

The Winter King stomps around the stalagmites and heads out of the white and blue cave. I tuck a fluffy towel around my frame before following him along the natural path. The smooth, round shape of his ass steals my thoughts, and a part of me is cross that I interrupted our lovely bath. Arguing with him is about as addictive as the touch of his hands—but not quite.

At the end of the natural cave, Elio finally wraps his towel around his waist and wrenches open the platinum door fitted into the rock opening, the exit leading directly into a study and library.

Large windows offer a wide view of the almost endless white plains at the bottom of the volcano's caldera. From the view, I figure we're at the top of the Ice City. Firelight flickers over the blue and silver tapestries hanging on the wall. Four floor-to-ceiling bookcases flank the hearth, made entirely of white wood. The beautiful pieces match the sanded matte finish of the desk.

Sara is sitting by the fire on one of two navy blue velvet loungers. She shoots to her feet at Elio's arrival and sets down her teacup on the ottoman. A smirk appears on her face as our gazes meet, but she quickly wipes it away. Elio marches past her without a word of greeting and beelines for the adjoining room on the other side of the study.

The woman I've seen with Elio in the castle gardens the night Aster died, and again at the carnival, is also sitting by the fireplace. I draw in a sharp gasp. "*Ohmygod.*"

She cracks a smile and sets her book aside, its small leather-bound cover catching the light as she discards it on the table next to her lounger. "Hi."

Celebrities are rare in Faerie, but all the more revered for it. In the new world, musicians, actors, athletes, and political leaders are held in high regard, yet none command the same level of adoration as the famous singer who reigns supreme in both realms. And it's not Morrigan.

"You're Elizabeth Snow."

She nods, and her long dark waves bounce around her face. "Call me Beth, please."

I can't keep from staring. Elizabeth Snow is Taylor Swift and Madonna rolled into one, topped with a zest of the Beatles. A living legend.

She stares right back, and the intensity of her gaze, the way it travels along my facial features and pauses on the curve of my ear tells me that she knew Iris. Just like Seth, Freya, and Elio himself, the ones who personally knew my doppelgänger look at me differently than those who didn't. Like I'm an infuriating puzzle that needs to be solved.

Elio returns from the adjoining room wearing pants and a fresh black button-down shirt and begins fastening the buttons. "See? She's my friend. The famous singer. Not Morrigan. She's been keeping herself hidden to avoid silly, awkward reactions like the one you just had."

"Be nice, Elio," Elizabeth Snow scolds him. "I think Lori has proven her allegiance."

Elio opens and closes his mouth, his fingers fumbling with a row of misaligned buttons. He grunts as he unbuttons and starts again. "How fucked are we? Did the cameras somehow broadcast the attack to the entire kingdom?"

"We weren't as unlucky as that, but it's still delicate." Sara makes a quick back and forth between the two rooms and returns with a plain white t-shirt for me to wear. "I'll show you. Let me set up the projector."

"Are the others alive?" I ask.

Sara's shoulders sag as she holds the door ajar and motions for me to go in and change. "All but one. One of the Reds didn't make it. She was killed in the mine, but your friend Daisy and the others are alright."

I nod with my bottom lip tucked between my teeth and slip past her before closing the door behind me. A large mirror is affixed to the wall next to a white wood dresser cluttered with papers, books, and quills. In one corner, a queen-sized bed with a white duvet and black pillows—simple, no frills—stands against the wall. Elio's platinum mask rests on the bedside table.

His bedroom... Wow.

I always assumed the Winter King resided in the castle, not the Ice City. I pull the oversized white t-shirt over my head, its hem falling just above my knees, and notice Elizabeth Snow's hooded cape hanging from a coat rack behind the door. I thought Elio was getting cozy with Morrigan, but perhaps I was just mistaken about his lover's identity.

A lump of saliva catches in my throat as I return to the study. While I was changing, Sara had set up a sleek black box on the desk, and video footage from the mountains now plays on the wall. I clutch the hem of the oversized shirt, feeling exposed.

"The camera following Lori through the challenge turned back on a few minutes after it was knocked down by the Tidecallers. The very end of the pursuit was broadcast to the entire realm, but there's no audio," she explains, pressing a button to start the video.

It feels surreal to see myself up close, snow clinging to my lashes as I reach out to Elio. I watch the moment I threatened to jump into the avalanche if he let go, our lips moving in silent dialogue. I only see our mouths move, but I remember every word.

The tear in my dress is visible from this angle, and my gut cramps as I recall how cold and listless my extremities felt.

But I couldn't let Elio slip through my freezing fingers.

The film replays the moment where he managed to pull himself up on the sleigh next to me and out of danger. My cheeks flush at how tightly I held him.

It was only because his body was warm, I tell myself.

I had my face buried in his stomach when it happened, so I remember his admonishment at how silly it was for me to try and save him, but I couldn't see his face then. He looks absolutely broken as I hold him, his eyes closed, and his limbs shaking.

It's such an intimate moment, and my throat shrinks at the thought that all of Wintermere witnessed it.

Sara lowers her voice. "Most people think it was all for show and part of the challenge, but others recognized the Tidecallers' helmets. I didn't want mass hysteria to settle in, so I promised you would explain everything during the live broadcast tomorrow."

Elio nods, his gaze riveted to the playback as he leans on the wall of his study, Sara and Beth now standing between us. What happened on the mountain could have had egregious consequences on the entire Fae realm, and I can't help but feel I'm missing some important information to make sense of it all, so I watch the feed intently.

The tree holding the dragon up splinters under its weight, and the beast flaps its wings in a frenzy to avoid being swallowed by the snow, ejecting me from the sleigh. The ice chain explodes in a flurry of pointy shards.

My fists curl at my sides as I see myself career toward the white flumes of the avalanche. I can't recall anything after that, but Elio's reaction knocks the breath out of me.

The Winter King doesn't waste a second and plunges headfirst after me. He didn't even hesitate, coming damn close to catching my arm before we disappeared. The rolling snow clears out about thirty seconds later, my unconscious body curled around a rock at the edge of the cliff, but Elio is nowhere to be found.

I risk a glance to the quiet man on my left, but he clears his throat without meeting my gaze. "Thanks for the swift rescue, Sara. Remind me to compliment Paul for his annoyingly resilient cameras, or you wouldn't have found us in time." He walks to the projector and smashes the power button.

The entire wall goes dark, jolting me back to reality.

Elio rubs down his face with a sigh. "Get Paul and Byron in here. We have a long night ahead of us. It's going to be damn-near impossible to spin this so the other royals don't blame us for the Tide-callers' foray inside the continent."

"There's something else we need to discuss—" Beth starts, her gaze darting to me for a split second.

Sara squeezes her shoulder, and something passes between them.

The royal chief of staff plasters an affable smile on her lips, the extra cheer in her voice reminding me of the tone she uses when she's speaking to the cameras. "I arranged for Lori to sleep in the guest's wing tonight. I'll take you there." She moves to open a third, unexplored door, but Elio beats her to the punch.

"No need. I'll show her myself. You go ahead and get things started." He motions for me to lead the way.

I offer the two women an awkward wave goodbye and tiptoe past Elio and into the hallway. The hairs at the back of my neck rise to attention when he slams the door behind us.

"What was that about? What do you need to discuss without me present?"

"I'm not sure," he answers darkly.

I brace my hands on my hips and pause in the dimly lit corridor, unhappy with his answer. "You mentioned the Tidecallers, but I thought they were extinct?"

"Rebellions are never truly extinct," Elio says tersely as he walks past me. "They simmer down, spreading silently through the cracks of rotten politics until they gather enough momentum to flare up again. The original Tidecallers were driven beyond the Breach to the Islantide, but their ideology endured. For centuries, their followers have been scuttling about the realm in their name."

I fall into step with him, my brows pinched in confusion. "I thought Tidecallers worshiped the Mist King?"

"That's a common misconception," Elio clarifies. "Tidecallers were mostly soldiers who wanted the endless wars to end. They believed that a new King and Queen should be elected every decade, so no one would ever amass as much power as the Mist King once did."

"That doesn't sound so bad," I quip, forging ahead.

The corridor opens up to a round staircase landing, revealing a dizzying view of the tiny streets of the Ice City below. We're at the very top of the fortress, and a sudden bout of vertigo blurs my vision.

"No, it wasn't such a crazy plan," Elio admits. "But harvesting and wielding power became addictive. Some crowns aren't meant to be survived... There was no guarantee that an elected monarch would willingly relinquish power once he had it, or that others wouldn't kill to steal it. The war grew more intense and violent with the spread of the jewels, so Mist Fae technology was outlawed, and all known jewels were destroyed.

"After the Summer King ordered the massacre of the Mist Fae, the rebel factions were pushed to repopulate the Islantide, never to return to the continent. Since then, every boat that tries to cross the Breach is blasted to dust on sight."

I crane my neck around to look at him, and the menacing look on his face flips my stomach. He's the same man who plunged into a torrent of ice to find me, yet the vibe rolling off him is more *predator* than *prince charming*. His fists clench at his sides like he's at war with himself, at odds with me, and daggers drawn with the rest of the world.

My bare feet test the feel of the cold marble, instinctively checking for its porosity and grip.

In case I need to run.

CHAPTER 30

DON'T BLAME ME

LORI

Darkness burns within the center of the round staircase, running at least twenty floors down. Shadows lick my skin as I trace the shape of the decorative wrought iron banister and start my descent.

Elio nips at my heels. The large windows on each of the landings light our path, but there's no torches or lanterns or electric lights to speak of. I glance at him over my shoulder—a mouse taking a stroll in front of a panther.

"So many shadows in your ice fortress…" I trail off.

"You must feel right at home."

"How could anyone feel at home on death's stoop?"

"I do."

The steep and narrow round staircase allows me to glimpse up at him as I skip to get ahead, the two of us now on opposite sides of the tight circle. Him lingering on higher ground, me feeling even more like a prey as we continue our descent.

An enigmatic smile glazes his lips, but he doesn't try to bridge the gap between us or engage in further conversation.

The Winter King is wearing black from head to toe, his hair about the only thing making him look human at all. The blonde locks have dried up since our soak, and they curl behind his pointy ears, softening up his lethal look.

After a couple more floors, I'm simply shaking with anticipation and stop on the next landing to look out the window.

From this height, the winding streets and tightly-knit townhouses of the Ice City are more visible, and I rest a hand on the glass. Painted signs wave in the winds above the shops and restaurants. Snow shovels are planted near each set of stone steps leading to the grim reapers' homes, stacks of firewood partially hidden under black tarps to protect them from the weather.

So...normal.

Elio stalks behind me until his chest is pressed against my back. His proximity sets my nerves ablaze, and yet it's also incredibly soothing. And maddening.

His breath tickles my ear. "Now, do you trust me?"

"No," I whisper back.

He combs my hair to one side and places a soft kiss on my bare neck. "You better not." He digs a hand in the flesh of my mid-thigh and drags his fingers up under the hem of my shirt until his palm is flat against my navel. "You look good in my clothes."

My lids flutter. "Are you sleeping with Elizabeth Snow?"

He presses me harder into him. "Are you jealous, my little spider?"

I choke on false words of denial.

Am I getting territorial over a man I don't even like? Elio is stubborn, cold, impatient, and totally *not* for me. So what if he's sleeping with the most famous singer in both the new world and Faerie? Our long soak in the healing springs paved the way for disaster, and yet our aborted dalliance has left me with more questions—and a terribly unsatiated need.

Every devious promise Elio made, every dark secret he unveiled, still pulses in my blood as he kisses a long, winding path from my shoulder to my ear. "Beth and I have never been involved."

"Why not? I mean—she's Elizabeth Snow."

Cold air washes along my back as Elio walks away.

"You're right. What was I thinking? I should go and propose to her now," he says in jest.

I grab his wrist to stop his falsely hurried retreat, and the light-hearted chuckle bubbling up his throat about kills me. It's an entirely new side of him.

"Stop making fun of me. You're the Winter King. It would make sense for you to be with her," I scold.

He prowls forward until my back is pressed up against the glass, and he's so tall that I have to gaze up at him to see the expression on his face.

"If we were interested in each other, we would have married as teenagers. It's not like her father wouldn't have been pleased," he says on a gruff whisper.

"Unless you didn't want to risk killing a national treasure."

Our gazes lock, and he rests his forehead on mine. "There you go again, reminding me about my dead wives."

I know what we both want, and yet I also know what it will cost me. I blink a few times, my mind struggling more and more to match the reality of Elio to the cruel, heartless portrait of the Winter King the rest of the world painted.

"Do you truly kill them? Your wives?"

"I don't strangle or stab them, if that's what you're asking, but I'm as responsible for their deaths as if I carried out the deed myself."

"So you're...cursed?" I think of Damian's curse and how hard he worked to hide it from everyone. Sounds like Elio is going through something similar.

I hold my breath when he gives a small incline of head. "It's an endless loop I can't escape..." With a sad smile, Elio wraps a hand in my hair. "Kiss me." He bends down, but I hold myself away.

"What about Iris? How did she die?"

Curses don't just appear out of nowhere.

His eyes darken. "Let's not talk about Iris."

If I push him on this, he's going to pull away. I'm the spitting image of the woman in question, yet the way he holds me drowns out the voice in my head that urges me to run. The magic between us is still powerful, but not as drugging as it was in the hall of mirrors. Not as desperate to *crush* us together.

I could turn and walk away. Or ask for answers.

I trace the bend of his brows instead, desperate to see him smile again, and link my arms behind his neck. "I'm done with my questions. For now." My gaze falls to his lips in invitation.

"Good."

Our noses bump. Elio's slow and tortuous kiss torments me more than all the ones that came before. Instead of rushing to the next part, we explore each other, coaxing sweet sighs and sharp breaths from one another in turn, riling ourselves up until we're restless and panting.

I unbutton his shirt and glide my hands under the fabric. The sleeves easily glide down his arms, and I test the feel of each defined muscle as I go. The button-down shirt falls to the ground, no longer encroaching on the view, and I bite my bottom lip. "I hate and love how good you look."

"Right back at you." He tugs on my hair, his eyes gleaming.

It's a total sham that any man would be so perfectly sculpted that each ridge and valley adorning his body would be enough to trip my brain up.

I trace the shape of his pec tattoo. "Why does it darken and lighten?"

"It's the Mark of the Gods. I got it when the old Winter King died, the gods designating me as his preferred heir."

As I continue my exploration, an area that's colder than the rest of him grabs my attention. Unlike the lesions on his shoulder blades, this one is a smooth and circular scar right above his left buttocks, and he shivers as I caress the shape of it. The skin smack in the center of the old wound is frozen and stiff.

Elio clicks his tongue in a chiding fashion before he spins me around to face the window, turning me away from the secrets written in blemishes on his body. He caresses my arms and laces our fingers before he raises our joined hands above my head and flattens my palms to the glass.

The chafe of the frosted window soothes the ache in my blood as Elio nuzzles the back of my ear. "Let me remind you of a universal truth that few people—mortal or not—manage to accept. Death isn't evil. There's no grand villain waiting to trip you up at the end. No dark machinations working against you."

The man holding me captive between his body and the splendor of his Ice City isn't as cold as he was the other night. Maybe the hot springs have melted a bit of the frost running through his veins, but he feels warm and human now. His behavior is more nuanced, adding a layer of complexity to his presence.

The Ice City is a silent witness to our addictive dance, a handful of reapers walking up and down the streets' steep network of stairwells, en route to collect souls and wreck countless lives.

The pressure of Elio's fresh, hard lips on my pulse point distracts me, the greediness of his tongue divine. His t-shirt shields my breasts from the sting of winter, my nipples hard as stone under the fabric.

"Death only stings for a moment. Love hurts for a lifetime," he says.

I force a deep breath down my lungs, about to lose it. "Love isn't supposed to hurt. Grief hurts. Wasn't Iris protected by the same magic as you? Unless you're the only one who can mark someone for death—"

He bites down my earlobe. "Reapers don't mark anyone for death. They collect the souls of those whose bodies stopped functioning. If they didn't, the souls would just stay trapped forever or fade away. I don't decide who lives and dies but act as their guardian and protector—and only for a short while."

The face of the reaper that took my dad's soul flashes into my memory once more.

"That goes against everything I've ever been taught," I say.

"Then you've been taught wrong. When grief hits, everyone looks for someone to blame, but reapers are not thieves. We guard the souls so that no one can harm them, and give them back to the gods on the solstice." He inhales deep, his nose buried in the crook of my neck. "Look down. Death is all around us." He sneaks one hand up my stomach and presses it firmly against my breastbone. "Feel your heart beating...ready to run. Don't run from me tonight, little spider."

I feel powerful in his embrace, more at home in death's arms than I'd care to admit.

"Deep inside, you crave death," he whispers.

I rake my nails through the coat of frost glazing the window. "I do *not* crave death. Death is awful. It took *everything* from me." The ashes of our last fight are like dry kindling waiting for a spark. One word out of turn and we could be at each other's throats again. "But I won't argue with you about death, because you are too stubborn to acknowledge one simple fact."

"By Thanatos," he says with humor, and maybe a little impatience. "I'm all ears."

"You are not death. You are no more death than Damian is the night, or your father the sun. You are her king. You're the most powerful Fae king alive because death is the most dangerous beast there is and needs to be ruled by a bigger, badder beast. So no, I don't crave death. But I do crave you," I taunt, spreading my legs slightly.

He teases my breasts, giving each hard peak a playful pinch before he slips a hand down between my thighs. A low hiss echoes in my ears when he finds out exactly how wet I am. "You're so ready for me. But you made me wait, and I have a few questions, too."

I hold myself up on the glass as Elio draws slow, impossibly careful circles over my sensitive spot. "Did you ever sleep with Damian?" he chucks out.

I shake my head. "Never!"

"And you wouldn't lie to me about that?"

"He's my boss. And in love with my best friend."

He lowers his voice even more. "What about Seth?"

"Look who's jealous, now." I grind my backside into his hardness, eager to hear every filthy little thought that runs through his mind. "Seth...is attractive."

Elio holds himself away, punishing me for my answer.

"But he's also a world-class fucker. Nothing's happened between us," I add quickly. "What difference would it make, anyway?"

"I guess it doesn't matter. You're mine, now." Elio brings both hands to my ass and scratches his nails along my curves. "Let me show you exactly what you do to me."

I bend forward and grip the windowsill.

He works his pants open and slides them down in seconds before he grabs my waist and lifts the hem of his shirt, baring me to him. The wide tip of his erection lines up with my entrance, and he rubs himself back and forth until he's coated with my juices. "Do you want me?"

I tense in anticipation, my knuckles white. "More than anything."

He thrusts inside of me without hesitation. *Oh fuck.*

I've never known a man who knows exactly how and when he wants it. I love the sound he makes when he's inside me. Crave the wicked games we play together. It's hot as hell, but I have to remember this king will break me a little more each time we do this.

It's better here, in the cold. The hot springs were way too romantic. It could have turned my head.

He gives a few, slow thrusts for me to adjust to his size, and his ragged breaths make my skin tingle. "You're so fucking tight."

He hits the aching spot inside me, over and over again, in the exact way my body needs.

"Harder." I arch my back, moving with him to increase the pace. Cries of pleasure echo up and down the stairwell, but I can't help myself.

The orgasm takes me by surprise. A white-hot line of bliss sizzles

up my spine, and I close my eyes, ridden to the peak with each invasion of his cock. My walls pulse around him, my body suspended in
rapture for the longest time. Warmth tingles in my extremities as I
taper down from the high, his hardness still rubbing my insides in all
the right ways.

I've always managed to steer clear of charismatic, powerful men.
Why is Elio any different?

We might be colliding with more finesse than last time, but I'm
still a meteor crashing into the sun. If I'm not careful, I'll become a
shell of a woman, addicted to some dark, magic rush I can't ever find
a proper replacement for—doomed to go through life with a Elio-
shape scar on my heart.

Without the shield of it being the first and last time, it no longer
feels like an indulgence, but a pattern. This is the last time I can be
weak.

A fresh wave of pleasure builds at the pit of my belly, but Elio
draws back. The tension between my thighs ebbs away, and I spin
around to scold him. "Don't stop now."

"Patience, little spider." He wraps his hand in my hair and pulls
me in for a long, soul-shattering kiss. After I'm nothing more than a
puddle, he grabs the hem of my shirt and pulls it over my head.
"That's better."

He bends down and places a sweet kiss over the long scar in my
side. "Change of plans. I'll keep you until the top three, so you win a
frost apple and heal this." He licks the shape of it with such care that
I struggle to stay upright. I know he sees someone else when he
gazes up at me with that look of adoration on his face, and that hurts
more than I ever thought possible.

Before I can say anything, he stands back up and pecks my lips.
"Now, get on your knees. I want to come deep inside your mouth."

My heart beats furiously at his demand. He's dangling immortality in front of me like it's nothing more than a party favor, and a
blazing heat engulfs me. "Are you proposing I whore myself out to
get one of your damn apples?" I snap.

His eyes flash with a hint of danger—and a truckload of grievances. "Don't twist my words like that. That was not what I meant, and you know it. But even if you don't want to get better—I'll still have your mouth."

He's mostly right, but I'm still torn by all the emotions running wild in my blood. "I can't believe you're going to go through with the rest of the pageant." I kneel and shoot him a dark look. "When you're so obviously crazy for me."

I arch a brow as if to dare him to say otherwise.

Desire and anger mingle on his breath, and his throat bobs. "I don't deny it," he whispers.

His admission sparks a soft glow between my ribs. I wrap my mouth around the tip of his cock and stroke the base with my hand, and the salty taste of his desire fills me with confidence.

Elio's hips jerk forward. "Oh! Your mouth is fucking insane." He cradles my head and grabs my hair at the roots. "I'm crazy for you, Lori."

I tease him with my tongue, and his jaw slacks, his chest rising and falling faster with each breath. Eyes half-mast, he tightens his hold on my hair and sets the pace. I rub my thighs together, about ready to come just from the sight of him so vulnerable and horny.

"Touch yourself," he orders, and I snake a hand down to obey. Elio's cock throbs inside my mouth as we reach a new climax together, and I suck him even deeper, swallowing his seed drop for drop, already addicted to the taste of his pleasure.

He pulls me up and presses his mouth to my shoulder, his lips curled in a smile. "Now, let's get you to bed." He picks me up in his arms and carries me to the guest room.

"I was there with you on the mountain. I stabbed the bad guy. Surely, that earns me a seat at the table in whatever secret meeting you plan to hold. And I'm not tired."

That last bit is a lie. I'm exhausted, but I'm not sure I can sleep, not so soon after I almost tasted the oblivion of death.

Elio lays me down on the mattress, his expression fierce and serious as he hovers above me. "I need to figure out how I'll present the Gray Man's incursion in Wintermere to the other royals, and to my people. Every kingdom has secrets, Lori, and my crown is coveted by many who don't understand its price."

I move to sit up. "I don't need to be tucked in."

He presses his forehead to mine with a sigh. "If I don't treat you like the foreigner you are—a Shadow huntress at that—the others will either believe I've lost it for good, or think that you've put a spell on me. You don't want the Spring Queen to ask too many questions about you, right?"

Ayaan's face flashes in my mind and acts as a lightning rod, freezing me in place. "Right."

"Sweet slumber, my little spider." Elio plants a kiss on my lips in lieu of goodbye, and I watch him leave with my heart lodged in my throat.

He's not seeing me as his enemy anymore, but he still doesn't trust me. And he won't share my bed. He's perfectly happy fucking in corridors and wagons, but the walls around his soul are not coming down. These stolen moments are merely allowing me a glimpse of what lies behind the ice, but it's never actually melting.

And I want it to, which is foolish and scary.

CHAPTER 31

TEARS THAT AIN'T COMING

LORI

Captive in Iris's body once more, I tease the knots of my long black braid, giving it more volume. My reflection in the full-length, standing mirror is one of pure annoyance as I secure a heavy pair of diamond ear cuffs over my pointy ears. "If you would only get off your high, frosty horse, you'd see there's nothing wrong with it."

A black sequin dress with a thigh-high slit flows around my body, revealing every curve, and underwear is conspicuously absent from my outfit.

"I'm not saying it's wrong. But two parties in that many days... All these people drunk together under one roof. It's a recipe for disaster," Elio answers from his piano bench, tickling the notes without thought. "I don't see why we couldn't celebrate both birthdays at the same time."

"Well... it's done now. The invitations went out weeks ago. The rooms are all made up and ready, and our guests are about to arrive. I can't tell them they're not welcome." I throw Elio a glance over my shoulder. "Are you ready?"

The fancy tuxedo Elio is wearing, combined with Iris's striking appearance, indicates some fancy birthday party, indeed.

Elio only sighs in response, his shoulders hunched. "Are you happy with me, Iris?"

His voice reeks of sadness. I yearn to spin around and walk to him, to see what is so obviously weighing on his mind, but Iris does no such thing.

"Of course! Why would you ask that?" I answer instead, touching up my braid and makeup one last time.

"All these parties...this noise... We can't get a moment of peace." He wraps his arms around my waist and meets my gaze in the mirror. "A moment alone together."

"You knew you married a spring fling, dearest. I couldn't survive on books, music, and solitude if I tried," I chuckle. A teasing smile glazes my lips as I spin around in his embrace and tighten his black tie. "You're a bit of a bore, you know."

"But you're happy?"

I slap his chest. "Shush. I'm perfectly happy. But there's one thing I've been meaning to ask you."

"What?"

"Can you ask Sarafina to skip it? It's Mother's birthday, and you know how she is... She can't stand the sight of death."

Elio lets go of me, my earlier annoyance reflected in his eyes. "Yet she manages to stand the sight of me."

"You're the king. And my husband. Sara is...depressing."

"A year ago, she was still princess of this castle, Iris. We can't cast her out now, not when she's decided to pledge her life to the realm."

"Fine. I'll tell her myself." I hurry down the staircase and curl my hand around the railing as I spot Sara reading by the window, sprawled over a velvet loveseat in a powdery blue dress.

Byron naps on the windowsill, the Faeling propped on his stomach, his iridescent wings folded over his back. If Sara's pimply face looks barely out of puberty, then Byron's round cheeks and chubby arms have not yet gone through it.

"Sara! There you are," I say.

But the most striking difference about this young Sarafina is her half-buzz cut and the vibrant blue runes carved into her skull. She's a grim reaper, but how? I reel, taken aback by the revelation, feeling disconnected from the scene for a moment.

It's impossible... grim reapers aren't supposed to retire. Once a reaper, always a reaper.

That's how death works.

"My guests are about to arrive," Iris says, her measured voice rising in excitement at the end—or perhaps warning.

Sara snaps her book shut and cradles her sleeping Faeling between her palms. "I get it. I'll make myself scarce."

She blows past me on her way up the stairs, and I stroll outside, where the Winter gardens aren't frozen or cold, but in bloom. The absence of snow between the stone paths reveals an emerald-green carpet interrupted only by cheerful mounds of moss campion with their star-shaped, pink blooms.

In the shade, creeping saxifrage snakes along the walls of the castle and weaves over the cedar hedges of the maze. Tables are set out under the branches of the Hawthorn. The sacred tree is all decked out in spring, clusters of delicate white leaves adorning its branches. Their silvery underside shimmers in the sunshine as though they are inset with diamonds.

Bronze cloths, matching silverware, and white orchids decorate the dozen or so tables, and a couple of servants hurry to get the details of each table right for the celebration.

I blow past them and slip inside the maze, walking around the tight corners like I know exactly where I'm going, and stop only at a dead end.

In the square-shaped clearing, an aspen tree towers above the hedges, the grass directly underneath its canopy overrun by alpine asters and various species of wildflowers.

Almost as soon as I stop walking, a hard hand covers my mouth, my back suddenly pressed against the hard planes of a man's chest.

If I were in charge, I would elbow his groin and spin out of reach, but my heart booms, and Iris relaxes against her captor, seemingly happy to surrender.

"You look glorious in that. Let's see..." The man slips a hand through the slit of the dress and growls as he buries his fingertips inside my flesh. "Good girl. I see you got my message."

"Oh, E... Where have you been?" I purr.

I feel on fire, like my body is going to flake off into ashes if he doesn't touch me right there, and I peer over my shoulder to look at him.

Same cheekbones. Same platinum-blonde hair. But the man snaking a shameless hand between my thighs isn't Elio. A gold-flecked pair of ivory wings are spread on each side of him, his chest bare. "You're hungry for my cock, my wicked weed?"

Iris backs up to grind against his crotch. His isn't the touch of a man feeling up another man's wife for the first time, but of a confident lover who knows exactly what he's doing.

"Yes!"

His hand knows every single button to push, and before long, Iris is panting and grinding against him for more friction.

"Does he make you feel like this?" he growls, picking up the pace until pleasure burns through Iris's body like flames.

"Never."

He spins me around to kiss me, and I've never been more acutely aware of the lines between Iris's body and my own consciousness because my insides curl up and harden in disgust just as Iris melts under the man's touch. Inside, I'm in tatters.

"Get on your knees," Ezra orders.

I want to stop, but I can't. Contrary to Elio's kisses in the other visions, this man's touch doesn't vanquish the hold of the vision. I want to run or leap or cry, but I can't.

I fall to my knees instead, the body I'm currently inhabiting only too happy to obey Ezra's command.

He grips my hair, his other hand busy unfastening the button of his white linen pants. "Good girl. Now suck me off and make me remember why I still fuck you even though you married my brother."

Eager to focus on anything else than what's about to happen, I catch a glimpse of long, aspen catkins tumbling down to the ground and a flutter of iridescent wings...

CHAPTER 32
DARK WHISPERS
LORI

A soft knocking sound wakes me. My eyes snap open, and I sit up on the unfamiliar bed, my spine straight as an arrow. *By the spindle...*

Sara creaks open the door. "Good morning, Lori. I've brought you some fresh clothes."

Blood gathers in my ears and cheeks, and I wonder if I look as guilty as I feel. Maybe it's for the best that Elio didn't spend the night in my bed, after all. I might have blurted out senseless apologies for accidentally dream-fucking his brother. A man I've never even met.

"Are you alright?" Sara asks as she lays down the clothes on the dresser.

Fuck no!

"Yes, of course. Morning," I say instead. The haze of the forbidden sex blazes inside my dumpster-fire brain, my pulse running off in spikes. "I had a terribly...sweaty night."

"You have time for a quick shower before I escort you back to Tundra."

"Tundra? I thought we were supposed to visit Glacier's Edge

next?" I shoot out of bed, but the bedsheet gets caught around my leg, and I untangle myself from the knot of fabric with a wince.

"That's canceled." Sara doesn't elaborate and glares at me instead. "You're all red. Are you sure you're okay?"

"Yes, why wouldn't I be?" I grab the clothes and cower inside the bathroom, slamming the door shut behind me.

The hot shower burns off the leftover bite of shame I carried back into my body with me, and I scrub myself down vigorously. Even though I couldn't control or change anything, I still *felt* it all. The taste of him is still in my mouth, for Morpheus' sake!

I brush my teeth three times and join Sara back inside the bedroom. Since my mask is still safely tucked inside Seth's lockbox, I need a babysitter to travel through the sceawere, but Sara doesn't look in a hurry to leave.

"Mortals and foreigners aren't usually allowed inside the Ice City, so you shouldn't mention your visit," she explains.

My fists curl and uncurl at my sides, adrenaline still sharpening my senses. "Right."

"And the healing springs are a royal secret. Each basin's energy takes years to replenish, so we have to keep them private."

"My lips are sealed," I answer, but inside, I'm eons away, straddling two timelines. Two bodies. Two men.

I can't pretend this isn't happening anymore.

The starkness in Elio's eyes when I asked about Iris last night tied a knot in my belly, and the revelations from my vision only deepened my anguish. Yet, I can't bring myself to believe that Elio killed the woman he loved out of jealousy. There must be another explanation. If his brother Ezra is as wicked as he seems, perhaps he was the one who killed her.

"What is going on with you today?" Sara interrupts my reverie by placing a soft hand on my shoulder. She pauses for a second, perhaps searching for a polite way to describe my erratic behavior. "Did something happen last night?"

"Sara... How did Iris die?" I whisper.

I have to know. I can't go to sleep tonight in fear of reliving every moment of her death—or suffer through another extramarital tryst with her winged fuck boy.

The royal chief of staff tucks her silver hair behind her pointy ears without meeting my gaze. "I can't say. All the facts pertaining to the investigation are confidential—"

"Was it Elio? Or his brother?"

Her face doesn't only fall at that, but becomes all shades of flustered. "His brother?" she squeaks.

"Ezra, the guy who was fucking Iris behind his back," I snap.

"How did you—"

"I *relived* it, Sara. In a multi-sensorial and vivid technicolor vision." I wave my arms at the pile of twisted bedsheets. "So don't give me some bullshit answer about confidentiality or write me off because I'm *just* a foreigner—"

She presses her lips together. "Has this kind of thing happened before?"

"Yes and no. I caught glimpses of Iris's past when I first arrived at court, but this was...all wrong." I suck in air. "So I'm done taking *none of your business* for an answer."

Up until last night, I'd mostly been treating the pageant as a simple exchange of services meant to save Ayaan, but I'm more involved than that now. Way more than I wish I was. No matter how deep I bury my head in the snow, that's not going away. And while I might have conflicting feelings about Elio and our magically engineered *connection*, it doesn't change the fact that me and his dead wife are most certainly linked somehow.

"I saw you, too. In the vision. You were a grim reaper," I murmur, unsure what Sara's reaction will be.

Blood drains from her features. "I was *almost* a reaper."

She sits at the foot of the bed, her white knuckles gripping the edge of the mattress. "Before the end of our training—before taking the eternal vows—we all get one soul to collect. At random. One chance to prove we can cut it. Some of us wait years to be called, and since I was the previous Winter King's daughter, Elio had allowed me to stay and live in my old room in the palace until the gods determined that it was my time to be tested." She screws her lids shut. "What else did you see?"

"I saw you talking with Iris. She was throwing a birthday party for her mother—I think. And you were wearing a blue dress with white ribbons."

She nods, like all of this is making sense to her.

"The very next day, my final trial came. I was called by the gods to collect none other than Iris's soul, but she had always despised me, and her opinion didn't change upon her death, so I failed. Spectacularly."

My eyes bulge. "That's...awful."

A small sniffle escapes her, her story coming in long, tortured rushes. "Many, many other *awful* things happened in the wake of her death. Elio was badly wounded—Iris's mother was wailing and Freya wanted to drill me full of arrows. The other guests only contributed to the general confusion. Iris's soul fled, and the Sun Court refused to do its damn job because of Ezra's sudden disappearance—"

"Ezra disappeared the same day that Iris died?"

A tight grimace overpowers her features. "Yes. Never to be seen again."

Wow. That's a checkmark in the *Ezra did it* column.

"I've relived that day a thousand times in my head... It was all my fault, really." She nods to herself a few times.

That's odd. Is she saying she killed Iris?

"How is it your fault?" I finally ask.

She traces the golden embroideries at the corner of the wrinkled duvet. "That's not important."

A flash of iridescent wings tickles my memory. "Byron saw Iris and Ezra in the gardens the day before she died, didn't he?"

Her eyes widen. "Are you saying Iris knew I was the one who

ratted her out?" she rasps, her voice brittle like I've just punched the air right out of her lungs.

I lick my lips and think about my answer. This is obviously of the utmost importance to Sara and has most likely haunted her for the better part of her life. "I'm not sure. She was otherwise occupied... I don't know if she connected the dots."

Sara wipes her tears and peels herself from the bed. "Anyway... What happened in the past usually stays there for a reason. Our priority should be to discover how you're able to see such things in the first place."

"I've thought about the possibility of reincarnation." I start, watching her face intently. "But reincarnated souls are more of a mortal belief, and even then, they're not supposed to share the same body as the one they had in a previous life. But if Iris's soul was never found—"

"Let me stop you right there. Of the very few lost souls the Sun Court catchers haven't captured, only one in a million is powerful enough to achieve true immortality and take on a new body. And even those who manage it don't change their vessel's outward appearance. You're in the clear, Lori."

Despite her reassurances, I'm not convinced. Iris fled her reaper, and there must be a reason why her soul was never found.

Sara's brows form a line, her eyes wrinkled at the corners as a newfound determination replaces the sadness on her face. "After you showed up, I made inquiries, too. So far, Beth and I only waded through false leads, but this vision confirms that you have a real connection to Iris. The most logical answer would be that you're related to her."

If my visions made something clear, it's that Iris was able to lie.

"She could lie, so she had to be half-mortal. Do you know who her real father was?" I ask.

"No. Freya denied that she wasn't a full-blooded Fae, and her mother refused to answer any of my questions." She rubs her face down with her whole palm before pinching the bridge of her nose.

"Your grandmother was a Spring Fae, was she not? What was her name?"

Names and magic go hand in hand, and sharing a family member's name—even after their death—is frowned upon, so I hesitate. "Yes, she was born in Amaria, on the coast of the Dark Sea. Her name was Riya Anisha Damore."

Sara salutes my confession with a gentle smile. "Thank you. I have just the idea on where to look next."

CHAPTER 33
BITTEN
LORI

"Welcome back," Daisy greets me from her cot. An intricate French braid pulls her long blond hair away from her face, and she's wearing a pink, strapless ballgown. She braces her hands on her hips and scours my body from head to toe. "You don't look quite as beaten up as I expected."

"They have good healers here. I heard I almost didn't make it." My lips twitch. "Happy to see you in one piece, too, partner."

It's easier to act as though I've just woken up from my injuries rather than explain what I've been doing with the Winter King in the Ice City, but it's weird to be back in the Spring dorms.

Daisy's gaze drops to the ground between us. "I saw the tape from the mountains."

"You did? I thought they weren't big on replays around here."

"You risked your life to save me, Lori. Thank you." She looks down her nose at the clothes I borrowed. "You should hurry and change. They're supposed to announce the three finalists in half an hour."

My throat shrinks.

"With only five of us left in the running, it should be quick," Daisy adds.

The tingles at the back of my neck spread to my chest. "Five? I thought only one Red had died?"

"Yes, the quiet one didn't make it, but her companions pulled out of the pageant, leaving you, me, Wendy, and the two other Winter seeds," she explains. "But don't fret. He's all yours."

"Oh?"

She shifts in her seat and adjusts the thick tulle of her crinoline. "After seeing him jump after you inside that avalanche, no one would doubt it. To be honest, I'm looking forward to going home. Maybe with a frost apple, if I'm lucky." She licks her lips. "What about you? Aren't you freaked out that he's going to kill you, too? Or is he that good in bed that you're willing to take your chances?" she says, wiggling her brows.

By the spindle... Am I really going to marry Elio?

I never thought this charade would go as far as that, but with everything that's happened, I'm not sure I can stand the alternative, either.

"Definitely freaked out," I answer under my breath, the weight of it all piling on my shoulders.

Seth enters through the door leading to the dressing room. "Lori, you're back!" He leaves the door ajar as he jogs to my side, his face heavy with relief—and maybe a hint of fear. "I need a word with you."

Daisy rolls her eyes. "Come on, guys. You can trust me. I'm the only Spring seed left, and I already know Lori's a spider."

"I'm sorry, Day. This is need-to-know only."

With a huff, she stomps toward the door leading out to the gardens. "Fine. Be that way."

Seth waits for the door to slam shut with a loud *bang* before he asks, "Where were you? Byron said you were alright, but they wouldn't let me anywhere near you—"

"The Ice City. They plunged me into a healing spring to keep me alive after the avalanche, but it's all a big secret," I whisper.

It's only the two of us, and the big dorms and adjoined dressing room feel so empty compared to how it was at the beginning.

Seth slips a hand inside his white tuxedo's pocket and hands over my mask. "Here. Put this on."

I pause, a nervous hiccup caught in my windpipe. "Where are we going?" I plaster the mask in place over the bridge of my nose, and the familiarity and safety of its size and weight soothes my nerves.

Seth walks to the door Daisy just stormed through and clicks the lock. "Nowhere, but my mother wants to meet you." He moves to close the intimacy drapes framing the windows, and the bright sunshine dims into a pleasant glow.

"Your mother, Freya, the Spring Queen? That mother?"

"It's a pretty common thing to only have one."

I punch his arm. "Why would I ever want to meet your mother? She's going to find out I'm a spider in *seconds*."

Seth looks me up and down with a knowing smile.

"What?" I bark.

"You called yourself a spider."

"And?" I breathe, suddenly engrossed in the small lint pieces floating about the room.

"You've never used the term before. Not since I met you. Are you finally making peace with that scar in your side?" His brows pull together. "Or is it healed?" he extends a hand toward my rib, but I slap his grubby hand away.

"Are you my shrink, now?" I slide out of reach. "Your mother, Seth. Let's talk about that, first."

He holds out his palms in surrender. "She freaked out when she saw you and grilled me with questions. I didn't want her to send her cupids after you, so I had to promise her *something*." He waves dismissively at that, like a promise to the Spring Queen is not at all cause for concern. "Don't worry, we'll tell her your resemblance to Iris is just a freak coincidence—"

"What if it's not?" I deadpan.

He frowns at that, his entire demeanor switching from apologetic to inquisitive in the span of one breath. "What else could it be?"

"I don't know."

I shouldn't spill my secrets just as we're about to face his mother. Seth can't lie, so it's better for him not to know.

"Right. Let's stick with the freak coincidence hypothesis, and whatever you do, do not mention Damian. Or Morrigan. Or my brother. Let *me* speak, really."

"She doesn't know about your brother?"

"She doesn't like to be reminded of my father's *real* family, as she puts it."

My top lip curls in disgust, all the gossip I've heard growing up about the woman in charge of mortals' love lives solidified. "That's horrible."

"Yes, well... That's my mother for you."

"A horrible mother. Is that what I am, Sethanias?" A sultry, amused voice booms from the surface of the mirror, the glass plying to let the Spring Queen through.

Eek. My eyes bulge, and I give Seth a pointed look, quietly mouthing, *"Sethanias?"*

His spine straightens as he offers his mother a sheepish bow. "I'm sorry, Ma'am. I didn't mean—"

"Shush. Didn't I always tell you to own up to your wickedness, my precious weed?" The woman I saw the other day at brunch—and a couple of times in Iris's past—glides over to me, her hand wrapped tightly around a peacock decorative fan.

A striking dress made out of a thousand rose petals gilded in thin sheets of gold hugs her curves. The tall white wig on top of her head and dramatic makeup give her a striking fairytale flair, and I lose my tongue for a moment.

She peels her golden mask away from her eyes, her lips pursed as she examines me.

A lustrous aura of power hovers around her bosomed frame, the Spring Queen made to compel all mortals to kneel at her feet and pledge their lives to her glory. If not for my mask, I would probably do the same.

"Marvelous. Absolutely flawless." She pinches my chin between her index finger and thumb. "What are you, child?"

"I'm Lori."

She flashes me a full row of perfect, straight teeth. "Lori of..."

"Of Chicago."

Seth clears his throat. "She's a spider. I found her and hired her to spy on the Winter King. I couldn't find any familial relation to Iris, so I think her appearance is a freak coincidence."

"Dearest Sethanias...such coincidences don't exist." Freya waves her fan vigorously at her chest. "I knew you'd dug up the girl from some dark hole in the Shadowlands. One look at her was enough for me to know she had more thorns than all the roses in my court combined." She turns her attention back to me. "So, Lori of Chicago. What happened on that mountain? They cut the feeds for minutes only to titillate us with one glimpse of the fleeing rebels..."

"I don't think they stopped the broadcast on purpose," Seth says.

Freya's lips tense, revealing fine lines around her mouth. "Did I give you permission to interrupt?"

The prince's purple gaze flies to the ground. "No, Ma'am."

"I've heard rumors of revolutionists slipping through your father's fingers and infiltrating the other courts, but none that were substantiated until last night..." She taps the tip of her folded fan to her bottom lip in a repetitive motion. "If an all-out war is about to break out, it wouldn't hurt to have eyes and ears in Wintermere."

Seth scoffs. "Lori's not going to marry Elio—"

"Why not? This year's pageant might be the most important since our dear Iris died." Her gaze softens as though she's seeing her niece in my place. "Spider or not, you can't go out there representing Spring in anything but the best."

Freya twirls her decorative fan around, and my clothes unspool like a ball of wool.

A strapless black corset appears around my body, combined with a long white tulle skirt. Studded velvet roses are sewn into the bodice of the corset, and the laced up front smashes my breasts together to create more cleavage than I ever thought I had. A truly original, rock-star-chic confection, polished with shiny leather flats. The shoe's black ribbons wrap around my ankles and make me feel like a naughty ballerina.

If I have to wear a dress, this one isn't half bad.

"Go and claim your prize, mortal. But never forget who put you there." There's no mistaking the clear *you owe me* in Freya's tone.

My very own Scary Godmother.

She secures her mask back on and waltzes out through the mirror.

After her departure, I peel off my own mask and study my reflection. A thick, glossy side ponytail cascades down to my waist, and smoky eyes paired with dark, matte lipstick complete the look. If it weren't for the sapphire mask in my hands, I wouldn't recognize the woman in the mirror. I paw at the unfamiliar contours of the corset.

Seth lets out a low whistle. "Wow. You look gorgeous. Now, we can only hope that icicle selects you to win one of his precious apples, and you can sneak inside his tower after the broadcast to look for clues—"

"Elio isn't in leagues with Morrigan. Her spiders were there on the mountain, but he had no idea. If not for me, Elio would have been killed up there," I blurt out.

"Something's changed..." Seth narrows his eyes at me like he's searching for something, and his jaw slacks. "Have you slept with him?"

"And what if I did?"

He shakes his head, over and over again. "No, Lori. You can't marry him."

A burst of heat engulfs me. "Was I supposed to fall for you in between brides? I've lost count of the girls you've fucked, Seth."

"I—No! Damn you, Lori. We're *friends.*"

I cross my arms over my corset, my legs jittery and restless. "Friends don't throw jealous fits and judge each other for who they sleep with."

"I'm scared *for you.*"

"Elio doesn't kill his brides. It's a curse..." I rationalize, but a small voice—perhaps the same voice who always pleaded with me never to stand out—agrees with him.

Seth holds out both arms in front of him in unequivocal dissent. "You've known him for what? Six days? That's not enough history to risk your life, even if you think he's innocent."

Has it really only been six days? *By Morpheus...* What if some magic is speaking here, and not me? I haven't worn my mask the last few days. Maybe the glitz and glamour of the Winter Court have drilled so deeply into my mortal brain that I can no longer tell death from candy.

"Morrigan's spiders guarded the entrance to the mines, so whoever the Gray Man is, he's in leagues with her. They're the bad guys—not Elio."

I might not be sure about the source of my feelings for him, but I'm sure of that.

"The Gray Man?"

"I think he's the one leading the Tidecallers," I say.

I quickly explain what happened on the mountains beyond what has been broadcasted, but Seth's expression remains unmoved.

"Damian will kill me if I let you do this—" he starts.

"I'm a grown woman. I can make my own decisions, and I've done my part." My heart beats in my throat as I roll my shoulders back. "The winter solstice is tomorrow. You need to make good on your promise."

Seth presses his lips together in a thin line. "A deal is a deal, of course. But I still think you're making a mistake."

A rapid succession of knocks interrupts our conversation, and Seth walks over to unlock the door while I hide my mask behind the skirt of my dress.

Byron's wings flap as he hovers in mid-air on the other side of the door with his trusty clipboard in hand. "Don't dawdle. The broadcast will commence in ten minutes. I need you two in the ball-room *now*."

CHAPTER 34
AND THE WINNER IS...
LORI

The ballroom has been rearranged to sit a few hundred courtiers, with an elevated stage set up in front of the frosted floor-to-ceiling windows. I recognize a few faces in the first row, mainly the other sponsors.

Anticipation rumbles through the audience at our arrival. A handful of cameras hover over the public, most of them glaring at the hosts. Sara and Paul sit in a pair of teal velvet armchairs, three empty seats lined up next to them.

Seth zooms across the room to rejoin his colleagues while Byron escorts Daisy and me to the side of the stage where the Winter brides are waiting. I haven't seen them since they left us to freeze on the mountains, and my nails dig into my palms.

"Look who finally decided to grace us with her presence," one of them grunts.

Wendy shoots me a glance that spells out exactly how disappointed she is to see me alive. The off-the-shoulder neckline of her dress highlights her smooth, pale skin, and her dark hair has been styled in an elaborate updo.

"The brides are here," Sara announces, drawing our focus back to the stage. She retrieves three small envelopes from the inside pocket of her glittering white jacket. "Since the last challenge was cut short, I now hold the names of the three finalists personally selected by our king."

Paul leans forward, his hands fanning in front of him in a show of machiavellian excitement. Despite his gray hair looking flat and oily, his black suit and matching bow tie lend him a more polished appearance than his usual white tuxedo. "Shall we invite them on stage, Sara?"

"Yes." Sara tears open the first paper envelope, and her voice trembles as she enunciates, "Daisy Sinclair."

The crowd claps. A full-bodied gasp erupts from Daisy, momentarily freezing her in place. She quickly regains her composure, striding forward with a blazing smile on her red-painted lips. She climbs the three little steps to meet Paul, who hands her a single blue rose, pecks her cheeks, and gestures for her to take one of the three empty seats.

Sara tears open the seal of the second envelope. "Wendy Frost."

A dozen High Fae rise to cheer her on, and I suppress the urge to roll my eyes.

Sara opens the third envelope and holds it over her chest. "And last but not least, Lori Lovegood," she announces quietly.

My shoulders sag in a mix of worry and relief. For a moment there, I was almost certain she wouldn't call my name.

I walk onto the stage amidst deafening applause. Paul hands me a blue rose and plants a peck on my cheeks as well, before I take my place between Daisy and Wendy.

Sara moves to shake our hands. "Congratulations," she says quickly, her hand clammy in my grip. "And good luck."

Her fake smile sends a chill down my spine as I lean in. "Is everything okay?"

She averts her gaze and offers Wendy the same lackluster words of encouragement before hurrying offstage. A molten heat pools in my gut. Something's wrong.

I scour the room, but between the cameras, the quiet gardens beyond the windows, and the eager spectators, there's no hint of trouble.

"How does it feel to know, one way or another, you're going to receive a frost apple?" Paul asks. "Let's start with you, Daisy."

Tears glaze over her eyes as she opens her mouth and swallows hard. "I can't find the words, Paul."

I play absent-mindedly with the long-stemmed blue rose and accidentally prick my finger on its thorns.

"What about you, Wendy? You're already immortal, and many of our viewers want to know exactly why you joined the pageant. As you know, you're the first Fae to do so in decades."

Wendy offers him a wide, beauty-queen smile. "I just thought Winter Fae shouldn't hide from their birthright, Paul."

"Is that the whole truth, though?" Paul motions to the empty wall behind him. "Let's take a look at some footage we recovered from the mountains. There's no audio, but I think the images tell a clear story."

A projector sparks to life. The zoomed clip shows Wendy by the entrance of the mine, helping one of the Tidecallers secure the last of his cargo. The two of them share a quick hug before he flees, and Wendy lies back next to the other unconscious girls on the floor of the mine.

"Wait! It's not—I didn't—" Wendy stammers, her knuckles white over the armrests.

Paul shakes his head with a reproachful scowl. "Guards, please escort Miss Frost to a holding cell."

While the cameras capture every moment of Wendy's arrest, a stage technician removes her chair.

Daisy grips my hand. "I knew it," she whispers only for my benefit.

I draw in a deep breath, vindicated that Wendy was working for the enemy, but I'm not sure what role she was supposed to play, or why she looked so disappointed to see me earlier if her mission had already failed.

"A formal investigation will determine the extent of Wendy Frost's involvement with the revolutionist group known as the Tide-callers." Paul turns to the side camera. "But first, let's welcome the Winter King to the stage."

My spine stiffens, and I grip the rose tighter. Elio climbs the stairs two at a time and sits on the other side of Paul, his chair brightening from dark teal to a soft blue as it ices over.

I try to cross his gaze, but he's pointedly not looking in my direction, focused on Paul as he unbuttons his jacket. Adrenaline rushes in my veins, the poise and nonchalance of the Winter King making me doubt he's the same Elio I've come to know.

"My king, can I ask you a few questions?" Paul asks with a sheepish grimace.

"Fire away, Paul. It's important to be transparent. Now more than ever."

Paul nods several times, his rehearsed, conspiratorial grin sending shivers down my spine. "In the spirit of transparency, let me show you the rest of the footage we recovered."

Elio opens and closes his mouth, his frustration evident. After a deep breath, he grits his teeth and gives a reluctant incline of the head. "Alright."

"Here."

Sharp whispers erupt from the crowd. Paul seems to be going off script, and my heart hammers in my throat as another clip lights up the wall behind us. I see myself trying to help Elio to his feet before he points an ice shiv at my neck, and the image freezes.

"Let's pause here." Paul licks his lips, drawing out the suspense to rile up the audience. "If I may ask, what happened right before this? You were bleeding?"

"The apparent leader of the Tidecallers tried to kill me, but Lori stabbed him, and he vanished," Elio explains.

Inaudible conversations rise from the sea of courtiers, the High Fae now gossiping openly among themselves.

"Had Tidecallers been spotted in Wintermere before this?" Paul asks.

Elio gives a decisive slice of the head. "Never. The only knowledge I had of them before facing them on the mountain came from history books and the scary Faen tales I heard around the campfire growing up."

The language used leaves no room for interpretation. Fae can't lie, so this serves as both the pageant's finalist round and a political inquiry. Everyone watching from home will know that the Winter King isn't in leagues with the rebels crawling about his glacier.

Paul nods emphatically. "And what were they after?"

"Power. They carved out scales from one of Wintermere's sacred dragons and stole precious jewels from the mines. They tried to abduct the brides—most likely to harvest their magic, too." Elio pauses and looks straight at the cameras before adding, "While most of the rebels were found dead after the avalanche, I want to send a clear message that any individual found to have participated in this attack—whether within this court or not—will be severely punished."

He's in on Paul's televised stunt after all.

Paul inches forward in his seat, his linked hands braced over his knee. "You look angry with Lori here. Was she involved in the attack?"

"No."

The projection resumes, showing Elio with a bloody lip and me in my white silk dress as we argue, before he kisses the life out of me...

The crowd goes wild for it. Our gazes meet across the stage for a split second, and my chest heaves, the rush of heat between my breasts almost too intense for me to bear.

Paul chuckles as the clip ends. "You two certainly have sizzling chemistry, but what our viewers want to know is how Lori Lovegood ended up hanging upside down from that sleigh. Let's hear from her, shall we?" He shifts in his chair to face me. "Lori, why did you risk it all? Why didn't you stay on the dragon's back?"

I suck in air. "I—I just couldn't let him fall."

Heartfelt *awws* and soft applause echo across the audience.

I need Elio to hold my gaze so I can vanquish the unease in my belly. I want the crowd to disappear so it can be just us. A fluttering sensation scatters across my chest. I want to spend the night in his arms. And make him laugh. I want to marry him so we can break his curse—together.

Maybe Seth is right, and I've actually lost my mind.

Paul jolts me out of my epiphany. "I can't begin to grasp the athletics necessary to slide down that chain and tilt upside down like that. You must be in very good shape."

My eyes narrow. I don't like his congenial tone one bit, and he seems to want to make some kind of point with it. "I am."

"Some have said that a mortal would need magic to achieve such a feat." Paul's eyes dance. "Are they wrong?"

"Err—"

Paul angles himself to the crowd and cameras and serves the viewers an exaggerated sigh. "I think it's obvious to everyone here that Lori isn't the Spring seed she pretends to be. After her truly impressive stunt—after she saved our king—it pains me to acknowledge it, but the rules of the pageant are all too clear. The brides that participate in the Yule pageant must come from the first kingdoms. Isn't that right, Your Majesty?"

"Yes," Elio croaks.

My heart shrivels at the disingenuity of the exchange. Paul's speech. Elio's answer. It's all *staged*.

The host tips his head forward for a moment, his shoulders hunched in defeat. "It's a pity, but the brave woman we've come to love isn't eligible to win, and is, as of this moment, disqualified." He draws in a deep breath, letting the news sink in, waiting for the crowd to settle down before he nails the punchline. "Which means Daisy Sinclair will be our new queen."

Sara strolls back on stage with a bushel of blue roses, and fucking confetti rains from the ceiling. "Congratulations, Daisy."

The lens of the closest camera zooms in on my face, and I squint at it, only vaguely aware of the unhappy chatter in the audience.

"The wedding will take place tonight, so the sacred rites of the solstice can be celebrated by the king—and our new queen—at the stroke of midnight," Paul announces. He turns to Daisy with a questioning smile. "How are you feeling, Daisy?"

Sara scurries over to me in the guise of shaking the loser's hand. "Let's talk after this."

A cruel snigger bubbles out of my mouth. I watch, petrified, as Elio grabs Daisy's hand and pecks her lips, my Spring friend pale as snow, her heart probably about to shrivel and die, too.

Oxygen is sparse as I tear every ounce of shadows from the stage to shield myself from the pity glances of the crowd and the vicious intrusion of the cameras. I take it all. The shade under the chairs, the gloom between the velvet cushions—even the darkness draped over Elio's face.

And I run.

CHAPTER 35
PIANO MAN
ELIO

The familiar glide of the piano notes under my fingertips leaves me hollow, and the flawless melody only exacerbates the dissonant agony at the pit of my stomach. After the announcement, Lori ran out of the ballroom cloaked in shadows so thick, I couldn't track her.

She left without saying goodbye.

My lovely spider. My pyre of hopes.

Given the circumstances, I thought she'd be relieved not to have to go through with a sham wedding.

The discreet creak of the hinges grates my raw nerves, but I let out a sigh of relief as I stop playing. The sensual bite of Lori's shadow magic sweeps across the secluded tower. She couldn't leave without seeing me after all. Judging by her expression back on that stage, she probably came to curse me to the seven hells, but it's better than nothing.

"I can hear you, little spider," I croak. Shame and guilt are like ashes in my mouth, breaking down the words.

Before I can move, the sharp tip of a dark, murky dagger presses into my neck. Dark tendrils slither within the confines of the blade, and I hold up both hands in surrender. Lori grips the hilt of her weapon, poised to sever my carotid if I dare to move.

I lick my lips and choose my next words carefully. "I thought you didn't want to kill me."

A snarl rushes down the slope of my neck. "I changed my mind."

My lids flutter shut, the heat of her body pressed against my bare back draining the fight right out of me. The scent of fresh rain and burnt embers wraps me up in a cocoon of regrets, and I angle my neck to the side to give her better access. "Do it. Take your best shot."

Her blade draws back an inch. I seize the opportunity, gripping her wrist and twisting around to face her as I stand. She's absolutely stunning in her black and white dress. The front of her corset reveals the shape of her breasts, and the tulle skirt is torn off at the hem, the fabric barely licking the ground.

The piano bench creates an awkward barrier between us as I press the tip of her dagger right over my heart. "I'd love nothing more than to perish in your arms."

She chokes on a quiet, heart-wrenching sob. "Did you know? Did you know Paul was going to disqualify me like that, in front of everyone?"

"Yes. It was my idea," I admit with a defeated tilt of the head. "I have to marry Daisy tonight, or the whole realm will fall apart."

Tears fill the cracks of anger in her voice. "Why? Why is getting married so damn important in this wretched kingdom, when every other Fae royal is free to remain single?"

"The gods gave Winter more power than the other kingdoms. It was needed to preserve the safety of the souls we collect, but it came at a price. So much magic, yielded by only one person, threatened the balance. Thanatos made it so the burden of replenishing the glacier's magic on the solstice always had to be shared. Both king and queen must allow passage to the souls that were collected during the year to the afterlife, or all of Faerie's magic might wither. Winter destroys one, but spares two."

She lowers her weapon, the blade flaking off into the ether. "Why not marry me, then?"

By the spindle...

My breath hitches, my jaw slightly open, but the fleeting spark blazing through my chest is quickly snuffed out by a cold, endless void. "I could never marry you. If I marry you, you'll die." I wrap a hand around her neck and bend down to kiss her, ravenous for one last chance to hold her.

One last taste of life.

She flattens her palms to my chest to stop me. "Every curse has a loophole. We could figure it out together."

"I couldn't take that chance with you."

The fire in her eyes returns full-force. "So you'll marry and kill Daisy instead? How is that fair?"

I caress the back of her ear with my thumb. "I want you to *live*, Lori. To be happy."

"Without you, you mean."

I hold her burning gaze, desperate for her to understand. "That's the only option. The Gray Man might have retreated the other day, but the Tidecallers aren't finished with me. If rebels and thieves were able to hide their presence in Wintermere for so long, they must have found a way to replicate outlawed Mist Fae technology and used it to steal an immense amount of magic. War is coming. Every Fae—royal or not—is in danger now."

"Is that why you think they tried to kill you? To suck out your magic?" she asks, tracing my features like she wants to draw them from memory later on.

I link our fingers and kiss her knuckles, walking around the piano bench to snake my other hand around her waist and hold her close. "I suspect that, if the Gray Man had succeeded in striking me down, he would have used my powers to take my place. Wendy already admitted that she was meant to win the Yule pageant so she could help him steal the souls."

"What do you mean by *taken your place*?"

"Controlling the light doesn't just allow me to become invisible." A stone sinks in my stomach as I adjust the million tiny scales of light magic covering my skin, tweaking them until the illusion I want to project is damn-near perfect.

I haven't used this particular power in fifty years, the repulsive subterfuge bringing bile to my mouth.

Lori gapes, her jaw slack as she tenses in my arms. The woman I'm projecting back to her is an almost perfect copy of herself but for the cold glint in her gaze.

"You can imitate anyone?"

"For it to look convincing, I have to know the person very well and move like they would, but yes. The voice is a different story, but a simple spell could bridge the gap," I explain before the illusion falters.

She molds her body to mine. "But the Gray Man doesn't know you."

"He must have watched the pageant to learn my mannerism, and while that might not be enough to fool the gods, it'd be enough to seize control of the realm for a few days. The souls are only accessible for one night a year, during the solstice ritual. It's the most potent well of magic in all the worlds. A jewel forged out of a hundred million souls would allow its wearer to obliterate all the Fae kingdoms' armies combined."

"Whether you marry me or not, I'm a Shadow huntress. I won't cower and hide in the new world. If a war is coming, I'll be ready." She stands on her tiptoes to kiss me, the invisible threads tying us together stronger than ever.

I shiver all over, addicted to the rush, and graze the length of her spine before slipping my fingers below the boning of her corset.

"Wait." She tears herself away, panting hard.

A heavy lump pulses in my throat as she flees from my grasp, and the sight of her standing by the window makes me quake with fear.

"How long were you and Iris married?" she asks.

"A little more than a year."

Her clear gray eyes widen, and I can tell it's not the figure she expected.

"Believe me, it felt a lot longer. My longest marriage to date," I chuckle darkly. "The poems I wrote after her death—those that Paul cherry-picked and published without my consent in a concerted effort to rehabilitate my reputation—sparked countless tales of sorrow and undying love. His efforts portrayed our marriage as tragic and romantic, ignoring how short and wretched it truly was." I tuck my hands in my pockets and look around the room. "No one but me has stepped foot in this room in fifty years..."

Has it always been this small?

Lori glances at the bed with her bottom lip tucked between her teeth. "I shouldn't be in here." She moves to leave, but I sweep her up in my arms.

"No, I hate this...shrine. I hate this bed. And those candles. I hate that it's all still here, untouched. Let's desecrate it together." I set her down on the piano.

The keys sink under her weight in a jarring cacophony as she spreads her legs and grabs a fist of my shirt, tugging me closer. "You only want me because I look like your dead wife. That's fucked up."

I bury my smile in her wavy hair. "If I'm so bad, why do you keep coming back?"

Every time we do this, she takes more and more of me. She thinks I only like her because of her resemblance to Iris, but that's actually what I hate most about her.

She fiddles with her fingers, suddenly absorbed by the shape of her thumb. "I thought—I figured that *maybe*, I could be Iris's lost soul."

"You're nothing like her."

She clicks her tongue in a chiding fashion. "Come on. I'm *exactly* like her."

I press my hand to her heart. "Not in here."

She doesn't meet my gaze, her eyes unfocused as though she's lost within herself, and the corners of her mouth curl up in a sad smile. "So it's only my body that's appealing to you. I get it."

"That's the opposite of what I said. Iris never cared about anything as fiercely as you do. She certainly never cared about me..." I cup her face and force her to look at me. "How do you feel when you're with me, Lori?"

Tears roll down her cheeks. "When I'm with you, I feel more alive than I ever did."

"I feel the same way." I kiss the salty tears off her smooth brown skin.

My heart feels like it's about to burst as I slide a hand down to the hollow of her neck. Her breasts strain against her studded corset with each labored breath, and I pinch the black bow holding it in place between my index finger and thumb.

A hiccup quakes her throat—almost a sob. "Please, I can't do this again."

"Do what? Endure all this pleasure I'm giving you?"

"Suffer the cold, empty loneliness that follows," she says, her voice more brittle and vulnerable than I've ever heard it.

"Spend the day with me. *Please*," I beg, the selfish impulse to keep her by my side eroding my resolve.

She plays with the lapels of my jacket, shaking her head. "One day...is not enough."

Despite her answer, she buries her hands in my hair and kisses me as though I'm the only oxygen in the room.

There's no hope for us, but she fits so perfectly in my arms, I could almost be convinced otherwise. I unfasten the knot holding the black ribbon in place and carefully unlace her corset, one criss-cross at a time.

She explores the lines of my shoulders with her hands, stroking the skin back and forth. "No more ice freckles?"

"You licked them all off."

"Well...yeah."

A full-bodied shiver rocks her from head to toe as I peel the corset from her frame and discard it to the side. I capture her breasts in my palms, testing their shape and weight until she writhes against me, her head falling back on a soft moan.

I move to kneel down, kissing my way down the valley between her breasts to her stomach, ready to tear what's left of her skirt off and make her come with my mouth again.

The sight of her blackened scab stops me cold, and I stand back up again. My heart gives a violent squeeze as I grip her waist, suddenly way more preoccupied by her health than her body. "Lori... I've got to get you that frost apple."

Her brows pull together in a frown, and she traces the shape of the inflamed scar with trembling fingers. "Weird. It was fine before."

Serpentine lines have spread from the M-shaped scar, the venom slowly spreading to the adjacent tissue

"Elio! Elio, are you up there?" Sara shouts. Her voice grows louder and louder as two sets of steps echo up the stairwell. She reaches the top of the stairs and stops herself short of entering the room, her arms braced on each side of the doorway. "Elio, we have to find Lori—"

I cover Lori with my body to shield her from Beth and Sara's noisy interruption, and glare at the last two friends I have in the world, ready to curse them to the seven hells for their constant meddling.

I bite back a scalding "fuck off" and settle for a grumpy eye roll instead.

Beth serves me a wry, knowing smile as she slips under Sara's outstretched arm. "Never mind. I found her."

CHAPTER 36

POISON APPLE

LORI

Sara shifts her weight from one foot to the other as she waits for me to button up the shirt Elio handed me after they interrupted our last—or should I say most recent—lapse in judgment.

"All clear," I call out, my heart beating in my throat at how relieved and excited she sounds.

"We found your grandmother's name in the castle's ledger. You and Iris aren't related like we thought. Your grandmother was working as a maid for the Spring Court during those years. She was part of the staff Freya brought along with her to Iris's birthday party."

"She was the one who washed off Iris's blood from the pavement," Beth adds quickly.

"She was pregnant at the time. With your mother, I figure. She reported that"—Sara opens the old ledger—"all the blood disappeared with a single swipe. It really freaked her out."

Elio steals the book from her hands and leafs through a few pages. "Why did no one tell me?"

Sara crosses her arms. "Tell you what? That the cleaning lady had a vivid imagination? Your wife had just died. They thought Lori's grandmother was either looking for attention or crazy and dismissed her."

"But they still made a note of it."

"Clearly, her direct superior believed her, but not enough to stick out his neck. He must have thought it wasn't worth mentioning. Nobody could've imagined this," Beth says in a pacifying tone.

"Magic sparked off in many dangerous currents that day, and blood magic is known to mess with cells and DNA. Iris's blood must have altered your mother's eggs as they formed in the womb. The more powerful the curse, the thinner the thread...but it's you, Lori." Sara takes a meaningful pause, her eyes glossing over as her high-pitched voice fills with hope. "You're the loose thread."

Beth pries the ledger from Elio's grasp with a smile. "She must be the only person who can cheat your curse."

My gaze bounces from Sara to Elio. "The curse that condemns all your wives to die?" I try to clarify.

Sara frowns. "That's not—"

Elio snaps back to reality, and the dark, guarded glint in his eyes sends a tingle of warning up my spine. "Shush. Give us a moment."

He walks to the coat rack and holds out his fancy wool jacket for me to slip on. I tie the sash around my frame. The oversized coat falls below my knees, and Elio guides me down the stairs. We exit the tower through the hidden door leading to the gardens, barefoot in the snow, his magic keeping us from freezing.

A heavy breath frosts in front of him as he glances up at the crooked branches of the Hawthorn. Moonlight reflects off his bare chest, licking the curves of his muscles.

I scurry behind Elio, the fresh snow sinking under my footsteps. His gaze darts to Iris's glass coffin before he extends an arm to the tree above.

The stem of a ripe frost apple ices over and detaches from the closest branch, falling straight into his hand. Shadows drape over his face as he extends the rare, precious fruit in my direction. "Here."

I shake my head. "Your curse made me look just like Iris for a reason. I will help you unravel it."

He walks over to me and tucks the frost apple in my hand. "I think the curse made you to punish me. To remind me that, no matter how many women I marry to appease the Gods—no matter how many of them I lose—my worst mistake will haunt me for all eternity." Elio guides my other hand over the shiny blue apple and presses my fingers closed around the sacred fruit. "Forget about me, little spider. Take the apple, heal yourself, and go live a long, happy life—away from the ice."

My chest shrinks, the single most coveted treasure in Faerie heavy in my grip. "You don't even want to try and break the curse?"

Elio presses his lips together. His fists curl and uncurl at his sides before the Winter King stands an inch taller. All the warmth drains from his cold, sharp features until he no longer looks like a man— but a cruel, impatient reaper. "You think I haven't tried? You think I just checked out at the first sign of trouble and let those girls die on my watch?"

"Of course not!"

"Olena died first. She was a Red with advanced weapon training, and when she stabbed herself to escape my company, I figured maybe it was my fault. Maybe I was indeed too cold for any woman to endure my presence. The next year, Deirdre started talking to herself as she wandered off on long walks to alleviate the homesick-ness. She fell straight through the ice of the lake and drowned even though it was twenty inches thick. That's when I knew winter would claim them all, no matter what. I spent the next two decades after that in a constant state of panic, following them around from dawn to dusk to catch whatever dark force was after them, but the more I tried to help, the more resources I dedicated to their safety—the quicker they died. One after the other, for *fifty* years. So don't you dare—"

His chest rises and falls, his fury burning out like a falling star. "The curse only prevents me from *loving* them. It shouldn't *kill* them, but ice breaks them because that's what ice does." He gazes off into the distance. "Why did you really come here, Lori?" he asks quietly.

My forehead creases. "I told you. I came to find Morrigan."

"You're lying." His hollow smile grates my insides, the walls around his heart thickening by the second. "And that's okay. Why not lie when you know you can get away with it? Given the opportunity, I'd probably do it, too." Elio's bitter, melodic chuckle sparks a fire in my stomach. "I know all about secrets, believe me. I've been keeping one for decades."

"I came to save my brother," I admit, the words flying out without nuance or pause, my soul a little lighter for it. "He's been rotting in a Spring prison for months, and Seth promised to save him from being hanged if I joined the pageant."

Elio's next line dies on his parted lips, and his anger evaporates. His blue gaze slips to the side, as if searching for the right words—perhaps summoning the courage to speak them.

"To answer your previous question, I did it. I killed Iris."

My mouth opens and closes, my mind silently praying for context. An explanation. A reason. Anything to soften the blow of the revelation.

The frozen glint in his eyes and the dire clench of his jaw don't offer any mitigating circumstance. "You've done a great job of running from death all your life, and I'm going to beg you to do the same now. I'd give anything to rewrite the past, but I don't deserve a second chance. I killed Iris, and if you stay, my ice will kill you, too. Do you understand?"

I nod once. Twice.

My silly fantasies crumble to ashes.

I've made my bed where Elio's concerned. Allowed him to skew my emotions and let myself forget who he was.

I've always known he was the King of Death.

CHAPTER 37
ELORI
LORI

Ink glimmers over the skin of my lower arm, the Fae runes meant to take me home a little blotchy because of my shaky hands. My mask is firmly planted over my eyes and prevents me from wiping off the cluster of dried, salty tears stuck in my eyelashes.

The frosty sting of the sceawere barely registers as I step out of the mirror. My entire body is numb after my conversation with Elio. The secret, half-formed hopes I'd begun to nurture are gone, and the hole left in their place created a raw ache in my ribcage.

The bite in my side sends a fresh flare of pain through my body as I walk to the desk in the middle of the Shadow Court's library.

This is where I belong, I tell myself, but the beauty of yellow, red, and teal hues streaming through the stained medallion window pales in comparison to the glittering lights of the ice gardens. The prospect of advising the High Fae on their next read and enduring their relentless gossip dulls my brain.

The only silver lining to my defeat is that I'll see Nell again, but I'm not ready to face my best friend. I not only failed to capture the wicked woman who almost killed us both, but also lost myself in the process.

The apple in my pocket could heal the venom that has been polluting my body, and yet I have no real intention to eat it. Blood fills my ears as her familiar head of white-blonde hair peers between the stacks.

"Lori! You're home!"

By Morpheus...

Nell is wearing her Shadow huntress uniform—a form-fitting black jacket and pants with knee-high boots, identical to what I'm wearing—but an entirely new aura of darkness slithers around her.

"You're..." I kneel in front of her out of instinct, the magic inside me bowing to the power that now drums in her veins. "My Queen."

"What are you— Get up!" Her entire face flushes with a deep shade of red at my allegiant impulse.

I chuckle and pull her into a hug. "Enjoy it, Old World. Royalty suits you. Truly."

"Oh, Lori! What are you doing here?" Cece shouts from the second floor. The Lil' Bit descends the stairs two at a time and races across the room to join the huddle, her long brown mane flying behind her.

But instead of celebrating my return, she pinches my arm. "Don't tell me you accepted this ridiculous disqualification—"

I shake off the sting of pain. "Erm... What?"

"Marrying Daisy is the worst idea in history. You could see on his face that he didn't want to do it," Cece says with a scowl. "I still can't believe Wendy was a spy. I bet she's the one who tried to drown you."

My eyes bulge, Cece's nails now digging deep into the flesh of my arm. "Wait..." I look between the two women. "Have you been watching the pageant?"

"Of course! Nell was on the fence for a while, but I've been rooting for Elori since day one," Cece declares.

"Elori?"

Her hazelnut eyes sparkle. "It's your couple name."

"My what?"

Nell's lips twist in a sheepish grin, like we're not having the weirdest conversation in the history of time. "Royals are allowed to watch the feeds, and even though no one knows about me, yet, I asked Baka to install a television in Damian's room—my room. I can't believe you've been watching television your whole life, it's absolutely enchanting!"

"You've been watching the pageant," I repeat, flabbergasted. I'd rehearsed a half-assed explanation on my way back, expecting to give Nell and Cece the cliff notes of what had happened back in Wintermere, but I *never* expected this.

Cece boosts herself up on the desk, her legs dangling from the edge. "Is Elio as gorgeous in person? What did it feel like to kiss him like that? What happened between you two off screen?"

"Cece! Give the woman some space." Nell scolds her sister with a *take it down a notch* motion.

"I—I need to lie down," I say, moving to the back of the room and settling into Nell's usual reading nook. My friend follows at a distance. "So... you've seen it all."

"All that was broadcasted."

I stare at the ceiling for a moment, hands braced over my stomach. "The dunk tank?"

"Yes."

"The kiss?"

"That, too."

"The kiss was the best part!" Cece chimes from afar.

I sit up with wide eyes. "You should know I had no idea I was wearing Iris's actual wedding dress at the ball."

"That's what we thought." Nell grips my hand. "Oh, Lori, I'm so glad to see you in person. When the feeds cut after you disappeared in the avalanche, I sent Damian to Wintermere, but Sarafina assured him that you were okay. How is the bite? Has it finished healing?"

Her healer gaze falls to my side, and the knee-jerk reaction to lie and ease her worries grips me. "Yes. All better now."

"What about Elio? Is he really going to marry someone else?"

"Yeah…"

"And is that…what you wanted?"

I press a pillow over my face for a long minute before a squeaky, "No," whistles out.

Nell peels the pillow away from my flustered face. "Crops! Cece was right! You're in love with him."

"Told you so!" Cece beams as she joins us in the secluded hideout.

My arms slice through the air in an emphatic gesture of denial. "No nononono. No!"

Nell gives me one of her most patient smiles. "Lori… I've never seen that look on your face."

I jolt to my feet and run away from her laser-like gaze, the Shadow Queen clearly using some dark mojo to pry the truth out of me. "No! That ice prick chose to marry someone else. As far as I'm concerned, he can choke on his damn curse and bring his entire kingdom down with him."

Cece tilts her chin up, giving me her best haughty princess glare. "He chose someone else *to protect you*."

"How do you know?"

"His wives all die before spring, right? It makes sense," she huffs.

"How does any of it make sense? How do you know he doesn't just kill his wives?"

Cece shakes her head like she finds me irritating and unreasonable. "Why would he willingly put himself through this every year? Nell and I figured he was cursed or something."

I raise a brow at her sister.

Nell's chest heaves in commiseration. "Moody, tortured kings can be incredibly stubborn. And stupid."

"Yeah, they are," I grumble.

The new Shadow Queen takes a measured pause. "The only real question is... Are you willing to fight for him?"

My mind reels at the implications. "Aren't you going to say I'm insane for falling for a man I've known for only a few days? That maybe I've been hit by a love arrow or a spell that stole my good judgment?

Her face crumples into a million lines. "Were you?"

"Not that I know of, but this conversation"—I gesture back and forth between the three of us—"is *crazy*. You're supposed to tell me to be careful and think this through. Talk me down from the ledge."

She holds up her hand in a halting motion. "Don't bother with what anyone else thinks. Trust your gut. What does it tell you?"

I grit my teeth together. "Nell!"

"Lori!" She imitates my angry voice and holds my gaze, her lips pressed together to suppress a laugh.

"Fuck-fuck-fuck!" I rake my fingers through my hair. "What am I supposed to do? Rush over there and *beg* him to marry me?"

"Maybe."

"He was so adamant that I should try and be happy without him. That all the Fae royals were in danger because of this coming war..."

A flash of worry shines in Nell's gaze. "Damian has been extra-broody since he learned about the Tidecallers. I bet that he would have sent me away, too, if we weren't already married," she grumbles.

"The man I stabbed—I call him the Gray Man—he wants Elio's magic."

The air inside the library suddenly booms with power, and the shadows around Nell skitter along her skin, the dark tendrils vibrating with excitement. I stretch my neck to glance past the corner of the stacks in time to spot Damian marching toward us with his long bow propped at his back.

The magic he collected during his latest hunt still pulses through his body. "Lori. You're back."

"Hey, boss..." I greet him. "What happens when a Fae king dies?"

The Shadow King places his weapon on the nearest table and walks over to kiss his wife. "When a King or Queen passes on, their crown—the magic that allowed them to rule—returns to the Hawthorn. I'm speaking only of a true ruler of Faerie, not their spouses. Spouses merely share in the magic; it doesn't belong to them." He glances at Nell for a moment. "A consort loses their powers once the true king or queen dies."

I nod, already aware of that asterisk. "And what would have happened, specifically, if Elio had died so close to the solstice?"

"A successor would have been marked by the gods as their preferred candidate to take his place. Each god is different, but Morpheus and Thanatos are actually more similar than not in this respect. They mostly care about raw power and strength of character when choosing their next heirs, so they're not easily swayed by bloodlines or politics."

Nell wrinkles her nose. "So the gods get to choose the next king or queen?"

"I'm not done. After the chosen of the gods is marked upon a monarch's death, he must drink from the Eternal Chalice to be anointed. If the other royals refuse him access to the Chalice and question his legitimacy, challengers have ten days to vie for the crown—typically engaging in a fight to the death or some other ridiculously violent task—and the winner of that challenge is crowned king."

"Or queen," Nell corrects him, and Damian nods in assent.

"Is that what happened with you? Did you challenge the chosen heir?" I ask.

Damian skims the tattoos snaking behind his ear. "Actually, I was the one who got challenged."

Nell caresses his upper arm in a soothing motion. "So it's not as easy as killing a king to steal his crown?"

"Most royals pretend that they want to uphold the will of the gods, but kingdoms can be stolen. A monarch deemed too weak to ensure his kingdom's safety or too dangerous to remain in power can be dethroned by the others. If a pretender is strong enough to kill a king *after* he's anointed, he's often perceived as worthy to succeed him. If Elio had died so close to the solstice, they would either have had to rush the challenge period or accept his heir apparent without questions, so replacing him would have been messy, to say the least."

I give them a quick recount of my encounter with the Gray Man and explain how he might have used Elio's magic to fool the public and taken his place upon the Winter throne.

"If the Gray Man wanted to take Elio's place, he never intended to become king. He merely wanted the souls to amplify his magic, and the aborted winter solstice ritual would have plunged the continent into chaos. But if he is as formidable as you say, he's not going to give up—" Damian's eyes darken. "We have a visitor." He slips out of the library's front door and returns a minute later with Seth in tow.

My mouth dries up. "Seth..."

After the terrible way the broadcast ended, I couldn't bear to face him.

"Looking good, Nell," Seth greets the Shadow Queen before his gaze finds me. "Lori... I managed for your brother's sentence to be reduced to life imprisonment. It's the best I could do for now." His lips curl down, his disappointment palpable. "There's a chance for you to speak to him, but it has to be now. He's being transferred to Murkwood Prison in a few hours."

The shadows draped over Damian's shoulders swell, and my spine stiffens. Murkwood Prison, as in the Summer stronghold from which no one has ever escaped, ruled over by dark forces that rival the worst nightmares in the Shadowlands.

CHAPTER 38
BROKEN ARROW
ELIO

Devi Eros enters my study through the mirror just as Beth is about to pin my wedding boutonniere. "Elio. Dashing tux, but you look a bit drunk, my friend." She removes her ruby-incrusted mask and tucks it inside her cleavage.

A dark crimson hooded scarf covers the roots of her flaming red twists, and the long sleeves of her shirt have thumb cuffs that run up to her knuckles. Criss-crossed leather straps wrap over her chest and hold her long bow and quiver, the otherwise monochromatic ensemble hugging her curves.

"Hey, Devi," Beth says on a cringe, the two women not exactly on speaking terms.

Devi crosses her arms at the sight of my unexpected visitor. "Elizabeth Snow... I thought the seven hells would freeze over before you came home again." Her red-painted lips purse in a sarcastic grimace, the constellation of dark freckles on her youthful face bunching together. "Was being adored by the masses too hard on you?"

"Devi!" I stumble over to the fallen Queen of Hearts and peck her cheek before wrapping her up in a hug. "Thank you for coming."

"Alright. No more Nether cider for you," she scolds me with a smile, patting me on the back a few times. "I see you're in need of some pest control."

"It's a shame that beauty doesn't come with a manual on how to be kind or show basic human decency," Beth quips behind me. "I imagine your exile must be quite lonely."

"It takes one to know one, moth. You let him get shit-faced an hour before his wedding?"

Beth's arms fly to the sky. "I found him like this!"

Their petty, teenage selves flare up every damn time they cross each other's paths, the two women on a life-long quest to piss each other off. The familiarity of it all takes me back to a past long gone. I can almost taste the ocean on my tongue and smell the seaweed littering the sand. The memory of those long, lazy mornings by the sea is almost unbearable given the circumstances.

I close my lids. "It's about time you two buried the hatchet…"

"You know me, E. I treat my grudges as treasure." Devi reaches behind her and grabs an arrow from her quiver. "Here. One arrow. One night. Same as always." She presents me with the arrow with a mock curtsy, and I swallow hard.

Ice frosts over the arrowhead as I pick it up and hold it to the light. Funny how something so small can destroy so many lives…or bring a lost soul one night of solace, in my case.

Beth's hand curls around the boutonniere she's still holding. "What? No… Don't do it, Elio."

"Why not? I do it every year."

Beth's jaw hangs open, shell-shocked, and Devi snickers.

"How do you think he's survived this long? With this stupid contest coming year after year, each new wife buried by the time spring comes around? Besides, its effects only last one night. For the wedding."

"It's fake love," Beth whispers, all the blood gone from her face.

I straighten my jacket, suddenly feeling a little hot. "If I'm cursed to cause my wife's death, over and over again, I might as well offer her one great night. It's bad enough to have an audience. I won't ask her to suffer my indifference, too."

Beth narrows her eyes at me before turning her ire to Devi. "If you were truly his friend, you'd stop carving forbidden arrows and help us figure out how to break his curse."

"Many curses were wrung the day Iris died. Not one of them has been unraveled to this day. But you weren't there, were you, moth? You were too busy wallowing in your self-imposed exile to show up to Iris's birthday—"

Beth points her index finger at her nemesis. "There's nothing I could have done to change what happened. I still can't believe Iris..." she shoots me a sideways glance.

I huff in frustration. "Say it."

She always tiptoes around my feelings like I don't remember what happened that day. Like I don't see it play out in heart-breaking detail every night before I go to sleep and wake up with the same gaping hole in my chest every morning.

"I still can't believe she jumped out the window. No matter how nasty things got back at the academy... I never meant her ill will. You loved her, and that was enough for me to believe she'd changed."

Devi and I exchange a glance. Beth doesn't know what really transpired between Iris and me, but what good would it do to set the record straight now?

"Did you hear? Aidan just got engaged," Devi rasps.

My eyes bulge, and I pinch Devi's arm as hard as I can, furious that she would bring this up now. "Shush!"

Beth's face turns from white to a sickly sheen of green, and the spark in her eyes dims, her gaze flying to the cracks in the stone floor. "I'll leave you two to do your thing. I can't stand by and watch you harm yourself like this. I'll see you later, Elio."

The tension in Devi's shoulders eases. "She'd forgive you if she knew the truth, you know. You shouldn't let the past gnaw at you anymore."

I grip the jug on the table and chug down what's left of the cider.

"Iris died, Ezra too, and I condemned an endless string of innocent women to cold, untimely deaths. I'm beyond anyone's forgiveness."

Devi purses her lips, deep in thought, before she says, "Ezra isn't dead...exactly."

I prowl forward, a fresh rush of adrenaline rising in my blood, making my cold heart stir. "Do you know what happened to him? If you've been covering for that fucker—"

"Settle down. He got what he deserved."

I curse myself for the cider I'd consumed, my mind too foggy to navigate this conversation. "Do you know where he is?"

Devi unhooks the clasp of her golden bow and pinches the string, tracing the entire length of it with a faraway look. "The only thing you need to know is that you didn't kill him, so you can wipe that clean from your conscience." A sigh heaves her chest, but she shakes the emotions off her face until only the smirk of the ruthless archer remains. "Now, strip. I don't want to miss."

A smile tugs at my lips. "Since when is the great Devi Eros scared to miss a shot?"

"Humor me."

I should ask for answers about Ezra, but I toss off my shirt and spread my arms instead, desperate for Devi to shoot the misery out of me. "Do your worst, devil of Spring."

She draws her bow, the string stretching with a low *creak*, but Sara bursts into the room with a frantic, "Wait!"

Oh for the love of Eros, how many interruptions can one man stand before he goes mad?

"Beth told me Devi was here," Sara says, scanning the room. "Where's Lori?"

"Who's Lori?"

"No one. Shoot the damn arrow," I clip.

The obvious confusion on Sara's face quickly switches from surprise to rage. "You still sent her away? After what we learned?" She puts herself between Devi and me to shield me from the arrow.

"Who's Lori?" Devi repeats, her voice laced with a hint of impatience, and my stomach flips as she lowers her bow.

Sara's arms fall to her sides. "Lori is Iris's doppelgänger. And the loophole to Elio's curse."

"Is that true?"

"You *think* she's the loophole," I grumble.

Devi squints at me and slinks closer, graceful as a cat. She takes a good sniff and retreats, her lips curled in a snarl, her wide black pupils swallowing the silver rim of her irises. "You're in love and you asked me to shoot you anyway? Do you know how dangerous that is? A love arrow isn't meant to supersede true love."

"What are you talking about? I'm not—" The untruthful words stick in my throat.

"Hmph." She raises a perfectly plucked brow. "Who are you kidding?"

Spring folks deal with love arrows, torrid affairs, and silly infatuations every day, but they're awfully touchy when it comes to true love.

"True love is a fantasy," I breathe.

"A friend of mine once wrote: True love transcends crowns, blood, and flesh," Sara declares.

I wince at the quote of my own words, and the dark hole in my chest swells. "The man who wrote that is dead."

Devi tucks her forbidden arrow back inside her quiver. "Yes, I see that now. If you're willing to walk away from love, then you're not the man I thought you were." With that, the archer presses her mask back upon her face and saunters off through the mirror.

CHAPTER 39
A RISING TIDE
LORI

S eth draws a rune in blood inside his palm to open the way to his mother's prison. I watch as he presses his hand flat to the pliable glass on our side of the sceawere, a spell clearly barring the way for anyone to enter that doesn't know the secret code—or possess the right pedigree.

Given the fact that Seth doesn't ask me to close my eyes, I figure it's the latter.

Considering Spring's acrimonious relationship with the Shadowlands, it's not surprising that they would take measures to prevent the Shadow King and his kin, along with the other high-born Fae who've been taught the ways of the sceawere, to walk in and out of their kingdom at will.

While runes serve as ever-changing addresses for the millions of mirrors peppered across the worlds, it's very difficult for a traveler to find a place he's never visited. And in this case, if someone managed to get to this mirror by design or chance, he simply wouldn't be able to walk through the glass.

Seth lowers his voice to a mere whisper. "The guard is an old friend of mine. We have maybe twenty minutes before her shift ends, and whatever happens, she can't know you're here." He points toward the corridor to our right and draws a timer rune over my arm, the clock set to fifteen minutes. "I'll make sure she's too occupied to bother with her last round and meet you back here."

With a rogue grin, Seth follows the path of bright torches on the left, and I wrap myself up in shadows. The mirror behind us is warded with a set of golden-leafed runes, confirming my hunch that even Damian wouldn't be able to enter this prison.

The ancient stones of the Secret Springs stronghold have been weathered by centuries of time. Moss creeps between the cracks, the murky air embalmed with pungent fragrances of mildew, overturned earth, and urine.

At the end of the hallway, a long, seemingly endless, corridor spreads on both sides. Doors of rowan wood, each with small, iron-barred windows, are set at regular intervals, all identical. There's simply too many of them to quietly look inside each one, but the low sound of water churning and frothing lures me to the northern side of the prison.

The stories my mother told about her time in captivity, with only the heavy rumble of the waterfall for comfort, are still fresh in my memory. If she knew her precious son had ended up in that place too... she would have been heartbroken.

After a dozen doors, cold sweat pearls above my brows, and I let my shadow cloak fall. "Foxtail? It's me."

My call reverberates along the claustrophobic walls. *"Leave this place..."* the night whispers, *"while you still can."*

"Hello?"

Faint footsteps echo through a few chambers, accompanied by the slow creak of chains dragging over stones. I catch a glimpse of long canines and black scales in the cell closest to me and grip my daggers tightly, my heart pounding.

"Foxtail?" I repeat, a bit louder and with more confidence, acutely aware that time is slipping away.

A rat scurries down the hallway.

"Nightshade?"

My boots thud along the long corridor until I reach the correct cell, where my brother's fingers are visible between the iron bars. "Foxtail!" I gasp, reaching for him.

Clammy fingers hook around mine, the space between the bars not wide enough for his entire hand to pass through, but my heart swells at the contact. I haven't seen him in almost a year, back when he formally decided to train as an arrow carver.

His hair has been buzzed off, his prisoner jumpsuit leaving his tattooed arms bare. Red, yellow, and blue patterns now cover his forearms, most of them new. Textured white scars streak along his neck and arms, the tattoos filling up the space between the marks, and I'm taken aback by the heavy muscles he's developed during our time apart.

"Oh, Foxtail. How did you end up here?"

He grins from ear to ear, his character unchanged despite his appearance. "Have you come to scold me or break me out?"

"Neither—" My fingers clench around his. "I got your sentence reprieved, but they're transferring you to Murkwood."

The joy on his face vanishes. "So instead of being executed, I'll waste away for decades? No one comes out of Murkwood alive, sis," he says in a scalding tone.

"Why would they send you there in the first place? It's a Summerlands prison."

Guilt flickers in and out on his face. His lips part like he's about to offer an explanation, but his features twist into a scowl.

"By Morpheus... you really carved a forbidden arrow. *How?* Freya herself isn't capable of sharpening them enough to pierce a Fae's heart."

"It's not that hard." He gives me the kind of nonchalant shrug that makes me want to strangle him. "With the right tools."

"You cocky bastard." I curl my fingers around the iron bars, testing their strength, but the metal doesn't budge. "Do you even know who it was for?"

Ayaan swats my question away with an awkward wave. "Oh, some spoiled Summer prince."

"The crown prince?" My eyes narrow, his evasiveness only sharpening my suspicions. "Was it the crown prince, Ayaan?"

"It might have been the crown prince."

"I will kill you myself! Who have you been associating with? Mom's old friends? She fled to the new world for a reason. You can't trust these people—" I press my lips together. My outcry sparked a multitude of footsteps in the neighboring cells, and I force a deep, cleansing breath down my lungs.

"What about you? Did you really enter the Yule pageant?" Ayaan asks, and the unspoken judgment in his voice irks me more than if he'd called me a whore to my face.

"How do you think I saved your sorry ass from being hanged?" I snap.

"I never asked you to do that."

I arch a brow that says, *Are you fucking serious right now?*

Ayaan crosses his arms, the red and blue shapes of his tattoos forming the silhouette of a crab over his chest. "Excuse me for not celebrating the fact that I'm about to be transferred to the worse prison in Faerie, when I know my friends will die thinking I betrayed them." He shakes his head. "Seth Devine might be a weed, but he's still one of them. Don't tell me you slept with that sly prince—"

"Who I sleep with is none of your business." I study the inked patterns, the crab flanked by a roaring wave.

Ayaan angles his gaze to the sky like I'm the unreasonable one, unaware of my sudden interest for his tattoos. "Thank Eros... You're out of Wintermere, now."

I know my brother like the back of my hand, and his apparent relief, along with the peculiar new ink, starts to form dangerous puzzle pieces. Old memories of the crab pendant lying at the bottom of my mother's jewelry box flash into my mind, and Elio's stern voice echoes in my ears. *For centuries, their followers have been scuttling about the realm in their name.*

Crabs feed at high tide, my mother once said.

"I'm going back in a couple of hours, actually," I lie, the words flying out of my mouth with ease.

He frowns. "Why?"

"I'm going to marry the King," I whisper.

"Oof. Nice one." A bright chuckle pops out of his mouth. "You really had me going there for a second, sis."

"I'm not kidding."

Even though I'm bluffing, the words ring true. So true in fact that I begin to believe them myself.

Ayaan rolls his eyes at what he clearly considers not only to be impossible, but absolutely ridiculous. "You can't marry the Winter King, Nightshade."

"Why not? He needs a wife, and he chose me. The solstice ritual starts in only a few hours."

My brother's brows furrow, the lines at the corners of his eyes making him look even more like our father. "You're lying to get me to talk about our plans. Who put you up to this?"

"What plans, Foxtail?"

"I'm not going to say another word. I know for a fact that the Winter King picked someone else."

"News travels fast here, I bet," I muse, injecting a shit-load of sarcasm in my voice. Without giving myself the time to chicken out, I reach into my pocket and pry out the frost apple. "Are you 100% sure your sources are correct?"

Ayaan's face loses all color. "Is that—" He draws away from the door, his gaze fixed on the mythical fruit.

I rub down the apple with the sleeve of my uniform, its vibrant blue peel like a beacon in the murky air. "What's going to happen, Ayaan? Because like it or not, it's going to happen to me. Not a stranger, and definitely not some spoiled Fae princess."

His gray eyes dim. "The tides will rise tonight and wash the Winter King from our shores. You can't be standing next to him when it happens."

A hot pocket of grief flares in my chest. "Who's their leader? Morrigan?" I search for hints of recollection on his face, and a small wince escapes him.

"Don't believe everything you've heard. Morrigan escaped the Shadow Court. Rye is one of us, now."

"*Us?*" I inch my shirt up to showcase my rotting scar. "See that? Your precious *Rye* did that to me." My teeth grit together as I summon the will not to yell. "Who's the leader? The Gray Man? Do you know who he is?"

"I've already said way too much. Just...don't go back to Winter-mere, and let the Winter King marry someone else."

The rune pinches my arm, signaling the fifteen minute mark, and I tuck the apple safely back inside my pocket. "I love you, Ayaan, but I have to go."

"Don't marry him, Nightshade! You're going to get yourself killed!" he shouts after me, the door of his cell rattling on its hinges.

Shadows glide along my arms and legs as I break into a run. Seth is already waiting by the warded mirror with his mask when I return, his bloody palm pressed to the surface of the glass. I slip inside the sceawere without a hitch, and he follows after me. His tie is undone, and a smudge of red lipstick mars the white collar of his undershirt.

"Is everything alright?" he asks, the cold kiss of the sceawere biting deep into the sensitive skin of my neck.

"We have to hurry," I rasp, the tightness in my chest morphing into a dull ache. "The Tidecallers are coming for the souls *tonight*."

CHAPTER 40
FOREVER
LORI

As her sponsor, Seth is supposed to give Daisy away. The ill-fated bride is sitting on a stool in front of the backlit vanity mirror of the dressing room, two women hovering around her.

The three of them are speaking in hushed voices, wrinkled cloth handkerchiefs tucked in their tight grips. The oldest of the two strangers is clearly Daisy's mother, with the same slim nose, blonde hair, and blue eyes.

The other woman gasps as we come in. "Oh my Eros. She's here." She's about my age, and I figure she must be Daisy's sister, the one that mysteriously fell sick the night before the pageant so Seth could squeeze me in the roster.

Daisy leaps from her seat. The wide skirt of her gown, adorned with silver roses, sweeps the floor as she hurries over to me. Her bridal up-do is decorated with a white veil and a platinum tiara—the perfect look for a Winter Queen.

"You're...gorgeous," I admit, my throat tight and painful.

The certainty I'd found back in the prison waivers, but Daisy grips my hands. "I can't do this, Lori. I can't sleep with him in front

of all these people. I'm not made for ice. I don't want to die, I—"
Adrenaline and fear crank up her sultry voice by a few octaves, and
my already racing pulse picks up speed.

A knock on the door startles us all, and I wrap myself in shadows
before Byron flies into the dressing room. The Faeling is wearing
black tails and a top hat, the usual shimmer of his wings at his back.
"Ha, Seth. Glad to see you finally deigned to join us. The broadcast
has commenced, so we need to cross the labyrinth."

Daisy nods emphatically at that. "I need a minute, please."

Byron hesitates in the doorway, adjusting his small glasses on his
nose as he observes the three women and Seth in turn. "Is something
wrong?"

Daisy serves him a wide, sugary smile. "Nope. I just need another
minute."

Her mother stalks forward to close the door with a feigned sniffle, her nose buried in her handkerchief. "Give us a moment." She
slams the door in Byron's face and turns to search the room for me.
"What are you here for?"

I loosen my grip of the shadows shielding me from her gaze. "I
need to speak with Elio."

"You heard Byron. The broadcast has already started," Seth says.

I wish there were time to do this properly and talk things out. I
feel as though I'm standing at the edge of a bottomless trench, ready
to rappel down without a rope, with no time to prepare.

The clock on the wall *ticks* and *tocks*, the meager minute Daisy
bargained for nearly over. Less than two hours remain before the
winter solstice ritual must take place—before the attack meant to
wipe out the Winter King.

"I hurried over to save the day, but now I'm not sure where to
start," I admit, my thoughts jumbling together and my palms sweaty
at the thought that, no matter what, Elio needs to wed in a few
minutes.

"Come with me." Daisy links her elbow in mine and whisks me
outside.

If Byron is surprised by my presence, he doesn't show it, the Faeling hurriedly crossing something off on his clipboard before he flies off.

Daisy and I walk in tandem along the parapet and down the stairs to the entrance of the maze.

Sara rounds the last kink of the cedar hedge just as we're about to head in, and a white puff of air mists in front of her face. "Daisy? Is everything al—" She freezes at the sight of me.

"I'll be the one walking Daisy down the aisle." I announce loud and clear, in case any hidden cameras are flying about.

With a grave nod, Sara guides us to the opposing end of the labyrinth.

Near the last corner, she stops and tips her chin toward the exit to give us the go-ahead. "Go and give him hell."

My spine straightens at her encouraging words, and I lean toward the royal chief of staff. "You should go to Elio's study. You're about to receive some visitors."

"Visitors?"

A fleeting smile glazes my lips, giving me another much-needed boost of confidence. "Daisy's not the only one who brought family."

I suck in air as we emerge from the maze and step directly onto the aisle.

The inner gardens have been decked out with thousands of lights for the occasion, with illuminated garlands of ice swaying to a gentle breeze from the branches of the Hawthorn. A spotlight highlights the position of a frost apple that looks ripe for the picking.

The one tucked inside my jacket pocket doesn't feel as heavy as it used to. Each step grows lighter as I make my way to the altar where Elio is waiting for his bride.

The Winter King stands next to Paul on stage, his gaze fixed straight ahead and his hands clasped at his front. His navy-blue suit, a deep and rich shade, complements his pale skin, and a high, starched collar adds to the formality of the occasion. His tie is fastened with a vintage platinum brooch, lending a touch of old-world charm to his otherwise modern look. His hair is tousled—chic yet rebellious.

The thick soles of my hunter boots squish the rose petals scattered on our path while Daisy's white fur slippers barely make a dent in the snow.

A string quartet accompanied by a pianist play the romantic melody of Elizabeth Snow's *Never to Be,* the most iconic Fae song of this century. I almost expect her to start singing when the first verse starts, but the famous singer is nowhere to be found. The forlorn notes of the piano send a shiver through my body, the absence of lyrics actually highlighting the melody, the theme strangely geared toward heartbreak.

Gasps, loud whispers, and a frantic buzz washes through the crowd of High Fae gathered on both sides of the aisle.

Paul raises a smooth gray eyebrow at us. "Another twist."

The master of ceremony feigns annoyance, but his shrewd gaze is practically scintillating as it meets mine, and one corner of his mouth curls up. I swear one of his nosy cameras must be broadcasting directly inside his damn skull.

Elio jumps off the stage and jogs toward us, and I dig the balls of my feet in the snow. My mouth hangs open as the angry, bitter words that were ingrained in my brain on my way over get strangled in my throat.

"You came back." He stops short of reaching for me, his fists curling at his side as his gaze darts to Daisy in her bridal gown.

She lets out a nervous chortle and lets go of my arm. "Your Majesty, it's obvious to see... Lori here is the one who holds your heart."

Elio shifts his weight from one foot to the other, his face ashen.

Daisy offers the guests and cameras a sad smile. "How could you choose anyone else after we all saw how bravely she risked her life to save yours? We all witnessed first-hand how fiercely she protected you, and she might not be from the first kingdoms, but if we know anything in Spring, it's that true love trumps tradition."

"What about the rules?" Paul quips, his intent gaze goading me to stake my claim.

My tongue finally starts working again. "True love transcends crowns, blood, and flesh. It doesn't care for common sense and doesn't play by the rules." A blush spreads across my cheeks, but my voice remains steadier than I'd hoped. "I love you, Elio. It doesn't make a lick of sense, but I do. And whether or not I wanted to say it for the first time in front of all of Wintermere... It needed to be said."

He brushes his thumb across my cheek. "I love you too, Lori."

I can see his resolve grow. He still plans to fight me on this.

I block Paul, the crowd, and the cameras out, focusing on the bob of Elio's throat and the fresh patch of blue freckles on his neck until all I can see is him. "The venom is spreading fast." I graze the festering wound along my rib. "I'm dying, and there's nothing you can do to stop it, unless..." I reach into my pocket to retrieve the frost apple and hold it up to the light.

The ethereal luster of the blue peel dries my mouth once more. Every time I've thought about eating it, I've felt sick, but not now. Without the apple—without Elio—I'm a dead woman walking. He can't expect me to accept it if he's not willing to let me save him, too.

The sea rolling inside his immortal gaze is bright and hypnotic as it slips to my lips. "If I marry you, you'll eat it? Is that your proposal?"

"Yes. Before I met you, I was already marked for death. If you want me to fight my fate and grab this opportunity to heal, you have to do the same for yourself."

"You're..." he pecks my lips, "evil."

"I'm your queen."

Elio offers me a wicked, filthy grin. "Yes. Yes, you are." His grip on the nape of my neck tightens as he tilts my chin toward him and swallows my next breath with a kiss.

He tastes of salt and bitter tears, mingled with fresh snow, pine sap, and a bite of Nether cider.

Paul clears his throat. "If the bride and groom could move up to the altar."

Daisy gives us an encouraging nod and gestures us forward. Under the watchful eyes of the High Fae, Elio extends his hand for me to take.

I lace our fingers together, tucking the apple back into my pocket before we walk up the aisle. The bright smiles and murmured approval of the courtiers spell out their enthusiasm for this sudden, unexpected turn of events.

They probably think it was all staged, too.

"Mortal love wanes. Fae love cuts to the bone." The master of ceremonies holds out a curved ice dagger with a platinum pommel and guard. "Will you cut yourself to honor your commitment to each other, from this moment forth to eternity?"

The tip of the beautiful blade gleams in the night as Elio picks it up and slides the edge across his thumb in one smooth, confident motion. "You belong to Winter, and Winter...belongs to you. Before I met you, I convinced myself that I didn't want to live, that death was my past, present, and future. But I want more than that, and it starts with you, Lorisha Pari Singh."

He swipes the blood across my cheek, and it frosts over, leaving only a trail of red snowflakes in its wake.

"Elio... All my life, I've been running. I fled from the painful memories of my childhood. I hunted nightmares but avoided every opportunity for greatness that came with training. I never allowed myself to take a risk with my heart. I ran from the grief I carried and anything that made my blood race too hard. I ran so far and with such ease that I forgot to slow down and truly live. I want a *life* with you."

I cut myself, too, and paint shadows over his full, masculine lips. The blood seeps into his skin as I rest a hand over his heart—the heart of the reaper king no longer frozen, but frantic. My *husband*'s heart. Beating for *me*.

He steals the apple from my unzipped pocket and hands it over. "We had a deal."

My mouth dries up. I wasn't lying when I said I was dying, so I give a small incline of my head. *Here goes.*

The peel of the frost apple yields with a heavy *crunch,* the burst of flavor like biting into a firm, sweet iteration of Elio's skin. Ice and sugar. Frosted sin. The juices dribble down my chin, the ripe flesh dissolving like a mix of crushed ice and cotton candy in my mouth.

"Eat it all," Elio murmurs, his eyes drinking in the sight of me munching on the apple until I've swallowed the last of it.

The core prunes and crumbles in my hand. I dust off the icy crumbs as Elio wipes the remaining sap from my lips with his thumb.

The powerful itch in my side is about the only clue of the apple's true power. Tingles rage war on the venom until the pain that had been a literal thorn in my side for weeks vanishes completely, and I hold my breath for a moment.

The corners of my husband's mouth twitch. "Long live the queen."

CHAPTER 41

FAMILY

LORI

Majestic ice wolves run in tandem in front of the royal sleigh, hauling us toward the lake. Moonlight reflects off their thick white fur, and warm exhales frost in front of their onyx-black snouts. Contrary to the wolves summoned by the Gray Man, these fantastical beasts are flesh and bone, and a keen intelligence shines in their yellow gazes.

Halfway to the solstice's shrine, the place where the winter solstice ritual takes place, Elio flattens his hand on my belly and presses me to him. His hold is desperate as though he expects me to crumble to ashes at a moment's notice.

"If they're planning an attack, it's going to take place on the lake, when we're at our most vulnerable," he says.

The rhythmic beat of the wolves' paws hitting snow, along with the glide of the runners, drown out our whispers and protect us from the cameras' nosy microphones. Our televised wedding didn't allow for the mention of the attack Ayaan warned me about, and there wasn't time to dawdle if I didn't want to alert our enemies. But I haven't stopped talking since we mounted the sleigh, trying to fill in the blanks as quickly as possible.

I lean into his embrace. "Sara must have strategized with Damian and the hunters by now. I'm sure they'll find a way to get near the shrine without being seen."

"It's risky. The other royals will wonder why they weren't involved. They don't like to be left out of the loop, especially when darklings form alliances."

I shrug, unperturbed by what the royals think of us at the moment, as long as we can prevent the Tidecallers from murdering Elio and stealing the souls. "We can deal with them after. They can hardly expect me not to involve my family in all of this."

I'm underdressed for a winter expedition, but the cold can't touch me here, in Elio's arms. Fae weddings are meant to link two individuals and their magic forever, the ritual completed upon consummation. I suspect that, even though we haven't gotten to that part yet, the new magic running through my veins has already started affecting how my skin processes ice.

Elio's breath rushes down the slope of my neck. "Do you really think of Damian as family?"

"His wife, Nell, is the sister I never had. You have her to thank for this wedding, you know."

He buries his nose in the crook of my neck and kisses the sensitive spot below my ear. "I'm sure she's lovely, but I'm surprised to hear he's married. That's not something he made public."

"They wed in secret, but if we can capture Morrigan tonight, they might not have to hide anymore."

The pressure of his lips near my pulse point blows away any strategic thought from my mind. "Careful. I need to focus."

"Focus on *me*," he teases, and the hunger simmering beneath the words melts my insides.

"Morrigan can morph into a spider. That's how she got away last time."

His brows furrow. "That's incredibly advanced blood magic."

"Yes. She leveled up since you last saw her."

The lake of souls—the frozen lake I caught a glimpse of from the castle's parapet on my first day—spans for miles in the center of the Frozen Hills. Elio and I hold hands as we walk from our sleigh to the open-air gazebo standing near the shore.

White, curved spires radiate out of the gazebo structure, round columns holding up the roof. A solid block of platinum-streaked marble hovers a few inches up from the surface of the ice, and the elevated platform allows for an unobstructed view of the lake.

Contrary to normal ice, the pristine coat of frozen water covering the lake is completely transparent, the turquoise lake beneath our feet even brighter in the dark. Thousands and thousands of lights swirl and move under the ice, one for each soul that has been carefully collected during the year.

Winter Fae lean into their craving for voyeuristic entertainment without scruples, so this wedding's consummation isn't expected to take place in a honeymoon suite or a tent in the middle of the gardens, but here, witnessed by the immensity of the lake—and one of Paul's cameras.

"Don't worry, the entire thing is not broadcasted live. I instructed Paul to record just enough to titillate the viewers before the camera pans to the sky to show everyone that the souls are safe, and that we've done our duty."

"Is that what we've been doing the last few days? Our duty?" I joke.

His eyes dance, their color mirroring the beauty of the torrent of souls below the ice. "That was only for fun."

"And tonight is not going to be fun?"

"Should be interesting." He kisses the root of my ear. "Can you see them, yet?"

I nick his earlobe with my teeth and sharpen my senses, trying to detect the enemies lying in wait among the peaceful scenery.

A dark spot behind the nearest column sends tingles up my spine. "See that shadow over there by the nine o'clock column?" I whisper. "That's her."

Morrigan's bite of power is faint, but I would recognize it among thousands.

"Sneaky." Elio's eyes narrow, fixated on the birth marks peppered across my collarbone as he bends down to taste them one by one. "They couldn't have brought their wolves or spiders here. There'd be no way to conceal them."

I pull his jacket from his shoulders, playing the role of a newlywed eager to get her husband naked, but secretly scanning the gazebo and lake. "I count only two."

"Two assassins of the Gray Man's caliber would be enough to kill or incapacitate me, considering you're supposed to be a defenseless Spring seed." He spins me around in his arms and guides me forward in the guise of showing me the lake. "This is the well of tears, where the ritual will take place."

I peer over the edge to the staircase leading to the ice. A circular hole the size of a large plate has formed, the water directly accessible at the center of the well. The roof above it is interrupted by a giant magnifying glass that condenses the moon rays in the exact spot where the ice is melted.

"It's the section of the lake that allows us to reach the water, but only when the moon is highest in the sky at the solstice. We have less than an hour to complete the ritual."

The icy crust around the small hole is probably thin enough for us to break through if we were ready to go down for a swim, and goosebumps rise on my arms. "An hour is enough."

"I've never seen you so...wound up. You truly hate her, don't you?"

I give a sharp incline of the head, quietly keeping track of the two shadows, and my heart shrivels as Morrigan slips out of the darkness in her huntress uniform and purple boots, her long black hair hidden below her hood.

My enemy chuckles, and her obvious joy makes my pulse swirl. "My, my. The world is a small place, Lorisha. Looks like it's my turn to interrupt *your* wedding night."

CHAPTER 42
EXPOSED
ELIO

Morrigan Quinn, the phantom queen, slinks around the closest column with a wry grin and lowers her big hood. Her black hair is braided away from her face, her brown eyes gleaming with a thirst for blood.

"I see you found a way to heal my venom after all. Are you really sure dying of a frozen heart is better than the fate I had in store for you, little huntress?" she says.

Back when I saw her last, she was equally wicked, but now, the bite of power spiking the air around her slender frame is laced with the same strange flavor of Tidecaller technology that the Gray Man possessed.

The plan was to stall the attack for a few minutes to give Lori's family more time to join us, but the devious grin Morrigan directs at my new wife turns my blood to ice. If it wasn't for Lori's insistence that we had to capture and not kill her, I'd gladly cleave that woman in two.

I summon my sword, and the familiar blade feels light in my hand, its cold edge at a sharp contrast to the fire in my chest.

Morrigan saunters closer, quick as an eel. "How did you know I'd be here?"

I instinctively sidestep to shield my queen, but Lori's daggers are extended on each side of her. Shadow magic slithers over the fabric of her black uniform, leaving no doubt that she was looking forward to this fight.

"Bring it, witch."

"Tut-tut. Patience. I want to see you squirm a little."

Lori points the end of her dagger at the second shadow she warned me about. "Is your boyfriend going to join us, or is he naive enough to think I didn't spot him?"

The air crackles with electricity. A muggy, nefarious cloud slowly sharpens to existence above our heads and obscures the moonlight as the Gray Man condenses into solid form next to his ally.

His thick, geodesic mask obscures his eyes, while the triangular metal plate covering his mouth and nose hides the rest of his face. "Let's not dawdle, Rye," he chucks out, his voice low and unrecognizable as it pierces the metal barrier.

"I know you," I say quickly, the peculiar piece of armor only making sense if he wants to hide his voice and identity.

Why else would he conceal himself so thoroughly?

He gives a low, croaky laugh, and shakes his head. "No, you don't, but I know *you*, Elio Lightbringer. I'm looking forward to taking *everything* that's yours." He angles his mask to Lori for a split second, and my blood howls for violence.

The current of animosity rolling off him feels familiar. I've been on the receiving end of many swords held by men that shared his sentiment. Whoever he is, he lost someone dear to him and blames me for their death.

"How did you know we were coming?" he asks.

"You tried to kill me on the mountains. It wasn't much of a secret that you'd try again."

"Elio killed his first wife, you know," Morrigan says with a smirk, clearly trying to drive a wedge between me and my new queen.

Lori tilts her chin up. "I know."

Morrigan's lips thin as her big revelation falls flat. "I didn't peg you for a power-hungry huntress."

"I'm queen now. And you're not," Lori taunts.

Angry fighters make sloppy mistakes, and Morrigan's failed life-long pursuit of a crown is her sorest spot.

With a flick of the wrist, the witch summons four Dreamcatcher spiders to her side like weaving nightmares is as easy as breathing. The creatures shimmer in the night, appearing out of nowhere as though they've just crawled out of hell.

By Thanatos!

Light undulates along their long, crooked limbs, their claws struggling to gain traction on the sleek marble floor. While the last batch were mostly black, this new model has blue, crystalline accents, and frosted over globulous eyes. Tiny overlapping plates decorate their front, reminiscent of the scales the Tidecallers harvested from my dragon.

A black and red metallic glint draws my attention to Morrigan's hand, where what I first mistook for a wrist guard is actually a metallic plate embedded with precious stones, inserted directly into her skin. The Mist Fae implant amplifies her magic, but what can be forged can also be broken—or cut off.

"No wolves?" I ask my opponent.

"I'd rather kill you myself."

His carefree demeanor sparks an itch between my shoulder blades as I inspect him for a similar trinket, but his arms and hands are concealed by tightly-knit fabric and heavy gloves.

"No one can kill death. If you strike me down, another will take my place. There is no escaping it."

"Death isn't necessary. Not for us. Immortal souls can endure death and be transferred into new bodies. You and your devil of a father just refuse to let us try," he adds. "You insist on wasting perfectly good souls, and now, I'm going to destroy you."

Goosebumps raise on my arms. The process he's alluding to is not only forbidden and heretical but also terrifying—especially for someone who has witnessed firsthand how wretched and deformed a dark soul can become.

Many flawed conclusions have emerged from the Mist King's experiments. The Gray Man is confusing possession with true immortality. While he's not the first to make this mistake, he is certainly the first with such raw power—and an army.

"The rituals you're referring to were outlawed for a reason. Besides, they wouldn't save whoever made you so angry with me."

His sword materializes in his hand, the long yellow lines on the dark hilt even more pronounced than before. He grips it with ease, the weapon held at the ready. The shimmer of the blade packs a mesmerizing punch, as if he has spent every waking hour sharpening it since our last skirmish.

"You're right about that. And I'm going to make you regret the day you stepped foot in her bedchamber if that's the last thing I do." The Gray Man pauses mid-step and angles his face to the side, switching his weight from one foot to the other.

Zip.

A shadow arrow pierces his shoulder, his last-second hesitation preventing it from reaching his heart. The arrowhead makes a sickening, squelching sound as it enters the flesh, and he howls at the impact.

Zip. Zip. Zip.

Shadow arrows ricochet off the nearest spiders, the projectiles ineffective against the creatures' new armor.

A hailstorm suddenly envelops us in a cocoon, erasing the outside world from view. I take advantage of the chaos to attack, while Lori moves to catch Morrigan off guard, too.

The Gray Man parries my attack with an angry grunt, and as much as I want to focus on him, half of my mind is on Lori. Morrigan is the greatest Shadow huntress ever to live—even without the obvious magical boost she acquired. She stabbed Damian through the heart and eluded justice for decades.

But my wife proves to be a better fighter than I anticipated, meeting the phantom queen's attacks with impressive stamina and flair, deflecting them left and right.

The Gray Man closes his hand around the arrow head sticking out of his body and pulls it straight through, his flesh melding back into fresh skin in less than a second.

By the spindle... this is the most advanced healing I've ever witnessed.

The audible smile in his voice raises all my hairs to attention. "Oh, let's go."

Sword fights hinge on footwork, timing, and analyzing subtle shifts in your opponent's stance—dancing on a knife's edge, as my father used to say. Once again, my opponent's impulsivity plays to my advantage, but when he strikes, he aims to kill.

The third slash of his sword misses me by a hair, and the momentum throws him off balance. My abs clench as the tip of my blade pierces his flesh, but the Gray Man heals as quickly as he did earlier. So quickly that I start to wonder if he can be killed at all.

His sword comes at me again and again, and my muscles tense under the relentless blows. A sharp rasp grates my throat as our blades lock.

A low metallic clink reverberates through the stillness of the frozen valley. We strain against each other, sweat gathering on our foreheads. The mask and metal plate concealing the Gray Man's face reveal no emotion, but his magic crackles with unrestrained hostility in the air between us.

I draw power from the glacier, the lake, and the souls beneath the surface. Ice thorns crawl over my arms in complex crystalline patterns, and each delicate shard pulses with a life of its own. With enough strength gathered, I unleash a blast of arctic wind that sends the Gray Man tumbling over the edge of the gazebo and onto the hard surface of the lake.

Ice embedded in his chest, he struggles to stand. Frozen fabric flakes off his shoulders, revealing the frostbitten skin beneath, and he trembles as he raises a hand to touch the cold injury. I might not be able to kill him, but I can certainly *freeze* him.

I flex my fingers, willing the ice to spread toward his heart, and dash forward to press my advantage when a pain-filled scream snaps my attention to Lori.

She's fallen onto her back at the opposite end of the gazebo, a set of spider fangs embedded deep in her ankle. Her arms shake violently as she slashes open the spider's stomach. The creature disintegrates into shards of shadow magic that quickly return to Morrigan, the witch now perched over my wife to administer a killing blow.

An ice spear flies from my hand before I can even think, slicing a deep cut into the witch's arm and disarming her. Lori shoves Morrigan down onto her stomach with a well-placed leg swing and tries to mount her to shackle her hands behind her back. Just as she's about to secure the restraints, another spider descends from the ceiling, splashing silk across Lori's face.

My wife jerks backward, desperately clawing at the sticky webs. Her panicked movements send a chill down my spine. I can't waste any time. I dash to her side and slice the spider in two, sparing her from the creature's venomous fangs.

The phantom queen remains sprawled on her stomach next to Lori. With an annoyed grunt, she pushes herself off the floor, baring her teeth in warning as blood drips from her injured arm. "Looks like chivalry isn't dead. Do you really want to win this fight only to bury her corpse next to the others, Elio?"

The jab grates my insides, but Lori seizes the moment to slam the hilt of her dagger into the back of Morrigan's hand. The impact shatters the metal plate molded to the witch's knuckles, sending a thunderous echo reverberating through the valley.

Morrigan shakes out her wrist, and her eyes widen as black tendrils slither through the sleet storm, the pulse of the Shadow King now palpable. Damian emerges from the veil of clouds behind me, with Seth close behind. The prince has created a protective bubble around them, and the blizzard fades.

The Gray Man watches us from a distance, pacing like a caged lion unsure of his next move. The ice injury he sustained glistens in the moonlight, its frosty surface contrasting starkly with the rest of his dark attire. Three other Shadow hunters encircle the gazebo, and he finally dismisses his sword.

"Sorry, Rye. You know we can't afford to be taken prisoner," he drawls in a dispassionate tone.

Seth's gaze snaps to him, and his throat bobs. "Luther?"

From the prince's reaction, it's clear he recognizes him. The Gray Man's grip falters for an instant, but he quickly recovers and hurls a dark, oily dagger at his associate.

Damian shields Morrigan with his body, the dagger intended for the phantom queen sinking into his chest instead as he lets out a low groan. *Did the Gray Man really just try to kill her?*

A warm wind lashes against my cheeks, lifting the snow from the ground to form a tunnel around the Gray Man as Seth rushes toward him. "Luther!"

Both men vanish into the storm, and when the white veil lifts, neither Seth nor the Gray Man is visible.

Dark blood gushes out of the laceration in Damian's chest, and Morrigan purrs, "It pleases me to see you so concerned for my well-being, darling."

The Shadow King snarls as he wrenches the blade from his flesh. When Lori insisted we capture Morrigan instead of killing her, I knew there had to be a reason. But seeing the Shadow King protect his ex-fiancée—the woman who nearly destroyed him—shakes me to the core. The oily dagger burns out as it exits his body, flaring into a flash of purple flames.

"What was on that blade? More venom?" Lori chucks out.

Morrigan sighs, her villainous grin faltering as she tightens her jacket around her frame. "Probably."

"Don't you dare try and transform, or I swear I will cut off each and every one of your limbs," Damian growls, his focus unshaken despite the blood streaming down his front.

Morrigan cowers closer to him like he didn't just threaten to maim her. "A girl knows when she's been bested. Take me home, then, my love."

If my relationship with Iris was toxic, these two are on a whole other level. Still, the way she coos the word *home* sends a sickening jolt of doubt through my stomach. I decide not to let Damian yield to her demand. If she's so eager to be locked in a dungeon, she'll have to settle for mine.

"I'll take her into my custody for now." Acid rises in my throat as I shackle Morrigan with solid ice and search her for more jewels. "Until we find her associate, he might return to finish what he started."

I can't shake the intuition that, if killing us was plan A, going home with Damian was plan B. I'll share my suspicions with Lori and Damian when the time is right, but that witch certainly looked too happy to get caught.

CHAPTER 43

NORTHERN LIGHTS

LORI

"Where do you think they went?" Sara asks as she examines the place where the Gray Man and Seth disappeared.

"I have no idea, but wherever they are, I hope Seth is okay," I answer.

From the strangled, desperate way Seth called out our enemy's name, I think he finally found his brother. Only a cocky, immortal Fae prince would say that his *baby brother* had been taken by Morrigan, and forgo the oh-so-important detail that he was in fact a grown man, but it's on brand with Seth's flippant communication skills.

If Ayaan had shown up to that fight only to flee in a cloud of smoke, I would have chased after him, too.

I walk over to Damian to check on his wound, joining him and Elio on the gazebo. "Are you alright?"

Damian grazes the stab wound near his collarbone. "Don't worry. This is not the kind of venom meant to strike down a Fae King." He looks to his prisoner. "But there will be time to discuss everything later. In private."

"Don't mind me. I'm enjoying this immensely," Morrigan cracks.

My fellow hunters—Misha, Cary, and Jo—keep an eye on her while we chat, and Jo growls, "Shut up, witch."

I offer my friend a warm wave. "Too bad Nell couldn't come along," I grunt under my breath, wishing she could have witnessed our victory first-hand.

"She stayed home with Cece, to heal her in case anything happened."

I arch a brow. "Yet you still took that knife to spare her the trouble."

"Like you said. I didn't know what kind of venom was on that blade."

I offer him a soft smile, thinking back to Nell's comment about Damian being extra-broody. "You won't be able to keep her locked away and safe forever, you know."

"You're right, of course." Damian scratches the back of his neck. "I'll take Morrigan away, now, so you two can have some peace for the next part."

Elio nods. "Take her to the Ice City. Kiro will know what to do. I wasn't okay with letting her go *home*, as she asked. Seemed too convenient."

"The furthest away she remains from my Nell, the better."

"I thought you didn't trust me, anymore," Elio says on a sad frown. "So thank you for your help."

"Lori trusts you, and that's enough for me, old friend." Damian extends a hand toward my husband, and the two men exchange a meaningful arm squeeze. "I'll talk to you both soon."

My chest constricts as Damian, Sara, and the other hunters escort Morrigan off the ice, leaving us behind to fulfill our duty. I brush my hand over the spot on my side where the spider venom used to fester. "We won, and yet she still came out on top, somehow. Look at her, cooing like she's happy to see her old pal, Damian. You did well to keep her in Wintermere."

But Elio's gaze is focused on the well of tears, his fists clenching and unclenching at his sides, and I realize Morrigan is now the farthest thing from his mind.

I walk behind him and brush his arm. "A penny for your thoughts?"

"Winter destroys one, but spares two," he muses. "We have to release the souls to the sky."

I inch toward the stairs leading down to the water, adrenaline still dispensing an equal dose of warning and euphoria in my blood. The water hole under the magnifying glass is almost frozen over, the window for the ritual quickly closing.

"Are we supposed to hold hands going in and swim a little?" I crack, the aloofness in my voice a little forced.

"Not quite."

"I figured." My gaze darts to the lonely eyeball still hovering in the air. "And the camera?"

"It's not as awkward as having Paul here. The camera will remain at a polite distance, and like I said, it will turn away to the sky when our duty is satisfied." Elio licks his lips, his cheeks still flushed from the fight, the knots in his arms flickering in and out of view. "Unless you changed your mind."

I unbutton his undershirt, a finely crafted piece with a classic V-cut, and slip my hands underneath the soft white cotton. My apprehension morphs to desire as I revel in the sight of his chest, bare and glistening. "Hush. I'm looking forward to planting my flag deep in your snow, Elio Lightbringer."

A small laugh quakes his body. "Shouldn't it be the other way around?"

We exchange a quick snicker, but he bites his bottom lip, looking more nervous than I've ever seen him. His platinum-blonde hair curls over his brows, and his breaths come in shallow gasps. Despite his attempts to maintain a stoic facade, worry and fear seep through, as if the Winter King himself is melting under the weight of his emotions—and the blaze of the solstice moon.

"Hey. Look at me." I flatten my palm over his heart. "You better get used to this face, because if Iris got to be your first wife, I intend to be your last. We'll laugh about it next year. Same time. Same place. You and me."

Tears glaze over his eyes. "I'd die for that to happen."

I stand on my tiptoes to kiss him, and the addictive brush of his tongue coaxes a heated moan out of my lungs.

Turning his back to the camera, Elio unfastens his pants and pulls them down, along with his underwear. My jaw hangs open as he stands stark naked in front of me—and most of Wintermere.

"I'll give the people what they want," he says with a wink, "But you owe me."

He picks me up, and I wrap my legs around him. The friction of my uniform against his bare skin makes me want to strip and say *to hells with the camera*, but I let him take the lead.

Elio breaks through the thin film of ice that formed over the well of tears and finds footing on the first water-covered step leading into the lake.

Water splashes out of the hole and caresses my calves, warmer than I expected. The souls scatter, clearing a space for us as Elio lowers us into the narrow passageway. It's not quite as spacious as a jacuzzi, but it's intimate.

An aquamarine glow dances across the frozen walls of the nature-made lagoon, the water's silky texture making me hum. Almost instantly, I yearn for Elio to touch every inch of me.

It makes sense that a ritual calling for sex would start with an aphrodisiac thrall, but the insidious current of energy rippling from the water is more potent than even the lure of a godlike king in a hall of mirrors.

The televised wedding ceremony was just a romantic premise to accommodate nature's will. Fae gods prefer to be worshipped with flesh, blood, and bones. My body vibrates to a new frequency as the water swirls around my waist, legs, and breasts—cold yet invigorating.

This is where Elio truly makes me his queen.

I can sense the immense glacier beneath the lake, the source of Wintermere's power. The crisp air, the snow-capped mountains in the distance, and the deep night sky are all ravenous for us to consummate this marriage.

Shivers rock my body as Elio freezes the fabric of my pants, then brushes it off my skin like fresh snow. He does the same to my jacket, followed by my shirt, until I'm completely naked.

"By Thanatos... I've got to have you now," Elio rasps, his cock hard against my bare thigh.

A starved, wet, and naked Elio is quickly becoming my favorite version of the Winter King, and I feel giddy. Not only do we get a do-over for our aborted tryst in the Ice City's hot springs, but this is no longer our last chance to find solace together. It's the first of many firsts. Our first night as husband and wife, with another to follow tomorrow—and the day after that. Joy sears my cheeks.

Elio lifts me up and adjusts the angle so he's prodding my entrance, the tip of him wide and delicious. The magic that has been rooting for us to get together from the moment our lips touched dizzies and suffocates me. I swallow his next command with a hot kiss as I lower myself onto him, taking him inch by inch.

He stretches me out slowly, my inner walls acclimating to his size, and we both groan in a mix of relief and greed. Power crawls along my skin and finally seeps inside me. The caress of winter buries deeper and deeper, rearranging the very fabric of my cells. Snowflakes crystallize over my skin, frosting my lips, brows, and collarbone. Elio darts his tongue out to lick the new icy freckles peppering my neck.

"Is it always like this?" I gasp.

"Never. It's *never* like this," he replies in a hushed drawl.

Elio combs his fingers through my hair, the dark strands now frozen solid. As the ice ensnares me, the cold remains at bay. I feel different. Energized.

I belong here, in the immensity of Winter. Ice can't hurt me anymore. My senses reach down to the bottom of the lake, to the bed of the glacier, and I feel its power mold me into something formidable and endless.

Something better.

I raise a trembling hand to my head and skim the edges of a heavy yet intricate feminine crown.

Elio's fingertips dig into the nape of my neck, his gaze riveted on my new accessory. "You're so fucking beautiful. That crown... I've never seen anything like it. The glacier always wanted you..."

I raise a brow, crumbs of frost falling between us. "*The glacier wanted me?*"

"*I* wanted you. I *love* you. You're my queen."

The sex isn't hard and fast, but slow and steady and maddeningly indulgent. Exquisite waves of pleasure lash through me as the union of our bodies consecrates my rise to Winter Queen.

Elio buries his fingers in the flesh of my waist and guides me up and down the length of his cock. I rock my hips, desperate to emphasize the grind, the pressure at the apex of my thighs spreading along my spine.

I want to see my husband reach his release inside of me—and only me. Forever.

He kisses my breasts with wicked intent, one hand snaking up to twist my cold, hard nipples. A gentle burst of ice zaps through them before he licks the frost off, my moans growing impatient and high-pitched as I curse him for playing with my body in such a cruel, cruel way.

"I'm close," Elio says in a hoarse whisper. "I want you to scream as you come."

He snaps his hips, filling me so deep, and my core throbs as I reach the peak. I scream, more than happy to obey his instruction, and the orgasm leaves me feeling intoxicated, happy, and boneless.

"Oh, Lori," he cries out, and I feast on the sight of him falling apart, his hardness pulsing inside me.

We ebb down from the high, my nails still embedded in his neck, and breathe together until our rushed breaths soften into loving whispers.

"Look," he says, spinning me around in his embrace. "It's done."

Sometime during our love-making session, the entire lake had melted, and I draw in a sharp breath, blown away by the beauty of the clear turquoise waters. The lights rise to the sky, joining their comrades in the vast expanse of the night.

Tears sting my cheeks as I think of the grieving families, but I can sense the souls' relief at being set free. Millions of them rise higher and higher before shooting upward with as many comets' tails. Falling stars burning in reverse, shining bright for one last time.

Northern lights paint the starry sky in green, pink, and purple streaks, as though the gods are throwing a party for the new arrivals.

"It's"—no adjective seems enough to describe this moment, my new husband's arm slung across my waist, holding me close as we watch the most beautiful spectacle nature has to offer—"perfect. I can't believe we'll get to see this every year."

Elio nuzzles the side of my face with a sigh. "You still don't fear my curse one bit, do you?"

"What curse?" I joke. "I made you a promise, and I intend to keep it. Next year, we'll laugh about this, you'll see."

"Promises can be broken, little spider. Even the most solemn of them."

I stand and stretch gingerly. "Stop pouting and take me home. We've had a grueling day. I want to sleep in your arms tonight."

Ice creeps along the rim of the lagoon, and I hold out a hand to help Elio up.

He rises to his feet and wraps a protective arm around me. "Let's go to my apartments in the Ice City. We can have some privacy before the reception tomorrow."

"No, the tower." The words leave my mouth of their own accord, as if the new magic inside me yearns to return to Iris's bedchamber —perhaps to desecrate it as Elio suggested earlier.

"Are you sure?" he asks quietly.

"Yes. There are some ghosts there that need to be put to rest."

CHAPTER 44

THE TRUTH IN YOUR LIES

LORI

I adjust my hair in the mirror of Iris's bedroom, wearing a white halter dress peppered with glittering sequins. The front of the skirt clings to my mid-thigh, while a long, dramatic train dips to the floor behind me.

"Breakfast is already in full swing, I figure?" I ask as Elio enters the room. "I overslept."

I move to look at my husband, but it's Ezra who has breached the peace of my morning routine, not Elio. Iris's lover crushes me against the wall at my back. "I ought to punish the birthday girl for being late to her own party..."

"What are you doing in here?" I seethe. My gaze falls to the discarded jacket sprawled over the piano bench, and I push against Ezra's chest. "Elio could come back at any moment."

He paws at my waist, his thumb slipping under the knotted bow at the nape of my neck. "I don't care. Turn around," he says in a hoarse whisper.

"Oh, E." Fire fills my blood as I obey. Ezra combs my hair to one side, and I arch my back, but instead of untying the knot holding my dress up, he scratches deep lines behind my ear. The motion is painful and unex-

pected, his nails peeling off a layer of skin and smudging the glamor runes hidden at the base. My entire body tenses.

"I knew it," he breathes.

I spin around, confused. "What are you—"

Ezra's face melts into one I know so well, and my soul screams. A heartbroken Elio stands in front of me, his powers of deception vanishing in a flash.

"You're not really Fae, are you?" Elio twists the round shell of my ear between his fingers almost viciously. "You've been lying to me all this time."

My throat bobs. "I had to. Freya and my mother tried to petition the old king for a frost apple through the official channels, but even their combined magic couldn't keep me from aging on the inside. I was dying, Elio."

"And to show your gratitude, you choose to fuck my brother at every single one of your parties, the two of you probably snickering in tandem, thinking you'd get away with it."

"I love him," I declare, as though it excuses everything.

My arms and legs shake, but I hold Elio's accusing glare with more poise and righteousness than I ever thought possible, considering the circumstances.

"Ezra only cares about himself. He's using you to get to me." Elio hits his breastbone with his fingertips a few times to emphasize his point. "He's punishing me for outshining him. You realize that, don't you?"

"You're wrong."

He hides his face in his palms with a dry snort and presses on his closed lids. "I can't leave you, as you well know. We could live apart or take turns touring the realm or whatever; we'll figure it out. But this affair ends now."

"Don't tell me what to do."

"Iris, we have a duty to our kingdom. To the souls. We can't be at war with each other."

"You talk about duty when you should be talking about power. You are

the most powerful Fae alive, yet you act like you're the same as before. A second-born son with no prospects."

Elio sucks in air, pupils dilated and dark. "That's cold, even for you."

"I want out." I bare my teeth. "You should have warned me about the ice. This magic you gave me... numbs me to the core. Ezra's the only one who makes me feel alive—"

"Believe me, I wish I could take my vows back, but you and I, we're forever." Elio rakes a hand through his hair. "And you know what's worse? If you had told me back in the maze that the real reason you wanted to marry was to get a frost apple. If you had told me in confidence that you were half-Fae and needed it to become immortal, I would have given you one."

"Just like that?"

"Thanatos help me, I loved you, Iris."

"But you don't anymore."

His eyes burn. "How could I love someone with such a black, rotten core?"

Ezra slithers inside the room, his voice almost teasing as he says, "That's no way to talk to a lady. What's going on here?"

"He knows about us," I sigh.

Elio turns his back to me, his fists balled at his sides. His feet remain firmly rooted in place, but his entire being shakes. It is apparent that he is clenching at every ounce of self-control he has left not to lunge at his brother. "Ezra Hermes Lightbringer, you get out of my kingdom before I kill you. I never want to see you again."

The order carries the weight of the glacier along with it, and magic frosts the air.

Ezra rubs his face down, unfazed. "Don't fuss over a pretty girl, kid. What am I always telling you? You take everything too seriously—"

"Are you proud of the pain you cause around you? Why do you want to be like him so badly?"

Ezra's face pales, and he stops breathing for the longest time, what little air is left in his lungs just enough to bark, "I am nothing like our father."

"*You need a better mirror,* kid," Elio drives his index finger against Ezra's chest. "*Because from where I stand, you're* exactly *like him.*"

Ezra slices his head from side to side. "*Iris knew she was fucking me. She wanted to.*"

"*Do you think that's what I meant? That you deserve a fucking prize for not passing as someone else? For not passing as me as our father would have done if he'd had the chance? Is that what allows you to sleep at night?*"

The carefully crafted mask of wicked nonchalance and fraternal condescension falls from Ezra's face, pinching his brows and clawing through his blue eyes until a completely different man stands in his place. "*You left me alone with him and never looked back. He took your wings in front of me, but you never stopped to ask what he took from me.*"

"*Why would he take anything from you when you just stood there and let him do it?*" Elio shouts as he pushes Ezra with all his might, thorns of ice sinking into his brother's shoulders.

"*You know damn well that if I had tried to help, he would have clipped my wings, too! He punished me for not telling him you were leaving, for not ratting you out when you made your plans. He destroyed her, Elio. Just for the hell of it. And you, with your new crown, your mighty throne, and immense power, did nothing.*"

For the first time, I feel Iris's emotions. Her jaw clenches, the realization that she's been a pawn in a much bigger war filling her with blistering fury. I watch helplessly as she summons a long, wavy-bladed ice dagger. My consciousness thrashes in the confines of her body, desperate to stop what's about to happen.

My wrist shakes in hesitation, and I hold my breath. The scene before me becomes clearer and more vivid, as though I have suddenly pulled a veil from my surroundings. Tears wet my cheeks, and I blink, but the strange phenomenon lasts only a moment.

Iris drives her weapon deep into Elio's backside, and he cries out in a mix of surprise and pain. A wave of ice unfurls from the wound as he falls to his knees, no blood leaking to coat my blade. Only ice.

The ground shakes, and the entire tower tilts under our feet.

I raise my dagger a second time, aiming higher, but Ezra dashes between us. "Iris, stop!" He knocks the blade out of my hands at the last possible second, and it ricochets off the wall with a loud clunk.

The Winter King staggers to his feet and spins around as I summon another dagger. Just as I am about to strike, he catches my wrist mid-air. The blue sea in his eyes is frozen, and a glacial flare jolts up my arm. Blue lines spread from my wrist to my elbow, mirrored on Elio's arm. A jagged bolt of ice surges up to our shoulders and snakes toward our chests, as though it's about to crack us in two. An arctic blast sweeps through my body, chilling me to the core.

Ezra pushes me off his brother with all his might, separating us. My body rams against the window, but instead of stopping my momentum, the glass explodes into a million pieces.

A warm breeze brushes my arms and legs as I fall, the long train of my sequin dress waving like a white flag above me. A sharp crack echoes in my skull, followed by a dizzying wave of nausea. The metallic tang of fear and blood fills my mouth.

The impact leaves me dazed. My lids are heavy as I blink and take in the shocked faces of my guests, who have stopped eating their breakfast. The music cuts off abruptly, and two women spring to their feet. Freya inches closer, covering her mouth with one hand, while Iris's mother rushes to my side.

"My flower!" Irene clasps my hand. "Iris, Iris, can you hear me?" She turns to a slender, young version of Seth. "Get a healer boy, quickly!"

He dashes into action and disappears between the onlookers, rushing off to find help.

"You'll be alright. Just hang on."

A crowd forms at a respectful distance, and shocked gasps buzz through the gardens. From the corner of my eye, I see Sara stumble out of the maze. The bright blue runes carved into her skull and hands glow with an eerie light, and the guests who haven't yet left their seats cower behind Freya as she approaches.

Irene wraps herself around me, growling, "Get away from her, you monster."

But the young Sara inches forward, her teary gaze fixed on the matching glow hovering above my chest.

Irene steps away from my side and shoves her with all her might. "Don't you dare take her soul! The healer is here now."

Sara falls to her knees on the stones as the crowd parts to make way for Elio and the healer. "I-I'm so sorry, Your Majesty."

A wrinkled woman in a long, flowing robe approaches, but all eyes turn to the Winter King. His gaze darts between Sara and me as he makes his way forward, one step at a time. Frost stains his shirt and pants, a flurry of snowflakes still spilling from his injury. Four guards in full uniform start ushering the guests inside, but Freya steps in front of Elio.

"What happened?" she snarls, her fists clenched at her sides. "How did she fall?"

The brown-haired healer slips past the angry Spring Queen and lays her hands on my chest, but her calm expression twists into a grimace almost immediately. She glances over her shoulder at Elio. "I can't do anything for her, Your Majesty. Her heart...is frozen."

The light emanating from Sara swells and condenses in her small, trembling hands, confirming the healer's prognosis. I realize with a jolt that my heart is indeed still and quiet. It isn't beating, even though my eyes are open. My consciousness is trapped in a cold, fading body.

Irene wails, "By Eros, not my girl. Please!" She turns to Elio. "You pushed her, didn't you?"

Elio shakes his head in denial. "I didn't."

"You coward—" She lunges to shove Elio, but two guards intervene, and she struggles helplessly against their hold. "Do something! Anything!"

"Elio... Her soul. It's calling to me—" Sara stammers.

"Give me a minute, Sara. I need a moment with my wife before you do your duty." A sob quakes in his throat as he sits down beside me and squeezes my hand. "Gods... I never meant for this to happen."

My breaths are soft and sparse, wheezing in and out of my lungs in faint rasps. Blue veins frost in and out of view along my arms as magic sparks nefariously through the air. "You're going to let her take me?" I croak. "You're the King of Death. You can stop this."

Tears glisten in Elio's eyes, but he remains silent.

And in his cold, frozen eyes, hidden beneath the shock and horror, I see a glimmer of light. A hint of relief.

I grip his hand. Hard. "Elio Hades Lightbringer, you'll regret this. Your heart shall remain emptier than your promises, and your next bride will wither at your indifference. Mark my words, Winter King, for you shall never love again."

CHAPTER 45
A CURSE THAT DEVOURS
LORI

Air fills my lungs, expanding my chest almost painfully, a sensation reminiscent of a newborn baby drawing her very first breath. After a second, more fluid gasp, I sit up straight.

The fresh sheets Elio used to make the bed after our journey back to the castle are drenched with sweat beneath my palms.

"Hey... are you alright?" Elio pats my back with a cool hand. "You were thrashing around in your sleep."

Darkness still reigns over the tower. The large window, through which I had fallen in the vision, is now a black void, the moon no longer brightening the night sky. I open my mouth to comfort Elio, but a strange pressure between my ribs prevents me from speaking.

"Did you dream? Is that something a Shadow huntress can do?" Elio asks patiently, rubbing my spine up and down.

I shake all over, my abs coiled in pain, and my knuckles turn white as they grip the sheets. Moving my tongue is in itself a spartan task, my lips and mouth clamped shut by some invisible force.

"Look at him. So ignorant. So...pathetic."

Wait. That voice... The same voice I've been hearing for a while now. First in the maze, then at the carnival, in the mountains, and inside the pit of Ayaan's prison... The voice that just condemned Elio to a cruel, lonely fate.

My voice, but different.

Iris's voice.

"Lori? Are you okay?" Elio repeats.

"Yes," I croak.

An insidious force compels me to relax my stiff muscles one by one, until I melt back into the pillows.

No! It's all wrong. It's my first night with him. You don't get to come in and ruin it.

"What are you going to do about it?" Iris answers. *"You came to me, over and over again. A bridge goes both ways."*

My eyes are glued to the dark window, my breaths steady as if I'm about to drift back to sleep, but inside, an all-out war is raging. Iris's soul stretches within me, her presence as vivid as if she were actually here, her twin form curling around my body.

Breathing in the air I'm breathing, and talking with my lips.

Setting down roots...

"I knew you were the chosen one. The other queens were too weak to withstand my influence, but you were tailor-made for me. A Shadow huntress with the skills needed to do what I couldn't," she explains.

Get out of my mind! I won't let you use my body.

"The curse made you so I could finally be made flesh again. I'm so grateful to you, sister."

No!

Curses might have a mind of their own, but I refuse to believe that the gods made me to serve as a second-hand body.

Iris prods at my memories, stomping around my brain as though it's hers for the taking. *"Do you know how lonely my death has been? I can only appear to the Winter Queen as part of the inheritance she gets when she's crowned. Except for you, of course. You could see and hear me well before Elio infected you with his ice."*

Wait a minute... you've been jumping from queen to queen ever since you fled Sara and the afterlife? You're the one who's been killing Elio's wives, one after the other?

"Like I said. They were too weak, but I knew my patience would one day be rewarded. Lightbringer men only use and abuse their partners. I've had years to mull things over, and Ezra was as much of a coward as his brother. You think I'm the villain, but you weren't there. Elio spent all his time playing the piano and moping around, desperate to suppress the power within him instead of embracing it. One day, you'll thank me for sparing you a lifetime with him. You'll see."

Our emotions blur together, and for a moment, I'm gripped by a flash of hatred. My mouth is pasty and dry, my heart pounding as if it's trying to escape my chest—or Iris's influence.

"Elio only cared about stupid poems and silly traditions. He never gave a damn about me or how empty I felt under his rule. In this cold, sterile castle."

Tears wet my cheeks, and Iris angrily wipes them away.

You lied to him and married him under false pretenses.

"I wanted to be immortal. And now I finally am. You and I are going to kill the Winter King, once and for all. And when it's done, I'll finally be alive *and free.*"

My knuckles clench around the edge of the duvet as I try to raise hell and warn Elio, but my eyelids are heavy, and a languid ache lulls me toward oblivion.

"Rest now, sister. I'll take care of things for a while."

The faint echoes of my heartbeat wane, creating a rhythmic thud that merges with the heavy silence dulling my senses. I catch only distant, fleeting scents—cold and metallic, like damp iron.

I can feel myself slipping away into a tiny, drugging crevice within my body—a cell far worse than the Spring jail or Murkwood could ever be. A prison within myself. No ice. No warmth.

Nothing.

CHAPTER 46

ROTTEN TO THE CORE

ELIO

D aylight blares through the tower window as I crack one eye open. I stir awake and reach out for the empty space next to me. "Lori?"

My lovely bride stands in front of the mirror, examining herself. The Winter crown Thanatos granted her during last night's ritual is no longer resting on top of her loose, messy black waves, but the new power flowing in her veins makes her gray eyes appear white as snow in the reflection.

I roll out of bed, eager to hold her in my arms again. "You look... fucking beautiful, Your Highness." I bow, coaxing a smile out of her.

She inspects her hands, cracking each finger one by one and rolling her wrists back and forth.

"Rough night?" I curl an arm around her frame and caress her smooth, bare thigh with my other hand.

"Not at all," she answers. "It was wonderful, actually."

The lull of sleep fades, replaced by a smoldering desire to make her mine again. I want to spend weeks with her in our bed. And in the hot springs. I want to take her through the provinces, just the two of us, and show her the wonders of our kingdom. We'll take moonlit strolls under the stars, barefoot in the snow—preferably naked.

Being in love certainly won't allow for a lot of time to rule, but the eerie, joyful excitement for all that's to come melts my insides. I'm not used to waking up with an unquenched thirst for life.

Lori pecks my lips and untangles herself from my grasp. "I need a shower."

"Can I come with?" I ask with a mischievous smile.

She pauses on her way to the adjoining room, as though my offer caught her off guard. "I guess."

Shaking off the urge to tease her about her less-than-enthused response, I switch on the light in the royal suite's bathroom. Even though I never use it, Sara had the whole place renovated in recent years, and the new marble rainfall shower is big enough for the both of us.

I thread deeper into the room to grab fresh towels and a bar of soap, placing them on the counter next to the shower while Lori figures out the functions of the different knobs and handles controlling the shower heads.

Steam quickly fills the room, fogging the large glass doors, and I step in next to her. My wife's body is perfect, but wet and glistening, it's damn near maddening, and my morning hard-on swells and throbs at the sight.

I move to stand behind her, admiring the view. "We should get you clean, my queen. I humbly offer my services."

Hot water sprays my face as I hold the soap underneath the jet for it to foam before slowly dragging it across her breasts and stomach before dipping lower to the place between her thighs.

She remains strangely stoic, and I hesitate. Maybe what I mistook for a sleepy answer earlier was actually her way of saying she'd rather be alone.

The soap slips from my grip, but I leave it on the floor and gather her hair to one side, nuzzling her neck. "Hey, how are you feeling?"

A sudden, violent wave of magic freezes the entire shower from floor to ceiling. We both tilt our heads up to examine the frozen shower head, the plumbing iced through.

"I-I just need a breather. I'm still adjusting to all this ice..." she stammers.

"Of course."

I'm all for giving her some space if she needs it, but I can't resist the urge to steal a kiss before I go. I slip my tongue inside her mouth with a low hum, savoring the moment.

She pushes me away with both hands, and my bare, wet feet scramble for traction on the marble. I brace myself against the wall of the large shower to stop my fall.

"Elio!" she shouts, clearly spooked by what just happened.

A pang of guilt shrinks my chest as I shake off the surprise and clear my throat. She did ask for space, and I crossed that line by kissing her anyway. "I'm sorry—"

"She's here."

The intense flash of fear and panic written in the gap between her lips sends my heart into a frenzy. I yearn to rush forward, itching to reach for her, but I force myself to stay back, keeping my arms close to my sides. "Lori, what's happening?"

Her lids close, and when they snap open again, a jolt of electricity runs down her body. Her muscles tighten and relax in uneven spasms. "I don't know what happened. I feel fine now," she croaks, but her body tells a different story.

I've seen that haggard, disoriented look before. I'd just never thought it would happen to Lori, too. And so soon after the wedding...

I hiss. "The curse is already working its way through you."

She gives me a decisive slice of the head. "Not the curse."

"What then?"

"It's I-Iris." Lori shakes as she raises her index and middle finger to her chest, and the small, trivial movement reeks of pain and agony.

Ice spreads in my chest, the name enough to kill what's left of my libido and send tingles of warning up my spine. "Iris?"

"Yes."

Her shoulders hunch, and the ice she mistakenly summoned melts all at once. The broken pipe above our heads erupts with hot water, the spray hitting us hard and interrupting our conversation. Steam clouds the shower and mingles with our startled gasps.

I turn off the main knob and rub the water off my face. "Here. Let's get you dry and figure this out." I wrap a towel around her shivering frame and gently guide her to sit on the cushioned bench in front of the vanity, kneeling in front of her.

With a stifled cry, she sobs, "I'm so sorry."

"Hey. Hey. You're safe, alright?" I gather her shaky hands in mine. "What about Iris?"

Her soft, heartbreaking sniffles morph into a bitter snarl. "Why did you have to go and be so...handsy? She won't shut up now, like you're some kind of prize worth fighting for."

I tilt my head to the side, and something inside me clicks. That voice... It's similar to Lori's, but sharper and full of reproach.

A ball of saliva burns my throat as I release her hands with a start, and when she combs her hair away from her face and looks down her nose at me, I see nothing but the ghost of my first wife, sitting right in front of me.

My soul shrivels with a mix of shame, horror, and rage. "You're not Lori."

"You figured it out, bravo," she says on a strangled laugh. "I can barely move, let alone stab you through. I was so sure this body was the one. Another disappointment," she mumbles to herself. "I guess I'll just have to wait and try again."

I stagger to my feet, widening the distance between us. "Where is Lori?" My voice hardens as the truth slowly sinks in. "What did you do with her?"

"Relax, she's here. Exhausted from what she just did, but she's here. With the others, it was like they were sleepwalking, and I felt groggy and numb all the time. But Lori... Lori cares for you something fierce. Her body was made for this, and yet she's clearly not willing to just step aside."

"What others? You've been haunting and possessing my wives?"

"Your queens, yes."

A hiccup quakes Iris, my first wife more honest in that moment than she's probably ever been with me.

I'm frozen, struggling to process the gravity of what Iris is saying. Grief slams into me next, a gut-wrenching weight that knots my stomach and blurs my vision with unshed tears. Olena, Deirdre, Hannah, Jillian... the haunting lullaby that sings me to sleep each night echoes in my ears. My teeth grind at the knowledge that, had I realized Iris's dark soul was killing them, I could have saved them. The crushing realization that I was blind to her presence and let them die in vain nearly chokes me.

My father had refused to send his soul catchers, but with my light magic, I should have been able to see her. I'd always assumed she'd fled to Spring.

"How did you manage to hide from me?" I rasp.

"You couldn't see me. Nobody could. Only the queens and the few odd brides I killed to gather my strength caught a glimpse of me," she explains, but instead of sounding satisfied and evil, she simply sounds... haunted. "I was so alone, Elio."

I arch a brow at the obvious remorse in her tone. "Why are you telling me all this?"

She tucks a strand of hair behind her ear. "Because Lori's making me. It's all very...muddled."

I search the room for a solution. I could throw on clothes and get Sara, but I don't trust Iris one bit. If her dark soul has taken over Lori's body, she might present a picture of defeat only to stab me when my back is turned. The large mirror catches my eye. Whatever is happening here, my mind is too clouded to understand it fully. I need backup.

I summon an ice blade to cut my thumb and draw a series of quick runes over the mirror. "Damian Morpheus Sombra, I pray to you. Shadow King, I implore you. Get the fuck over here, and quickly. We need you."

The glass shimmers as it absorbs the blood, and I wrap a towel around my naked bottom.

Iris shakes her head, a mix of exasperation and resignation in her eyes. "He's not going to know what to do with us. By Eros, I don't even know what to do with myself."

"Hush. I need to think." I hand her one of my old shirts from the closet. "Just put this on for now."

Iris scoffs and lays the basic cotton shirt down in her lap. "Really? Preventing another man from seeing me naked is at the forefront of your mind, right now?"

My mouth hangs open at her jab. "You were always so obtuse! I'm not dying of jealousy, here. I was just trying to preserve your— Lori's—modesty."

"Pfft," Iris snickers. "Sure. And I'm not here to cause any trouble. I just stopped by to say hello."

My lids close for a fleeting moment. A few minutes in, and we're already back at square one, arguing over meaningless stuff. Iris so quick to believe the worst about my intentions. Me so damn tired of having every single word and action spun out of context, always relegated to the role of the overbearing husband.

Less than a minute later, Damian slips out of the glass, the morning light filtering through the windows snuffed out by his presence.

"I came as soon as I could. I thought maybe the Gray Man was back..." He removes his mask, and his brows raise as he takes in our appearance, clearly taken aback by our blatant state of undress. "But that's obviously not the case."

I force my fists to unclench, my gaze skidding over Iris. "Lori managed to warn me... Iris is in there with her, somehow."

Iris raises a hand in the air and wiggles her fingers at the Shadow King in a sassy, impertinent wave. "Hey, Damian. Long time no see."

The shadows around Damian swell and writhe along his skin as he considers the naked huntress in a new light, and he quickly presses his mask back in place. "How did this happen?" he asks.

"I don't know. According to Sara's research, Lori and Iris look the same because her grandmother was somehow infected with Iris's blood upon her death, but we don't know much more than that."

The room settles into an awkward, miserable silence. Damian shifts uncomfortably, his eyes averted as he avoids looking at Iris. The shadows around him twist and pulse, mirroring his unease.

The soft sounds of shifting feet and the constant drip of water from the broken pipes whip my heart into a frenzy, each drop a relentless reminder of the chaos we're engulfed in. The rhythmic *plop* of water against the cold marble echoes through the room, amplifying the oppressive silence.

Damian finally clears his throat, breaking the tension. "Lori?"

Her eyes water, her confidence shattered, replaced by a trembling uncertainty that hangs in the air like a heavy fog. "Hey, boss."

"Lori," I murmur, reaching out to touch her bare shoulder, overwhelmed by the slight shifts in her expression that reveal who's truly in control. "I love you."

She places her palm over mine and gives it a sad squeeze.

Damian rakes a hand through his hair, pulling at the roots. "Fuck. I don't know much about blood magic, either. We need a witch."

The meaning of his words sinks in, and I bite the insides of my cheeks. "I'm not willing to strike a deal with Morrigan—"

"Not Morrigan," he interrupts. "I wouldn't trust her with this, either, but her grandmother might help us."

Iris raises one brow at that, her arms crossed over her breasts. "Are you saying you know where the Old Queen is hiding?"

Damian clicks his tongue and angles his face to me. "I didn't spend decades hunting for Morrigan without covering my bases. But

Mabel isn't exactly in the business of granting favors. We'd have to barter, and she drives a hard bargain."

"Can we trust her?" I ask. "Mabel was fond of Ezra, but I never knew her well."

"You're her grandson. I don't think she'd cross you on purpose."

My jaw clenches, but there's no doubt in my mind we need to do something drastic. And quickly. "Let's go."

CHAPTER 47
MARASSA
LORI

Fighting Iris for control is exhausting. When we're both too tired to truly hold the reins anymore, our shared senses become dull and painful, and just keeping our eyes open demands a buttload of energy.

We're at such a crossroad, now, our body curled around itself, waiting for the rematch as Damian instructs us to dress and get ready for traveling. I obey in a robotic fashion, each movement dragging on like I'm navigating a murky lake.

When we woke up this morning, I let Iris believe she was in control only to keep my strength and warn Elio. She was eager to get some time alone to practice and access my magic and skills.

While we were in the shower, she quietly ran through possible violent scenarios, plotting the best way to kill Elio. His touch repulsed her, so she distanced herself mentally to avoid revealing her true intentions. I took advantage of the moment, disrupting her plans before she could act on them.

I'm damn proud of myself, but terrified.

"I died too young, but the curse has allowed me to possess my succes-

sors for a reason. The Gods must believe I deserve a second chance, or they wouldn't have made you," Iris whispers.

Your curse made me so I could save Elio from this dreadful fate you inflicted on him.

"Let's agree to disagree, sister."

Don't call me that.

"Why not? We're twins. Stranded in time, maybe, but twins all the same."

I bite my bottom lip, a headache pounding against my forehead. As much as my love for Elio drove her to say things she didn't want to say earlier, I also share her bitterness and blinding hatred for the Winter King. I feel her emotions and hear her thoughts, and her crushed hopes for a new chance at life are debilitating.

"Should I be worried that you're going to attack me?" Damian asks, his voice tinged with concern. "How much does she know about your powers or how to use them? Do you guys share memories in there?"

My tongue feels heavy in my mouth as I answer, "Yes and no. I don't seem to be able to access hers unless I'm sleeping, but she's persistent."

"Then you'll forgive me for my prudence." The Shadow King tucks my mask in his jacket and hands me a scarf. "I'll escort you through the sceawere myself. Whatever you do, don't lie or play on words. The Old Queen can always tell when someone is lying." He angles his mask to Elio, my husband keeping close to our rear. "Ready?"

"Yes," Elio says, his voice faltering. The distance between us feels like an insurmountable chasm, and it breaks my heart to see him so broken and distant.

With my eyes closed and the scarf securely fastened around my head, I let Damian guide me inside the sceawere.

A soft, almost timid knock echoes in from our side of the glass, and I hold my breath. Damian never knocks. The Shadow King typically strides in—and rightly so—like he owns the sceawere and anything connected to it, never bothering with such formalities.

"Mabel? Are you home? We're coming in," he announces, his voice carrying a rare hint of uncertainty.

The space between worlds leaves a cool, tingling sensation on my neck, but the usual sting is absent thanks to my new magic. I adjust the scarf on my brow and look around. We've emerged from a round, wall-mounted mirror into a quiet living room. A plush purple corduroy couch sits in front of a sleek plasma screen TV, and a bowl of fresh wildflowers adds a splash of color to the serene space.

The scent of dried herbs soothes my raw nerves—lavender, sage, and thyme mingle with hints of patchouli and the subtle sweetness of rose petals. The bay window reveals the overgrown green bushes outside, framed by a tall rowan tree. The red, orange, and yellow leaves block the view of the street beyond the rusty iron gates. Inside, the multi-level Victorian house exudes old-world charm, with its wooden sash windows and grand high ceiling.

"And to what do I owe this...polite intrusion?" a woman's voice calls from behind us. We all turn to face our hostess, who stands poised and curious.

The elderly woman we came to visit is holding a dark wooden cane, though her grip wavers as her weathered gaze finds Elio. She pauses, both hands resting on the carved raven adorning the tip of the walking stick, her thin lips pressed together. "Surely, if you were here for my soul, you would have been enough of a gentleman not to bring guests into an old lady's home?"

A dry grin curls Elio's lips. "I have better manners than that."

Mabel appears to be around seventy years old, but given that she's Morrigan's grandmother, she must be way older. Her bite of power is faint—almost imperceptible, really—but I suspect it's a deliberate disguise. Despite its subtlety, it has a strangely comforting effect.

"I can't believe you've never heard of Mabel Bloodsinger," Iris chokes

out, her inner voice laced with a mix of fear and awe. *"She's the most powerful witch to ever live."*

I dig the balls of my feet into the thick cream carpet, Iris's panic prompting me to run. But as Mabel's gaze crosses mine, the blazing impulse to flee dims into a warm haze.

A few gray streaks are peppered throughout Mabel's white hair, and she squints at Damian with a careful, muted expression. "What has my granddaughter done now?" she asks, heading for the cupboard and retrieving a plate of biscuits covered in transparent wrap.

"For once, Rye isn't to blame for my visit," Damian says quickly.

"But she's alive?"

"Yes. I have her in my custody," Elio answers.

"Why is she alive, if you finally managed to catch her?" the witch muses, her wide hazelnut gaze fixed on Damian.

The Shadow King shifts his weight from one foot to the other. "She joined her fate to that of a Shadow seed who is precious to me."

Mabel's wrinkled hands still over the plastic wrap covering the biscuits. "Are you saying my granddaughter bound herself to a mortal?" She sets the plate down in the middle of the dining table and motions for us to sit.

"Yes."

She licks her lips. "And where is this special girl?"

How did she know Cece was a girl? My eyes narrow, but I walk around the table to sit beside Elio. A glass curio cabinet set along the wall displays antique teacups with beautiful hand-painted patterns.

"She's safe in my care." Damian takes his seat at the end of the table. "This is the new Winter Queen and one of my Shadow huntresses. She's been possessed by a dark spirit."

"Come here, child." Mabel reaches into her pocket and unfolds her glasses as I walk back around the table to join her in the kitchen. The deep lines creasing her mouth deepen as she examines me. "A spirit, you say? A dark worm is more like it."

She grabs a tissue from the counter and slowly wipes down each of the long, narrow lenses in thoughtful silence. "Alright, I'll help you. But in exchange, I want to meet this mortal my granddaughter entwined her fate with."

The muscles in Damian's jaw tick, but he offers the witch a small bow. "You have a deal."

"So, who are you?" Mabel asks me.

"I'm Lori," I reply, my voice steady despite the swirling confusion in my mind.

The corners of her mouth quirk. "Are you really?"

"I don't know," I admit. "Everything is muddled."

"Two souls, one body. One body, two souls. Such is the Marassa's fate. Two sides of a coin. One light. One dark." The old woman turns to Elio. "I'm not sure why you came to me, King of Death. Witches deal in flesh, blood, and bones. The Dark One himself couldn't touch a soul if we wanted. Only your father, the King of Light, could divide the two twins and kill only the dark half."

"My father would rather burn his cities to the ground than grant me a favor. Hell, he'd probably spare Iris and kill Lori just to spite me." Elio's chest heaves, his jaw clenched on a bitter sigh. "Are you saying there's nothing that can be done?"

"I didn't say that." The witch raises and lowers her hands in an orchestral conductor fashion, a gesture that signals us to simmer down. "The dark twin is weaker than she lets on. She might be persuaded to...rest for a while."

I instinctively walk toward her. "How?"

"Patience." She inches toward the sink. "The Standing Stones won't topple over in the next hour. Help me with the tea, dear, so I can get to know you better." She passes me the infuser and motions toward the glass cupboard. "Eight spoonfuls should be enough." With these incomplete instructions, she clicks on the stove and fills a water boiler to the brim.

I open the cabinet door and grab the closest tea box, but the witch clicks her tongue. "Not that one. It's as dark as the highlands on a stormy night. That one"—she extends her wrinkled hand to the metal box at the very back of the shelf—"will do nicely."

I crack open the lid, and a bittersweet, herbal scent supplants the others. The tiny, dried sun-shaped flowers of the herb ring a bell, but I can't quite place it.

We wait in stifled silence while Mabel adds milk and honey to the table. The metallic teapot shows signs of wear and tear. A bump in its side gleams under the electric lights, while freckles of heat discoloration and welding marks decorate the handle.

The high whistling sound of the boiler sends goosebumps up my arms. Mabel gives me the go-ahead, and I place the infuser into the pot before pouring the hot water over it. The tea steeps, its color gradually deepening as a sunny fragrance fills the room.

We exchange weary glances while we wait. Elio's expression is a mix of frustration and exhaustion, and Damian's eyes reveal a guarded patience. Mabel's gaze, though calm, holds an unspoken scrutiny. The minutes stretch, each of us lost in our own troubled thoughts as the tea continues to infuse.

Finally, I serve us each a cup of tea in vintage porcelain cups. The delicate aroma wafts up, a small comfort amid the tension. After I'm done, I join Mabel and the men at the table, sitting opposite the old witch. She stirs her tea with a small golden spoon, dipping the tip of her biscuit into the cup.

Elio stares down the brown liquid with his brows furrowed. "So... How would you go about making Iris sleep?"

"Tea, first," the woman orders with a scowl.

I swallow a long swig, eager to get this part over with. The beverage's muted floral taste is oddly enticing, and before I know it, I tilt my head back and finish the whole cup in one go.

Mabel sets her spoon down with a satisfied nod. "Well done."

Iris curses me to all hells before she slowly slips away, as the old witch clearly planned. I sigh in relief, finally regaining control over my body. Her influence dissolves, leaving my muscles spent and aching but fully mine once more.

Mabel takes a measured sip of her tea. "I didn't want to alert the dark twin. The tea you've been drinking is made from St. John's Wort. It grows during the summer solstice and brings light and positivity to the mind and spirit. Drink it every morning and night, and it should be enough to keep the dark soul from taking control and spreading its roots too deep inside of you."

"But Iris will still see and hear everything?" Elio croaks.

Mabel shows off her pearly white teeth. "I expect she will remain mostly dormant, with the occasional bout of consciousness."

Elio and I exchange a heavy glance. While that compromise might sound perfectly acceptable to Mabel, it sure as hell isn't enough of a solution for us. But the old witch is not our friend, so I swallow back my reckless, biting comments and take solace in the fact that I can't hear Iris's thoughts or feel her emotions anymore. Wherever she went, she's far enough away for me to feel like myself again.

My hands shake, and the teacup clinks repeatedly against the golden-rimmed plate as I set it down. "Thank you for your help."

"Eat a biscuit, dear, before you pass out." She turns to Damian. "Now... about that meeting."

CHAPTER 48
SONGBIRD
LORI

Sara clicks her knife on the side of her crystal flute, interrupting the guests' chatter and the live band. "Thank you all for coming. After the week we've had, I knew we needed a wedding reception to honor our new queen, a chance to celebrate and lift our spirits as this year comes to a close."

Elio and I are sitting at the sweetheart table, the ballroom all decked out for our wedding reception. The royals from the other kingdoms were all invited to attend so we can smooth things over with champagne as we address the failed attempt by the Tidecallers to steal souls.

All have come, except for Elio's father. From what I understand, the two men haven't set foot in the same room outside of their royal obligations in Eterna since the bastard clipped his wings.

To my regret, Nell couldn't attend. Damian is still too wary of announcing their wedding, the secrecy of their union preventing any associate of Morrigan from targeting her. The phantom queen might be safely imprisoned within the confines of the Ice City, but she's still breathing. As long as she lives, we'll be in danger.

Sara claps her hands, a bright gleam dancing in her eyes. "And now, ladies and gentlemen, I give you Elizabeth Snow."

The announcement sends a ripple of excitement through the crowd. The High Fae erupt in cheers, their voices rising in a collective roar, while the royals shift in their seats, eager to catch a glimpse of the singer's entrance.

"Thank you, thank you." Beth sits at the piano, her stunning blue gown shimmering under the frozen chandeliers. Snowflakes dust her tulle skirt, and two jeweled straps glint like strands of stardust against her pale alabaster shoulders. "As most of you know, I usually don't play at Elio's wedding*s*." She pauses for effect, the emphasis on the "s" coaxing genuine laughter from the crowd. Winter Fae certainly don't cry over spilled milk, and her dark humor coaxes a smile out of me. "But this one is different."

She cranes her neck around and meets my gaze. "Lori... of all the women who won this cruel, cruel pageant, you're the only one who's truly won Elio's heart. And for that, I salute you. And I wish you both a lifetime of happiness."

Contrary to her popular, revenge-filled pop songs, this one begins slowly, barely above a whisper. Her voice is soft and haunting, with an ethereal quality that captivates the audience as soon as she hits the first note.

"I never knew a love
Quite so rare as yours
Never knew a gaze
Quite so entrancing
You held out your hand
By the river bank
And asked me for a dance

Just one night; in lieu of forever
One chance; it was now or never
As luck had it, my star-crossed lover

I was promised to another
But I only wanted you

I never knew a name
Quite so forbidden
Never knew a love
Quite as doomed from the start
We were oil and water
Sweet and sour
It was never to be
Never to be
But I only wanted you

Just one taste; in lieu of forever
One summer; it was now or never
As luck had it, my star-crossed lover
I was promised to another
But I only wanted you

Yours was a crown of gold
Mine only a shard of cold
A piece of coal
Safe from my cruel shadow
I risked it all to hold you
And lost it all in one go
It was never to be
Never to be
But I only wanted you"

The tempo of the music softens, and the mournful piano notes ring out, filling the silent room with their melancholic beauty.

"Such a lovely, heartbreaking song. Do you know who she wrote it for?" I ask, my curiosity piqued.

Elio laughs softly. "Not me, I assure you."

"I wasn't—" I cut off my husband with a sharp look. "I'm not jealous of Beth anymore. Just curious."

"Thank Thanatos, you've stopped using her entire name," he quips.

I give his arm a playful slap. "Shush."

"But you just gave me an idea. Beth might be able to help us barter with Thera for your brother. It's a well-kept secret, but Beth almost married her son."

"Is he the guy from the song?"

"Yes, and I'm sure Thera would give anything for them not to meet again. But let's not involve Beth just yet. The apple I gave the Summer Queen should buy us enough goodwill to tip the scales on this." He kisses the back of my knuckles. "Don't worry, we'll talk to Thera later tonight."

He skims the skin of my naked back with his fingertips, my black halter top and leather pants more my style than a wedding dress. "I love you, Lorisha Pari Singh. And not just because you kicked ass out on that lake, or for the courage and patience you show every day."

"No?"

He flattens a hand over my chest, his thumb dangerously close to brushing my nipple through the thin fabric. "I love your smoking-hot—" I glower at him, but he pecks my neck with a chuckle. "It's your heart. Your warm, passionate, electric heart."

I dig my fingers into his blonde locks and tug before giving his scalp a playful knock. "And I love you in spite of your big, stubborn head."

"Take that back."

"Kiss me." I slip my hands under the lapels of his jacket and hide my face in his chest. "She shrivels when you're near."

Elio's brow furrows, and instead of giving in to my demand, he draws back an inch, clearly spooked. "She's awake?"

"Yes, but barely." I hate how he's nervous—and frankly hesitant—to touch me when he knows Iris is lurking around the fringes of my subconscious. "I better get my tea." My chair creaks as I stand, but Elio follows my lead and wraps an arm around me, his touch gentle but firm, delaying my departure.

"I'm sorry I cringed. I'm just not used to the idea of Iris living inside you, yet," he whispers.

"That makes two of us."

"We'll find a way to cast her out for good. Even if I have to slay my father and beg his successor for help, I promise we'll find a more permanent solution."

"Another empty promise... he should really stop doing that," Iris chants.

While I'd love nothing more than to slay her, our consciousnesses are already starting to barter—to compromise. The most she can do now is talk, and she takes every opportunity to do so. The tea buys me about eight hours of peace, but Mabel warned me against overusing it. She explained that all magic needs balance, and that shutting Iris off completely could create problems later on.

I don't want to live the rest of my life with a whispering devil on my shoulder, and I inhale deeply to keep her at bay. "I know we will. And now that we know exactly what's been killing your wives and why, you don't have to worry about me dropping dead before spring."

A dark glint burns in Elio's eyes. "Don't joke about that."

"I'm just being honest."

"Come here."

Howls and applause resonate across the ballroom as my new husband kisses my dark thoughts away. Most of our guests are unaware of our recent challenges, and I let myself pretend, if only for a moment, that we are just carefree newlyweds—not immortal royals with more problems than we can handle.

The embrace of the Winter King is warm and perfect. Iris retreats, unwilling to witness our happiness, and I know we will beat her, in the end.

For true love.

LOVELY READERS

Thank you so much for reading. As you can see, Elio and Lori's story is far from over. Rest assured, their happy ever after is coming. I invite you to visit the Summer Court next, as Beth deals with some ghosts of her own.

This book will feature many of the characters you already know and love.

See what Damian was like as a young lord, and find out why Elio lost his wings.

A momentous wedding looms on the horizon. Will Beth lose the love of her life forever, or find him again?

The royals are all invited, and so are you.

See you there,

xoxo

Anya

THE PRINCE FROM A CRUEL SUMMER

Summer love cuts to the bone.

I didn't choose to attend Royal Academy, an elite school full of vicious Fae. I never wished for an arranged marriage to a nasty shadow prince.

I especially never wanted to meet Aidan Summers. He was the most beautiful man I'd ever laid eyes on—the one who broke my heart beyond repair.

He was the fire to my ice. Our relationship was forbidden, and the fallout almost cost me my soul.

A century later, I have it all—money, fame, power—but none of it matters. I'm still his. And when I receive an invitation to sing at his wedding, I can't resist the flames.

Has he really forgotten about me? Or does he want to destroy what's left of my soul?

This novel is a full-length romantasy with a happy ending, and though it's part of an interconnected series, it can be read first.

Join Elizabeth Snow down memory lane as she attends her ex's wedding and awakens the ghosts of a past long gone. Steamy. 18+. Full list of triggers inside.

Enemies-to-lovers
He falls first
Second chance
Forbidden romance

THE SHADOW WITCH TRILOGY

R ead the series that started it all! *Fall for the shadows. Kiss the enemy.*

The complete trilogy in one place! More than 1000 pages of fast-paced action and slow-burn romance with a steamy finale!

Nothing stays black and white in a world full of shadows.

I'm Alana, and for my birthday, I got a brand-new magical destiny instead of the laptop I was saving for. Surprise! I'm a witch.

Demons, glamors, potions, and spells... Nothing is as it seems in this ruthless new world, and the rules of the game are stacked against me. I have powers I can't control and a throng of enemies vying for a chance to drain me dry.

In the midst of all this chaos, the Walker brothers are determined to save my life. Well...sort-of.

Liam wants to eat me about as much as he means to help me, and Thom's made it his life goal to protect me from demons—his brother included—whether I want him to or not.

If only I wasn't attracted to both of them... But the last thing I need is a boyfriend. At this rate, I'll flunk Witchcraft 101.

To survive, I must embrace the darkness simmering inside me and unleash the devil within, no matter the consequences.

The Shadow Witch trilogy is a completed urban fantasy romance (MF) filled with action, humor, and smoking-hot men. It's a slow-burn, forced proximity, enemies-to-lovers adventure with a steamy happy-ever-after on top and sprinkles of touch-her-and-die. In this series, the heroine has to choose between light and dark, though both will steal pieces of her soul in the process.

https://bit.ly/shadowwitch

Printed in Great Britain
by Amazon

55492390R00199